The
Italian
Girls

ALSO BY DEBBIE RIX

The Secret Letter

The Italian Girls

Debbie Rix

FOREVER

New York   Boston

Forever
Hachette Book Group
1290 Avenue of the Americas, New York, NY 10104
read-forever.com
twitter.com/readforeverpub

Originally published in Great Britain by Bookouture in 2020
First American Edition: November 2022

Forever is an imprint of Grand Central Publishing. The Forever name and logo are trademarks of Hachette Book Group, Inc.

The publisher is not responsible for websites (or their content) that are not owned by the publisher.

The Hachette Speakers Bureau provides a wide range of authors for speaking events. To find out more, go to www.hachettespeakersbureau.com or call (866) 376-6591.

Library of Congress Cataloging-in-Publication Data has been applied for.

ISBN: 978-1-5387-2345-6 (trade paperback)

Printed in the United States of America

LSC-C

Printing 1, 2022

For Luisa—
whose extraordinary story inspired this novel

"It is easier to forgive an enemy than to forgive a friend."
—*William Blake*

This novel is a work of fiction, but it is based on the real-life experiences of Italian women during the Second World War. The character of Livia is an amalgam of two university students in Florence who worked for the Resistance. The character of Isabella is based on the life of the film star Maria Denis, who was caught between the Fascist authorities that ran the film industry in Rome and her devotion to Luchino Visconti, a film director and member of the Resistance.

CAST OF CHARACTERS

The main characters in this novel are fictional, but their stories intersect with those of real individuals, who are highlighted here in italics.

Isabella's Story
- Isabella Bellucci: film actress
- Giovanna: Isabella's mother
- Ariana: Isabella's aunt
- Maria: her personal assistant
- Ludovico Albani: Isabella's first boyfriend
- Peter: the man she eventually marries
- Stefano: her "tennis pro" friend
- Count Vicenzo Lucchese: a film director
- Count Vittorio Lucchese: Vicenzo's father
- Contessa Alessandra Lucchese: Vicenzo's mother
- Luciana Torelli: Vicenzo's sister
- Carlo Torelli: Luciana's husband
- Raffaele: Vicenzo's brother
- Amadeo: Vicenzo's cousin
- Anna: Vicenzo's assistant
- *Karl Wolff:* head of the German SS in Italy
- *Herbert Kappler:* head of the Gestapo in Rome
- *Pietro Koch:* head of a special Fascist police unit in Rome
- *Commissario Guarnotta:* of the Fascist police in Rome
- *Pietro Mocci:* a Resistance member, killed in the Ardeatine massacre

- *Salvato Cappelli:* a journalist and Resistance member
- *Gianni Cini and his father, Vittorio Cini:* cabinet minister in 1943
- *Mario Chiari:* a film designer
- *Count Galeazzo Ciano:* Minister of Foreign Affairs and Mussolini's son-in-law
- *Arturo Orvieto:* Isabella's defense lawyer
- *Alessandro Pavolini:* a cabinet minister in Mussolini's government
- *Eitel Monaco:* the director of cinema at Cinecittà
- *Doris Duranti:* an actress
- *Elsa De Giorgi:* an actress
- *Alida Valli:* an actress
- *Elsa Merlini:* an actress
- *Massimo Girotti:* an actor
- *Clara Calamai:* an actress
- *Princess Matilda of Savoy:* an aristocrat

Livia's Story
- Livia Moretti: young Florentine student and *staffetta*
- Giacomo Moretti: her father
- Luisa Moretti: her mother
- Alberto Moretti: her grandfather
- Angela: the housekeeper
- Gino: the gardener
- Elena Lombardi: her best friend
- Benedetta Lombardi: Elena's mother
- Cosimo de Luca: her boyfriend and fellow Resistance member
- Sara, Jacob, and Matteo: the Jewish family sheltered by the Morettis
- Valentina: her friend in Verona
- Pietro and Sergio: Resistance members
- *Mario Carità:* head of the Fascist Police in Florence

The
Italian
Girls

Prologue

Florence
2019

Livia Moretti stepped out onto the street and closed her eyes against the dazzling brightness. After the darkness of her top-floor apartment, the glare of bright white light felt almost shocking. The heavy oak door slammed shut behind her and she leaned against it, steadying herself, sensing its heat through her faded cream linen summer coat. She fumbled for the fastening of her handbag, and felt inside the silk pocket for her door key. As was her habit, she checked for the other contents, ensuring everything was in its place. Her elegant fingers touched her small emerald-green leather purse, followed by the engraved silver money clip—an antiquated but neat contraption for keeping notes orderly—and finally, the little jewel-encrusted powder compact her mother had given her over seventy years before. In the bottom of the handbag was a small silver-handled magnifying glass. Livia snapped the bag shut, content that all was well and slipped it into position in the crook of her arm; with her other hand, she reached for her white stick leaning against the stone surround of the front door.

She walked along the cobbled street at a slow but even pace, her head very erect, even in her ninth decade, having been drilled as a child to stand up straight by her German governess. Fräulein Schneider had strapped a board across her charge's back, pinning Livia's shoulders into position. It had seemed harsh at the time, restricting her movements, preventing her from lolling and slouching as she would have liked. Even on holiday in the resort town of Forte dei Marmi on the Ligurian coast, where the family went to escape the heat of the city, the board was still worn at mealtimes. Livia remembered the ecstasy as it was removed and she was allowed to slip into a loose white linen frock, her bare feet on the white sand, her dark hair covered with a straw panama. Her mother, meanwhile, would be sitting upright in her rattan chair, her white skin protected by a parasol.

A gaggle of tourists fluttered toward Livia. Their features and bodies were indistinct; they were just an amorphous grouping of people, barring her way, standing gawping at the Duomo, flapping their arms and clicking. She often complained about them to her cleaner, Monica. "Why must they stand in the middle of everywhere? They make it so difficult to get around. And what are they doing—making these clicking noises all the time?"

"They're taking photos...selfies."

"Selfies, what on earth are 'selfies'?"

"Photos you take of yourself."

"Well, how ridiculous. They've come all the way to Florence to take photos of themselves? Why don't they at least take pictures of the beautiful buildings?"

"I don't know," Monica had replied, as she plumped the needle-point cushions on the battered linen sofa. "They're not interested in the buildings, I suppose. They just want to prove they've been here."

Livia shook her head, bewildered. Everything changes, she thought. Everything moves on. Life cannot stay the same.

Her route that morning was imprinted on her memory. Although she was unable to see the precise details of the buildings around her, their familiar shapes loomed on the edges of her vision. She knew how many steps it was from the Duomo to the small café in the Piazza della Repubblica, and counted silently to herself as she walked: "One hundred and forty-eight, forty-nine...and stop." The roar of a motorbike, as it rushed past her, created an eddy in the air, rustling her silk dress.

"Can I help you cross the road?" The man's voice was young and friendly. She would usually have declined, preferring to manage herself, but he had already taken her elbow—the arm that carried the handbag—and was edging her forward. She found herself walking faster than she would have liked across the road and up onto the pavement on the other side.

"Thank you," she said crisply.

"You're welcome," he replied. "Can I take you anywhere?"

"No, thank you. I'm just going to Café Paskowski. It's only a few minutes from here."

"I'm going there myself," he said. "May I accompany you?"

They walked the last hundred yards together. His touch on her arm, as he guided her through the crowds, was gentle and deferential.

"It's a delightful café, isn't it?" he said, gazing up at the large glazed windows and the Edwardian signage above the door. "I've been here several times since I arrived in Florence. I've seen you here occasionally—it's obviously your favorite haunt too."

His knowledge of her daily activity unnerved her. She wished he would leave her alone. She felt the familiar edge of the pavement with her stick. Just five more steps to her table. Angelo, the head waiter, always kept it for her so there was no embarrassment, no need to move someone else on. Her hand reached out for the familiar back of the chair and she sat down.

"Well," the young man said, "it was lovely to meet you...I've often wondered about you."

It was such an odd thing to say...so intrusive. She looked up and could see his outline. He was tall and dark-haired. But in spite of his forward manner, she felt drawn to him; she wished she could see his face properly.

"I'm sure I don't know why," she replied.

"Oh, I don't mean to be rude—forgive me." He sounded nervous. "I merely meant that you are so elegant, and every day you sit here, drinking your coffee, studying the paper with your magnifying glass."

"Well," she said, smiling faintly, wishing to bring an end to the conversation. "Goodbye then. And thank you again."

He bowed and moved out of her field of vision.

Angelo placed a cup of coffee on the table, together with a folded copy of *La Stampa*, her daily newspaper.

"Ecco, signora," he said politely.

"Grazie."

Livia took a little sip of the coffee and felt it reviving her. She opened her handbag, retrieved the silver-handled magnifying glass and laid it next to the coffee cup. Unfolding the paper, she spread it out, holding the magnifying glass to her eye so she could follow one line of print at a time.

She perused the headlines, before turning to the inside pages, where her eye was drawn to a story about an Italian actress who had just died. The name was familiar—Isabella Bellucci, otherwise known as *la fidanzatina d'Italia*—Italy's little sweetheart. She had risen to stardom in the late 1930s, the paper said. She had married a British businessman after the war, and retired to the hills around Rome. Her son had died twenty years before, leaving one solitary grandson.

Livia felt her pulse quicken. She began to turn the pages of the paper, searching for a longer obituary. As she read about Isabella's life—of her wartime experiences, of the scandals, the trial—she thought back to those days during the war, when trust in Italy was in short supply, betrayal was everywhere and the world went mad.

PART ONE

THE FASCIST YEARS
1941–1943

"Fascism is a religion. The twentieth century
will be known in history as the century of Fascism."

Benito Mussolini, known as "Il Duce,"
the Prime Minister of Italy 1922–1943

Chapter One

"Signorina Bellucci, they're ready for you now."

It was Mario, the assistant floor manager, poking his head around the makeup room door.

Isabella took one last look at herself in the mirror. Her dark hair was waved to perfection, her rosebud mouth rouged. False eyelashes had been painstakingly applied one at a time to her top lids, giving her the wide-eyed girlish look her fans adored.

The makeup artist brushed away the excess powder from Isabella's flawless pan-caked complexion, put a smudge of Vaseline on her lips to add a little shine, and removed the cape from the star's shoulders with a flourish.

"Perfetto, signorina," she said, "you are ready for your close-up."

A star's close-up was a constant source of friction between actor and director. The actors demanded it for the simple and straightforward reason that the more close-ups you had, the more the public loved you and the more important you became to the studio. Directors, however, found them irritating: they got in the way of the story, they took time to set up and they pandered to the worst excesses of an actor's ego. All the female stars at Cinecittà had a certain number of close-ups written into their contract for every film. Isabella—by nature, shy and lacking in confidence—had realized early on in her career that if she was not to be pushed around by the studio, she would have to play the part of the "Diva." Her performance over the years had been so effective that she had earned the unfortunate moniker of "The Tyrant" among some members of the crew. Isabella was rather hurt by the nickname, because she knew it was both inaccurate and unjustified. But she played along with it, and in her latest film had demanded no fewer than eight close-ups. In order to be ready she had to spend two hours in makeup to ensure that her complexion, her hair, her eyes were as perfect on camera as possible. Inevitably this meant an early start—rising at five o'clock. So, when the time came to negotiate the contract for this film, she had decided to put her foot down.

"No more early mornings," she had said firmly to the director when they were planning the filming schedule. "To be on set at eight, as you demand, is simply unreasonable. I'm exhausted before the day even begins. How can I be ready for my close-up if I have dark rings beneath my eyes?"

"Now, Isabella," Lorenzo purred, "you know how these things work. If we don't start filming at eight o'clock, we'll never get the film completed in time."

"That's your problem, not mine," retorted Isabella. "You can shoot other scenes that don't include me first thing in the morning. I'll be on set at nine o'clock and not before."

He flushed—with fury, she supposed—and bit his lip.

"Do you have something to say?" she asked imperiously, inwardly nervous of his reaction.

"I was merely wondering…" he hesitated, "…if perhaps it would be better not to do a close-up, as they present such a problem for you. The story doesn't really demand it."

She smiled like a cat, her blue-gray eyes flashing. "No, perhaps not, but our public demand to see as much of their stars as possible, and the authorities agree with them; so I think that's the end of the matter, don't you?"

Relieved to have won that particular argument, she stood up and pulled her cream coat around her shoulders, put on her sunglasses and swept out of the room, leaving a haze of Arpège perfume behind her—complex, sexy and feminine.

Isabella arrived on set amidst a flurry of attendants. She stood in the shadows being primped and prodded; the makeup artist's assistant dabbed powder on her already perfect complexion and the dresser tweaked her Edwardian gown, tilting her hat just so. Isabella turned to her personal assistant Maria, and handed her a letter.

"Get this delivered for me, will you?"

"Of course, signorina," the girl said, glancing down at the envelope. It was addressed to a young army officer, Baron Ludovico Albani, a member of Rome's aristocracy. The pair had enjoyed a whirlwind romance that summer—dining à deux in Rome, walking arm in arm down Via Veneto, and spending their Sundays bathing at the beach at Fregene. The relationship had been captured for Isabella's fans by photographers and printed in the press beneath ecstatic headlines:

Movie Star Finds Love with
Aristocratic War Hero

Ludovico had been elusive for the previous couple of weeks and Isabella was worried. She had begun to believe that she had found love at last. Now she feared that, as far as he was concerned, it had merely been a summer fling. In her darker moments she worried that he had already forgotten her. But as usual, she did her best to bury these concerns, and concentrate on her work.

The film she was shooting that hot day in September was set in rural Tuscany. Isabella played the part of a kindly schoolteacher who had been unlucky in love. When she arrives in the countryside to take up a new post, the local mayor is determined to win her heart. Location scenes for the film had already been shot on the shores of Lake Orta. Now the village school had been re-created in the vast sound stage at Cinecittà. A painted backdrop featuring rolling olive groves set the scene. In the foreground stood the schoolhouse—a wooden building, artfully disguised by scene painters to resemble Tuscan stone. Mature trees stood on the edge of the set, their vast pots hidden from the camera by flowers and plants.

That morning's scene featured Isabella hugging a small child playing the part of one of her pupils. The moment the director called "Action," Isabella—professional as always—smiled beatifically at the child, as the camera tracked onto her exquisite face. Under the hot lights, her flawless smooth skin glowed, her cat-like eyes sparkled, and her dark hair gleamed. Irritated though the director was by his star's demands, Lorenzo had to admit she was "the image of perfection."

At six o'clock, the day's shooting over, Isabella emerged from the dark studio building into the blinding summer sunlight. She felt in her Hermès crocodile handbag for her sunglasses.

"Buonasera, signorina." The uniformed doorman tipped his hat to her. She nodded her head discreetly in acknowledgment, and looked around the parking lot for her black open-topped Mercedes.

"Do you remember where I parked my car?" she asked him.

"Yes, signorina...it's just over there, by the gate."

"Oh yes, thank you. I was thinking about something else this morning, and I'd quite forgotten."

"Have a good evening, signorina," he said, delighted to have been singled out for this "chat."

"And you," she called back over her shoulder.

She threw her handbag onto the passenger seat and turned the key in the ignition. It always gave her a thrill to hear the roar of the engine. She remembered the first time she had ever driven a car—it was just after she had been signed to the studio, aged sixteen. Isabella had been "discovered" while walking with her mother in the parkland surrounding Villa Borghese, Rome's famous art gallery. Until that moment she had never considered acting, nor any kind of performing, as a potential career; on the contrary, she was a serious, academic child with a knack for mathematics and languages. Born in Argentina to an Italian mother and an Argentinian father, she and her mother, Giovanna, had returned to Italy after her parents' marriage collapsed. Her father had had a nervous breakdown, and her mother was determined to provide a better life for herself and her child. Back in Rome, they had moved into the small, shabby apartment of Giovanna's mother and widowed sister, and there the four women had lived for the rest of Isabella's childhood.

When a young director searching for a "new face" for a film project spotted Isabella in the park, her mother realized it was an opportunity Isabella couldn't afford to miss. This was just the kind of chance she had been hoping for when they ran away from Argentina, and offered an escape from their poverty. After a successful screen test, Isabella had been quickly signed to the studio, which schooled her in elocution and etiquette, before casting her in what would be the first of numerous films—with sometimes as many as six shot in a single year.

Isabella drove her Mercedes out of the studios and headed up the Via Tuscolana toward the center of Rome. It was Saturday evening, and she was looking forward to Sunday, her only day off a week. With the roof down, she enjoyed the sensation of the wind whistling through her dark hair. She felt relaxed, driving with one hand on the steering wheel, the other resting along the edge of the door. She now lived in an area of the city called Parioli, adjacent to Villa Borghese and its parkland. It was filled with wealthy and ambassadorial residences—most with three, or even four stories, stuccoed and painted in various shades of terra-cotta, apricot and cream.

Isabella's house was called Villa Rosa and, as its name suggested, was a shade of pink that cheered her the moment she first saw it. Sandwiched between two much larger properties, the house was a low two-story building, with a row of arched windows on the ground floor overlooking a terrace at the back, beyond which stretched a private garden—something of a luxury in Rome. It had the advantage of being surrounded by high walls, which provided both security and seclusion—a key consideration for the stars of Cinecittà who were often dogged by fans curious to see the homes of their screen idols.

The house itself was not grand, but Isabella immediately realized it had enough space for both herself and her mother, Giovanna, who having persuaded her daughter to become an actress, saw Isabella's success as something of a personal achievement. To share in her daughter's prosperity was her right, Giovanna felt, and Isabella would not have dreamed of refusing her mother—however overbearing she could be.

When she had first viewed Villa Rosa, Isabella was delighted to discover a small cottage in the garden, which seemed ideally suited for her mother. But Giovanna made it quite clear that her rightful place was in the larger house, and the cottage was now home to a married couple who worked as housekeeper and gardener.

Now, as she approached her pale-pink house, Isabella tooted her horn and almost immediately the large metal gates swung open. She swept into the drive, the gardener closing the gates behind her.

"Buonasera, signorina," he said, taking the keys from her.

"Buonasera, Giuseppe."

She scanned the front garden, with its flower borders and lawn, overshadowed by two arching pine trees.

"It all looks very tidy, thank you."

"Grazie, signorina—I've been sweeping up the pine needles all afternoon."

That evening, Isabella was holding a party. Most of the guests were from the film industry—her fellow actors and actresses, directors and writers, alongside a sprinkling of aristocrats. Inevitably she also had to invite representatives of the Fascist authorities who controlled much of the film industry, and Cinecittà in particular. They saw films as a useful vehicle for their political propaganda, and many of the stars were on intimate terms with senior figures in the government. Although Isabella didn't count these men amongst her friends, it was prudent to maintain good relations. Besides, she rather enjoyed their devotion.

It seemed harmless enough, Isabella thought, as she pulled out dresses from her walk-in wardrobe, searching for something special to wear. She had no particular interest in politics. Why should she? After all, she was only an actress. But she had worked hard, escaping poverty in Argentina; she had made something of herself, and if she was required to be charming for an evening, where was the harm in that?

The guests began to arrive at eight o'clock. Soon the drawing room was heaving with actors in full evening dress. They jostled for space with "the bohemian set"—young directors and writers, dressed more casually in cream linen suits, or pale trousers and waistcoats. The air was filled with cigarette smoke, and the drinks flowed.

Isabella, wearing a sheath of white silk, mingled with her guests, keeping an eye out for her handsome army officer. Maria had assured her that she had hand-delivered the invitation to his parents' palazzo. Isabella checked her diamond evening watch—it was already half past nine and there was still no sign of him.

The actress Doris Duranti arrived just before ten. Clearly determined to make an entrance, she swept into the drawing room wearing a long silver-pleated Fortuny gown. Her companion for the evening was the Minister of Popular Culture, Alessandro Pavolini. Although married with a family, he was famously besotted with Doris. He dropped her off at the studios each day in his chauffeur-driven car and it was rumored that he even accompanied her to the hairdressers. Men generally envied his ability to ensnare such a beauty, while despising his slavish devotion. Women, on the other hand, disapproved of the illicit liaison, but secretly admired her hold over him. He was not a particularly attractive man, Isabella observed, as the couple glided through the drawing room toward her. He had cruel dark eyes—slightly too close together—and his upper lip was dominated by a small mustache. His thinning dark hair was slicked back over his high forehead. Doris, by contrast, was exquisite, with a fine long nose, wide dark eyes and full lips. She had an exotic quality that could be mesmerizing—both on screen and in person.

"Isabella, darling." Doris grasped Isabella's arms, kissing the air on either side of her face. "How lovely...Is everyone here?" She looked around her, as if vetting the room.

"Pretty much," said Isabella. "Did you have to bring him?" she whispered.

"Oh, he's no trouble. He's a little lamb really. He wanted to come, how could I say no?"

"Doesn't he have a family to go to on a Saturday evening?"

Doris glared at Isabella, her nostrils flaring.

"That's the problem with you, Isabella. You are so... bourgeois."

Doris plunged into the crowd, dragging Alessandro behind her. She made a beeline for Cinecittà's Director of Cinema, Eitel Monaco.

"Eitel, darling, you know Alessandro, of course."

Isabella turned away and picked up a dry Martini from a tray, trying not to show her growing disappointment that her lover, Ludovico, had still not arrived.

"Lovely party, Isabella." Princess Matilda of Savoy had maneuvered through the crowd and stood at her side holding a glass of champagne. "But you look a little sad."

"Do I? I'm sorry—I was just hoping someone would come..."

"Who? Would I know him?"

"I'm not sure if you would. He's an army officer—Ludovico Albani."

"Ah! Ludovico—yes. He is a charming boy. I've known his family for years. They used to entertain lavishly before the war, in their palazzo in Rome."

The Princess waved to someone across the room and drifted away, leaving Isabella with the sense that her interest in Ludovico was not to be encouraged. He was an aristocrat, after all, while she—in spite of her star status—was just a poor girl from Buenos Aires.

Chapter Two

Livia Moretti came into the hall from the garden, barefoot, wearing a light-blue summer dress. The villa was cool after the intense heat of the terrace. The stone floors felt soft beneath her feet as she padded across to her father's study. The only sounds were the ticking of the clock, her grandfather Alberto snoring quietly in the sitting room, and the distant chatter of her mother, Luisa, and the housekeeper in the kitchen. In her hand, Livia carried a letter confirming her a place at the University of Florence. It had arrived a few days before, and she was anxious to show it to her father, Giacomo. He had driven up earlier that day from Florence, where he had a legal practice. During the week he lived in a small apartment in the city, only returning to his family at weekends.

Livia was about to knock on his study door, but could hear him talking on the telephone. Reluctant to interrupt his work, she slipped the letter back into her dress pocket, and retreated to the terrace. Her father had been enthusiastic about the idea of his eighteen-year-old daughter attending university, but Livia knew that her mother did not see the point of girls receiving an education. She feared there would be an argument, but hoped they could resolve the matter amicably over dinner.

This large airy villa, deep in the Tuscan countryside, and a small apartment in Florence were all that was left of the family's estate, after decades of financial mismanagement. Giacomo was the first generation of his family to work for a living, but he was untouched by the loss of their fortune.

"Money," he often said to Livia, "can be a curse as well as a comfort. Better to spend your life making a difference to people's lives, rather than counting coins in a vault."

In spite of their reduced circumstances, the family were nevertheless comfortably off. As a young girl, Livia had been educated at home by a German governess, Fräulein Schneider. A strict disciplinarian, she insisted on her charge becoming fluent in German, French and English—something the child had railed against at the time. She had also emphasized the importance of perfect posture, and employed a technique of inserting a board down the back of her pupil's dress, requiring her to sit bolt upright when working at her lessons, or eating her meals. This torturous training had given Livia a sense of rebellion against figures of authority, but it had also produced the desired effect. She now had a grace and elegance—her head always held high, her neck elongated, her shoulders square—that drew admiring glances from everyone.

At the age of eleven, Livia was sent to boarding school on the southern outskirts of Florence. Here she flourished, excelling at foreign languages and the arts. The pupils rarely went unaccompanied into the city itself; instead access was limited to supervised trips to art galleries, or guided tours of historic sites. Crocodiles of little girls were led around the center of the city, before being shepherded back onto a bus or the train, and returning to school in time for supper.

Occasionally, at the start or end of term, her mother would venture into the city and take Livia shopping at one of the big department stores such as La Rinascente in the Piazza della Repubblica. After lunch in one of the grander hotels, they would visit the Boboli Gardens to escape the crowds, or if it was raining go to the cinema. The films they usually saw were innocent, light-hearted stories of love and romance. Known colloquially as *Telefoni Bianchi* or "White Telephone films," they were set in opulent Art Deco surroundings, and featured the glamorous stars of the day—Doris Duranti, Elsa Merlini and Isabella Bellucci—starring opposite tall handsome men like Vittorio De Sica and Osvaldo Valenti. For Livia, who had been brought up in the countryside in a rambling farmhouse filled with ancient furniture and crumbling infrastructure, the sight of these men and women, living in extravagant modern homes, wearing beautiful clothes, was as far removed from her own life as she could imagine.

Clutching her letter of acceptance, Livia waited anxiously on the terrace for her father to emerge from his study. It was his habit to join the family before dinner, where he would sit beneath the vine that rambled over the pergola, a glass of wine in hand, his newspaper placed conveniently on a small side table. Livia placed the letter on top of the paper and sat down expectantly. Meanwhile, her mother was quietly sewing, a glass of Amaretto by her side. As the sun set across the garden, Giacomo, wearing a crumpled linen suit that had seen better days, wandered onto the terrace. He ran his hands through his thinning silver hair and poured himself a glass of white wine.

As he sat down, he noticed the letter. "This isn't for me," he said to Livia, "it's addressed to you."

"I know," Livia replied, blushing. "I've already read it. I wanted you to see it."

He ran his eye over the contents. "Well done, Livia." He looked up at her with tears in his eyes. "This is exactly what I had hoped for. English Literature and History of Art—an excellent combination."

She rushed over to him, and crouched down next to his chair and kissed him. "Thank you, Papa."

"Well, I'm not so sure it's a good idea," her mother interjected from the other side of the terrace, "what with the war and everything. Surely it would be better if she stayed at home with me."

"Tied to your apron strings?" Her husband smiled indulgently. "The girl has a fine mind—what on earth would she learn at home?"

"How to cook, how to be a good wife."

"She's barely eighteen. She needs an education, and she's a clever girl—an intellectual. Plenty of time to learn how to be a wife."

"But is getting 'an education' so important? I didn't get one."

Giacomo looked up from his newspaper. "You use the word 'education,' Luisa, as if it's something to be ashamed of. If not an education, I'd like to know what your definition of 'important' is. What, for example, is so important about learning to cook?"

"Well, you'd be in a fine state if you didn't have me and Angela to cook for you."

"I'd eat in a restaurant," he replied loftily. "I certainly wouldn't starve."

"Oh, Giacomo!" Luisa stood up irritably. "You're impossible! The point is—I'm worried about her. How will she get to university each day, for example? We live nearly forty kilometers away. It's not like when she was at boarding school. She'll have to take the train or a tram, or even drive."

"If that's what you're worried about, let's move to the apartment," her husband suggested.

"To your apartment in Florence? How on earth could we all live there? It's far too small," Luisa complained. "It's fine for you to spend the odd night there when you're working on a case, but not for the whole family day in, day out. Livia won't even have her own bedroom—where will she sleep?"

"In my study, of course. I only use it in the evenings when I'm working on a long case. I can work at the dining table instead."

"But I don't like the city," Luisa persisted. "It's so crowded. And what about bombs? The government say we should be leaving the cities and moving to the countryside if we can—not moving back into them."

"That's up in the north," Giacomo reassured her. "Turin, Milan, Genoa. Not here."

"The Anglo-Americans bombed Naples the other day," she interjected. "I heard about it on the radio. Who's to say they won't bomb Florence too?"

"The day may come, of course, when they do bomb Florence, but it has no real strategic importance. The Allies' chief targets are our troops fighting in Russia and North Africa, plus our industrial heartlands in the north."

"How can you be so calm?" Luisa snapped.

"What is the point of becoming exercised?" Giacomo glanced at her over the top of his newspaper. "Our government is intent on a mad strategy which is doomed to failure. I sincerely hope the whole fiasco will be over soon—before too many young men are sacrificed on the altar of Mussolini's ego."

Luisa slumped back down into her cane chair, her dark brown eyes filling with tears. Giacomo patiently folded his newspaper, laid it on the side table, and crossed over to her. He knelt down at Luisa's side and took her hands in his.

"Look, my darling. If things do get bad in Florence we can always move back here to the villa. But, in the meantime, let the girl continue her education."

Luisa, who was not to be so easily placated, changed tack. "And another thing—who will look after Alberto if we go away? You know how helpless your father is."

"Angela will take care of him," Giacomo suggested calmly, as he sat back down again.

"She's getting too old," Luisa insisted. "And her cooking is appalling…and Gino's is no better." Gino was Angela's elderly husband who tended the gardens of the villa.

"Well," said Giacomo, finally becoming exasperated, "if you really don't want to come, you can stay in the country with my father, and Livia and I will live in the city alone. I'm sure we'll manage."

"What a ridiculous idea!" Luisa protested. "You are as bad as Alberto—incapable of looking after yourself. And Livia is just a young girl; she needs her mother."

"So we are agreed then," said Giacomo smiling, "we shall all live in Florence together."

Luisa could see any further argument was pointless. Over the following days, she resentfully packed various essentials: suitcases filled with clothes and extra linen for the beds, along with her sewing basket, cooking utensils and supplies from the larder. Finally, with their possessions safely stowed in Giacomo's old black Lancia, they gathered outside the villa, Luisa tearfully hugging her father-in-law and offering last-minute instructions to Angela and Gino, before they climbed into the car and drove away down the winding road to Florence.

They arrived outside the apartment building late in the afternoon. It was an exceptionally hot day and the city throbbed with late summer heat. Luisa sweated slightly beneath her summer straw hat, and as they unloaded their suitcases and baskets of provisions, piling them up in the entrance hall on the ground floor of the building, Livia braced herself for her mother's inevitable outburst.

"Oh Giacomo, why have we come here?" Luisa complained, leaning against the cool walls of the lobby, removing her hat and wiping her brow with a lace handkerchief she kept in her sleeve. "It's so hot in the city, and these stairs to the apartment will kill me." She gazed up at the staircase winding its way inexorably to the top of the building. "Five flights—how are we to manage? I can't think why your family didn't buy an apartment on the ground floor. Perhaps we should have stayed in the country after all."

Giacomo put down a large brown leather suitcase and cupped her face in his hands. "Luisa my dear, we're here for Livia, remember. Come…give me your case to carry. Let's get everything upstairs."

With their belongings in an untidy pile on the landing outside the apartment, Giacomo wrestled with the multiple locks on the heavy chestnut door. As the last of them gave way, the family almost fell into the tiny entrance hall. Sunlight filtered through a pair of glazed double doors that led to the sitting room, illuminating the dust-filled atmosphere.

Giacomo dropped their bags on the floor, and walked purposefully through to the sitting room, where he opened the windows and unlocked the shutters. The room flooded with air and light, revealing a charmingly proportioned room ideal for a small family. A long biscuit-colored linen sofa stood against one wall, opposite two armchairs with cane backs, upholstered in dark-red velvet. A pair of dark, impressive portraits of Giacomo's grandparents hung on the wall between the two windows.

While her mother began to unload baskets of provisions in the small kitchen, Livia walked down the corridor, inspecting the rest of the apartment. A bathroom stood on the left-hand side. It was dark, tiled and entirely functional. Next to this stood her father's bedroom. It had none of the femininity of her parents' bedroom in the villa, with its painted furniture and flowered linens. Standing in the doorway, Livia noted the small double bed covered with a dull green bedcover and a bedside table, on which stood an untidy pile of papers, jostling for position with a reading lamp. The only other furniture was a wardrobe. Opening it, Livia found it contained nothing more than a spare dark suit, some items of underwear, and a pile of shirts still in their wrapping from the laundry. She carried on down the corridor toward her father's study. This room, which overlooked the street below, would now be her bedroom. Beneath the shuttered window stood Giacomo's desk. It was covered with books and papers, and a bookcase along one long wall was filled with legal textbooks—so much so, that it had virtually collapsed under their weight. Further books stood in tottering piles on the floor. A tiny daybed, where Livia would now sleep, was wedged against the opposite wall, covered in a dark-red toile fabric that seemed strangely out of keeping with the rest of the apartment; Livia presumed her mother, or possibly her long-dead grandmother, had chosen it. She laid her suitcase on the bed and began to hang up her clothes in the wardrobe.

Those first few days in the apartment were a whirlwind of cleaning and sorting. Livia and Luisa stripped the beds and made them up with the fresh linen brought from the villa. Slowly a pile of dirty washing accumulated on the kitchen floor.

"Before the war, I had an arrangement with a laundry round the corner," Luisa sighed. "Your father would drop his shirts in to them on his way to work—and once a fortnight they'd wash his sheets. But the thought of staggering down all those stairs carrying all of this seems impossible." She gazed down at the untidy mountain of washing. "I think it would be easier if we washed it ourselves."

"But where will we dry it all?" Livia asked sensibly. "Should we hang a line across the front of the house, between the windows?" On their way through the outskirts of the city, she had noticed how people strung up their washing lines between apartments.

"Absolutely not!" her mother retorted. "What a disgraceful suggestion—we are not peasants, Livia. No, we shall dry the laundry on the roof terrace."

"Do we have a roof terrace?" Livia asked.

Her mother took a set of keys from a kitchen cabinet, and unlocked a narrow door at one end of the hall. Livia had assumed this was merely a cleaning cupboard, but as Luisa opened the door, Livia was surprised to find a set of steep stone steps leading upward.

"Go and have a look," her mother said, handing her a piece of rope she'd found in a drawer. "And put up this washing line while you're there...and please be careful, the railings are not safe."

At the top of stairs was a landing with three doors leading off it. Livia tried the handle of the first door, which opened to reveal a dark attic space, illuminated only by a tiny window, and filled with wooden tea chests, an old desk and a couple of broken chairs. Peering into the chests, Livia saw they contained nothing but old legal files of her father's clients. Opening the second door revealed a minuscule space filled once again with tea chests. The final door was part-glazed, and although its windows were smeared with years of grime, Livia had a tantalizing glimpse of the roof terrace beyond. On it she could see a rusting pergola, and a battered metal table and chairs.

She opened the rickety door, and walked out onto the terrace, instantly feeling the sun beating down on the back of her neck. The terrace itself was about three meters square, edged by a low wall into which was concreted a flimsy metal rail running around the perimeter at waist height. Her mother had been right: the rail wobbled when she pushed it. But in spite of the shabby surroundings, Livia could imagine the family eating up there, the old plant pots filled once again with scarlet geraniums and flowering climbers.

At one end of the terrace, there was a fixed ladder which led to a flat roof above. Intrigued, Livia climbed the ladder. Disappointingly, the roof contained nothing more than the water tank for the building, but the view was spectacular. Shielding her eyes against the fierce Florentine sun, she admired the three-hundred-and-sixty-degree panorama of the city. To the south, the terra-cotta cupola of the Duomo, and further west the angular blond splendor of the church of Santa Croce. To the north, the city was framed by the soft green hills on top of which stood the village of Fiesole, behind which, much further away, she could imagine the family villa. In the foreground, and surrounding the terrace, were the rich-red terra-cotta roofs of the neighboring buildings.

She clambered back down the ladder and began to look for a way to attach the washing line. An old hook projecting from a wall seemed sturdy enough, and she tied the other end to the rusting pergola.

"It's wonderful," said Livia, coming back into the kitchen. "The view is so beautiful—we should eat our meals up there. And if we cleared out Papa's papers, I could move into that little attic room, so Papa could have his study back."

"Don't be so ridiculous!" Luisa retorted. "Where would we put all his papers? He won't hear of getting rid of anything, and his office in the city is completely full up. Besides, the attic room has no insulation. Really, you wouldn't like it—it's boiling hot in the summer and freezing in the winter. But the terrace is a good place to hang the laundry. Now help me."

In the first few days of living in Florence, Livia found it thrilling to walk down the narrow cobbled road toward the Duomo each morning and feel that she was really part of this bustling city. She was fascinated by the eclectic mix of people she encountered on her daily journey—the street traders calling out to passers-by; the clerics rushing to church to conduct morning prayers, their black robes flapping; the ladies who, in spite of the war, maintained a certain elegance, clicking down the road in their high-heeled shoes, on their way to coffee or lunch. Livia often wondered who they were meeting, dressed in such finery.

Gradually, the family settled into city life. Luisa coped with the privations, as she saw them, of urban living. Food was getting scarce all over Italy and supplies to the markets were dwindling. Meat was almost unobtainable and all the staple foods like flour, sugar and salt were rationed. Giacomo appeared to be unconcerned about such trivialities and simply buried himself in his work. Livia relished the freedom her studies gave her. She quickly made friends at the university, and enjoyed spending time with them—roaming the streets with a gaggle of girls, or lying on the grass in the Boboli Gardens. One young girl in particular became her closest friend.

Elena Lombardi was studying the same subjects as Livia, and the two girls quickly formed a bond. Slight in stature, with bright blue eyes and golden curls that framed her pretty face, Elena was the physical opposite of Livia, who was taller, with shoulder-length dark hair and large brown eyes. Brought up in Florence, Elena had attended a day school for girls near the Duomo. Her life had been much freer than Livia's strict boarding-school upbringing. To Livia's delight, she knew the city well, and together they visited quirky little cafés and out-of-the-way bookshops. Elena even had male friends—young men who held no romantic attraction for her, but were simply people to have coffee or lunch with. This made her, in Livia's eyes, both sophisticated and worldly and she felt lucky to have such a knowledgeable friend.

For her part, Elena loved Livia's enthusiasm and original way of looking at the world.

"You're not like other girls I've met," she said one afternoon, as they lay on the grass overlooking the central pond in the Boboli Gardens, listening to the refreshing sound of splashing water from the fountain. It was late in the afternoon, and the sun's heat had begun to ebb away.

"In what way?" asked Livia.

"You don't follow the herd—you make up your own mind. I like that."

"My father's influence, I suspect. That, and years of boarding school. It made me rather rebellious."

"What was it like?"

"It was…restrictive," Livia replied, her hand running over the grass, feeling it cool beneath her fingers. "Although less restrictive than having a governess who insisted on putting a board down my back." She giggled.

"Did she really do that?" Elena was aghast.

"She did—even on holiday. We used to go and stay with friends who had a villa on the coast, near Forte dei Marmi—do you know it?"

Elena shook her head.

"I was only allowed to take the board off when I went swimming."

"Did your parents approve of this torture?"

"My mother did. She always told me I'd be grateful in the end. I don't think my father really noticed."

"Your childhood sounds fascinating, if a little claustrophobic," said Elena, laughing. Secretly she was intrigued by her friend's genteel upbringing. "Did you live on a big estate, growing up?"

"No! There used to be a lot of land with vineyards and so on, but it was sold off a long time ago. My grandfather, and his father before him, were no good with money, or so my father says."

"Well, I think you look very aristocratic." Elena cast a shy glance at Livia's elegant profile. "Like one of the Medici beauties we were looking at yesterday in class."

Livia blushed. "Don't be so silly."

"Are you ashamed of your background?" Elena asked. "You always seem embarrassed talking about it."

"I suppose I am," Livia said shyly. "My father despises inherited wealth. In his work as a lawyer, he always supports the 'little man': people who can't fight for themselves—the worker, the tenant, the shopkeeper fighting injustice from a domineering landlord, that sort of thing. I suppose it's rubbed off on me. Besides, we don't have much money now." She looked over at her friend lying on the grass. "Now, that's enough about me. I want to know all about your family."

"My life is much less interesting. My mother looks after the house—although she used to be a secretary. My father's a doctor; he's a surgeon at the hospital."

"That must be challenging—particularly at the moment with the war going on."

"He gets very depressed," said Elena, sitting up, and wrapping her arms around her knees. "The hospitals don't have the supplies they need—it makes him angry."

"I'm sorry, that must be hard. Do you have brothers and sisters?"

"No. I'm the only one, like you."

The two girls' History of Art lectures were held in an airy paneled lecture theater, its walls covered with impressive religious works of art. They usually sat together at the rear of the hall, and Livia, who preferred her English Literature classes to History of Art, often found her concentration wandering.

One warm afternoon, she felt her eyelids drooping as their tutor showed slide after slide of works by Verrocchio, a Renaissance artist and mentor of the great Leonardo da Vinci. Livia's eyes began to wander sleepily around the lecture theater and settled on an intense young man sitting a few places away. He was scribbling notes in a leather-bound book on his lap, his metal-rimmed glasses slipping down his nose. He had dark hair that flopped over his face, which he pushed back distractedly from time to time. Perhaps sensing he was being observed, he looked around and noticed the delicate, dark-haired girl watching him. He smiled at her. She blushed, looking away embarrassed, and hooked her own shoulder-length hair behind her ears. Elena, sitting next to her, noticed her friend's reaction.

"He's good-looking, isn't he?" she whispered. "I know his family a little...his father's a surgeon at the same hospital as my father. Cosimo's doing a doctorate here—philosophy, I seem to remember."

"What's he doing in our lecture then?" Livia whispered back.

"He must be interested in Verrocchio, I suppose," Elena replied. "And now, it seems, he's interested in you too."

When the lecture was over and the students were milling about outside the hall, the young man weaved through the crowd, heading straight for the two girls. Livia blushed slightly as he approached them.

"Cosimo," said Elena, "how lovely to see you again."

He bent down to kiss his friend on the cheek, but he was clearly transfixed by Livia.

"Cosimo...may I introduce Livia, a new friend of mine."

He bowed his head a little. "It's wonderful to meet you."

"Well," said Elena tactfully, "I ought to be going—I've got a tutorial. I'll see you later, Livia."

As the summer faded into autumn and the air grew cooler, Cosimo and Livia were inseparable. They wandered the streets, holding hands and talking feverishly. They discussed everything—their studies, their families and, of course, the war. Nothing was off limits. They discovered that their fathers—both men with a strong sense of public duty—shared a hatred of Fascism.

"Do you know what I like about you?" Cosimo asked Livia one chilly afternoon as they wandered around Piazza della Repubblica, the wintry sun sinking in the west, casting long shadows.

"No," Livia replied playfully.

"You never annoy me."

She came to a halt outside a café and stared at him. "What do you mean? Are you often annoyed by people?"

"Constantly. Most people speak before they think, and have no sense of humor or irony. You're not like that. For someone so young, you're very wise."

He turned and gazed down at her. She sensed his desire to kiss her, and tilted her face toward his. At that moment, a strong gust of wind blew through the piazza, and she shivered slightly.

"You're cold," he said. "Let's go in here." He pointed toward an impressive-looking restaurant with tall glazed windows. It was called Café Paskowski.

"It looks rather expensive." Livia peered anxiously at the elegantly dressed customers sitting inside.

"No, it's not really. It's popular with poverty-stricken artists and rich aristocrats alike—it's an interesting place." He smiled and winked at her, took her by the elbow and steered her firmly inside. They chose a table by the window from where they could view the comings and goings in the piazza. Lights were coming on in the shops, making the scene outside the window feel inviting.

"My mother and I used to shop in the department store over there," Livia said, indicating La Rinascente, "but we always ate in one of the hotels afterward—all very safe and respectable. I suspect she would have thought this place was too..." she paused, searching for the right word, "...bohemian." Livia looked around her at the glamorous clientele.

Cosimo laughed and beckoned the waiter over. "Two glasses of sweet vermouth, please."

"I've never drunk this before," said Livia, as the waiter laid their drinks on the table with a flourish. She lifted the glass nervously to her mouth and took a sip. "Mmmm...It's delicious."

"Good, I'm glad you like it." Cosimo sipped his drink thoughtfully.

"What's the matter?" she asked, reaching across the table and touching his hand gently.

"I'm just a bit worried about something," he replied.

"What? Tell me."

"It's not a very romantic subject."

"Don't worry about that. What is it?"

He put his drink down on the table and grasped her hand in his. "I can't stop thinking about what would happen if I got called up."

"I understand—it must be a frightening prospect."

"I've heard such bad things from my father—so many young men have been wounded, their lives destroyed." He lowered his voice to a whisper. "It seems such a waste, especially for a cause I don't believe in."

"My father says it's madness to be invading Greece, and even Russia, when the army is so massively under-resourced. It is the work of an 'egomaniac,' he says. I can't understand how some people still think Mussolini has brought some honor to this country."

They sat for a moment, lost in their own thoughts.

Livia broke the silence. "What would you do...if you were called up?"

"I'd try to get into the Medical Corps, I suppose."

"I thought they only took medical students for that."

"They must need orderlies," he said. "Or maybe I could work as a radio operator. I'm good at that sort of thing. Anything but proper soldiering—I've never fired a gun and I'm not sure I could kill anyone." He put his head in his hands. "Oh God! I don't know...I just want to go on with my studies."

"Try not to think about it," she said comfortingly. "With luck, it will be over soon."

As Christmas approached, the days grew shorter and the sun began to disappear behind threatening dark clouds scudding across huge skies. When Livia went up to the roof terrace with a basket of washing first thing in the morning, her fingers were often red with cold as she hung the sheets and towels on the line to dry. Sometimes, when she returned to collect it later in the afternoon, the laundry was frozen solid and she and her mother would drape it across the backs of the dining chairs where it dripped water onto the parquet flooring.

Livia and Cosimo still met every day—once on their way into university and again in the evening, when he would walk her home. Sometimes they would stop to buy a bag of steaming chestnuts from one of the traders who had set up small braziers at the side of the road. Between mouthfuls, they would warm their hands on the hot paper bag. Before they reached her apartment, he would pull her to one side, and wrap his arms around her. When he kissed her, she felt as if her body was melting into his. But knowing that her mother would be waiting for her, she would reluctantly pull away.

"I must go in," she would say.

"Stay a little longer," he would plead.

On the last day of term, they stood together, out of sight of the apartment, dreading the moment when they would have to part.

"I have to go back to the country tomorrow, with my family," she blurted out. "I wish we didn't have to, but my grandfather is all alone."

"I understand," said Cosimo, holding her heart-shaped face in his hands and kissing her gently on the mouth. "But I will miss you."

"And I'll miss you—desperately," she replied. "I can hardly imagine not seeing you every day. But we'll be back early in the New Year. Perhaps you could come to dinner and meet my parents. I'm sure you'd get on with my father very well, and I know he would love you."

"I'd like that."

"Why not come in with me now?" she suggested. "It's so cold today. I'm sure my mother could make us something nice and warm to eat."

"No," he replied. "When I meet your parents, I'd like to do it properly. It's not fair on your mother—she may not have enough food."

"That's very thoughtful of you."

"I have a mother too, you know—I know what they are like—and they don't enjoy surprises." He laughed and kissed her again. "Can I write to you while you're away?"

"Of course, I'd love that."

When they finally parted and she walked toward her apartment building, she instantly missed him. She was about to run back to him, to kiss him one more time and feel his arms around her, but he had already gone—swallowed up in the Christmas crowds.

Chapter Three

Rome
December 1941

The stars of Cinecittà were expected to support the war effort over the Christmas period. Isabella had invited her grandmother and aunt to join Giovanna and herself on Christmas Eve. The women arrived early and set to work in the kitchen preparing meat sauces and pasta, while Isabella retreated to the sitting room where a huge bag of fan mail had been deposited by the studio. The letters were predominantly from soldiers heading off for the front in Russia, or North Africa. As she dipped into them, laying them out on a long table overlooking the garden, she was touched by their simple faith that a kind word and a photograph of her would "give them strength to go into battle." And so in the days after Christmas, Isabella and her mother, together with her assistant Maria, sat at the dining table in Villa Rosa, piled high with stacks of letters, photographs and envelopes.

"These boys," said her mother, putting a letter on the "answered" pile, "they think they are in love with you, don't they? It must be wonderful to be so adored."

"Not really," said Isabella, sensing her mother's petty jealousy. "I feel sorry for them, to be honest. I mean, it's not real is it, this passion they have? They don't even know me, and I certainly don't know them."

Giovanna gave the impression that she thought her daughter's life was one of lazy self-indulgence, which irritated Isabella. Her mother rarely acknowledged the hard work involved in being an actress—the weeks spent learning her lines, the grueling early starts, the constant arguments with the company lawyers for better pay, better hours and better parts. Giovanna simply saw a young woman with a beautiful house, fabulous clothes and the admiration of men she didn't even know. But what really irked Isabella was that her mother had never thanked her for their comfortable existence. Isabella had supported her mother financially since she was sixteen. She had given her a better life than she could ever have hoped for back in Buenos Aires, and it was hurtful that her mother could not be more grateful.

Giovanna pushed a letter across the table, signed by someone called Ludovico. Isabella's heart stopped. Was it her Ludovico? As she quickly scanned the letter, she realized this man was not her lover but another young soldier with the same name. She was reminded of their last afternoon together, when she lay in Ludovico's arms on the beach in the closing days of summer.

"I'd love one of your photographs," he had said, kissing her hair. "You know, one of your official ones, with your signature."

"Don't be so silly," she had replied. "They are for strangers. We are lovers. Wouldn't you prefer a photograph of us together?"

"I have photographs like that already," he'd insisted, "but I'd like one of your official ones...really I would. I can keep it with me always, next to my heart." He had laughed, dramatically tapping his chest. "And I could show it off to my friends. This is my girlfriend, the movie star!"

When they got back to the villa, she had reluctantly signed a photo and handed it to him: "To my love from your love, Isabella."

"Have you heard from that handsome soldier of yours?" Her mother's voice startled her. "You know, the one you were going out with in the summer? He was called Ludovico, wasn't he?"

"Yes," said Isabella evasively.

"And?" Her mother's curiosity about her love life was irritating.

"He wrote to me, yes. A lovely letter as it happens."

In fact, the letter had haunted her. Written the day before he was sent to North Africa, the words were loving enough, but she had felt a distance—both physical and emotional. He had made no declaration; nor had he suggested a meeting. It sounded almost like a farewell.

I miss you and think of you constantly. We are moving off tomorrow. I shall be stationed in Libya—I don't know for how long, nor do I know how easy it will be to write once I'm there. I'm sorry I had to leave so suddenly. You must understand—I am a career soldier and I have my duty to perform. But I regret how we had to part.

I keep your picture with me at all times, next to my heart—just as I promised.

Take care of yourself,
With love
Ludovico.

"He was a good catch," said Giovanna, adding another letter to the pile. "I'm surprised he's not arranged to see you over Christmas."

"Maybe he's busy, fighting the war," Isabella replied sarcastically, pushing a photograph into an envelope and sealing it.

"Still…" her mother went on, ignoring her daughter's tone, "you should keep up with his parents. Go and see his mother, the Baroness, and ask her how he is."

"No," said Isabella firmly. "She was never very friendly to me."

"Well, she should be—you're a movie star. Her son is just a soldier. He'd be lucky to have you."

"He's not just a soldier. He's an officer—and an aristocratic one at that."

"Exactly," said her mother, licking an envelope and sticking it down. "You go and see her. Just think, you could become 'La Baronessa' one day."

The following day, against her better judgment, Isabella found herself standing on the marble steps of Ludovico's parents' grand palazzo. Wearing a smart dark-red dress and her best fur coat, she fiddled nervously with her leather gloves, regretting she had allowed her mother to talk her into the visit. She was about to turn tail and leave, when the butler opened the door and ushered her into the grand salon.

The spectacular high-ceilinged room was decorated with florid paintings of fat-bottomed cherubs frolicking with bare-breasted women in classical dress. A pair of gilded sofas sat on either side of an ornate marble fireplace. Uncertain if she should sit uninvited, Isabella hovered anxiously by the long windows overlooking the elegant formal gardens.

The sound of high heels on a marble floor presaged the entrance of Ludovico's mother. She swept into the room, her silver hair coiffed to perfection, a tight-fitting gray dress emphasizing her slender frame.

"You asked to see me?" The Baroness stood in the doorway, studying Isabella disdainfully.

"I just wondered if you'd heard anything," Isabella asked, her voice uncharacteristically tentative, "from Ludovico . . . as it's Christmas."

"Well, if I have, I don't think it's any of your business."

"It's just that I haven't heard from him since October."

Ludovico's mother sat down wearily, gesturing to the silk-covered sofa opposite. "You'd better sit down."

Isabella sat nervously on the edge of the seat, fidgeting with the buttons of her dress. "He wrote to me from Sicily," she began. "He said he was about to move on . . . to North Africa."

"Yes." His mother pursed her rouged lips.

"I just wanted to know . . . if he's all right."

"As far as I know." The Baroness stared down at her manicured hands.

"He explained it would be hard to write from Libya."

"Did he?" She looked up at Isabella. "Well, he's written to *me*." She emphasized the word.

Isabella bit her lip nervously.

"You might as well know," his mother went on, her voice conveying profound irritation, "Ludovico's commanding officer, Marchese Alfonso di Castelnuovo, made it quite clear that he should dispense with this unsuitable *liaison*." She spat out the word as if it were an unpleasant taste in her mouth.

"What on earth do you mean?" Isabella asked defensively. She could feel her eyes prickling with tears of humiliation.

"A man has a duty—to his country, in particular. Ludovico is a serving army officer. He has a reputation to maintain. He can't be seen in the company of an *actress*." Again she spat out the word. "We are at war, you know—or maybe you don't understand that in your strange little film world."

Isabella had never heard anyone speak so harshly—either to her, or about her profession. She felt reprimanded, like a naughty child at school. "I'm sorry," she said, suddenly rising to her feet.

"Yes, it's better that you go."

When Isabella reached the door of the grand salon, Ludovico's mother called after her. "It would never have worked between you—your backgrounds are too different. Please don't come back."

Isabella hurried down the long drive and climbed into her car, slamming the door. At least now she knew the truth: his last letter had been a goodbye, perhaps demanded by the army, or more likely by his parents. She was not good enough, not aristocratic enough, to be the young Baron's wife. Humiliated, she quickly drove back home, where she ran upstairs and locked herself in her bedroom. As she lay sobbing on her bed, she heard a knock at the door.

"Isabella…Isabella, what's happened?" It was her mother.

"Just go away…please."

"Oh Isabella, don't be silly…let me in."

"No! I should never have listened to you. I knew it was a mistake to go there. His mother hates me. She told me to go away and not come back. I'm not good enough for him, apparently. Please just leave me alone."

She lay in the dark, listening to her mother's retreating footsteps.

The following morning, Isabella emerged wearing slacks and a sweater, her makeup done, her hair perfectly arranged. In the dining room, she drank a cup of coffee and sifted through her mail in silence.

Her mother, sitting at the other end of the table, looked up from the newspaper. "Are you feeling better this morning?"

"Of course," said Isabella crisply. "I have a busy day...it'll take my mind off things."

"Good." Her mother poured herself another cup of coffee. "Are you filming?"

"No, photographs—but I am going to the studios. 'Today we are knitting!'" she announced, with an ironic smile.

The Ministry encouraged actors who worked for Cines, the State-sponsored production company, to take part in staged photographs. These were then sent out to the press and film magazines to cheer the population. The pictures showed them performing everyday activities like knitting scarves and hats for the troops in Russia, or shopping on a bicycle, their baskets filled with produce.

"But you hate knitting," her mother pointed out.

Isabella drained her coffee cup and stood up to go. "I'll see you later."

Isabella did indeed hate knitting. She also rarely shopped for food—her housekeeper or her mother did that. And yet, apparently, these were the photographs that people wanted to see. Photographs that proved what delightfully "ordinary" people the stars really were. Isabella convinced herself that it was harmless publicity, and yet there was a dishonesty about it. Ordinary people's baskets were not filled with produce from the markets; in fact, they were increasingly empty. Actors like Isabella were spared the worst of this hardship—after all, they had enough money and could buy food on the black market. Besides, the restaurants they frequented with their influential friends had an almost limitless supply of food and drink, which the general population could only dream of.

Another PR photo-shoot had been arranged a few days later by the minister, Alessandro Pavolini. Isabella and several other actresses were to visit wounded soldiers in a military hospital just outside Rome. To ensure they arrived at the hospital in good time, a taxi collected them.

"No Doris today?" asked Isabella, as she climbed into the back seat.

"No," said Elsa De Giorgi, making room for her. "She's coming down separately, apparently—in Alessandro's car."

"Trust her," said Isabella, settling into her seat and smiling at the others.

The women were all immaculately dressed, wearing fur coats and hats, as if they were off on a glamorous outing.

"I wonder who they've lined up for us this time?" asked Isabella. "The last visit we did, the soldiers were so handsome they could have been chosen by Central Casting. I don't think any of them had anything worse than a broken arm."

"Our brave soldiers!" said Elsa sarcastically. "So talented and clever that they never even get injured!"

When the actresses arrived, they were surprised to find themselves shown into a ward filled with badly wounded men. One bed was surrounded by bulky studio lights, their cables trailing across the floor. A studio movie camera had been set up on a tripod pointing at a heavily bandaged man. Nurses trying to attend to him were having to step over the cables, and squeeze past the film crew, idly standing around, waiting for the director to start.

"What's going on?" Elsa demanded.

"Isn't it obvious?" said the unit manager. "We're shooting a movie, signora."

"We thought we were here for photographs," protested Isabella. "Not a movie."

"Those are my orders, signora," said the director apologetically, shrugging his shoulders. "I'll run you through your lines."

"What lines?" Elsa asked.

"Look," said the director wearily, "Pavolini will be here soon. Just cooperate…all right? Then we can all get home a bit quicker."

Throughout the morning, the cameras rolled and the actresses delivered their hastily memorized lines. But it was an uncomfortable situation, made worse when a doctor arrived for his ward round.

"What is going on here?" he demanded of the director. "I will not have these men subjected to this sort of disturbance. Who gave you permission to film here?"

"Alessandro Pavolini," said the director. "It's a ministerial order."

"But my patients are desperately ill—in some cases, dying. Is this how you think wounded men should be treated? Is this the sort of spectacle you think our people would enjoy? It's not make-believe, it's real life and death. To make propaganda out of it is an outrage."

"I'm sorry," said the director. "But I've got my orders…there's nothing I can do about it."

Isabella had some sympathy with the doctor's point of view. Acutely aware they were in the medical team's way, she did her job as professionally and swiftly as possible—smiling gracefully, touching a hand or an arm, trying to show genuine concern for the patients. But the scowls of the injured soldiers disturbed her. It could have been Ludovico lying there…with a leg missing, or his handsome face disfigured by shrapnel. And how would he feel being used in this way?

"That was embarrassing," she muttered to Elsa at the end of the day, as they climbed into the taxi.

"Embarrassing is not the word," Elsa replied, lighting a cigarette. "It was an outrage—as that doctor said."

"But what can we do about it?"

"Make a complaint."

"Should we?" Isabella was nervous. "We don't want to upset the authorities. Besides, who would we complain to?"

"Pavolini, of course. I noticed he never turned up—nor Doris! I shall speak to him." Elsa blew cigarette smoke out of the window impatiently.

"She might not like you doing that," suggested Isabella, recalling how Doris had clung possessively to Pavolini at her party a few months earlier.

"I can handle Doris," said Elsa dismissively, "and I suggest we refuse to take part in such disgraceful propaganda again."

*

The hospital filming gave Isabella an insight into the terrible suffering of the young men fighting for their country. For the first time, she began to understand the true devastation of war. She realized how fortunate she was: she had enough food, she earned a lot of money, her family were safe, and Rome was untouched by bombing or invasion. The sight of those young men lying broken in their beds disturbed her, and she was relieved to get back to work in the New Year and lose herself in a project.

The film was a historical drama about two orphaned sisters played by Isabella and a young dark-haired actress called Alida Valli, who had been dubbed "the next Garbo" by the press. Isabella's part was a beautiful but blind young woman who is forced into a life of poverty. Alida won the role of her sister, kidnapped by an unscrupulous marquis. Isabella's role was physically demanding—not least because she spent most of her time with a blindfold over her eyes, bumping into pieces of furniture on the set. At the end of a day's filming, her legs and arms were covered with bruises, but when she thought of the men lying in that hospital, injured and dying, she knew how lucky she was to live in the rarefied world of the film industry.

As the winter of 1941 drew on, there was news of food riots spreading around the country. Rationing was so tight that people were at starving point, and the food that was available was increasingly expensive. Even in the State-owned Cinecittà canteen, the lighting men and sound recordists struggled to afford much more than an egg sandwich. When Isabella joined them at lunchtime, she would often buy a large plate of salami or ham and share it with the crew. But not everyone was so supportive of the workers.

One afternoon a young actress called Elsa Merlini, the highest-paid star at the studio, ostentatiously purchased an entire roast chicken, and fed it, piece by piece, to a stray dog. The workers looked on with a growing sense of anger.

Isabella was appalled at the woman's behavior.

"What on earth do you think you are doing?" she asked angrily.

"What's it to you?" Elsa replied.

"Don't you understand? People are hungry—they're starving, and you waste good food on a dog."

Elsa shrugged her shoulders.

"It's all right for us," Isabella went on. "We have connections, we earn good money, but these people," she lowered her voice, gesturing to the film crew angrily staring at the slavering dog, "they can't afford such luxury. You should show more respect."

Isabella could feel her cheeks burning with fury and indignation. But Elsa ignored her, throwing the last pieces of the chicken carcass to the dog, finally licking her fingers, one by one.

"The dog was hungry too, doesn't he deserve a treat?" Elsa gathered up her belongings. "I can see why they call you the tyrant," she called back, as she headed for the door. "Maybe you should learn to mind your own business."

That evening, Isabella was due to attend a dinner at the Acquasanta Golf Club, south of Rome. This prestigious club had been laid out by a British groundsman just after the Great War, and its greens were considered to be amongst the most beautiful in the world. The clubhouse itself was a peach-colored villa, with an elegant lounge decorated with chintz and antiques, and terraces overlooking the greens. The arching pines and meticulous landscaping gave one a sense of being in the middle of the countryside, although only a few miles from the busy center of Rome. Isabella had been a member of the club for several years and enjoyed her time there, playing bridge, golf and tennis. But at the start of the war, Count Galeazzo Ciano, who was both Mussolini's son-in-law and the Minister of Foreign Affairs, had adopted it as his unofficial headquarters. Now he held court there, surrounded by senior Fascists, aristocrats and movie stars. Isabella felt the whole atmosphere at the club had changed for the worse. That evening's dinner was to be hosted by Ciano, and she regretted accepting the invitation.

"I really don't want to go," she said to her mother, while she powdered her face at the dressing table. "I'm tired after a day's filming. Frankly I'd rather just go to bed."

"You must go," her mother insisted, sitting down on the edge of the bed. "These people are important—Count Ciano is Il Duce's son-in-law, for heaven's sake. You're lucky to be invited."

Isabella looked at her mother reflected in the dressing-table mirror. "You think so, do you? Do you have any idea what he's like?"

Her mother shrugged.

"He's too fat," Isabella said, "and he has a voice like a clucking hen."

Her mother laughed. "You're very wicked."

"Well it's true. He's a ghastly person."

"Well, it's your duty to go," her mother insisted, "and wear something glamorous."

"Isabella, darling." Ciano kissed her on both cheeks when she arrived, and whispered into her ear, "I hear our friend Elsa has been a naughty girl."

Isabella looked at him, surprised. "What do you mean?"

"Oh come on—everyone's talking about it—the chicken in the canteen..."

"Oh that. Yes, it was rather disgraceful."

"Il Duce heard about it," said Ciano, giggling. "He was furious, apparently."

"Oh dear," replied Isabella.

"'Heads will roll!'" Ciano's impersonation of Mussolini was remarkable. "I fear salaries will be capped," Ciano went on. "He was apoplectic, shouting at anyone who would listen: 'They're paid too much.' He's even talking of banning you all from driving to the studios. 'They can all take the bloody tram from now on,' he said. Wouldn't that be funny?"

Isabella smiled uncertainly. "Yes," she said nervously. "Screamingly funny."

*

There was something slightly unhinged about Ciano, Isabella thought. Over dinner, where he insisted on sitting next to her—so he could "keep an eye on her"—he ordered course after course, ostentatiously demonstrating his generosity to his "friends"—the sportsmen and aristocrats keen to toady to the authorities and be on the edges of power. Once, as the main course was cleared away, Ciano's hand delved beneath Isabella's silk dress, and slid up her stockinged thigh, only stopping when his fat little fingers touched flesh. He pinched it between his thumb and forefinger, making Isabella jump. But when his fingers began to inch toward her underwear, she gasped audibly.

"Are you all right?" asked the man on her right—a tennis player, himself with a reputation as a ladies' man.

"Yes, perfectly," she replied weakly.

Ciano smirked, as his fingers slithered back down toward her knee, which he patted affectionately.

At the end of the evening, Ciano insisted on driving her back to her villa.

"But I have my car here," she argued.

"My people will bring it back for you."

Nervously, she climbed into the back of Ciano's chauffeur-driven black Alfa Romeo. He sat beside her and leaned toward her, clearly hoping she would respond. She shifted away from him, moving closer to the door, but he lurched toward her every time the car swerved around a corner, until eventually she could feel his breath against her neck. By the time the car finally arrived at her villa she was wedged uncomfortably against the door handle.

"Thank you," she said hurriedly, opening the door and leaping out.

"I hope to see more of you soon," replied Ciano lasciviously.

Isabella had never before heard such an innocent phrase spoken with such menacing sexuality. She slammed the door and watched with relief as his car slid away.

Her mother was waiting for her when she came in. "Did you have a lovely time? Do tell me what everyone ate."

"I really can't remember. But the food was very good."

"And Ciano?"

"He was fine, as always. He drove me home—insisted on it."

Her mother's eyes lit up. "Really? He likes you then. How useful."

"I'm going to bed, Mamma."

As she walked upstairs, Isabella sensed her mother watching her. When she reached the top step, she turned around. Giovanna's expression was one of disappointment.

As she took off her dress and makeup, Isabella shuddered to recall Ciano's fat fingers on her thigh. She must be more careful, she realized, not to be alone with him. Being one of the chosen is sometimes a dangerous place to be.

Chapter Four

The country villa felt cold and empty when Livia and her family arrived a few days before Christmas.

"Why is there no fire lit in here?" her mother asked, gesturing toward the fireplace in the hall.

"I have no idea." Giacomo wearily put down a suitcase.

"I'll go and find Angela," said Luisa, heading for the kitchen.

While Giacomo brought in the rest of the luggage, Livia went in search of her grandfather, Alberto. She found him sitting in an armchair in front of a meager fire in the large drawing room, a rug over his knees. She knelt in front of him, and took his hands in her own. "Your hands are like ice," she said, rubbing his fingers. "Let's get the fire lit properly. Hasn't Gino brought in any wood?"

"I don't know." Alberto looked around him. He appeared confused. "I've not seen him today, and Angela spends all her time in the kitchen."

Outside in the hall, Giacomo was hanging his overcoat on the coat rack.

"Papa, Nonno is next door and he's freezing," Livia complained. "There doesn't seem to be any wood for the fire."

"Let's go and find Gino," sighed her father, wearily putting his coat back on.

They discovered Gino alone in a garden shed. He was sitting on a dilapidated kitchen chair, smoking a cigarette. An ax lay at his feet, a small pile of wood stacked along one wall.

"Gino," Giacomo asked convivially, "how are you?"

"Well enough, sir, thank you."

Gino stood up awkwardly. His limbs seemed stiff, and he was thinner than when she had last seen him, Livia thought.

"Sit, sit, please," said Giacomo. Gino sank down gratefully, as if exhausted. "Tell me," asked Giacomo gently, "how are the family?" Gino had two sons, both of whom had been drafted into the Italian Expeditionary Corps. "Have you heard from the boys?"

"Not for a while." Gino pulled on his cigarette. "The last I heard they were in Ukraine—wherever that is."

Giacomo touched the old man's shoulder. "Perhaps we'll get some news in time for Christmas, eh? Now, be a good man and chop up plenty of wood. The whole family are here, and we need to get the place warmed up."

While Gino began to stack piles of seasoned wood outside the back door, Giacomo brought the first barrowload into the house. He loaded up the sitting-room fire and soon got a blaze going. He was pleased to see Alberto smiling at the flames.

"There you are, Father, that's a bit brighter, isn't it?"

The old man looked up at his son with rheumy eyes. "I've missed you."

"I know, Papa, and we've missed you too. Now, while Luisa prepares something nice to eat in the kitchen, you and I will have a little glass of wine together. Would you like that?"

The wintry sun had long since set, and night enveloped the villa as Alberto dozed in an armchair in front of the fire. Livia sat with a book on her lap, while Giacomo closed the heavy curtains and covered his father's legs with a rug.

"Livia, I have some work to do before dinner."

"All right, Papa," she replied, scarcely looking up.

She heard her father unlocking the door to his study at the back of the house. The fire was beginning to die down and Livia picked up the wood basket to refill it from the log store outside on the back terrace. The wood was stacked beneath her father's study windows, and as she loaded up the basket, she noticed her father leaning over what looked like a radio. Intrigued, she stopped to listen. She could hear a cacophony of voices, occasional bits of music, mixed with strange hissing noises. He was obviously turning the radio dial, searching for something specific. Finally a voice with a crisp English accent began speaking in perfect Italian:

Germany and Italy have announced they are now at war with the United States.

Today, Italian dictator, Benito Mussolini, pledged that the Patto d'Acciaio, his "pact of steel" with Germany, would ensure the Axis Powers' final victory.

From the Reichstag in Berlin, Adolf Hitler announced that under the Tripartite Agreement signed on 27 September 1940, Germany was obliged to join with Italy to defend its ally Japan. "After victory has been achieved," he said, "Germany, Italy and Japan will continue in closest co-operation with a view to establishing a new and just order."

In Washington, President Roosevelt told Congress the free world "must act quickly and decisively against the enemy."

The news was grave, Livia thought, but not a surprise. The newspapers had been full of jingoistic headlines for days. What disturbed her was that her father was listening to a foreign news station—something which she knew was illegal. She smiled ruefully. Her father had always been a bit of a rebel. She picked up the basket of wood, took it through to the sitting room and loaded up the fire.

Luisa called out to her from the kitchen. "Can you fetch your father for dinner?"

Going into the hall, Livia knocked on her father's study door.

"Who is it?"

"It's me, Papa. Dinner is ready."

"I'm coming," he said.

When he opened the door, she was still standing outside. "What were you listening to?" she asked.

"Just a local news station," he replied dismissively.

"It didn't sound like it," she persevered. "The announcer was English, wasn't he?"

"No!" His tone was uncharacteristically stern. "Now let's go and have that dinner."

*

The following day, while her mother went shopping for provisions, Livia suggested to her father they should put up a Christmas tree in the large entrance hall. "Can we take one from the copse in the corner of the garden?"

"All right," her father agreed, "I'll get the ax."

Livia chose one the same height as herself and they dragged it inside and wedged it into an old terra-cotta pot.

"Can you manage to decorate it by yourself?" Giacomo asked. "I've got some work to do."

"Yes, of course," said Livia. "I'll go upstairs to the attic and find all the decorations."

The attic was approached via a narrow staircase, and lit from a pair of grubby skylights. Livia soon found the old trunk where the decorations were stored. Mice had been at work nibbling at a Nativity scene made of straw, but the glass baubles had survived, carefully wrapped in tissue paper, along with little brass candle holders, and strings of sparkling tinsel.

Back in the hall, as Livia busied herself decorating the tree, the front door suddenly blew open and her mother appeared—slightly windswept, her face pink with cold.

"Well," said Luisa, putting down her basket, and hanging up her coat and hat, "I am shocked."

"What about, Mamma?"

"I have been trying to buy flour in the village. With Christmas coming, I need to bake and make pasta."

Livia nodded.

"In October," her mother continued, scarcely pausing for breath, "the ration was two hundred grams a day per person, which was hardly generous. Now they have reduced it to *one* hundred grams. How on earth are we to survive on that? The baker in the village offered me a little extra, as long as I was prepared to pay some exorbitant sum for it."

"And did you?" Livia asked, half-hoping her mother had abandoned her principles.

"Of course not!" Luisa retorted. "As if I would conspire with the black market! He's a rogue, that man. No, we will just have to manage. Angela told me she had collected chestnuts a few months ago. Perhaps we can grind those up and make flour." Luisa walked off briskly toward the kitchen at the back of the villa, calling for Angela.

Livia smiled. Although her mother could be infuriating at times, she had to admire the way Luisa never faltered in her views of what was right and wrong.

She walked into the sitting room and lit a taper from the fire, intending to light the candles on the tree. It was getting dark outside, and she was looking forward to seeing the candlelight flickering. She was interrupted by the sound of knocking on the front door. She blew out the taper, and laid it on the hall table. Opening the door, she found three men wearing dark overcoats and homburg hats standing on the doorstep.

"Can I help you?" she asked politely.

"We are here for a meeting with Signor Moretti."

"Oh, please come in. He didn't mention he was expecting anyone." She paused, waiting for an explanation, but the men simply huddled together in silence. "I'll go and fetch him," Livia suggested, hurrying to knock on her father's door. "Papa, there are some men for you." She heard him unlocking the door.

"Ah, I've been expecting you," he said, ushering the three into his study. "Livia, my dear..."

"Yes, Papa."

"Tell your mother I must not be disturbed."

Livia was used to her father holding meetings at home, both in the villa and in the apartment in Florence. Although he had an office in the city, clients often sought him out in his private residences, anxious to escape prying eyes. But for clients to seek legal advice so close to Christmas seemed unusual, even for him.

Intrigued, she loitered in the hallway, lighting the candles, and tidying up the boxes of decorations. From time to time, she crept over to listen at the door to her father's study, hoping for some clue about the identity of the three strange men. But much to her irritation, the thick chestnut door was virtually soundproof. Finally she gave up, and was just taking the spare decorations upstairs, when she heard the door to her father's study being unlocked. She stopped on the landing and listened as the men, accompanied by her father, emerged into the empty hall.

"So, you will get the papers finalized as soon as possible?" said the tallest of the three men.

"Of course," Giacomo replied. "But you must understand, nothing will happen now until the New Year. The transfer of a business like this—to a fabricated individual—is very involved. The creation of your non-Jewish partner will take a lot of doing."

"We understand, and hope it does not bring you trouble."

"So do I," said Giacomo.

At that moment, the back door that led to the garden opened, and Gino came into the hall, carrying a basket of logs.

"Well, thank you gentlemen," Giacomo said briskly. "I wish you a happy Christmas."

"And to you, Signor Moretti—you are a good man."

Giacomo showed the men out and closed the door behind him. "Ah...Gino—good. Stoking up the fires?"

Gino nodded, and took the firewood into the sitting room.

Giacomo glanced up and saw his daughter observing him from the landing. "How long have you been there?" he asked.

"Long enough," she replied.

He frowned, beckoning her into his study. "Come in, sit down." He pointed to a chair opposite his desk. "You shouldn't listen to my business, it's private—I have people's confidences, do you understand?"

"Yes, Papa. But those men, what business are you transferring? I don't want you to get into trouble."

"Too late for that," said Giacomo with a smile. "There are terrible injustices, Livia. Our Jewish friends are being forced out of their businesses as well as their homes. I'm just doing what I can to help. Theft is theft, even if it's done by the State, and I won't have it. But say nothing of this—especially to your mother."

"I understand." Livia stood up to leave, but at the door she turned. "Papa..."

He looked up from his desk. "Yes, darling?"

"I'm proud of you."

The following day was Christmas Eve. The family attended Mass, and then exchanged presents. Luisa had knitted a dark-red scarf and matching hat for Livia. She also gave her a powder compact inherited from her own mother; the lid was studded with red jewel-like stones.

"They're only semi-precious," Luisa explained, as Livia unwrapped it. "Garnets, I think, not rubies."

"But it's so pretty. Thank you, Mamma."

"Yes, it is a pretty thing; you do like it, don't you?"

"Yes, Mamma, I love it." Livia kissed her mother fondly.

In return Livia gave her mother a tiny pill box decorated with a cameo.

"Oh Livia," her mother protested, "it's too extravagant!"

"Papa helped me choose it," said Livia, glancing shyly toward her father.

Her gift to Giacomo was a small anthology of American poetry she had found in a second-hand bookshop in Florence. Her father opened the book straight away.

"This is one of my favorites; it's about hope," he said, reading out loud an Emily Dickinson poem. Livia was touched by the idea of hope being like a little bird.

"It seems appropriate at this time, I think," said her father. "We must all have hope; and however delicate, however vulnerable it is, it must be nurtured, especially now."

As soon as Christmas was over, Livia was eager to return to Florence, and sought ways to distract herself, helping her mother in the house, or offering to collect supplies in the village. This at least gave her the chance to buy a newspaper and read it while she drank a coffee in the village café. In spite of her father's insistence that the papers were full of government propaganda, she was nevertheless curious to see how events in the outside world were being reported. One headline announced an Italian victory on the Soviet Front.

Christmas Battle! Victory Is Ours!

She brought the newspaper back to the villa and laid it on her father's desk. "I thought Gino might like to see this," she suggested. "He's been so worried about his boys."

"That was thoughtful," said Giacomo. "Let's go outside and find him."

Gino was piling up firewood in a neat stack near the shed.

"Gino, my friend," her father began, "Livia's brought you a copy of the newspaper. There's a story about your boys' regiment."

Gino looked up brightly. "Really? Are they all right?"

"Well, they've beaten back a counter-attack by the Soviets. It's being hailed as a great victory."

Giacomo handed the old man the paper, who glanced at it briefly before handing it back.

"Is that good?" Gino asked.

"It is," said Giacomo.

"Do they mention casualties?"

"Only minimal Italian casualties, it says; so that's good news, isn't it?" Giacomo smiled encouragingly at the old man who nodded and lit a cigarette.

"We'll pray for them, Gino. I'm sure they'll be home soon."

In the first week of January, snow began to fall. It drifted in graying piles at the sides of the road as the family drove down the winding hill toward Florence. Once in the city, the Lancia began to skid on the cobbled streets, forcing Giacomo to drive at a snail's pace to avoid hitting any parked cars. It was already dark by the time they arrived at the apartment, and a full moon hung low over the city, casting a pale silvery glow on the snow-covered steps that led to the front door. Giacomo wrestled with the key, his fingers blue with cold, and once the door was open, went back to help Luisa out of the car. "Be careful, darling," he said, as he opened the passenger door, "it's very slippery."

"I'll go and open up the apartment, shall I?" Livia suggested, rushing into the lobby. She was eager to see if there had been any post for her while the family had been away, and was anxious to conceal it until she had had a chance to introduce Cosimo to her parents. In the lobby of the building, she quickly unlocked the postbox for their apartment, and removed the pile of mail, sifting through it. To her delight, there was Cosimo's letter, which she slipped into her coat pocket to read later, just as her father was helping her mother into the hall. Livia handed him the rest of the mail.

"Take it upstairs for me," he said, "and one of the suitcases as well."

Inside the apartment, Livia put her father's mail on the hall table, and retreated to her room. The air was so cold that when she exhaled, her breath turned to mist. She lay down on the little divan bed, covering herself with a woolen rug and eagerly took the envelope out of her pocket. Next door, in the sitting room, she could hear her mother complaining to Giacomo about the lack of firewood. Confident she would not be disturbed, Livia began to read.

21st December 1941

Cara Livia,

My darling… I miss you. Without you the Christmas holiday stretches away interminably. I think of you constantly. My parents and sister are all here and we will try to have an enjoyable time. My father needs a few days off. You remember I told you he was a doctor? He is exhausted—the hospitals are filling up with wounded soldiers. We will do what we can to cheer him.

My little Livia, let's meet as soon as you are back, shall we? On the first morning of term at eight o'clock outside Palazzo Strozzi? Can you manage that? I shall have a sleepless night, so excited will I be at the prospect of seeing your perfect face again.

Until then, my love,
I am yours… Cosimo.

*

The following day was the first day of term, and Livia awoke filled with excitement. She dressed carefully in her best black skirt, a cream silk blouse and a dark-green cashmere cardigan of her mother's.

"I hope you have a lovely day," said Luisa, as she poured coffee into a cup for her daughter. "You look very smart, are you meeting anyone important today?"

Livia blushed. "No, I just wanted to look nice."

"Well, you do. But I worry it might snow again later. Are you dressed warmly enough?"

"Yes, Mamma, I borrowed your cardigan—I hope that's all right."

"Yes, of course it is, but what coat will you wear?"

"My dark-red one—you always say it makes me look rosy-cheeked." Her mother smiled. "It's a very pretty coat."

"And it matches the new scarf and hat you gave me for Christmas," Livia said delightedly. Her mother smiled.

Livia arrived at the meeting place with ten minutes to spare. She waited, pulling her dark-red muffler more tightly around her neck, as the minutes ticked by. She paced up and down looking around her, but Cosimo was nowhere to be seen. She checked her watch again—it was now fifteen minutes past eight. Perhaps he'd had to help his father with something, she told herself; or maybe his mother needed him to go to the market before college. She tried to relax, stamping her feet to keep warm.

At half past eight, wondering if she had perhaps misunderstood his instructions, she took his letter from her coat pocket and read it again. But there was no mistake: it was Thursday morning, the first day of term, and she had arrived before eight o'clock and was waiting at the correct location.

Her feet were frozen and her fingers blue with cold, before she finally decided to leave. It was nearly nine o'clock, and she would be late for her first lecture. She hurried to the university building and slid into her seat next to Elena.

"You're late," her friend whispered.

"I know. I was waiting for Cosimo outside Palazzo Strozzi, but he didn't come."

Elena blushed slightly and bit her lip.

"What?" Livia asked. "What's the matter?"

"Haven't you heard?"

"Heard what?" Livia was suddenly apprehensive.

"He's been called up. A lot of them have. He's in the army."

Livia was in a state of shock, her mind whirring. She recalled a conversation with Cosimo before Christmas. He had been so downcast about the prospect of joining the army. It was as if he had had a premonition. "I've never fired a gun and I'm not sure I could kill anyone," he had said to her when they had last met.

"I can't believe it," she whispered at last to Elena. "He loathed the idea of fighting."

"I know. But they need new recruits. There have been so many casualties."

"When did it happen?" whispered Livia. "He wrote to me just before Christmas and mentioned nothing about it."

"He got a letter on Christmas Eve. Quite a few of the students did. They had to report somewhere before the New Year. It was all very sudden."

"Do we know where they are being sent?" Livia asked finally, dreading the answer. She could think of only two theaters of war where recruits might be urgently needed—one was the frozen wastes of the Eastern Front, and the other the deserts of North Africa. In either case, Cosimo would be unlikely to survive. She felt sick with nerves, tears spilling down her cheeks.

Elena took her hand in hers and squeezed it. When her friend's answer finally came, Livia's heart almost stopped.

"They're being sent to Russia, I think."

Chapter Five

Rome
April 1942

Isabella stood for a few moments outside Hotel Flora, breathing deeply, trying to calm her mind. She had been invited to audition for the director Vicenzo Lucchese, one of the few directors who famously refused to work for the Fascist film industry. Isabella had never met him before, but his reputation had gone before him, and she was nervous. "Bewitching" was a description people used about him. "Impatient" was another. What was generally agreed was that he was "a genius." Although the descendant of an old aristocratic Roman family, his political leanings were widely known to be left of center, and he rarely used his title of "Count" Lucchese.

In her handbag was the letter she had received, inviting her to the audition. She took it out and reread it.

> *The film will be based on the novel* The Postman Always Rings Twice *by James M. Cain. Have you read it?*

Isabella had not.

> *The part I think you could play is that of the young wife, married to an older man—a bar owner. A young, handsome drifter arrives at the bar one day, and she falls in love with him. Together they conspire to kill her husband. I need to see emotion, passion, despair, desperation. I think you could do it.*

Standing outside the hotel, she quickly scanned the scene they were going to shoot. It involved her and her lover arguing about the best way to kill the old man, before making up and kissing passionately. The woman's impetuous actions were alien to Isabella, who was more inclined to careful consideration; neither was she cruel nor vindictive. But she was an actress, and should be capable of summoning up any emotion required. For this scene, she had to demonstrate both lust and an icy determination to commit the most terrible crime. She had to be demanding, persuasive, erotic. Isabella wanted the part badly, but feared that none of her previous roles—the prim schoolteacher, the poor blind girl—had prepared her for the volcanic passion this character demanded.

Filled with nerves, she finally pushed through the revolving doors of the imposing nineteenth-century hotel, and hovered anxiously in the lobby.

"Signorina Bellucci." A tall elegant young woman was walking toward her with an outstretched hand. "I'm Anna, Vicenzo's assistant. Please come this way."

The hotel ballroom had been set up like a film set, with two cameras and lights. It was already hot, and beads of sweat broke out on Isabella's forehead as she walked into the room.

A tall fine-boned man, his dark hair slicked back from his high forehead, turned to greet her. She presumed he was the director, Vicenzo.

"Ah," he said, holding out his hands to her, "here you are…our little Isabella." It was such a tender thing to say. His voice was gentle and seductive, but his eyes—deep set, and almost black—looked as if they wanted to possess her. She felt herself trembling as he squeezed her hands between his. They were cool and dry to the touch.

She was to play a scene with the young male star of the movie—the actor Massimo Girotti. He introduced himself to Isabella, and he too held her hand. "You're shaking," he said.

She blushed. "I'm terrified," she whispered.

"But you're a big star, what do you have to be nervous of?"

She glanced over at Vicenzo who was watching her intently.

"Oh him," said Massimo. "The 'genius.' He can be intimidating. But he wouldn't have asked for you if he didn't think you had what it takes."

"That's just the point. I'm not sure I do have what it takes."

"Perhaps you need a little help," Massimo suggested.

Isabella looked at him wide-eyed. "What do you mean?"

"A little something to calm your nerves."

He pulled a small pill box out of his pocket—gold, with an amber-colored jewel on the lid. It looked like a citrine, Isabella thought. He opened it and removed a small blue pill.

"Here, this will make you feel better."

"I'm not sure," Isabella replied hesitantly. "I don't usually take anything like that."

"Neither do I, normally. It's just something to soothe you. A doctor gave them to me—they're quite safe. Take it." He handed her a glass of water and she discreetly swallowed the pill.

Within minutes she felt unnaturally calm—as if she had just enjoyed a long, hot bath. She yawned and rolled her head around, cracking her neck, easing the tension. Vicenzo watched her keenly.

"Are you ready to begin the scene?" he asked.

"Yes," she said. "Perfectly ready."

When she was filming with a director for the first time, it was quite normal for her to feel nervous. Her heart would beat faster, thumping hard in her chest. She had learned to breathe through it, exhaling, bringing her pulsating heart under control. It was part of the process, and channeling those nerves ultimately resulted in a fine performance. But now, as the pill did its work, she felt no excitement, no sense of threat or danger, and her heart remained stubbornly steady and slow. It was as if she were wading through emotional and physical treacle, she thought. Even her legs and arms felt heavy and clumsy. The scene called for her to push her lover away, to shout at him, to tell him to leave her, before he pulled her toward him, kissing her passionately. But she was incapable of showing the right amount of anger—or indeed any emotion at all.

"Try it one more time," said Vicenzo gently, after the first couple of takes.

"Remember, Bella—may I call you Bella? I want to see passion, fury. Can you do that for me?"

He took her hands in his once again and stared deeply into her eyes, as if willing her to succeed. But far from feeling encouraged, she began to feel woozy, and stumbled slightly.

"Are you all right?" he asked.

"Yes...No, not really. I'm so sorry. I don't feel very well." Embarrassed, she began to walk unsteadily toward the door.

Vicenzo chased after her and swung her round, studying her face. "Something's happened to you. I know this is not the performance you wanted to give. Would you like to try again?"

She shook her head, as tears of shame spilled down her cheeks. "No, but thank you. I'm really not well...I can't do it."

"All right," he said kindly. "Are you sure you can get home by yourself?"

"Yes," she said uncertainly. "I live just across the park. The walk will do me good."

"I hope you don't feel it's been a waste of time."

"Oh no, of course not. I'm just so embarrassed. I feel I've wasted your time." She glanced across at Girotti, who was smirking slightly.

"Well," said Vicenzo with a wink, "at least you got to kiss Massimo. He's a handsome rogue, isn't he?"

As she walked home, past the beds of tulips glowing in the spring sunshine, she wondered how she could have been so naïve. To take a pill of any kind was so out of character, but to allow Girotti to control her had been madness. And what had been his motivation? Perhaps he had been trying to sabotage her.

She got back to her villa, climbed into bed and slept deeply.

The following day a huge basket of lilies arrived. She searched among the flowers for a card.

*Sorry it didn't work out this time, but come and visit me on
set in Ferrara. I'd love to see you again.*

Yours, Vicenzo

Her mother, predictably, was intrigued. "Flowers, Isabella? Who
is your admirer?"

"No one you know," Isabella replied brusquely, slipping the card
into her pocket.

Her mother lingered next to the flowers, inhaling their scent.
"Still, these are expensive. Whoever he is, he must like you."

"It's just a professional relationship," Isabella said defensively, as
if to convince herself. But long after the lilies had faded and died,
Isabella re-ran the encounter with Vicenzo over and over in her
mind—his intensity as he watched her performing, his black eyes
flashing, the amused smile on his lips, the gentleness of his touch
as he held her hands between his.

But it was his reaction to her inability to perform that touched
her most. He had every right to be angry with her for wasting his
time. But, on the contrary, he had seemed most concerned for her
welfare. "Our little Isabella" he had called her when they first met,
as if he wanted to protect her—an unusual experience for someone
more used to fighting for her own survival. She had taken care of
herself and her mother for so long, she'd forgotten what it felt like
to be protected. Vicenzo had made her feel special.

Over the next few months, Isabella took every opportunity to talk
to people about Vicenzo. Had they ever worked with him? Who
did he live with? Who did he love? Her friends at the Acquasanta
Golf Club were dismissive.

"He's very left-wing, you know," one of the old ladies pointed out
one evening during a bridge game. "I knew his mother years ago.
They're a good family, but he's always been a bit wild." She raised
her eyebrows in a knowing way.

Acquaintances at the studio were more forthcoming. As usual, all the best gossip was found in the makeup room. Everyone knew a woman who had been in love with him. One famous actress had even tried to commit suicide over him.

"Oh, he knows how to break hearts, that one," said a makeup artist, as she brushed powder over Isabella's face. "He's just got that...something, hasn't he? You'd give up everything for him."

With such a formidable reputation, Isabella knew she should have dismissed him from her mind. But instead, the talk and the gossip simply fueled her fascination. She felt compelled to seek him out—after all, he'd sent her a note after her disastrous audition, making it quite clear he was keen. *I'd love to see you again*, he'd written.

An invitation to appear at the Venice Film Festival in September presented her with the perfect opportunity. Fuel shortages made driving to Venice difficult—and besides, stars were now being encouraged to use public transport as a show of solidarity with the general population. If she took the train to Venice, she could break her journey in Ferrara, the location of Vicenzo's film. As she settled into her first-class carriage, she mused on the wisdom of her decision. She had no idea what sort of reception she might get: it was possible that Vicenzo might have forgotten her already—it had, after all, been five months since they'd last met. Perhaps she had been deluding herself all this time.

En route to Ferrara, the train stopped in Florence. She leaned out of the carriage window and called out to a paper boy. "Do you have a copy of *La Stampa*?"

He handed her the paper, and as she sat back down in her seat, it occurred to her that she had never been to Florence. She had lived in Italy for ten years and in that time her life had revolved completely around work, spending six days a week in a darkened studio in Rome. Perhaps now would be the time to get off the train and explore this beautiful city. The idea seemed momentarily enticing, but before she could make the decision, the guard had blown his whistle and the train pulled out of the station.

As they headed north, clattering through the Tuscan hills, Isabella read the paper. It carried depressing news of the war. Italian troops had been withdrawn from Libya to Tunisia with huge losses. Further down the front page was a devastating headline:

British Murder Cream of Italian Youth

An Italian hospital ship called the *Arno* had been torpedoed and sunk in the Mediterranean by British aircraft. Isabella, who was not a particularly political animal, wondered about this story—surely it was illegal to blow up a hospital ship full of injured men.

For the first time in months, she thought about Ludovico. Her obsession with Vicenzo had almost driven her ex-lover from her mind. Now she wondered if he had been on the *Arno*, or was one of the soldiers battling hopelessly against the British in the North African desert.

Forty minutes later, the train pulled out of Bologna heading for Ferrara. Leaving the apricot-colored city behind, it traveled through soft rolling hills and fields of wheat, burned dark gold by the sun.

Isabella gazed at the passing countryside, intermittently trying to concentrate on her newspaper, but the closer the train got to Ferrara, the more nervous she became, and she spent the rest of the short journey filled with indecision about the wisdom of visiting Vicenzo. Firstly, he might have forgotten her—a kind note in a basket of flowers sent months before was not the same as an actual invitation. Secondly, she would be bound to meet Clara Calamai, the actress who had won the role, and it might be awkward. Actors could be possessive of parts they had won, and she might resent Isabella's presence on set. It was also possible, given Vicenzo's reputation, that he would now be in a relationship with his leading lady. Finally, Isabella would have to face Massimo Girotti—the man who had knowingly, or otherwise, sabotaged her audition. She could still recall him smirking when she had left the ballroom at Hotel Flora.

The guard announced Ferrara would be the next stop. Isabella's head told her she should stay on the train and continue straight on to Venice. But as they drew into the station, she took an impulsive and instinctive decision, gathered up her luggage and got off the train. After all, she reasoned, walking toward the taxi rank, if the encounter went badly she could always get the next train to Venice. She hailed a taxi with a renewed sense of determination.

"The whole of Ferrara is excited about the filming," said the taxi driver. "The bar they're using is on the outskirts." He studied Isabella in his mirror: she looked elegant in her cream coat and high-heeled shoes. "It's not a very nice part of town—maybe I should wait for you, yes?"

"Oh that's kind, but I'll be all right. I'm meeting someone there."

The bar was just as the driver had described—a shabby building on one side of a piazza. A crowd of eager onlookers had been fenced in on the opposite side of the square. They parted as Isabella approached them, muttering amongst themselves. Many recognized her and asked her to sign their autograph books. She graciously stopped for a few moments, before walking across the piazza. Harsh light spilled out from the windows of the bar, which was surrounded by tottering piles of metal camera cases, film lights and foldaway chairs. A group of technicians hung about outside, smoking and chatting quietly. They recognized Isabella as she approached, standing up awkwardly and stubbing out their cigarettes beneath their shoes, like naughty schoolchildren caught out by a teacher.

"Hello everyone," she said cheerfully. "Don't mind me, Vicenzo invited me."

They visibly relaxed; one or two lit up again and a young props assistant took her suitcase and picked up one of the foldaway chairs. "He's still shooting a scene," he said, offering her a seat, "but they'll be finished soon. It's nearly six o'clock."

They made whispered conversation, while in the background she could hear the familiar sounds of a film in production—the clapperboard at the start of each shot, the raised voices of the actors, punctuated by the comments of the director.

"You must hit her, Massimo," Isabella heard Vicenzo shouting. "You hate her now, remember..."

She heard a slap, and then a woman—presumably Clara Calamai, the actress—crying out. The technicians glanced uneasily at one another.

"Cut, cut!" Vicenzo said irritably. "Harder, Massimo. Really hit her—two or three times."

"But if I do that, I'll kill her!" the actor protested.

Finally, a voice called out: "It's a wrap." The film lights spilling out from the bar were instantly extinguished, and slowly the crew emerged into the evening sunlight—among them Clara, her face red and raw. It was obvious she had been crying. She glanced briefly at Isabella, before walking hurriedly toward a caravan that had been set up on one side of the square as a dressing room.

As the crew packed up the equipment into the metal boxes, Isabella could hear Massimo Girotti arguing with Vicenzo inside the bar. She couldn't make out what they were saying, but it was clear from the actor's raised voice that he was angry. Suddenly she felt like an intruder. A film set was a private, secretive place reserved for the family of actors, and not for casual visitors. She began nervously to look around, searching for another taxi, but the only people in the square were the eager onlookers. If she were to leave now, she would have to run the gauntlet of the fans, carrying her suitcase. She felt trapped and awkward, regretting she had not stayed on the train.

"Little Bella!" Vicenzo's voice interrupted her thoughts. He was standing in the doorway to the bar, wearing dark-blue jeans and an open-necked black shirt, his dark hair flopping over his forehead. He rushed toward her, put his arms around her and kissed her on both cheeks, before standing back, his hands on her shoulders, just as he had done that day in Hotel Flora, gazing at her intently. "You came! You actually came!" He sounded so delighted that all her anxieties melted away.

"I did," she said shyly. "I hope it's all right—I don't want to interrupt."

"You're not." He lit a cigarette and exhaled. "We've finished for the day—it's perfect timing."

Girotti followed him out of the bar, shading his eyes against the evening light with dark glasses. He looked tired, Isabella thought, his shoulders slumped. He too lit a cigarette, inhaling deeply, before noticing Isabella.

"Hello," he said. "What are you doing here?"

"Just passing through," she replied casually. "I'm on my way to Venice—to the film festival," she added superfluously.

He didn't reply. He just shrugged, before shuffling across the square and into his caravan, slamming the door behind him.

"It's been a difficult day," said Vicenzo. "But we're getting there."

"I see." Isabella nodded toward the pair of caravans. "I hope they don't mind me being here."

"Why should they?" he asked. "Now, I insist that you have dinner with us. You can't get to Venice now—it's far too late. Besides, we have a big villa here for the artists, with plenty of room. Please say you will stay?"

She blushed with pleasure. "I'd love to, thank you."

Vicenzo looked around for his assistant. The tall girl Isabella remembered from the hotel appeared magically at his side, clipboard in hand.

"Anna, could you please take Signorina Bellucci to the villa and arrange for her to have a room? She is joining us for dinner this evening." He turned to Isabella. "Darling, I must sort out a few things here—but we'll meet later, yes?"

During the drive with Anna to the villa, Isabella thought about what she had just witnessed. She had been in the film industry long enough to know that directors could sometimes push their stars to the limit. She had experienced some demanding parts herself, but what Clara and Massimo had been asked to do was different. It was as if they were being asked to really inhabit the parts they played. Massimo must really love, but also hate, Clara. She must really feel pain—not just pretend to do so. It was disconcerting, but they should remember that Vicenzo was an artist, a true visionary, and it was the actor's duty to interpret the director's vision. They were lucky, she reasoned, to be in the presence of such a talent. And the thought that this man—this genius—had been so delighted to see *her* was thrilling. Here was a man she could really admire, a man she could adore. A man who was worthy of her love.

She could feel herself falling hopelessly under Vicenzo's spell.

Chapter Six

Florence
August 1942

Florence had become a scalding cauldron and the buildings throbbed with heat. Pedestrians clung to the shadows, retreating to their apartments in the early afternoon, reappearing only when the sun had begun to go down. The university term now over, Livia and Elena filled their days with visits to cooling museums and occasional strolls in the Boboli Gardens.

One afternoon, they emerged from Palazzo Pitti into the bright sunshine, arm in arm, and headed north across the river.

"It's so hot," Livia said, "I think I'll just go back home, do you mind?"

"Not at all," replied Elena. "It's a good idea—I need a sleep too."

They crossed the Ponte Vecchio, stopping from time to time to admire the jewelry displays glittering in the shop windows.

"Are you staying in Florence for the rest of the summer?" asked Elena.

"I doubt it," said Livia. "We'll have to go back to the villa and see my grandfather, and I think my mother wants to visit some friends. What about you?"

"We're not going anywhere," Elena said wearily. "Papa has to work, and Mamma won't leave him. Besides, we have no friends we can stay with."

Livia felt a tinge of guilt. Her life could sometimes seem so much more interesting than Elena's. She wondered if she should invite her to join the family in the country, but her mother could be difficult about spontaneous gestures involving people she didn't know.

"Have you heard from Cosimo?" Elena asked, changing the subject.

"No," sighed Livia, as they walked into a small stationery shop. "It's been months. I do worry about him—have you heard anything?"

"He wrote to his mother a few weeks back. I only know because she told my mother about it. But it was one of those letters, you know, where he wasn't really telling the truth."

"What do you mean?"

"Oh it was all, 'I'm well, I'm doing fine, it's not as bad as I thought…' All nonsense, of course. My father says it's the most ill-judged military campaign in history. Even Hitler doesn't want us in Russia."

Livia had been examining a small notebook covered in turquoise marbled paper, wondering if she could afford to buy it; she now looked up at her friend tearfully. "Poor Cosimo. I think about him every day, you know. But I feel so helpless. What can we do?"

Elena shrugged. "Nothing… nothing at all."

The shopkeeper cleared her throat, clearly irritated by the girls' reluctance to buy anything.

Livia returned the notebook to the display. "Elena, we'd better go," she said quickly. "Let's get together tomorrow. I don't think I can bear another museum, but we could go back to the Boboli Gardens—at least there's a bit of shade there."

"I'd like that," Elena said, kissing her friend. "See you tomorrow then."

The moment Livia arrived back in the apartment, her mother started complaining. "It's so hot it's almost unbearable," Luisa exclaimed, mopping her forehead and peering at the thermometer she kept on the windowsill. "It's forty-one degrees!"

Livia moved the thermometer into the shade. "I don't think it's quite that hot, Mamma, but it is very warm, I agree. What's that odd smell?" she asked, looking round the kitchen.

"It's this, I expect," her mother said, pointing to a large bubbling pot of steaming liquid. Livia peered inside; pieces of something spongy and rubbery were floating around in the water. "What is it?" she asked.

"Cow's lung," her mother said defensively. "And before you say anything, it's the only meat I've managed to get hold of in weeks."

"Ugh . . . they had it in the university canteen last week—I remember now, I couldn't eat it."

"Well, there's nothing else." Her mother sounded impatient and angry.

"But Mamma, it looks and smells disgusting."

"I know, but we were lucky to get it. There was a queue outside the shop—women were fighting for it." She peered into the pot and sniffed. "I still have a couple of onions left. I'll try to make it a bit more palatable."

Livia retreated from the kitchen and was heading down the corridor toward her bedroom, when her mother called after her. "Livia! There's a letter for you, it's on the hall table."

The letter—stained and battered—lay on the polished walnut surface. She grabbed it and rushed up to the roof terrace. She sat down, leaning against the hot metal side of the water tank. The sun hung low over the Duomo, casting pink light all over the city. A faint breeze blew over the rooftops, while flocks of starlings swirled above her head swooping and diving in unison. She tore open the envelope.

June 1942

My darling Livia,

I have not been able to write for some time. I cannot tell you how awful it is here. I know I should be brave and write of my manly achievements—fighting for a cause I believe in, standing shoulder to shoulder with my comrades-in-arms. But the truth is, none of us believe in the cause and my comrades are already exhausted. The food is terrible—but perhaps for you also? My mother's letter reached me a few weeks ago and she told me that everything is rationed now in Florence. People are so hungry, she said, they are eating rats and the lungs of cats. Is that really true? I cannot bear to think of you all starving.

We are in Russia—I cannot say where. The plan—if there is one—is to capture a coal-mining basin nearby. We move off tomorrow and I pray we survive. I'm working as a radio operator, so am not in the front line, thank God. But I fear we will all have to fight in the end; I just pray I never have to kill someone, as I really don't think I could, although it's unlikely as our guns don't work properly. Even the hand grenades are faulty!

My darling, I must go now. I kiss you. I kiss your tiny beautiful wrist.

I love you
Cosimo xxxx

One evening before he had left, long ago in the cold, icy winter, Livia remembered that Cosimo had taken her hand to his lips and kissed it. Then he turned her hand over and kissed the inside of her wrist. The skin was so soft, he said, like a bird's wing. Now, Livia imagined his lips kissing her, his arms around her waist. She kissed his letter and slipped it into her dress pocket. The letter had been sent weeks before. Whatever battle he had gone into the following day had long since finished. Had he killed someone by now? Had he even survived?

Reluctantly, she left the terrace and was assailed by the putrid odor of cow lung as she descended the staircase to the apartment. She had still not told her family about Cosimo, and a letter from a young man serving at the front was bound to cause interest. She prepared herself for the inevitable interrogation from her mother, but as she opened the door onto the corridor, she heard raised voices. Her mother and father were arguing in the sitting room.

"Why do you always have to put yourself at risk?" Luisa sounded frightened and angry.

"I don't know what you mean," replied Giacomo soothingly.

"It's always the same! You don't care a fig for me, or Livia," she shouted. "We are incidental to your existence! All that matters is the cause!"

"I've simply joined a political party, for heaven's sake."

"The Partito d'Azione is not just a political party and you know it. They are a rabble of left-wingers." Her mother spat the words out as if they disgusted her.

"No, Luisa, you are quite wrong," Giacomo said calmly. "Firstly, they are not a rabble, in fact quite the reverse. They are a united front of intelligent people—lawyers like myself, university professors, bankers, industrialists—who all care about this country, just as I do. And they are not left-wingers. Again, quite the opposite: they reject Marxism, and instead are intent on building a republic, supporting civil liberty and true socialism. They believe in a European federation of free democratic states. They have a vision of the future—and one which I share."

"All very laudable, I'm sure," Luisa said. "But they will get you imprisoned—or worse."

Livia could hear her mother's voice quivering with emotion. She stood silently in the hall, as her mother, flushed and wiping the tears from her cheeks, rushed out of the sitting room. Luisa shook her head at Livia as if to say "you talk to him" and went through to the kitchen.

"What's going on, Papa?"

Giacomo was standing in front of the window. It was open to allow a breeze, but the shutters outside were closed, so the sitting room remained dark and humid.

"Your mother is upset," he said calmly, sitting down on the sofa.

Livia closed the doors behind her and perched on the arm of a chair. "I can see that, but about what?"

"I've joined the Pd'A, that's all." He picked up a newspaper lying on a side table and studied the front page, as if the subject was now closed.

"I heard your little speech about them," she persisted, "but is it safe? Can they be trusted?"

"With what?" He looked up irritably. "Our freedom?"

"I just mean…you shouldn't take any unnecessary risks. They are enemies of the Fascists. Mamma's right—you could end up in prison."

"If I do, I do," he said phlegmatically, and resumed reading his paper.

Livia began to understand why her mother found him so irritating. He seemed incapable of seeing any problem from an alternative point of view. "What made you join them now?" she asked gently.

He sighed and put his paper down. "They've been in existence for a while. I was approached a long time ago and I've been thinking about it. They need people in Florence. And I must do something, Livia." He stood up and walked across to the window; he pushed the shutters open and a draft of warm air washed over them both. He turned to face her. "We cannot stand around anymore, watching that madman destroying our country. Mussolini's on the wrong side of history and it's time to put a stop to him."

That evening, as Luisa ladled out three bowls of cow lung broth, she announced her intention to leave Florence. "I can't stay here anymore, in this heat. Livia must come with me. We'll go back to the country—for a month at least. Yes?" She looked hopefully at Livia.

Livia nodded uncertainly. "I suppose so. Will Papa come too?"

Giacomo looked up distractedly from his food. "Where?"

"To the villa!" Luisa said impatiently. "To see your father, to get away from the heat and the filth, and this disgusting food." She threw her spoon down onto the table and stormed out. They heard her bedroom door slam, followed by muffled sobbing.

Giacomo rose patiently, smiled at Livia and went to comfort his wife.

Livia retreated upstairs to the sanctuary of the roof terrace. She climbed the ladder to the upper level, where she sat down, leaning against the water tank.

Her father found her there half an hour later. "So this is where you escape to." He sat down heavily beside her. His hair smelled of cigarette smoke as she leaned against his chest. "Your mother said you had a letter today."

"I did," she replied.

"She wondered who it was from."

"I thought she would."

"You don't have to tell me, I just thought you should know."

"It was from a friend—from university. He's away fighting on the Russian Front..."

Her father nodded, and lit a cigarette. "Poor man."

"It sounds pretty bad from what he said in the letter."

"You must be worried." He put his arm around her.

"Yes, I am. I feel so helpless."

"I understand that feeling. It's why I've joined the Pd'A."

"I think you're right, Papa. We have to do something."

"Yes, but there's not much *you* can do right now." He gave Livia a hug. "You should go to the country with your mother."

"I feel guilty—as if I'm running away."

"What from? Don't feel that way. Your grandfather needs you and your mother too, think about that."

"What about you? Don't you need a break?"

"I have work to do. Meetings and so on—I must stay here. But I'll try to come at weekends, if I can get hold of enough petrol."

"At least it will be cooler in the country," said Livia, flapping her blouse up and down, trying to create a breeze.

"Yes...and your mother says you have been invited to spend a week with the Luccheses."

"Have we? I knew she was planning something. We haven't seen them for years. I wonder why she wants to visit them now."

"I would have thought it was obvious," Giacomo said, smiling. "They're old friends, they have a beautiful villa, they live near the sea and they are rich. Seriously though, Livia, your mother needs a rest, and so do you. You should go."

That weekend, Giacomo loaded their belongings into the car and set off with the family for the villa. Driving through the olive groves, a cool wind blowing through her hair, it seemed to Livia that the war was far away. The horror of the Eastern Front being endured by poor Cosimo was unimaginable up here in the hills, surrounded by the scent of rosemary and the pale gray-green of the olive trees.

The villa was approached down a long drive and Livia's spirits always rose when it came into view. Its familiarity was comforting.

The house felt cool, shaded by the heavy shutters, as they carried their belongings inside.

While Giacomo unlocked his study, Luisa went into the sitting room, looking for her father-in-law. Throwing open the shutters, she wiped her fingers judgmentally through the dust on the side tables. "I don't think Angela does a stroke of work when I'm not here," she tutted, "and where's Alberto?"

They found him outside on the terrace at the back of the house, dozing in the shade of a Russian vine that scrambled over the metal pergola. He looked thin but peaceful, with a battered straw Panama hat covering his face.

"Nonno?" Livia knelt at his side and touched his arm gently.

Alberto awoke startled, his hat falling to the ground. "Who's that?"

"It's Livia."

"Livia?" He opened his eyes and stared uncertainly at her. "Oh yes, Livia," he said more warmly. He offered his cheek, and she kissed him. "Is it really you?"

"We've come home for the summer," Luisa explained. "Have they been feeding you properly?"

Alberto shrugged. "It's hard for everyone to get enough to eat," he replied stoically.

Livia and her mother found Angela and Gino sitting round the table in the kitchen, stripping the leaves off what looked like weeds.

Gino stood up. "Signora, signorina—we weren't expecting you."

"I can see that," said Luisa irritably. "What is that you're doing? Are we eating grass now?"

Angela shook her head ruefully. "There's nothing else. We've already had our ration of flour for the week. I cannot make pasta. And there's no bread in the shops—unless you're prepared to pay. So we picked these wild greens from the hedgerows. We used to do it as children."

"This is intolerable," Luisa retorted. "I'm going to ring Contessa Lucchese and see if we can visit them a week early."

*

The following day, Giacomo packed the whole family, including Alberto, into the car and drove them all the way to the Luccheses' villa on the Ligurian coast.

The villa was set amongst the pine forests that surrounded the ancient town of Forte dei Marmi. This elegant resort had been the summer playground of the rich and successful since the nineteenth century. Industrialists such as the Agnellis, the owners of Fiat, kept a villa there, as did the Siemens and Marconi families. Here, they rubbed shoulders with famous writers, artists and sculptors, along with a sprinkling of Italian aristocracy.

As Giacomo drove his old black Lancia up the Luccheses' long drive, Livia peered excitedly around. Through the lush gardens, she glimpsed the dark-red clay of a tennis court. As a child, no older than nine or ten, she had played there with the Luccheses' children. A decade older than her, the two boys, Vicenzo and Raffaele, had indulged her, throwing balls to her on the tennis court, or taking her down to the beach and overseeing her attempts at swimming. Vicenzo had been very kind, she remembered—holding her gently beneath her stomach, encouraging her to take her first few strokes in the water. The boys' elder sister, Luciana, had resented Livia's presence and cut her dead most of the time. She had an unhealthy obsession with Vicenzo, or so it had seemed to Livia.

The family were greeted by the Contessa herself. Dark-haired, with hooded black eyes like her eldest son, she wore a pale-blue fitted dress over her surprisingly plump figure, and a large straw hat.

"Luisa, my dear, how lovely to see you. It was fortunate, when you rang last night, that we had room for you. You were originally supposed to come next week."

"I know," said Luisa, "and I do apologize, Alessandra, but I couldn't bear to wait any longer... the heat, the war, the rationing..." She paused nervously.

"I understand, of course," said the Contessa, inspecting the motley group. "And you are all most welcome. And little Livia is here too—how delightful, and how you have grown, my dear."

Alberto hovered in the background, shuffling slightly. He had known the Contessa all her life, having been in the army with her father.

"Alberto," the Contessa began, taking the old man's hand. "Luisa didn't mention you were coming." She left the comment hanging in the air.

"Oh…" said Luisa nervously. "I hope it's all right. I couldn't leave him alone in the villa—the servants, you know, they are absolutely useless."

The Contessa smiled graciously. "I'm sure we'll find somewhere for everyone. Do please come with me."

A servant gathered up their luggage and they were shown to a set of elegant bedrooms on the first floor, all with a distant view of the sea.

Clearly, "finding somewhere" was not the problem the Contessa had implied, Livia thought, as she threw open the turquoise shutters. She sat for a while on the edge of the windowsill, admiring the tranquil, inviting water in the distance. Inevitably, her thoughts turned to Cosimo. While he was fighting for his life, she was here, surrounded by this luxury and comfort. Unable to reconcile her guilt, she resolved to try to enjoy herself. She hung up her few clothes in the wardrobe and changed into a pale yellow summer dress.

When she came out onto the landing, intending to go downstairs, she overheard the Contessa, standing below her in the hall, complaining to her husband. "Not only are they here a week early, but she's brought her father-in-law! He's the most awful old man."

Livia coughed quietly and the Contessa looked up. "Livia, how lovely you look! Do come down, dear. Join us on the terrace."

She led the way through the elegant house, past sofas upholstered in turquoise linen. The terrace overlooked a lush garden, and was arranged with cane chairs.

"A Campari, Livia?" The Count, Vicenzo's father, was standing next to a large table laid out with bottles in all shapes and sizes. He was tall and slender like his children, his silver hair slicked back over his tanned forehead.

"Thank you," said Livia uncertainly, for she had never tasted one.

"Are the children expected?" Luisa asked, settling into one of the cane chairs. The "children" were, of course, the Contessa's three adult children—Vicenzo, Raffaele and Luciana. But to Luisa, who had known them all since birth, they remained permanently infantilized.

"I'm not sure," said the Contessa. "I think Vicenzo might join us for a day or two. He is filming in the north, you know, in Ferrara. Raffaele and Luciana will come later in the season."

Giacomo left early the next morning, explaining he had to get back to his work. But he promised to return the following Saturday and collect his family.

Livia kissed him goodbye on the steps of the villa. "I'm not sure they really want us here," she said.

"I know," said Giacomo. "The Contessa is a tricky old thing, but she and your mother have known each other for a long time—it will be all right. I had a word with her and explained how very tense your mother is. She'll be able to relax here, and you'll have fun. The house is comfortable, the sea is warm, and they have lots of food!" He laughed. "Try to enjoy it, darling."

Alberto spent the next few days sitting quietly in the garden, and gratefully eating everything that was put in front of him. The Contessa had a remarkable ability to obtain extra food rations, and the whole family enjoyed the soups, pasta and wild boar that she served up each evening.

Livia and her mother were driven down to the sea each day by the chauffeur, taking up residence in one of the *bagnos* that lined the white sandy beach. These private beach clubs were reserved for the rich residents of Forte dei Marmi, and were equipped with everything needed to make a day on the beach comfortable. A *salvataggio* stood guard at the water's edge, raising a red flag if the current was too strong for guests to swim safely. There were changing rooms complete with showers, and daybeds stood in neat rows on the raked sand, protected from the fierce sun by large umbrellas.

Luisa, wearing a patterned cotton dress and a straw hat, chose to sit in a comfortable armchair in the shade, cooling herself with a paper fan, but Livia lay on a sunbed in her new halter neck swimming costume, tracing patterns in the soft sand with her fingers and relishing the cool breeze blowing in from the sea.

By the end of the week, Luisa had finally relaxed, and Livia had even managed to set aside some of her lingering guilt about Cosimo. She had eaten well and put on a little weight; her skin was tanned and her dark hair was streaked with gold by the sun.

On their final day, she was reading on a sunbed, when she was interrupted by an unfamiliar voice.

"It's little Livia, isn't it?"

She looked up from her book, and there was Vicenzo—tall and more handsome than she remembered, but with the same dark eyes, his hair swept back from his high forehead. He was tanned, wearing an open-necked white shirt and cream trousers. He looked more like a movie star than a director, she thought.

"Vicenzo," she said gaily, leaping to her feet. "I hoped you would come."

He leaned down and kissed her.

Her mother, who had been snoozing, her head lolling forward onto her chest, suddenly woke up. "Oh Vicenzo," she said, fanning herself coyly, as he kissed her hand. "How marvelous. We've had such a wonderful time at the villa. Your mother has been so kind."

"I'm sure she has loved having you here. These days, we don't often get the chance to see you all—it's not like when we were young. Have you been in?" He gestured toward the sea. A red flag flew overhead, warning bathers to beware the dangerous current.

"Not today, I was too nervous," admitted Livia.

"Come in with me. I know where it's safe to swim."

He walked back toward the bathing huts and emerged a few moments later in a pair of white swimming trunks that showed off his tanned torso. He put his arm around Livia's shoulders, guiding her toward the water's edge, but left her standing in the shallows while he strode in.

"Stay in that area," he called back to her. "Make sure you can still touch the seabed, and you'll be fine. The current gets a bit stronger further out."

She watched him crawling athletically back and forth, while she swam a few tentative strokes. Although she remained in the shallows, she could still feel the pull of the current around her legs. She felt relieved when Vicenzo finally swam back and emerged from the sea, his dark skin glistening in the sunlight.

That evening, as Livia was changing for dinner, there was a knock on the door.

"Who is it?"

"It's your mamma." Luisa came into the room, wearing a formal black dress decorated with beadwork. Her silvery dark hair had been pinned up at the neck.

Livia, sitting at the dressing table, swung round and admired her. "You look very smart. Why are you so dressed up?"

"Well, it's our last night." Her mother was anxiously checking her reflection in the long mirror. "What will you wear?" she asked.

"I don't know," said Livia, "the dress I had on this morning, I suppose."

"Oh no, you can't wear that." Her mother flung open Livia's wardrobe, and began to riffle through her clothes. "Didn't you bring a proper evening dress?"

"No, Mamma. You know I don't have a proper evening dress."

"What about this?" Her mother held up a white cotton dress with a sweetheart neckline, edged with broderie anglaise.

"Oh not that," said Livia. "It looks like the sort of thing you wear to your first communion. Anyway, why does it matter what I'm wearing?"

"Because Vicenzo is here," her mother replied, laying the dress on the bed.

"So what if he is?" asked Livia.

Her mother blushed slightly. "Because..." she hesitated, "I've always thought it would be nice if you two..."

Livia looked up at her mother's reflection in the mirror. "If we two what?"

"You know... if you two got married."

"Married? Me and Vicenzo? I hardly know him, Mamma—I haven't seen him for years. Don't be ridiculous."

"All right," said her mother, smiling. "But do wear the dress—it's very pretty."

When Livia came onto the terrace that evening, Vicenzo's father rose to greet her. "How charming you look." The Count kissed Livia's hand; she blushed slightly, her tanned skin glowing against the white of her dress. "I'll mix you a cocktail," said the Count.

Vicenzo sauntered onto the terrace, dressed in his customary black—a silk shirt and linen trousers—and joined Livia. Together, they looked like the perfect couple, thought Luisa; she smiled approvingly.

"Now," said the Contessa, "where are we all going to sit? Vicenzo, you sit here." She indicated a chair in the center of the table. "I'll put Livia next to you—and Luisa, you go opposite them."

"What a beautiful table," Luisa gushed, as she sat down. "The candles, the crystal—it's all so lovely."

Vicenzo pulled out Livia's chair for her. "You should wear white more often," he murmured in her ear. "It shows off your tan."

She sat down, blushing, and Luisa kicked her daughter playfully beneath the table. Livia glared back at her.

As Vicenzo poured them both a glass of wine, he opened up the conversation. "You're at university now, I hear."

"Yes, I'm studying English Literature and History of Art."

"That's a wonderful combination. I studied art too, but I soon realized I had no real talent for painting. So after university I traveled a lot. I ended up in Hollywood and fell in love with film."

"It all sounds impossibly glamorous," said Livia shyly.

"It's not really. Most of the time the film business is hard work. We film in all weathers, and have early starts and late finishes. And actors are the most egotistical people on earth." He laughed. "They all think they can do the job better than you. It's a nightmare." He drained his glass and refilled it.

"Well, it sounds more interesting than sitting in a lecture theater all day," replied Livia with a smile. "Your mother said you were filming in Ferrara. What's the film about?"

"It's about death, treachery and jealousy..." then, dropping his voice, he whispered in her ear, "...and it's very dark."

Luisa, sitting opposite them, looked on approvingly.

"Anyway," he said, "that's enough about me. I'm sorry your father couldn't be here. I would have liked to speak with him."

"He had to go back to Florence. He has a lot of work to do."

"He's still practicing law, then?"

"Yes, he's a lawyer with a heart." Livia smiled. "He takes on all the cases no one else wants—defending those who cannot defend themselves."

"He sounds very interesting...and honorable. Of course, I remember him from when we were young, but somehow I never really got to know him then. I'm sorry to have missed him."

"Perhaps you could come and see him in Florence."

"I'd like that. We need as many people as possible who are..." He lowered his voice, and narrowed his eyes as if sizing her up, "...committed to a new way of life."

"You mean people who oppose the government?"

He smiled. "Exactly. I see you speak your mind. I like that. But you should be careful. My family are open to these ideas, but many others are not. They refuse to see what is in front of their eyes."

"My father and I discuss politics a lot," replied Livia. "In fact, he recently joined one of the anti-government parties." She stopped, suddenly aware that she may have revealed too much.

"Good for him," said Vicenzo. "It is incumbent on all of us to make a stand at this time."

"How do you intend to do that?" she asked.

He laughed. "You are very bold! I'll tell you something that you must keep to yourself."

Livia leaned forward eagerly.

"In spite of my comfortable background," he said quietly, "I am also on the left of the political spectrum."

"Really?" She sat back, studying him. In his dark silk shirt, his face tanned and smooth, he looked more like a playboy than a revolutionary.

"You think because I have a title, because we live in such luxury, that is not possible?"

"No, not at all." She blushed, embarrassed. "I'm just a little surprised, that's all."

"Don't allow appearances to blind you to the truth," he said, patting her hand. "Not everyone is what they seem." He refilled her glass. "As for your father—I will come to Florence one day soon and meet him."

Luisa overheard the comment and smiled knowingly at her daughter.

"Papa's coming back here tomorrow to collect us," Livia explained. "You could meet him then."

"I will be leaving very early, unfortunately," said Vicenzo. "I must get back to Ferrara. But we will meet another time…I promise."

Chapter Seven

Rome
October 1942

Isabella returned to Rome after the Venice Film Festival feeling tired and distracted. With no new film project to concentrate on, she found herself dwelling on the evening she had spent with Vicenzo in the villa in Ferrara. He had made such a fuss of her in front of everyone, insisting she sat next to him at dinner, directing all his conversation toward her. It made her feel special, and she began to truly believe that he was deeply attracted to her. To Isabella's relief, it became clear during dinner that Clara Calamai had no personal interest in Vicenzo. In fact she had almost completely ignored everyone that evening, and instead was deep in conversation with her leading man. Perhaps she and Massimo Girotti were having an affair—it would certainly explain Girotti's earlier fury with the director. It was bad enough, Isabella thought, having to hit an actress across the face, but when that actress is the woman you love, it would be intolerable.

At the end of the evening, as the group began to break up, drifting off upstairs in ones and twos, Isabella lingered at the table. She wondered if Vicenzo might try to seduce her—in fact, she rather hoped he would. But he didn't, joining in with the banter of the remaining film crew—the hard drinkers who enjoyed the late nights after filming. Eventually, Isabella realized that Vicenzo would never make the first move, so she left the table, saying it was time for her to go to bed.

She hesitated at the bottom of the stairs, hoping he might follow her, and when she saw him coming into the hall behind her, her heart began to race in anticipation.

"Well, goodnight little Bella." He cupped her face in his hands, and gazed deeply into her eyes. "You must be tired after your journey."

"I'm not that tired," she said teasingly.

To her disappointment, he kissed her chastely on the cheek. "Sleep well," he murmured. He then returned to the dining room; she heard the sound of male laughter, and a cork being removed from a bottle.

She waited in her room for half an hour, hoping he would come to her. Finally she undressed and got into bed. Perhaps, she reasoned, he didn't want to embarrass her in front of his colleagues. Or maybe he was just an old-fashioned gentleman.

When she woke the following morning and went downstairs in search of him, she found a note addressed to her on the hall table, written in his elegant graphic script.

> *My little Bella—it was wonderful to see you. We had to leave early and I'm sorry I couldn't say goodbye. Enjoy Venice and let's meet back in Rome…*

Back in Rome, she waited eagerly for his return to the capital and, true to his word, as soon as his film project was completed, he phoned her one evening.

"I'm back at last," he said, "and wondered if you'd have dinner with me."

"I'd love to," she replied enthusiastically.

"Tonight?"

"Oh dear." She couldn't keep the regret out of her voice. "I can't tonight. I have another engagement."

"Tomorrow then?"

She was nervous of seeming too eager but was desperate to see him. "Yes," she said—too quickly.

"I'll pick you up at home, at eight o'clock."

That evening's "engagement" was a dinner hosted by Count Ciano at the Acquasanta Golf Club. Work had kept her away from the club over most of the summer—which was convenient, as Ciano's overt flirtations had become tiresome. She loathed his attention, and yet to display any irritation or displeasure would be career suicide. Instead, she walked a tightrope between charming indifference and politeness. It infuriated her, because the club had always been something of a second home—a refuge from the film industry and her mother, where she could enjoy a game of golf or tennis, and in the evenings play cards. But since Ciano's arrival, the atmosphere at the club had become increasingly oppressive. Instead of the usual games and idle chat, members hovered nervously around the bar, hoping to be part of Ciano's court.

When she arrived, Isabella hung back, standing to one side of the room. The Count was surrounded by his usual coterie of adoring followers, including one or two representatives of the German Embassy in Rome—stiff men wearing Teutonic jackets and wing collars. Ciano was in the middle of a long diatribe about the Africa Campaign and the battles that were currently raging in Egypt between the Anglo-American "Allies" and the "Axis powers" of Germany and Italy.

"We have virtually no transport, nor munitions," he said in an almost amused fashion, sipping a large whisky. "Really it's quite absurd. How Il Duce thinks he will bring the whole campaign to a successful conclusion is beyond me. He spent three weeks over there in the summer, thinking he would be making a triumphal march into Alexandria, before he had to admit defeat and slink back to Italy."

The Germans laughed. It was widely known that Hitler disdained his Italian counterpart.

Isabella, observing from the shadows, was struck by Ciano's disloyalty. He loved to entertain and be the center of attention—that was his weakness. The more his audience laughed, the more indiscreet he became.

"The Allies have appointed a new man, a funny little chap called Montgomery," he went on, tipping whisky down his throat. "It's obvious they're not giving up the Suez Canal without a struggle. What with that and Stalingrad, it's not looking good, it really isn't."

One or two of the Italian guests began to mutter and shift uncomfortably in their seats.

Ciano looked around, beaming at his audience, and noticed Isabella. "Isa, darling," he began. He had taken to calling her "Isa" and she hated it. "What on earth are you doing over there? Come and sit by me." He patted the leather sofa next to him, and two young actresses, who had been sitting on either side of him, were moved to make room for "my favorite." The women seemed unconcerned, happily joining a group of German embassy officials, laughing on cue and fluttering their eyelashes. The men appeared delighted, whispering into their ears, their hands sliding up the young women's thighs.

Isabella dutifully took her place on the sofa next to Ciano, while inwardly resenting the assumption that actresses were there for the taking.

"What are you doing about the strikes in the north?" one of the guests asked him.

"It's a problem, I admit," said Ciano. "Genoa is full of discontent. Il Duce is unhappy about it. 'They are afflicted by moral weakness,' he says."

"Perhaps it's the relentless bombing that's making them so unhappy," ventured one of his entourage. "After all, I hear the Allies have been attacking them mercilessly."

"Possibly," Ciano replied. "In any case, the Neapolitans are Mussolini's favorites. He respects their fatalism, caused by years of hardship. They have even composed some ironical songs about the English which they sing loudly during bombing attacks!" He laughed gaily, his audience dutifully following suit.

As the evening wore on, Isabella thought wistfully of Vicenzo and his sensitive, fascinating conversation. By contrast, Ciano was an egotistical bore. By nine o'clock, she'd had enough and made her excuses.

"Count, I'm so sorry, but I suddenly have a blinding headache. I really think I should go. Will you forgive me?"

"I don't believe it," Ciano sulked, "you can't leave now—we've not had dinner yet."

"I'm so sorry," she said, "but I really must go."

She turned at the door of the club room to wave goodbye, but Ciano was already deeply engrossed in another of his own anecdotes.

The following day, Isabella eagerly anticipated her dinner with Vicenzo. He had promised to collect her in his car at eight o'clock, and late in the afternoon, her mother found her, dressed in a slip, trying on various outfits. Those she had rejected lay in an abandoned tangle on the bed.

"Wear this," her mother advised, extracting a fitted dress made of fine scarlet wool from the bottom of the pile. "It's very ladylike, but sexy—men like that."

"I'm not sure." With one hand Isabella held the red dress up to her body, while clutching a pale-gray suit with the other. "I was thinking about wearing this."

"Oh no!" Her mother snatched the suit away. "You'll look like someone's mother in that."

Vicenzo arrived on the dot of eight, while Isabella was putting the finishing touches to her makeup. He tooted his horn and swept into the drive. From her bedroom window she watched him striding toward the house. Her heart beat loudly in her chest as she picked up her handbag and gave herself a final look in the mirror. Her lipstick matched the red dress perfectly. As she walked along the landing, she heard the front door opening, and Vicenzo beginning to chat amiably with her mother. At the top of the stairs, she coughed discreetly to attract his attention.

"Goodness!" he said, glancing up at her. "Very femme fatale."

At that moment she earnestly wished she had worn the gray suit. Being a femme fatale was the last impression she wanted to give. She blushed with embarrassment as Vicenzo helped her on with her coat.

Before Isabella left the house, her mother hugged her. "Don't lose this one," she whispered.

The restaurant Vicenzo had chosen was a small family-run affair in Trastevere—a charming part of Rome that had the feel of a village, with its cobbled streets and little shops and cafés. The tables were covered with red-checked cloths, lit by candles, inserted into empty raffia-covered Chianti bottles. The other customers stared openly as the glamorous couple entered, squeezing past the tables. Isabella felt overdressed, and nervously sipped a glass of mineral water the moment they sat down.

"The menu is not huge here," Vicenzo explained. "There's not much meat—rationing has seen to that—but the pasta is good."

He was an attentive host and she began to relax. Over dinner, Vicenzo probed her about her acting aspirations. "The films you do, about schoolteachers and orphans, do they give you pleasure?"

"Yes, I suppose so." She felt a little confused by the question. "Although the one about the orphans was exhausting," she continued. "Playing a blind woman is not easy. They made me wear a blindfold, and I bumped into so much furniture on the set, I was black and blue." She laughed, but Vicenzo wasn't smiling. "It's just my work... it's what I do," she went on nervously. "I've made films like these since I was sixteen. It's all I know."

He sipped his wine thoughtfully. "You don't feel they are..." he paused, choosing his words carefully, "... restrictive at all?"

"Restrictive? In what way?"

"Emotionally, as an actress. What I mean is, these films are not true to life, are they? They are fantasies, fairy stories."

"I've never thought about them like that. They are simply stories which make our audience happy. That's what people want from us, isn't it—escapism? For a few hours to forget about the war, the rationing, the suffering."

"You see, Isabella, for me, cinema is about realism. To show things as they really are, not how we wish they could be. Anything else is propaganda. People don't run about in pretty dresses, or have perfect makeup all the time, or use white telephones for that matter." He was laughing now, and for the second time that evening she felt embarrassed—and patronized.

"But what if they make people happy?" she asked uncertainly.

"But do they? I think what would make them happy is having a proper job, enough money and a benign government. People's lives are not simply happy or sad—they are complex. I believe our audiences want to see this in the films they watch. They need something they can relate to. Do you understand?"

Isabella felt stung by his criticism. "So you think the films I make are trite, unworthy in some way?"

"No," he said, reaching across the table and taking her hand. "But I think *you* are capable of so much more. You have great depth, Isabella, genuinely you do."

"You really think so?"

"Of course. Why else would I have asked you to audition for me? I can see something special in you, Bella, something very special."

He drove her home in silence. It had been a strange evening. He could wound her deeply, only to buoy her up moments later. He rejected her with one hand, while attracting her with the other.

Sitting in the car outside her house, he held her tightly in the darkness, kissing her ear, caressing her hair. "Little Bella," he whispered.

She inhaled his scent and ached for him.

Suddenly the mood changed. He leaned across her and opened the car door. "Goodnight," he said softly.

She turned toward him, expecting him to kiss her, but instead he wound down his window and lit a cigarette. She sensed him withdraw, as if a door to his emotions had been shut in her face. She climbed out of the car, and he closed the door behind her, with a slam.

Through his open window, he simply called out: "Goodnight," before driving off, leaving her alone and confused.

A few days later, Isabella received a phone call from a French film director called Marcel L'Herbier. "I wonder if you would do me the honor of meeting me?" he asked. "Could you come to Nice?"

"To Nice?" she said with surprise. "You mean in France?"

"Yes, I would like to cast you in my next film."

"Don't you want me to audition first?"

"No," he said simply. "I know you are right for the part."

"What is the part?"

"Oh, I'm sorry, did I not say? It's based on the opera *La Bohème*. You would play the part of Mimi, opposite Louis Jourdan. It will be shot in French at the Victorine studios here in Nice."

She sat in stunned silence for a few moments. "In French? You want to shoot it in French?"

"Oui, I hear you speak French very well."

"I speak it a little, but really not well." She could hardly believe her schoolgirl French would be good enough.

"I'm sure we'll manage," he said.

As she replaced the receiver, it occurred to her that Vicenzo might have had something to do with it. She was tempted to call him but decided against it; she could ask him about it when they next met. If he had encouraged L'Herbier to cast her, then she was in his debt, if not, then it was just a coincidence. She hoped she could live up to the director's obvious faith in her, but the tragic story of Mimi would certainly stretch her talent. Perhaps it would also win Vicenzo's approval.

That afternoon, her mother came into the room carrying a basket of white roses. "Look what you've got...who are they from?" Giovanna poked nosily around in the basket. "Ooh!" she said, brandishing the card, "they're from Vicenzo; he must be keen."

Isabella took the card from her mother. "Give me that—it's private." She picked up the basket of flowers. "And I'll take these to my room if you don't mind."

Upstairs, she placed the roses on the chest of drawers in the window where she could admire them, and lay down on the bed to read his note.

I hear you are off to work in France. Come and see me before you go. My mother, the Contessa, would like to invite you to dinner tomorrow night to meet the family. Come at eight.

With love,
Vicenzo

Isabella felt the familiar mix of excitement and fear. A few days ago, Vicenzo had driven off without even a goodnight kiss. Now she was to meet his family. Why would he offer her something like that, unless he cared for her?

She could think of nothing else, and spent the rest of the day working out what to wear, determined not to repeat the mistake of the tarty red dress. She tried on several outfits before finally deciding on something simple, elegant, and black.

The Luccheses' Roman villa was approached through tall, ornate metal gates. The house itself was painted terra-cotta and covered with ivy.

As Isabella parked in the drive, a man in a neat dark-blue uniform opened the car door and offered to take her keys. "The family are waiting for you inside, signorina," he said, guiding her toward the impressive marble porch.

A pair of greyhounds lay on the steps. They stood up as she approached, wagging their tails but, rather than gamboling toward her as she had expected, they remained on the porch. She put her hand out to offer them her scent and they nuzzled her fingers with their soft noses.

Before she had a chance to knock, a butler opened the door. He clicked his fingers discreetly, and the dogs instantly lay back down, sulkily looking up at Isabella. "Signorina Bellucci, please come in."

She was shown into a large salon with high ceilings and long windows down one side. It was furnished in delicate shades of apricot, with high-backed silk sofas on either side of the fireplace, and a pair of gilded Bergère chairs, embroidered with bucolic scenes. The walls were covered with classical paintings, some modernist sketches and even the occasional impressionist canvas.

Vicenzo came toward her, his hands outstretched. "Carissima Bella," he said, wrapping her in his arms and kissing her on both cheeks. "You look lovely," he whispered. With one arm protectively around her shoulders, he guided her toward an elegant, if slightly plump, woman seated on one of the sofas.

"Mamma, can I introduce you to my friend Isabella Bellucci. Isabella, darling, this is my mother, the Contessa di Lucchese."

The older woman proffered an elegant hand wreathed in diamonds. She had sparkling black eyes and an eager smile; she was also, Isabella was relieved to see, wearing a black evening gown. "Isabella, call me Alessandra, please." She smiled and patted the sofa next to her. "Come and sit here by me—I've heard a lot about you. Vicenzo, get your young friend a drink."

Sitting opposite Isabella was a younger woman, elegantly dressed in a cream figure-hugging dress. She looked remarkably like Vicenzo, with the same hooded eyes, angular face and high forehead. "I'm Luciana," she said, "Vicenzo's sister. And that's my husband Carlo." She waved a hand toward a tall fair-haired man, leaning languorously against the fireplace, smoking a cigarette. He wore pale-cream trousers and a dark-blue silk shirt with a spotted silk cravat tied at the neck. He crossed the deep-pile Turkish carpet, took Isabella's hand in his, and kissed it.

Vicenzo returned carrying two cocktail glasses filled with crimson liquid. "Here you are. I hope you like Negronis?" He chinked his glass against hers.

She took a sip of the sweet-sour cocktail, and felt its warmth spread through her body. "It's delicious. I've never had one before."

"Oh," said Luciana, with just a hint of scorn. "We drink them all the time. I'm surprised you've not tried one."

"I don't drink very much," Isabella explained shyly.

Luciana glanced amusedly up at her brother, a look that didn't go unnoticed by Isabella.

"Ah, and here is my little cousin, Amadeo," Vicenzo announced, welcoming a tall young man into the room, who sat down next to Luciana. "He's a dreadful little boy," Vicenzo said, ruffling the boy's hair affectionately, "but we have to look after him."

Amadeo blushed slightly.

"Oh leave the boy alone," said the Contessa, turning to Isabella. "I'm afraid my other son, Raffaele, is not with us this evening. He had business out of town, but hopefully you'll meet him soon."

An older man—tall and slender, with the same high forehead and elegant profile as Vicenzo and Luciana—entered the room.

Vicenzo leapt to his feet. "And here is my father. Papa, can I introduce my friend, Isabella Bellucci. Cara, this is my father Vittorio, Il Conte di Lucchese."

"Forgive me," said the Count, bowing low to Isabella. He took her hand in his and kissed it. "I was just collecting this from my room." He held up a silver cigarette case and sat down on a gilded chair, next to his eldest son—the king and his handsome heir, Isabella thought.

The family seemed universally attractive and charming. It was as if they had been blessed at birth not only with wealth, but also beauty and wit.

As the evening wore on, they chatted incessantly, laughing uproariously, and interrupting each other constantly. Vicenzo's parents and cousin did their best to include Isabella in the conversation, but his sister Luciana treated her with a faint air of disdain, either by ignoring her, or by reminding Vicenzo of special moments that only they could share. The phrase "Do you remember, Vicenzo..." peppered her conversation. Meanwhile, Carlo appeared merely bored. He drank constantly, replenishing his glass from a decanter set up on the drinks tray behind the sofa. His wife admonished him from time to time, but her mother constantly intervened. "Oh leave him alone, Luciana. If a man can't drink with his own family, who can he drink with?"

After dinner, which had been served in the grand dining room, the family returned to the drawing room.

Vicenzo's father stood next to the drinks tray. "What does everyone want to drink?" he asked.

"Brandy, please, Papa," said Luciana. "Let's play the truth game."

"Oh darling!" The Contessa, settling herself back on the sofa, looked exasperated. "Must we? I'm not sure our guest is quite ready for the truth game yet."

"What's the truth game?" asked Isabella.

Vicenzo handed his sister a brandy. "It's a silly game that we've played since childhood. It can be fun, but I think Mamma is right. Let's not play it tonight."

"What are you frightened of?" Luciana asked her brother.

"Nothing," he said. "Certainly not you." He leaned down and kissed her.

Luciana pouted childishly, stroked his cheek and blew him an imaginary kiss.

"All right," Vicenzo agreed. "If that's what Luciana wants, let's play."

Luciana sat up eagerly and began to explain the rules. "One person is the leader, I'll do that. Someone else is chosen to leave the room—in this case we'll make it Carlo."

Carlo raised his eyes heavenward and refilled his glass.

"Everyone else has to tell me an embarrassing, but true, fact about him," she continued breathlessly. "They whisper it to me, of course, so the others can't hear. Then, when he comes back in, I reveal the secrets, and he has to guess who said each one. It's great fun."

Isabella thought it sounded rather cruel, and was relieved when the Contessa declared that she would be unable to take part. "There's no point in poor Isabella playing as she's never met Carlo before. But she can watch."

"And learn," said Luciana pointedly.

Luciana listened to the revelations about her husband with intense delight, giggling uproariously as her brother or mother exposed some tantalizing but embarrassing fact about her husband.

Carlo returned and poured himself yet another large brandy. Luciana began, gleefully, to reveal his "secrets." He was clearly both hurt and embarrassed, and with each new revelation, drank another slug of brandy. It struck Isabella as an odd sort of game, designed purely to humiliate and hurt the victim. She was glad she had been excluded.

When it was Vicenzo's turn to leave the room, Isabella was selected as team leader—on the basis that, as a new friend, she would have no secrets to reveal.

"He was afraid of mirrors," his mother whispered to her. "As a child, he would scream if the light was turned out and he could see any sort of reflection in the mirror in his bedroom. I had to remove it eventually."

"He used to cheat at tennis," Luciana told Isabella. "Calling the balls out when they were definitely in. He thought I didn't notice, but I notice everything," she said with a wink.

Amadeo, who was younger and sweeter than the rest, knelt at Isabella's side and whispered in her ear. "He once said he wanted to be a film star, like you."

When it was Carlo's turn to reveal a secret about his brother-in-law, he sat down heavily next to Isabella, reeking of alcohol. "He's not all he seems," he said darkly, leaning toward her. She looked at him questioningly. He nudged her. "You understand?"

She smiled nervously.

When Vicenzo returned, he sat calmly on the sofa and looked around at his family. "Come on then, all of you, do your worst."

As Isabella revealed the secrets, he identified their authors instantly. When it came to Carlo's comment, he said merely, "Ah, that would be the opinion of the drunk."

Carlo responded by pouring himself another drink.

"Let's change the game," said Luciana suddenly. "I'm bored with this. What about the tower game?"

"What's that?" asked Isabella.

"It's a sort of 'what if' game," replied Luciana. "Say, for example, you were on top of a tower and there was only room for one other person, who would you choose to save?"

The Contessa was first to play, and chose Vicenzo.

"She never chooses me," her husband remarked *sotto voce* to Isabella. "She says it's a mother's instinct to save her young." He laughed uproariously. Vicenzo nodded gracefully to his parents, acknowledging his mother's devotion and his father's forbearance. His sister, meanwhile, visibly sulked. But when it was Luciana's turn, she also chose Vicenzo, staring pointedly at Carlo. Now seriously drunk, he left the room in fury.

"Luciana," her mother said gently. "You could at least have chosen him. You know how hurt he gets."

"He's just like a spoilt child," Luciana declared. "He's behaved badly all day—why should I reward him?"

When it was Vicenzo's turn, both his mother and his sister sat up eagerly. He surveyed the group teasingly, letting his gaze linger on each member of the family, finally settling on Isabella.

She blushed as he called out her name. "Oh don't be ridiculous," she blurted out, "you should choose your mother or your sister . . . or your best friend—you've only just met me." But secretly she was thrilled.

He sat down next to her and kissed her cheek. His mother studied them together, her black eyes flashing.

At the end of the evening, Vicenzo showed Isabella into the hall. "Thank you so much for coming," he said, kissing her hand.

"Thank you for asking me." She looked up at him, anticipating a kiss on her lips. But instead he kissed her on each cheek—blushing slightly, she noticed.

"Will you be all right driving home?" he asked tenderly.

"Oh yes, I'll be fine. I only live ten minutes away. I could practically walk it—although maybe not in these shoes," she indicated her little satin evening slippers.

He ran his hand down her back as they approached the door. She trembled, and once again thought he was going to kiss her properly, passionately. But Luciana called him from the sitting room.

"What are you doing?" she shouted. "Do hurry up."

"Goodbye then," he said. As the door closed behind her, the greyhounds, lying on the stone step, stood up and nuzzled her hand.

Chapter Eight

Florence
October 1942

It had been months since Livia had heard from Cosimo, and she had learned to live with the dull ache of anxiety and uncertainty that filled her waking hours. Even her dreams were dominated by surreal images of him lying in agony in a pool of blood by the roadside. She was haunted by the newspaper photographs of Italian troops who had been left for dead on the Eastern Front. She was grateful for the comforting distractions of her university course and friendship with Elena.

Standing in the canteen queue one lunchtime, Livia chose the least unattractive option on offer—a pale, watery soup served with a small piece of bread. She was placing the bowl on her tray, when Elena suddenly appeared at her side.

"Elena, there you are!" Livia said. "I missed you this morning—where have you been?"

"The hospital."

"Why?" she asked, taking her friend's hand. "What's wrong—are you ill?"

"No, I'm fine, but a boy I know, an old family friend, has just been sent back from the Russian front. He's very badly injured—God only knows how they got him home. I went to see him this morning as he's in my father's hospital." She put a bowl of soup on her tray. "It was a terrible shock, seeing him like that."

"I'm so sorry. Will he recover, do they think?"

"I don't know. It's rather touch and go. I thought he might have news of Cosimo. They were friends, you see, in the same division."

Livia put her tray down next to the cashier, her heart racing. "And?" she asked.

"I'm afraid I don't know," Elena said, getting her purse out and paying for her lunch. "He was asleep when I got there, and the nurse wouldn't let me wake him."

The pair moved away from the line and sat down at a table.

"Perhaps we could go back there now?" suggested Livia eagerly. The thought that someone in Florence might have seen Cosimo, might know something about him, was almost more than she could bear.

"They won't let us talk to him," said Elena flatly, eating her soup.

"But I must try," Livia insisted, "surely you can see that?"

"All right," Elena agreed. "But eat your food first—there's no point in starving." She reached over and squeezed Livia's hand. "He may know nothing, so don't get your hopes up."

Later that afternoon, Elena led Livia onto the ward. The tightly packed rows of beds were filled with young men—their faces pale and gray, many with missing limbs. They looked exhausted, defeated and hopeless, Livia thought, as if old before their time.

Elena's friend lay at one end of the ward, his face turned to the wall. She sat down gingerly on the edge of his bed. "Mario, it's me Elena," she murmured.

He rolled over, groaning slightly. One half of his head was covered in bandages. Judging by the shape, he had lost part of his skull, and possibly one eye. Blood seeped through the white muslin dressings.

"Oh Mario." Elena took his hand, her eyes filling with tears, "you poor, poor thing. Can you speak?"

"A little." His voice was hoarse and very weak.

"What happened?" she asked gently.

"A mortar attack," he whispered.

"Are you going to be all right? What have they said?"

He shook his head.

"Well, you're back now, thank God. They'll make you better."

His good eye filled with tears.

"They will," she said earnestly, "I promise. My father's a surgeon here. It's amazing what they can do."

They sat for a moment in silence, each reflecting on Elena's optimism. The soldier caught sight of Livia standing nervously to one side.

"Mario, this is my friend, Livia."

Livia crouched down at his bedside. "I'm so sorry. It must have been awful."

"It was a living hell," he said quietly. "Bodies everywhere...no guns, no support...the things I have seen. I can never get them out of my mind." He began to cry and a nurse bustled toward them.

"What are you doing here? I told you this morning—he can't have any visitors."

"I'm sorry," replied Elena, "but he may have some vital news for my friend here." She stood up, smoothing the bedclothes.

"Please," Livia pleaded, taking the nurse's hand, "let me ask him one more thing."

"All right—just one question," the nurse replied crossly, "and then you must leave." She stood sternly at the end of the bed while Livia sat down at Mario's bedside.

"Elena thought you might be stationed with another friend of ours. His name is Cosimo de Luca."

"Cosimo," he murmured. "Yes, I know him."

"Is he alive?" Livia asked, suddenly terrified by the answer she might receive.

"Yes...At least, he was when I left." Mario sighed, closed his one eye and turned his face back to the wall.

"I insist you leave now," interjected the nurse, grabbing Livia by the elbow and ushering both girls briskly out of the ward.

Walking back toward the university, Livia and Elena were lost in their private thoughts. It was Elena who eventually broke the silence. "It's good news about Cosimo, don't you think?"

"I suppose so." Livia was close to tears. "At least we know he *was* alive."

"And probably still is," Elena encouraged her, taking her arm. "Really, you mustn't give up hope."

"I'll try," sobbed Livia, tears cascading down her cheeks. "But it's so hard. That poor boy back there—he looked so...broken. What are we doing, Elena, fighting a war in Russia we can never hope to win? What are we trying to prove? It's madness."

Later that day, still worrying about Cosimo, Livia climbed the stairs toward the apartment. As she reached the landing on the fifth floor, she could hear her father shouting. This in itself was an unusual experience, for her father rarely lost his temper. As she opened the glass doors into the sitting room, her father was standing between the two windows, his face puce with rage.

"How dare they?" he was saying, to no one in particular.

Luisa was on the sofa, staring open-mouthed at her husband, clearly alarmed at this outburst.

"Giacomo," she said softly, "please calm yourself. It will do you no good, all this shouting. You'll make yourself ill."

"How do you expect me to react?" he replied, pacing the room.

"Papa," Livia called out. "What on earth is the matter?"

"You've not heard, then?" he demanded.

"No, what?"

"Pisa? Have you not heard the news about Pisa?"

"No, Papa. I've been..." She paused, unsure if she should reveal her hospital visit. "I've been in lectures all day."

"The Pisans have been attacking Jewish shopkeepers. Our fellow Tuscans have been looting their premises, defacing their shops with smears and lies, denouncing good Jewish citizens as traitors and spies—when it's those vandals who are the real traitors."

"How did you hear about it?" asked Livia, sinking down into one of the armchairs.

"I have clients with connections," replied Giacomo, his anger surging again. "It's appalling. This is the end, do you hear? The absolute end. We will rise up and stop this. It cannot go on."

Luisa rose to her feet and began to pace the floor agitatedly. "Now Giacomo, you cannot take the world's problems on your own shoulders. You cannot help everyone."

"So what do you suggest?" he asked, rounding on her. "That I sit back in comfort here in my apartment and do nothing? Say nothing? No, Luisa, the time has come for action." He stomped out of the room; a few minutes later the front door of the apartment building slammed shut.

Livia stood up suddenly and announced to her mother, "I have to go out too, Mamma."

"But you've only just come home."

"I know, I'm sorry."

Livia ran down the five flights of stairs and, emerging onto the street, she glimpsed the tails of her father's coat as he swung round the corner. She raced after him. "Papa, Papa…"

He stopped and turned around. "Livia, what are you doing?"

"Coming with you," she said defiantly.

"No, Livia, no," he said firmly. "Go home and help your mother with supper. I'll be back in an hour or two."

"No!" She pulled his arm until they both stood facing one another at the edge of the road. "Wherever you're going, I'm coming with you. I can't stand aside anymore either. I can be useful, you'll see."

He gazed down at her with tears in his eyes and stroked her cheek gently with his hand. "Your mother will never forgive me," he said, smiling. "Come on then. We have a meeting to go to."

The meeting was held in the cloisters of a church—a gloomy space that smelled strongly of wax candles. A group of about fifteen men sat in a semicircle facing the door. A tall man with silvery hair stood up respectfully when Giacomo and Livia arrived.

"Ah, Francesco," said Giacomo, "I hope we're not late."

"Not at all," he replied.

Giacomo put his arm around Livia's shoulders. "This is my daughter, Livia. She is a student here at the university, and would like to help. I trust that's all right?"

"Of course, she's welcome." Francesco pointed to two empty chairs next to him. "Please, do join us."

The discussion began with what could be done to prevent further attacks on Jewish citizens in Tuscany.

"This is just the start," said Giacomo darkly. "You mark my words. There'll be more atrocities to come."

"It's strange, because the Fascist government does not officially support anti-Semitism," interjected Francesco. "It goes against everything we stand for in this country."

"Mussolini is under pressure from Hitler," argued another. "And it will only get worse—Giacomo's right. We need to identify the most vulnerable and find hiding places for them if necessary."

"Yes, yes," Giacomo sounded impatient. "Individual acts of human kindness are important, of course they are. But our role in this must be more strategic. We need to build a political coalition—working with the Communist Party, the Liberals, all of them. At the moment we are just five or six disparate groups all trying to make a difference. We need to become a movement."

The others nodded.

"And part of that," Giacomo went on, "is to get our message out there. People are sympathetic to our cause, but they need to know that others agree with them, that there is a plan. We need a rallying call and a way to get information out to the general population. I think we need a newspaper."

Livia listened respectfully as the men talked. They were mostly academics, interspersed with industrialists and a few professionals like her father. They were intelligent and well-meaning, but inwardly she felt a sense of frustration: how could producing a newspaper really turn the tide against the power of the Fascist government? How could sheltering a few Jewish families really make a difference? It was time, she decided, for direct action, before the lives of all the young men like Mario and Cosimo were destroyed, fighting for a cause no one believed in. It was time to fight back.

Chapter Nine

Rome
Christmas 1942

It was Christmas Eve and a blanket of snow covered Isabella's rose-colored villa and the surrounding gardens. The pine trees that dominated the front garden were so weighed down that with each gust of wind huge piles of snow fell dramatically onto the lawn. Upstairs in her bedroom, Isabella could hear the muted tones of her mother and Giulia, the housekeeper, as they prepared the evening meal. She had invited her grandmother and aunt to join them for Christmas and she knew her mother was planning a traditional celebration.

Pulling on her fur coat, she looked out of her bedroom window. Outside, Giuseppe the gardener was doing his best to keep the drive clear, shoveling snow into a large graying pile in one corner of the garden. But as fast as he shoveled, fresh snow fell, and Isabella's car appeared to be completely blocked in the drive. If she wanted to go out, she would have to walk.

Wearing her best snow boots, she adjusted her hat in the mirror and picked up a small parcel wrapped in hand-blocked paper. Slipping it into her coat pocket, she went downstairs to the kitchen.

"Mamma," she said, pulling on her gloves, "I have to go out for a while. But I'll be back in time for dinner, I promise."

"Where are you going?" her mother asked. "Your grandmother and aunt will be here soon."

"I promised to see a friend who's all alone this Christmas."

"Invite her to dinner," her mother suggested.

"No," said Isabella evasively, "I don't think that would be a good idea. She's quite shy." It was a lie, of course. But if she told her mother where she was really going, there would be no end to the interrogation when she got home.

The roads felt eerily quiet as Isabella strode out in her thick winter boots and fur coat. She imagined families tucked away inside their houses preparing for the holiday—lovers draped in one another's arms sharing their first Christmas, or married couples with small children, sitting in front of the fire or cooking together in the kitchen, excitedly wrapping presents for one another. Imagining all those other people enjoying Christmas made her heart ache. For, while she loved her family, and felt a strong duty to them, they could never be a substitute for the intimacy she yearned for, and the desire she felt to create a family of her own with Vicenzo.

She touched the parcel in her coat pocket. It contained a silver cigarette lighter engraved with the words: *To Vicenzo with love your Bella.*

As she walked up Vicenzo's drive, there was no sign of the dogs. Normally they would be on the stone steps outside, but perhaps they were indoors, lying by the fire. She knocked on the door and was relieved when it was opened by the butler.

"I'm afraid the family are not here, signorina," he said. "They are in the country."

"Vicenzo too?" she asked.

"Yes, signorina," he replied. "Can I give him a message? I will be going there myself this afternoon." He gestured toward his suitcase, standing ready in the hall. "We are closing up the house, you see."

"Oh," she said, trying to hide her disappointment. Her fingers touched the parcel in her coat pocket. Should she leave it with the butler to give to Vicenzo? She could imagine him announcing it when he arrived at their country house. "Signorina Bellucci brought this for you," he would say. If Luciana was there, she would doubtless find it hilarious—the idea of yet another actress besotted with her brother. His parents would be more generous, she thought, but they would all inevitably pity Isabella, and she would emerge as a tragic figure—desperate and pathetic. That was the last thing she wanted.

Determined to appear unconcerned, she pushed the parcel back into her pocket, and muttered, "No...no message. I was just passing. I'm sorry to have bothered you."

She decided to walk back through the park. To return home too soon would only invite her mother's inevitable curiosity. She walked around Villa Borghese until the sun began to set, the sky glowing dark pink, fused with violet, casting shadows across the snow. The colors reflected her mood—pensive and melancholic.

Vicenzo really was the most perplexing man, she thought. To go away for Christmas without even saying goodbye seemed heartless. He could be filled with love and affection one day, sending her flowers and little intimate messages, only to ignore her for weeks at a time. How could the man who had chosen her over his own family in the "tower game" be the same person who could go away without a word?

Isabella was relieved when Christmas was over. *La Bohème* was due to start production early in the new year. At least she would be busy and less likely to brood. It was to be shot at the Victorine Studios in Nice, which since November had been part of the Italian-occupied section of southeast France.

"I should be coming with you," her mother said, as she watched Isabella pack her trunk. "I don't like to think of you being there all alone."

"Mamma, what on earth would you do all day in Nice? Much better that you stay here and look after the house."

"You talk to me as if I were the housekeeper," her mother bridled.

"Mamma..." Isabella put her arm around her mother's shoulders. "You know I didn't mean that. You'd be bored up there, all alone."

"Well at least it wouldn't be so cold there." Giovanna stared miserably out at the snow-covered garden. "Firewood is running low again and the house is freezing."

"I suspect it's even colder in the south of France, Mamma," Isabella argued, throwing a pair of shoes into her suitcase. "Besides, the film budget is very tight. I've already had a terrible battle over my contract, and they're not paying me very much. They're putting me up in a hotel and they'd never agree to pay for you as well. And much as I'd like to, I can't afford to pay your hotel bill myself."

"So I have to stay here," her mother replied petulantly.

"Mamma!" Isabella, exhausted by the argument, sat down on the bed. "Please don't be like that. I'm sorry it has to be this way, but I have to work to earn us a living. Now," she said, "I still have a few things to pack, and then we'd better get Giuseppe to take the trunk downstairs. I'm leaving first thing tomorrow."

Isabella intended to break her journey in Genoa. An old school friend had recently moved to the city with her husband. Mimi was a teacher, her husband, Daniele, a doctor. It had been years since the two women had seen each other. They had been close at school; both had been academic, good at maths and languages, but their lives had diverged the day a film director in Villa Borghese had catapulted Isabella into the rarefied world of the film industry.

"I wondered if I could stay with you," Isabella suggested, when she rang to tell Mimi about her trip. "It's such a long way from Rome to Nice, I'll never do it in one day. I've got to break the journey somewhere, and I thought it would give us a chance to catch up."

"I'd love to see you, of course," said Mimi. "But I should warn you—there has been bombing up here. The last raid was just a few days ago. Fortunately, our apartment is still standing."

"I've heard about the bombing." Isabella recalled a conversation with Count Ciano at the golf club before Christmas. "But as I say, I've got to stay somewhere, and I'm just as likely to get bombed in a hotel as with you." She laughed nervously. "How long has it been since we saw one another?"

"Eight...nine years maybe?"

"Really, is it that long? So much has happened to both of us. I'm so sorry I had to miss your wedding. My problem is that I'm always working."

"Yes, that was a shame," Mimi observed. "It was a lovely day—just family, really. We're very happy together. Are you married?"

That innocent question felt like a stab in the heart.

"No," Isabella replied quietly, "but I have met someone."

"How exciting!" Mimi's enthusiasm was obvious. "You must tell me all about him."

Isabella instantly regretted saying anything. "Oh no, there's nothing really to tell. I'm more excited at the prospect of meeting Daniele."

"And he's thrilled at the idea of meeting you," said Mimi. "He's a huge fan."

This one simple statement somehow shattered their shared intimacy. Isabella no longer felt they were just two friends chatting quietly, catching up on old times. It revealed the chasm between them. She was a movie star and her friend's husband was a typical fan.

"I hope I won't be a disappointment," murmured Isabella.

"How could you be?" Mimi sounded genuinely shocked. "Now, talking of disappointment, you must understand that we just live in an ordinary apartment. It's in the old town, in a rather beautiful building, but the apartment itself is quite small. On our salaries we can't afford much."

Isabella reassured her. "Mimi, I'm sure it's wonderful. I'm really grateful to you for putting me up."

The journey to Genoa would take all day. Isabella had to change trains in Florence, and as they left the city and traveled west, she spent the afternoon admiring the rolling Tuscan countryside through the carriage windows. When she realized they would be passing through Pisa, she hoped to catch a glimpse of the famous Leaning Tower, but was disappointed it was not visible from the train. After Pisa, the railway line turned north, passing through small coastal towns along the Ligurian coast.

As the train pulled into Forte dei Marmi station, Isabella had a sudden flash of recollection. Wasn't that where Vicenzo had a house? Was this the "house in the country" where he and the family were spending Christmas? It seemed unlikely. Forte dei Marmi was a summer resort, but even so, Isabella had to fight the impulse to get off the train and go in search of Vicenzo's villa.

When the train finally arrived, it was already early in the evening. The porters unloaded Isabella's trunk from the train and wheeled it to the taxi rank. As she traveled the short distance from the station to Mimi's apartment, she was shocked by the damage Allied bombing raids had inflicted on the harbor. She was relieved to find Mimi's apartment building had survived unscathed. The concierge offered to take care of her trunk until the following morning, and directed her to the third floor.

Mimi opened the door, carrying a small white fluffy dog in her arms.

"Isabella! How lovely to see you. Please come in—meet little Minou."

Isabella kissed her friend and stroked the little dog's head. She was introduced to Daniele, who blushed as he shook her hand. He was tall and dark-haired, with a kind face. While Mimi showed her to her room, Daniele poured them all a drink. Back in the sitting room, Isabella sat down on the sofa, with Minou at her feet.

"She likes you," said Mimi. "She doesn't normally sit next to strangers."

"I love dogs," Isabella replied, thinking of Vicenzo's two splendid greyhounds.

"Do you have one at home?" Mimi asked.

"No, sadly. I'm away working so much, it wouldn't be fair."

"You mentioned you live with your mother—couldn't she look after it?"

"I'm not sure. My mother is a rather complicated woman. Besides, I don't expect to live with her forever."

"When you get married, you mean?"

"Yes, I suppose that's what I mean."

"So tell me all about him," said Mimi, leaning forward eagerly. "When we spoke on the phone, you mentioned there was someone."

"It's complicated," Isabella began cautiously. "There *is* someone I like, maybe love, but I'm not sure if he feels the same." She laughed nervously as Daniele handed her a drink. "It's tempting fate to talk about it...So tell me," she went on hurriedly, "where did you two meet?"

The young couple gazed at one another lovingly, and both began to speak at once.

"You go first," Daniele said, laughing.

"We met on a bus in Rome, didn't we?"

"We did." He took her hand in his and kissed it. "I was there for an exam and I sat behind her. I thought she had the most beautiful neck I'd ever seen. When she got off the bus, I followed her."

"I didn't notice him at first," Mimi continued. "I sat down in a café and this man..." she stroked Daniele's cheek "...this very handsome man, sat down at the next table and introduced himself."

"You're very lucky," said Isabella. "It can be hard to meet people in my situation...to make relationships."

"I'll get on with dinner, shall I?" suggested Daniele. "Then you two can talk."

"He's wonderful," said Isabella, when he had gone through to the kitchen.

"He is," Mimi agreed. "He cooks and cleans and he loves me. What more could I ask?"

"And there are no problems?" asked Isabella.

"What sort of problems?"

"Well, he's Jewish, isn't he? And you're Catholic."

"That's not a problem for us. His family are all in Genoa, which is why we chose to live here. They were perhaps a little disappointed that he'd chosen to marry a gentile. But they've accepted me now and are very kind."

"The bombing must be hard to live with," Isabella suggested.

"The planes aim for the industrial areas—shipbuilding is important here."

"Yes, I noticed the damage when the taxi drove past the harbor. Still, it must be frightening."

"You get used to it," said Mimi calmly. "Besides, I'm on the Allies' side."

"Really?"

"Of course. The government are beginning to stoke up such bad feeling about Jews. Until now we've always felt safe here. But recently there have been a few attacks on Jewish businesses and shops. It's a worry—you know?"

"But Daniele is a doctor, surely no one would do anything to harm him?"

"I'm afraid being a doctor is no protection." Mimi's eyes filled with tears. "People who hate Jews just see a person who is less than human."

"Surely, that can't be true?" said Isabella, shocked.

"I think perhaps you live in a rather different world," Mimi replied quietly.

Isabella thought of the evenings she had spent at the Acquasanta with Count Ciano and his cronies. She knew Jews were not allowed to become members, but it was not something she had ever given much thought to. And while Count Ciano was not himself anti-Semitic, she had often heard unpleasant remarks about Jewish people during his dinner parties—casual throwaway comments that she had chosen to ignore. But now she felt guilty that she had remained silent.

Over dinner, the couple were keen to know about her life. Where did she live? What was it like making a movie? Who was her favorite leading man? All simple enough questions—the sort of questions she answered every day in fan letters. But it made her feel awkward: her life seemed too far removed from theirs and the dangers they faced every day.

That night, Isabella was taking off her makeup, when she suddenly heard a siren, followed by a knock on the bedroom door.

"Isabella! Isabella!" It was Mimi. Her tone was urgent.

Isabella opened the door to see Mimi standing on the landing wearing a thick dressing gown, clutching Minou to her chest.

"The planes are coming," said Mimi. "Quick, we must go downstairs."

"What do you mean?" Isabella was confused.

"To the shelter...in the basement. It will be cold down there," she said, looking at Isabella's silk nightdress. "Do you have a dressing gown?"

"Yes, but it's in my trunk downstairs. I'll just put on my coat."

As Isabella pulled her fur coat on over her nightdress, she noticed the sky was filled with aircraft heading toward the harbor. Terrified, she followed Mimi and Daniele downstairs.

The basement rapidly filled up. Three elderly couples arrived in quick succession, well prepared with blankets and baskets of provisions. They leaned against the wall in a corner of the room, covering their legs with the blankets, and laying out thermos flasks of coffee and packets of playing cards—clearly ready to occupy themselves through the long night.

A young woman arrived in floods of tears, her face smeared with mascara. "He wouldn't come," she kept saying. "I think he's really left me this time."

Mimi glanced across at Isabella. "She says the same thing during every raid," she whispered.

Last to arrive were a middle-aged woman and her young daughter, clutching what looked like a stack of film magazines. The girl sat down, stared at Isabella and then pointed at her photograph on the cover of *Star* Magazine.

"Is that you?" she asked Isabella in amazement, showing her the cover. Her mother nudged her daughter in the ribs. "Sssh, don't be so rude."

"It's all right," said Isabella. "Yes, that's me. Would you like me to sign that for you?"

The girl nodded wide-eyed, her mother rummaging in her bag for a pen.

When they came, the bombs were unrelenting. Isabella instinctively gripped Daniele's arm.

"Don't worry," he said, putting his arm around her, "we should be safe enough down here."

As waves of bomb blasts ricocheted through the air, the elderly couples clung to one another. One lady began to say the catechism: "Hail Mary, mother of God…" Her husband wrapped her in his arms and rocked her like a child.

Suddenly a massive explosion shook the building above, and the air filled with dust. The hysterical young woman leapt to her feet and began to scream: "We're all going to die!" She ran toward the door and yanked at the handle.

Daniele jumped up, and tried to pull her away. "You must stay here. We'll be all right, I promise you."

The woman looked at him, wild-eyed. "You're mad. This place is going to come down on all our heads. My husband's out there somewhere. I have to find him."

"Wherever he is," said Daniele, guiding her back to her place, "you can't help him now. You must look after yourself."

She slumped against the wall, wiping away her tears. The girl with the magazines handed one to her. "Here," she said, "read this...it will take your mind off it." But the woman stared back at her uncomprehendingly.

By dawn, the bombing was over. They all emerged from the basement, congregating in the communal hallway. Through the tall glazed doors, they could see vast craters in the road.

"We were lucky last night," said Daniele. "That was close." He ushered his wife and Isabella back upstairs.

"Mimi, I can't believe what you have to cope with," Isabella said, as they made coffee in the tiny kitchen. "In Rome there has been no bombing at all. Apart from some food shortages and a lack of firewood, you would hardly know there is a war going on. I feel I have been living in a dream, while you have been trapped in a nightmare all this time."

"You get used to it," Mimi replied wearily. "But it takes its toll, you know? We've lost so many good friends killed by the bombs. The hospital was hit the other day. We just pray it will end soon."

"But how?" asked Isabella gloomily.

"The government needs to change course. Fighting the Allies is madness." Mimi handed her a cup of coffee. "You said you knew Mussolini's son-in-law. He must have influence. Can't he do something?"

"I don't know." Isabella blushed, embarrassed at her ignorance. "Count Ciano prefers to gossip and show off. We don't talk about politics much."

Mimi stared at her, disbelieving. "Well, maybe you should," she observed coldly.

Back on the train, traveling along the coast toward Nice, Isabella realized that Mimi had been right. She had spent ten years feeling she was entitled to the rewards of her hard work, that the money and position were what she deserved. Her relationships—such as they were—with the Fascist authorities were a necessary evil. But she had been lulled into a sense of false security; she had stopped seeing the world through other people's eyes and as a result had failed to understand the extent of their suffering. For the first time in her life she felt guilty about her privileged position.

Isabella had been booked to stay in a grand hotel on the Promenade des Anglais. Gleaming white against the pale blue winter sky, it overlooked the beach fringing the Bay of Angels. No longer an inviting place of relaxation, it was now lined with barbed wire and anti-aircraft guns. The sea beyond was gray and forbidding, and not the turquoise idyll of her imagination.

At the hotel, a pair of doormen arranged for her luggage to be brought inside. The lobby was filled with people. They gathered noisily around the desk, and sat in groups on the sofas, or drifted toward the bar.

"You're busy this evening," Isabella observed to the desk clerk. "Are they all here for a New Year's Eve party?"

"No, madame," the clerk replied. "These people are residents. We are full up."

"How astonishing, I had no idea so many people took holidays at this time of year."

"They are not holidaymakers, madame," he explained quietly. "They are refugees."

"Where from?" she asked confused.

"From the north of France. They are Jewish—escaping from the Nazis."

Isabella was disturbed by this revelation—that people should be forced to seek sanctuary in a hotel, merely for being Jewish, was incomprehensible.

Over the following few weeks, once the filming began, Isabella became aware of the resentment of the local people, who were angry at "the Italian invasion," as they saw it. There were times when waiters and shop assistants could be rude or dismissive. But Isabella learned to smile and turn on her charm.

Her co-star Louis Jourdan was, without doubt, the most handsome man she had ever met. Tall and slender, he kissed her hand when they were introduced, and flirted effortlessly with her. To her relief, she felt no attraction for him; to be in love with one's co-star is never a good idea. Besides, he had a terrible reputation for breaking women's hearts, and over the course of the filming she observed him in action, as he seduced one member of the cast and crew after another. A succession of broken-hearted young women were often to be found sobbing in the makeup room after their night of passion with Louis.

She wrote regularly to her mother.

> *The filming goes well… but I am exhausted working in French all day. I get back to my room each evening, and just sleep. I'm glad you didn't come—I'm no company for anyone.*

Her mother wrote back, complaining that the housekeeper and the gardener had left. Giuseppe had been called up into the army, and his wife had decided to leave Rome and move in with her sister.

> *I have been abandoned. I can't cope alone, so have invited Mamma and my sister to stay.*

Isabella was mildly irritated at this development, but was nevertheless resigned. Her mother at least would have company and help in the house. Her only anxiety was that with no prospect of another film after *La Bohème*, the money she made from this film would now have to support four people.

When the film project began, she had hoped for a few words of encouragement from Vicenzo, but had heard nothing. At first she felt hurt by his lack of interest, but she convinced herself that he was simply busy. After all, he was an artist with an artist's temperament. He was not like other men, weighed down by petty jealousies and trivia. She frequently took up her pen to write to him but, fearful of appearing too desperate, abandoned every letter. No man wanted to be chased by a woman. But eventually she could bear it no longer, and one Sunday afternoon, as she gazed out of her hotel window at the gun-metal-gray sea, she put pen to paper.

Dearest Vicenzo,

I hope all is well with you. I trust you had an enjoyable Christmas.

I am quite settled here in Nice. It would be marvelous to see it wreathed in sunshine, but most of the time it has rained—a dark leaden rain that falls continuously from a gray sky. I imagine before the war it was a wonderful place. Now it reminds me of a beautiful woman trapped in an unhappy marriage—all is gray and gloom, the beaches covered with barbed wire, the hotel guests filled with sadness and woe.

The film is going well, and I hope you would be proud of me. I am working very hard. It is "realistic"—filled with tragedy and sadness—so I hope you approve! The part is stretching me, both emotionally and intellectually. I spend all day weeping in French—it's utterly exhausting!

My co-star, Louis Jourdan, needs no introduction from me. Perhaps you know him already. His exquisite beauty is well documented, but he has talent too. Off set, I keep my distance, you'll be glad to hear. His reputation precedes him! He has taken a villa in Nice and has invited me to a couple of parties. They are enjoyable enough, but Louis is always

*surrounded by women who are hopelessly lost in love with
him. I fear he torments them mercilessly and I am relieved
not to be among them!*

    *Well...I must end now. I'm tired and we have an early
start.*

    I miss you.

With love,
Isabella

Two weeks later, she received a reply.

*I am so proud of you. I know you have such depth and will
do the part beautifully. Just make sure you don't fall in love
with the intoxicating Louis...*

This last comment gave her hope. The idea that he might be
jealous of her working with the famously handsome actor suggested
that he did feel something for her after all.

As winter turned to spring and the rain finally retreated, Nice
recaptured some of its pre-war beauty. In the evenings when she
emerged from the darkened studio into the sunshine, Isabella would
stand for a while, relishing the setting sun's rays on her skin and
think of Vicenzo. She resolved that when she returned to Rome, she
would finally declare herself to him. It was time, she realized, to be
honest...time to tell him that she loved him.

Chapter Ten

The hills above Florence
Christmas 1942

It was late in the afternoon when the Morettis' black Lancia drove through the wintry olive groves. The pale-gray sky was heavy with snow and the gray-green leaves clinging to the trees glowed in the watery sunlight.

Returning to the villa for Christmas, Livia sat in the back seat, gloomily staring out of the car window. She had been reluctant to leave Florence, and had begged her father to let her stay in the city.

"Please let me stay here."

"Why?"

"It's my friend...Cosimo. I've already told you about him. He's away on the Eastern Front and if I'm in Florence I can get news of him from Elena or his mother."

"But Livia, nothing will happen over Christmas. Come with us to the villa. If you don't, your mother will be so disappointed."

Now, as the car swept up the long drive and the pale-gold villa came into view, Livia's heart lifted. This house, the place of her birth and her childhood, gave her a sense of security. Perhaps it was the fact that nothing seemed to change: the arching umbrella pines that loomed over the house, the olive trees that stood in large pots on either side of the door. As a child, they had reminded her of two elderly gentlemen, standing to attention, their bark twisted and gnarled. Even the fig tree that rambled up the south-facing wall, its branches now bare, offered the promise of summer when it would be groaning with ripe fruit. The house and its grounds provided a sense of continuity where everything remained the same, and in spite of her initial reluctance, Livia was pleased to be home.

As soon as they arrived, Luisa went through to the kitchen to discuss meals with Angela. Livia and Giacomo discovered Alberto asleep in the sitting room. In spite of the rug over his knees, his hands were like ice.

"Why is there no fire lit in here?" Giacomo asked irritably. "I'll go and find Gino and bring in some wood. Livia, wake Nonno, will you, and try to warm him up—perhaps with some hot tea or soup?"

"Of course," said Livia, kneeling at her grandfather's side and rubbing his hands warm.

Once the fires had been lit, the house began to come back to life. They had no Christmas tree that year—it seemed too frivolous. Instead Livia decorated the sitting room with tinsel and glass balls, which glowed and twinkled in the firelight.

In spite of the food shortages, Luisa managed to produce some tasty meals. Fresh vegetables were scarce, but she bartered some of her fig jam for a neighbor's store of beans, and Giacomo took his guns from the cabinet and went out into the fields and shot game—hare, rabbit and pigeon. In the evenings, the family sat together in the sitting room, warmed by a roaring fire, reading or playing games.

On Christmas Eve, Giacomo went down to the cellar and brought up a couple of bottles of wine.

"This is the last of the vintage I bought some years ago," he said, caressing the dusty bottles. "I was saving them for a special occasion—Livia's marriage perhaps." He winked at his daughter. "But I think we should drink a couple this year." He uncorked a bottle and poured the dark liquid into crystal glasses.

As she sat by the warm fire, sipping the wine and watching the snow falling outside, Livia thought it was almost possible to imagine the war was over.

*

A couple of days after Christmas, Livia went to the village to collect her father's newspaper. The headlines brought the war back into sharp focus.

Italian Troops Fight Bravely on in Russia

As she hurried back to the villa, her thoughts turned to Cosimo. While she had been spending Christmas in front of a warm fire, he had been in the frozen wastes of Russia enduring terrible suffering. She remembered his friend Mario talking of "the living hell" they'd experienced on the Eastern Front. But this headline made it sound as if the battle was being won. Could it be true?

Keen to discuss it with her father, she found his study door closed. Standing outside in the hall, she was about to knock, when she heard voices coming from inside. Straining to listen through the thick chestnut door, she was unable to make out who was speaking. Intrigued, she tapped at the door.

"Who's that?" her father called out.

"It's just me, Papa. I've got your newspaper. Can I come in?"

"Just a moment," Giacomo replied.

The voices fell silent; Livia heard the key rattling in the lock, and Giacomo finally opened the door. He resumed his place behind his untidy desk, where she laid the newspaper on top of a pile of folders stacked in front of him.

"Sit down, sit down," he said distractedly, as he tied a sheaf of papers together.

She sat down on the battered sofa. "Papa…" she began.

"Yes, Livia?" He slid the sheaf of papers into the desk drawer and locked it.

"I heard voices just now. Who were you talking to?"

"No one." He peered at her over his rimless glasses.

"Well I definitely heard voices," she persisted.

He paused for a moment and picked up the newspaper absent-mindedly, studying the front page. "I was listening to the radio, if you must know," he said.

"Why did you turn it off?" she asked. "I was hoping to get some news myself—the headlines don't say very much."

"I think that's rather the point," he replied, throwing down the newspaper dismissively on the desk. "There is no truth in Italy anymore, Livia, only propaganda. Our newspapers and radio programs are controlled by the government and filled with lies. You know that, don't you?"

"Why listen to the radio, if it's all lies?"

He studied her for a moment. "Can you keep a secret?"

"Yes, of course. I'm part of the Pd'A now, aren't I?"

"Yes you are, forgive me. I forget sometimes that you're no longer a child. But this is an important secret—and a dangerous one which, if it was discovered, would get us all into terrible trouble."

"I won't say anything, I promise," she said with conviction.

"I was listening to a foreign radio station called *Radio Londra*. It's broadcast by the BBC in England."

"In England? But that's against the law, isn't it?"

"Yes. We could all end up in prison if they found out. That's why I keep the radio in here, locked away. I don't want Angela or Gino to know anything about it—or your mother, for that matter. But the fact is, it's the only way to get anything like accurate news." He picked up the newspaper. "Did you read this rubbish?" he asked scornfully.

She nodded.

"Anyone seeing this headline would think we were doing rather well, wouldn't they?"

"Aren't we?" Livia asked, inwardly dreading the answer.

"Of course not! We are losing—badly. Russia is a bloody, frozen nightmare. Stalin's troops are well supplied and there are lots of them. Whereas our boys are short of munitions, shelter and food. The Battle of Stalingrad is all but over . . . and we're being annihilated."

Livia suddenly stood up, walked over to the window and looked out onto the snow-covered garden. "Did they mention casualties on the radio?" she asked, trying to hold back the tears.

"I'm afraid they did," her father said dispassionately, "sixty thousand prisoners and as many as twenty thousand dead."

Livia began to sob. Her father crossed the room and wrapped her in his arms. "What's the matter? I know the news is terrible but—"

"My friend Cosimo is there," she blurted out.

"Oh, of course! How stupid of me." He turned her round to face him and wiped her tears away. "I'm sorry, darling, that was thoughtless."

She bit her lip. "Do you think Cosimo might be dead?"

"I'm sure he's all right," Giacomo said comfortingly, holding her to him.

"No, Papa." She pushed him away. "Don't patronize me. I need the truth now."

"Well," he began, gazing down at her, "I think, my darling, it will be a miracle if he is still alive."

In early January, with Christmas over, the family headed back to Florence. As they unloaded the car, Giacomo handed Livia a small black suitcase. "Take this up to the attic for me, will you?" he said quietly. "And don't tell your mother."

"Why, what is it?" Livia whispered.

"The radio. We'll need it here now—to get information for the Pd'A. We'll keep it up in the attic. Your mother never goes up there, so it should be safe enough."

Later that evening, Livia was getting ready for bed when Giacomo knocked on her bedroom door. "May I come in?" he asked. "I want to ask you a favor—it's something I'd like you to do for the Pd'A."

"I'll do anything, you know that," she said eagerly.

He sat down on the edge of her bed. "Would you monitor the news on the radio for me?"

"Of course, but why me?"

"Because I think you'd be good at it. And now you're part of the group, I'd like you to have a proper role."

"Well, thank you." Livia was delighted.

"It's important that we spread real information about the war. Once people realize how badly our army are doing, any support for the government will begin to recede. The workers in the north are already striking, thanks to the encouragement of the Communist Party. People are losing heart, but they need information."

Livia nodded.

"Do you remember at the last meeting of the Pd'A we discussed starting a newspaper? Well, the radio broadcasts will form an important part of that. I need you to listen to the news, and write up a report each day. That information will form the basis of an article for the newspaper. We're calling the paper *L'Italia Libera*, and I believe we can really turn the tide in this country, and help people understand what an unmitigated disaster the war has been."

"Do you really believe it will help?"

"I do. We'll soon have Mussolini on the run."

"And you think I could do this—that I'm up to it?"

"Livia," her father said, taking her hands in his, "I have infinite faith in you. You can do anything you set your mind to. We'll start tomorrow."

The following evening, Giacomo and Livia set up the radio in the attic. Luisa had been preoccupied making dinner, and had scarcely noticed the pair disappearing upstairs.

"I'm just going out with Livia for half an hour," Giacomo, standing in the hall, called out to his wife.

"Another of your meetings?" said Luisa, hardly looking up from her pasta making.

"Yes, something like that," he answered vaguely.

"Well, don't be late for dinner."

"We won't."

Her father went through the pretense of putting on his coat and opening the door. But instead of going outside onto the landing, he slammed it shut and then, followed by Livia, crept up the stairs to the attic.

"Where did you hide the radio, Livia?"

"Here," she said, opening a cupboard in an old desk that stood beneath the window overlooking the terrace.

Giacomo took the radio out of its case, and set it up on the desk, draping a thin wire up and over the top of the window frame.

"This is the aerial," he explained, "the higher it is, the better the signal."

He hauled a battered armchair over to the desk and sat down, twiddling the dials of the radio. Eventually, through the static, came a man's voice, strong and clear, with a slight English accent.

"Here we are," said her father. "They call him 'Colonel Buonasera,' but his real name is Colonel Stephens. He's half-Italian, but quite fluent, I think. Did you bring your notebook?"

Livia nodded, and perched on the arm of her father's armchair, they listened to the broadcast. When it was over, they crept back down the stairs and went through the motion of opening and closing the front door.

"We're back," Giacomo called out to Luisa.

"I'll serve dinner then," she said from the sitting room.

"If you could tidy up your notes this evening," Giacomo whispered to Livia, "I'll write them up as an article and get it into the paper."

The following day, Livia woke early and opened her shutters. Fine powdery snowflakes floated down from a dove-gray sky. Her room felt cold and she shivered as she pulled on corduroy trousers and a jumper.

In the kitchen, she searched for a piece of bread, but there was none. She took her coat from the rack in the hall, and was just putting it on, when her mother appeared from her bedroom.

"Where are you off to? Term doesn't start till tomorrow."

"I'm going to visit Elena," Livia replied.

"This early?" Luisa asked, incredulous.

"She won't mind. I'll see you later, Mamma." Livia opened the door to the stairs.

"You've not even had breakfast," Luisa called after her.

"There isn't any," Livia called back up the staircase.

Elena's family lived in a top-floor apartment overlooking the market square of Piazza Sant'Ambrogio. Normally it was filled with shoppers, but this morning it was deserted, the market stalls virtually empty.

Livia climbed the stairs to the apartment and knocked on the door. It was answered by Elena's mother, Benedetta. Small and fair-haired, she looked like an older version of her daughter. "Ah, Livia—come in. Can I make you some coffee?"

"Thank you, only if you can spare it."

"Yes of course. Elena's in her room."

Elena was reading, propped up on pillows. "Livia!" she said, throwing her book down on the bed. "I'm so glad you're back. I've missed you so much." She stood up and wrapped her arms around her friend.

"I've missed you too," said Livia. "What are you reading?"

"Oh, just a textbook. Very dull."

Livia sat down on the bed next to Elena. Her friend's room was even smaller than her own room at her father's apartment. The bed was under the window, and a chest of drawers served as a bedside table. The only other furniture was a bookcase on the opposite wall.

"Have you had a chance to see Mario again?" Livia asked. "I wondered how he was."

Elena flopped back down onto the bed. "He's making very slow progress, I'm afraid. My father is not optimistic. I don't think he'll ever really recover."

"Poor Mario," said Livia. "I hardly like to ask, but I don't suppose he's mentioned..."

"Cosimo?"

Livia nodded.

"No. But I do have news of him."

There was a knock on the door, and Benedetta came in with two cups of coffee. "I'll leave them here, shall I?" she said, putting the cups down on the chest of drawers.

"Mamma," said Elena. "We were just talking about Cosimo. I was going to explain what's happened to him."

"Explain what?" Livia asked, suddenly nervous.

"Ah, yes, poor Cosimo." Benedetta leaned against the doorframe.

Livia felt her heart thudding in her chest. "What?" she asked urgently. "Tell me. What's happened?"

Benedetta knelt next to Livia. "Well, the good news is that he's alive."

"And what is the bad news?"

Benedetta took Livia's hand in hers. "He's been injured. I'm so sorry."

Livia looked at her wide-eyed.

"He got frostbite," said Elena, wrapping her arms around her friend. "Then gangrene. So they had to amputate, I'm afraid. He lost part of one leg."

"His leg..." Livia repeated slowly, as if struggling to understand.

"Not his whole leg, you understand," said Benedetta calmly. "Just above the ankle, we think. Really, he's lucky to be alive. He's on his way home now. Heaven knows when he'll arrive, but his parents were told to expect him in the next few days, and I'm hoping he can be transferred to my husband's hospital."

Livia scarcely knew how she got back to the apartment. She walked robotically up the stairs and unlocked the door. She could see her father working at the dining table as usual, but said nothing, and headed down the corridor to her room.

"Is that you, Livia?" he called out. "Are you all right?"

"No," she replied flatly. She went into her room and closed the door.

A few moments later, there was a knock on the door. "May I come in?" When he got no reply, Giacomo pushed open the door. Livia was lying on the bed, facing the wall.

"Tell me, darling, what's the matter?"

"Cosimo is alive," she murmured. "He's coming back to Florence."

"But that's wonderful news!" cried Giacomo. "I must admit, I'm surprised—and delighted, of course." He sat down on the edge of her bed and stroked her hair.

She turned and looked at him, her face stained with tears. "Papa, you don't understand."

"Why, what's happened?"

"He's lost his foot—frostbite, they said, and gangrene. I don't really know what that is."

Giacomo blanched. "It's a dangerous infection," he began calmly. "To save the man, the limb has to be severed. It sounds like he's lucky to be alive."

"But his foot, Papa. He was so strong and handsome, and now he has only one foot—how will he get about?"

"I don't know, Livia. And it's a terrible shock, I understand that. But he's alive. This is the miracle you were hoping for."

Over the following weeks, Livia adjusted to the idea of Cosimo's injury, grateful for the distraction of monitoring the radio. The calm, gentle manner of the BBC presenter, Colonel Stephens, gave her a sense of optimism. Once the bulletins were over, she would return to her room and write up her notes. But one evening she decided to present her father with a finished article.

Glancing through it, he looked up at her with surprise. "You write very well," he said eventually. "You have a confident style. I like it."

"You can change it, obviously," she said nervously. "The notes are all there. But I thought it might save time, if I just wrote it up as a finished piece."

"Well it saves me a lot of time," her father agreed, "and I think it's excellent. You must carry on."

Filled with enthusiasm for her new role, Livia's only problem was concealing her activity from her mother who, her father insisted, must be kept in the dark about their activities.

"She would become hysterical if she knew you were involved," he said. "You must promise me that we will keep it between us."

This secrecy involved considerable subterfuge. In order to get upstairs to the attic in time for the bulletin at nine o'clock each evening, Livia had to go through an elaborate ritual. If her mother was in the sitting room or bedroom, it was simple enough: she would appear to leave the apartment, slamming the door, before escaping upstairs. But if her mother was in the kitchen, which overlooked the hall, she would have to actually leave the flat—sometimes even walking down the road if she felt her mother might be watching from the kitchen window—and return quickly and silently, slipping back into the apartment and up the staircase to the attic. In the winter months this worked well enough, as her mother rarely left the sitting room after dinner. But when summer came, Livia was concerned that it would be harder to conceal her clandestine activity.

She discussed the problem with her father one evening. "Even Mamma sometimes goes upstairs in the summer to hang up the washing, or look at the view."

"Well," he said, "we'll deal with that problem when it arrives."

One bitterly cold evening in early March, Livia came out of the house, going through her ritual of pretending to leave. Her mother was in the kitchen and as Livia glanced up, she noticed her in the window. She began to walk down the road, irritably checking her watch. The bulletin was due to start in ten minutes.

As she reached the corner, a tall man came loping toward her, using a pair of crutches. He wore a dark overcoat and a trilby hat pulled down over his eyes. Poor old man, she thought—and was about to hurry on when she heard him call out.

"Livia..."

She turned round. "Cosimo! Cosimo—is it really you?" She ran toward him; he stooped down, allowing her to wrap her arms around him. She kissed his face, his cheeks, his lips. "I thought I would never see you again," she murmured.

"And I you. But here I am—only not quite as I was." He looked nervous, she realized, as if he was frightened, scared perhaps of rejection.

Suddenly all her fears of the previous few weeks evaporated. Nothing mattered except him being there in front of her. She took his face in her hands and kissed him again. "The point is, you're here and that's all I care about."

PART TWO

FORTY-FIVE DAYS

"I had lived, grown up and, you might say, been born under Fascism. I did not know anything else. I thought everything was going to be fine."

Maria Denis, the actress—writing in her memoir,
Il Gioco della Verità, 1995

Chapter Eleven

Rome
July 1943

With *La Bohème* finally behind her, Isabella returned to Rome, where she had a part in a new film—a Roman epic starring a clutch of Cinecittà luminaries, including Doris Duranti, the lover of the Fascist minister, Alessandro Pavolini.

Inevitably, given everyone's uncertainty about the future of the war, the conversation among the cast and crew was all about politics. When the U.S. and British forces landed in Sicily, the makeup room was abuzz.

"They'll be in Rome before you know it," the leading man said to Doris one morning. "I'm rather worried, if I'm honest. What's going to happen to all of us?"

"I wouldn't worry," Doris drawled, "Alessandro has it all in hand."

Isabella, who was having her hair arranged at the neighboring mirror, listened anxiously to the conversation.

"I wouldn't be so sure," said the leading man. "Cinecittà is an arm of the State. I can't see them keeping it going if Il Duce is out of the picture."

Doris waved his concerns away with her manicured hand, and swept out of the makeup room.

Isabella had never imagined Cinecittà being closed down. The idea that her career, something she had worked so hard for, should be brought to a halt by the war seemed unimaginable. She tried to envision a future for herself without the movie industry. She had three dependents now—her mother, her grandmother and her aunt. How would they all survive without her income?

*

Isabella buried her anxieties and once the studio sequences were completed, the cast and crew moved onto the location scenes to be shot at the ancient Roman Baths of Caracalla.

One morning, as they were about to shoot a scene and the film director called "action," the sound recordist, listening through his powerful headphones, held up his hand. "Hold it!"

"Cut!" called the director. "What's the matter?" he asked irritably.

"I'm sorry," said the sound recordist, "but there's some sort of engine noise cutting through—it's a long way off, but I can definitely hear it. We'll have to wait, I'm afraid."

Within minutes, the engine noise was audible to everyone on the set. It soon turned into a roar as a large plane flew overhead, quickly followed by twenty, thirty, forty more, until the sky was dark with hundreds of aircraft. Moments later, there was a series of terrifying explosions and the sound of distant screams. Dust filled the air, and soon everyone was choking, coughing and rushing for cover.

This was the first time Rome had been bombed since the beginning of the war. The actors removed their costumes and rushed to their cars, all in a state of shock. The day's filming was canceled.

As soon as she got home, Isabella collapsed onto the floor in the hall in floods of tears. Her mother helped her to her feet. "Cara Isabella, what's the matter? Come into the kitchen."

"Did you hear the bombing this morning?" Isabella asked.

"Of course I heard the planes—they flew over here. It was terrifying. The news is saying that there are thousands of casualties. It was an Allied bombing raid on the freight yards and steel works at San Lorenzo."

Later that day, Giovanna and her sister were preparing supper, when the bombers returned. The women lay in terror beneath the kitchen table as the planes flew over, heading for their target.

The morning newspapers reported that Rome's two airports had been hit. Although filming continued, everyone in the cast and crew was uneasy, braced for another attack. By the weekend, Isabella was exhausted, and on Sunday, after a quiet day at home, she listened to a concert on the radio to calm her nerves. But at ten forty-five the concert was suddenly interrupted by "a special announcement by the Commander of the Army, Marshal Badoglio."

"*Italians!*" he declared. "*By order of his Majesty the King and Emperor, I am assuming the military government of this country with full plenary powers. The war against the Anglo-Americans continues.*"

Il Duce appeared to have been overthrown.

To Isabella, for whom life under Mussolini had been all she'd known, this seemed impossible. She rushed to the kitchen, where her mother was kneading dough on the table, the radio playing quietly in the background.

"Did you hear the announcement, Mamma?"

Giovanna nodded.

"Do you think Mussolini has really gone?"

Her mother shrugged.

"Mamma, don't you understand? What will happen to us now? To me? To the film company? It's owned by the government."

Her mother looked up. "We will manage," she said calmly. "We managed before, when we had nothing—do you remember? We can do it again."

Over the next few days, the streets of Rome were filled with people surging into the piazzas. Isabella walked into town and was soon caught up in a throng heading toward Piazza Colonna. The crowds were singing patriotic songs and shouting "Down with Fascism." Pictures of Mussolini on public buildings were torn down and set on fire. The protesters danced around the flames, screaming and whooping. Isabella returned home through the park, feeling frightened and disturbed by what she had seen. Rome appeared to be in a state of anarchy.

The phone was ringing in the hall as she let herself in. It was Elsa De Giorgi. "The studio is closed," she said, "We can't get back in."

"Closed?" Isabella felt as if her world was imploding. "I don't understand, Elsa. What about the film?"

"It won't be finished for a while, I suppose," Elsa said phlegmatically.

Isabella began to cry. "I thought it was all going to be all right," she blurted out through sobs. "That the war would come to an end eventually and things would go on as before."

"Don't be so foolish, Isabella. Have you been living in a dream? It's all over, the whole thing. If we have any sense, we must side with the Anglo-Americans now. They're not our enemies anymore, they're our liberators."

That evening, desperate for reassurance, Isabella drove to the Acquasanta Golf Club, hoping to see friends. In spite of the bombing and the rioting in the city center, at least here she was confident there would be no anarchy. The members had a quality of steadfastness that she always found comforting.

Stefano, the tennis pro, was there, propping up the bar as usual. For once she wasn't irritated by his presence, but fell into his arms.

"Darling," he drawled. "How lovely to see you. It's been months."

"I know. I've been away in the south of France, filming. I only got back about a month ago."

"So you've missed all the gossip," he said. "Have you heard the latest?"

"Well, only what we've all heard on the news. And Elsa just told me that the studios have closed down. To be honest, I'm in rather a state of shock."

"Let me buy you a big drink." Stefano clicked his fingers at the barman. "Vermouth?"

She nodded vaguely. "Is Ciano here?" she asked, looking around. "I thought he might give me some advice."

"Ciano? Oh no, darling. You really are out of touch. He lost his post as Foreign Minister back in February and was made Ambassador to the Vatican—a real demotion. That was the last we saw of him."

"You mean he's disappeared? I thought he'd be with Mussolini."

"Hardly." Stefano laughed. "I'm pretty sure he was part of the group who kicked the old boy out."

"Really? But Mussolini was his father-in-law."

"I know, and he was fond of the old man, but he was never really on board with the whole foreign policy, was he? Constantly damning with faint praise."

Rootless and afraid, Isabella reached out to the only person she felt could provide her with some kind of security. The following day, she walked across the park to Vicenzo's house on Via Salaria. The door was opened by the maid, just as Vicenzo came into the hall. Isabella pushed past her and fell weeping into his arms.

"Isabella, little Bella," he whispered into her hair. "What on earth is the matter?"

She sobbed, unable to speak.

"Don't cry. You're safe now. Come inside and let's talk."

He guided her onto the terrace, where he settled her on a comfortable cane sofa and poured her a drink. "Now," he murmured, sitting next to her and taking her hand, "tell me what's upset you so."

"The studios are closed, my film has been stopped and I don't know who I can trust anymore."

"You can trust me," said Vicenzo. "As for the studios, in the present political situation, it's hardly surprising is it?"

"I suppose so," she sniffed miserably.

"Now, you must give me all your news. How was France?"

"It was not as I expected," she said. "The place felt so sad."

"What do you mean?" he asked.

"When I arrived, it was full of Jewish refugees escaping from the Germans in northern France. I was really shocked—I had no idea people were being persecuted like that."

He took her hand. "Terrible things are being done in our name," he said. "It has to stop."

"The people there—the waiters in the cafés and shop assistants—they were so rude to me, simply because I was Italian."

"Can you blame them?"

She looked up at him, bewildered.

"Darling," he said gently, "we have invaded their country. What else should they do—welcome us with open arms?"

"I suppose not. I'm so confused and frightened. I had thought our world was safe, that it would go on forever. But that was naïve, wasn't it?"

"Perhaps, a little." He refilled her glass. "You believed what you wanted to believe. It's understandable—you knew nothing else. You've been cocooned in that world since you were a child."

"I'm sorry for the Jewish people in France, of course, and for my Jewish friends in Genoa; they're being persecuted too, and he's a doctor—a good man. But if I'm honest, I'm frightened for myself. What will happen to me? What will happen to you?"

"Well, you don't have to worry about me. I've always been an outsider. I loathe Cinecittà, as you know, and everything it stands for. But I'm lucky. I have money, and that helps. But I have something else too, something better than money. I have conviction, and a belief in the strength and valor of the Italian people. We will get through this, you'll see. Mussolini and his like are finished, thank God. There's a better life waiting for us . . . once this war is over. And we artists must stick together."

He put his arms around her and kissed the top of her head. Isabella rested against his chest, inhaling the scent of his aftershave, and felt safe, completely enveloped in his arms.

Chapter Twelve

Florence
July 1943

It was a hot, steamy evening; Livia, Elena and Cosimo were sitting at a table outside Café Paskowski, when news of Mussolini's overthrow broke.

"He's gone! Il Duce's finished," shouted a young student, running through the piazza. The friends rushed into the busy café, demanding the barman switch on the radio. The room fell silent as the announcer declared: *The King Emperor accepted the resignation of the Head of Government, Prime Minister Cavalier Benito Mussolini, and appointed the Marshal of Italy, Pietro Badoglio.*

The café erupted, as people cheered and leapt to their feet, but the barman, still with his ear to the radio, shouted over the hubbub. "It's the King, be quiet!"

Through the noise came the voice of King Emmanuel III. *Now, more than ever, I feel inextricably linked to you all in the certainty of the immortality of the Fatherland.*

"What does he mean," whispered Livia, "by 'the immortality of the Fatherland'? I thought now we'd got rid of Mussolini, we'd be free of Fascism too."

"I don't really know," said Cosimo, shrugging his shoulders. "But Mussolini's gone. Isn't that all we should care about?"

The three of them left the café and joined a larger group of students, running toward the Duomo. They leapt and shouted, hugging one another. Passers-by out walking in the cooler night air acknowledged them, smiling and laughing. There was a palpable sense of relief in the city, as if the worst was finally over.

Livia and Elena parted, kissing each other and making plans to meet the following day, before Livia and Cosimo walked together toward her apartment.

"Are you happy?" she asked.

"Of course," he replied. "We have to believe the worst is over now. The tyrant has gone." He leaned down and kissed her.

"Come up with me," she urged him, as they stood outside her building. "I'd like my father to finally meet you."

"But it's late. Won't he be in bed?"

"I doubt it, not on a night like tonight. Besides, my father never goes to bed early, he's a nocturnal animal. Please?"

Standing in the lobby, Cosimo peered up into the darkness. "You live on the top floor?"

"Yes, it's five flights. Can you manage, do you think?"

He grinned. "I think so."

As Livia held his crutches, Cosimo began the long climb, half-hopping, half-dragging himself up the stairs, stopping on each landing to catch his breath. He was sweating heavily by the time they finally arrived outside the apartment.

As they entered the hallway, she could see the lights were still on in the sitting room. She poked her head around the door. Her father was in his favorite armchair.

"Livia, darling, I've been worried about you. Have you heard the news?"

"Yes, Papa—isn't it wonderful?" She turned around, and beckoned to her friend. "You remember I told you about Cosimo, Papa?" Her father nodded. "Well he's here . . ."

"Of course I remember." Giacomo stood up and held his hand out to the young man. "Please, do sit down, Cosimo. I'm sorry we're on the top floor. It must have been very difficult." He glanced down at Cosimo's crutches. "But I'm delighted to meet you at last—thank you for making the effort. Livia's told me a lot about you."

"Thank you, sir. I'm very pleased to meet you too. There was a time when I thought I'd never see Livia, or anyone else I cared about, again." He sat down heavily on the sofa, leaning his crutches against his good leg.

"I'm sure," said Giacomo kindly. "Can I get you a drink? I think a celebration is in order, don't you?"

"Where's Mamma?" asked Livia.

"She went to bed, soon after the news broke."

"Isn't it exciting?" exclaimed Livia, pacing around the room. "Perhaps now we can all get back to normal."

Her father handed round three small glasses of grappa. "Maybe. But I think it will not be so easy, or straightforward."

"But Mussolini's gone!" Livia protested, sitting down next to Cosimo.

"Yes," said her father cautiously, "but the people who have taken over are nevertheless still Fascists. As far as they are concerned, the war with the Allies still continues."

"Is that what the King meant by the 'immortality of the Fatherland'?" asked Livia. "Does that mean that our work goes on too?"

Giacomo nodded, glancing nervously at Livia, and then at Cosimo.

"If you're worried about the Pd'A," she said, "I've already told him."

Giacomo frowned. "Livia, I don't think you should have done that."

"I'd like to join you, sir, if I may," Cosimo interjected. "I want to do something. I *need* to do something."

"You have a right, certainly," said Giacomo, "after what's happened to you. But it's a big step joining an organization like ours. Who knows what the next few months or years will hold? The future is uncertain. At the moment we are still technically at war, although that may change. But either way it won't be easy or bloodless. The Germans are in the north. The Americans and British are in Sicily and have already begun to bomb Rome. We might be next, caught in the middle—like rats in a trap."

There was a noise outside in the corridor. Livia leapt to her feet. "Is that you, Mamma?"

"Yes, it's only me." Luisa stood in the doorway wearing a pale-blue silk robe over her nightdress, her dark hair unraveled around her neck. "I thought I heard voices."

"Come in, darling." Giacomo leapt to his feet, beckoning his wife. "Have a grappa with us. Meet Livia's friend, Cosimo."

"You know I hate the stuff," said Luisa, sitting down in an armchair, waving the glass of grappa away. "Cosimo..." she said sweetly, turning to him, "...such a lovely name. I had a friend many years ago called Cosimo." She smiled but then noticed his crutches and missing foot. "Oh!" She blushed, obviously shocked. "I had no idea, I'm so sorry."

"I lost my foot in Russia," he explained calmly. "I developed frostbite. I'm lucky to still have the rest of my leg, or so they say. I've been promised a prosthesis. But with the war, it's taking a long time to be made and fitted."

Luisa smiled nervously.

"I hadn't told my mother," Livia murmured to Cosimo, by way of explanation. "Mamma, we were talking about Mussolini going at last—it's exciting, isn't it?"

"I suppose so." Luisa looked pointedly at her husband. "What were you saying about the Americans bombing Florence? Are you serious?"

Giacomo sipped his drink. "I fear we must be prepared, cara."

"Then we must leave immediately." Luisa stood up. "Livia's term is finished for the summer. We should all go back home to the villa, as soon as possible."

"Luisa, please sit down," began Giacomo gently. "Whatever happens, we're not leaving now. And you know as well as I do, that I can't leave. I have too many responsibilities here."

"So you'd rather stay here and be bombed—is that it?"

"Darling..." Giacomo's tone was soothing. "Please."

"Don't 'please' me, I want to leave!"

Giacomo put his glass down on the table and stood up, taking her hands in his. "Well, if you really want to go, I can take you home, of course."

"And Livia, she must come too," said Luisa firmly.

"No, Mamma." Livia looked desperately at her father for support. "My place is here."

"Don't be ridiculous. You're a young girl and my only child. You must come with me to the country, where we'll be safe. Giacomo, explain it to her."

"Please, Mamma." Livia walked over to her mother and held her firmly by the shoulders. "Let's talk about this tomorrow. For tonight, let's just enjoy the sense of freedom... please?"

The following morning, the family rose late. Livia joined her father in the kitchen. They made coffee and ate a little stale bread, toasted on the gas ring. The peace was interrupted by the phone ringing. Giacomo, still in his dressing gown, went into the hall to answer it.

"I'm so very sorry." His tone was muted, Livia thought. "Please tell him, from me, that he has my deepest sympathy."

He came back into the kitchen and slumped down at the table. Livia poured him another cup of coffee.

"Papa? What is it?"

"That was a colleague from the Pd'A in Puglia. A group of young people, demonstrating against Fascism, were attacked last night by the Italian police. Twenty-three were killed, including the son of the local leader of the Pd'A. He's devastated, of course."

"I knew it," said Luisa, coming into the kitchen. "I heard all that, Giacomo. There is danger everywhere. I insist you take us to the villa. Nothing is worth the risk of staying here."

"Now, Luisa—" Giacomo began.

"Don't you try to persuade me," Luisa shouted. "I've heard enough of your arguments to know how it will go. But I will not change my mind!" She left the room and they heard the thud of her suitcase falling onto the floor—she had obviously dragged it down from the top of the wardrobe.

"Papa," Livia pleaded, "I can't leave now. Cosimo is back at last, and there's the problem of the radio. Who will monitor it if I'm away? Perhaps you should explain to Mamma what we're doing—and how important it is."

"I can't tell her about the radio," he said. "She's already hysterical. Firstly, she would never forgive me, and secondly, I worry that if she was arrested or challenged she might inadvertently give us away."

"Well, think of another excuse—please, Papa."

"Look," he said, taking Livia's hand, "I can monitor the radio for a few weeks. It's wonderful of you to do it, but the situation is too confused here... it's not safe." He lowered his voice to a whisper. "I hadn't told you this, but our leader in Puglia, Tommaso Fiore, has been jailed by the Fascist police. There is danger everywhere, and in some ways I agree with your mother. You should go home."

Livia's eyes filled with tears. "But who will protect you?"

"I'll be all right," he said cheerfully, "you mustn't worry about me. But if anything happened to you, I couldn't forgive myself. Just go to the country for a few weeks, until we have a sense of what is going to happen. I'll cover the radio, and with luck you'll be back in September."

"Are you sure? I worry that Mamma will expect me to stay up there in the hills forever."

"I won't let that happen," her father assured her.

Luisa appeared in the hall, her bulging suitcase by her side. She was already wearing her summer coat and hat.

"I'm ready," she said. "Livia, go and pack."

"I can't leave straight away," Livia pleaded. "I have to say goodbye to some friends first." She looked at her father for support. "Please, Papa."

He smiled. "It's all right. You go and say goodbye to your friends, we can leave after lunch."

"But don't be too long," Luisa said desultorily, taking off her hat.

Livia was in a quandary. She wanted desperately to see Cosimo but knew she should also visit Elena. As her friend's apartment was closest, she went there first. She arrived to find Elena and her mother washing up at an old stone sink in the kitchen.

"I'm so pleased you're here, Livia," said Elena, drying her hands. "What shall we do today?"

"I can't do anything, I'm afraid, I'm leaving Florence."

"Why?" Elena looked puzzled.

"My mother insists we have to go back to the country—she's frightened."

"Of what?" asked Elena.

"Everything, really, but bombing in particular. My father is concerned that the Americans have already attacked Rome and we might be next."

"I agree with him," said Benedetta as she put the washed china back in the cupboard. "No one seems to know which side we're on anymore."

"My father says that Mussolini's supporters won't give up without a fight," Livia continued. "The Germans have over a hundred thousand troops in the north. The Anglo-Americans are in the south and we're caught in the middle."

The three women stood around the kitchen table considering the implications of Livia's news. Eventually Elena broke the silence.

"I'll miss you if you go away," she said, sitting down gloomily at the table.

"And I hate the idea of leaving you," replied Livia. "Why don't you all come with us?" she asked brightly. "We have plenty of room."

"Thank you, Livia," said Benedetta, "that's very kind, but I must stay here. My husband's work is at the hospital. He'll never leave Florence. But Elena could certainly go with you."

"No, Mamma," Elena insisted. "I must stay and look after you."

"Don't be ridiculous," her mother chided. "I don't need looking after, but you would have a nice time in the countryside."

"Oh, do say you'll come, Elena," Livia pleaded.

"All right," said Elena uncertainly, looking at her mother. "If you're sure?" Benedetta nodded. "And you promise your mother won't mind?" Elena asked her friend.

"She'll be fine," said Livia. "I know she can make a bit of a fuss, but she'll be happy to have you. But we really need to leave today."

"Will you tell Papa for me?" Elena asked her mother.

"Of course! Now go and pack some things."

The girls left the apartment excitedly.

"I'm so pleased you're coming," said Livia, as they crossed the piazza. "But before we leave Florence, I must go and see Cosimo. Maybe he could come too?"

"Really?" Elena was slightly disappointed. The prospect of spending a month or more with her best friend had seemed so enticing. She was less sure about the wisdom of being stuck between the two lovebirds.

Elena led the way to Cosimo's parents' apartment, which was on the ground floor of an elegant nineteenth-century block. Livia found it strange to be going there for the first time under such curious circumstances—even stranger that she had never met his parents. They rang the bell, and waited on the marble steps outside.

Cosimo's mother opened the door. Tall and dark, like her son, she smiled broadly when she saw Elena.

"This is Livia," said Elena. "She and Cosimo are...friends."

"Ah! I'm so pleased to meet you at last. Cosimo's told me all about you. Come in, won't you?"

Livia blushed, as she and Elena shuffled into the dark hall. "I wondered if Cosimo was here," Livia began nervously. "I have to go to the country today, you see, with my mother. Elena is coming with me. But I couldn't go without saying goodbye to your son."

"I'm afraid he's out," his mother replied. "But I'll tell him you called round."

Noting the look of disappointment on Livia's face, she added: "I'm sorry he's not here, but you'll see him soon. After all, you'll be back in the autumn, won't you?"

"Yes, of course," Livia replied. "Well, goodbye then."

Reluctantly, she left the apartment. As they walked down the street, she peered hopefully around, looking for Cosimo, but he was nowhere to be seen.

When the two girls finally arrived at Livia's apartment, they found Luisa waiting impatiently in the hall. "Livia, where have you been?" she asked, looking pointedly at Elena.

"Mamma," said Livia, "you know Elena."

"Yes of course. But—"

"She's coming with us," Livia interjected firmly. "It will be fun to have a friend. Please say she can come."

"Of course she can," said Giacomo, emerging from his study. "Come on, let's get the bags in the car. We have a long drive ahead."

Chapter Thirteen

Rome
August 1943

Through the long hot summer months of July and August, Rome was declared an "open city," favoring neither the Germans nor the Allies. With no work to occupy her, Isabella increasingly spent her afternoons at the Acquasanta Golf Club. A game of cards, or tennis with Stefano, provided some stability in her otherwise empty life. Everyone was anxious. People who had for years socialized with the Fascists now found themselves uncertain which way to face. Count Ciano hadn't been seen for months; it was rumored that he was secretly negotiating a peaceful solution with the Allies. Meanwhile, senior German officers were increasingly found mixing with the Italian elite.

Isabella had been invited to a dinner party at the home of the socialite, Princess Virginia Agnelli. It was not uncommon for beautiful actresses to be invited to such gatherings, merely to add glamour. Isabella often declined these invitations, but the Princess was a good friend and always made her feel welcome. As Isabella was removing her fox-fur wrap in the entrance hall of the palazzo, the Princess came over to greet her.

"Isabella, how wonderful to see you. I wanted a quick word. I've got a rather special guest this evening, and I want you to pay him some special attention. His name is Karl Wolff, and he's the Supreme Commander of the SS in Italy—a very important man. I'm hoping to arrange a meeting between him and the Pope."

Isabella looked surprised.

"The Vatican is desperate to avoid a full-out war," the Princess explained. "Wolff is minded to help, to broker some kind of peace between Germany and Italy. I've placed you next to him at dinner. Look after Wolff for me—you'll like him, he's a very cultured man."

As her guests began to gather together in the dining room, the Princess introduced them. "General, I'd like you to meet a good friend of mine, the actress Isabella Bellucci."

Wolff bowed low and kissed Isabella's hand. "How delightful," he said.

He was tall and not unattractive, she thought, with a high wide forehead, fair hair and gray eyes. But his mouth was a little too thin, and his eyes, overshadowed by heavy brows, were perhaps a little too close together. He guided her to her chair, and sat down heavily beside her.

"I visited the gallery at Villa Borghese yesterday," he told her, as the wine was served. "I saw the Venus and Cupid exhibition. I particularly enjoyed the painting by the German artist, Lucas Cranach."

"I loved that exhibition," Isabella said, "although I can't remember the Cranach offhand."

"You've seen it?" he asked, clearly surprised. "So you're an art lover then?"

"Oh yes," Isabella replied, mildly irritated to be so patronized. "I don't pretend to be an expert, but I go to the gallery quite often. I live just across the park."

"I must call in and see you when I'm next there," he said.

The following day, Isabella received a note from Wolff, inviting her to dinner. She instantly regretted being so charming the evening before. Why did powerful men always presume that actresses existed purely for their pleasure? But to refuse him could be dangerous. It would draw attention to herself and risk his anger. Equally, it would be madness to agree to meet him.

She wrote back explaining she had contracted the flu and would be forced to stay in bed for the next week.

A bouquet of flowers arrived the following afternoon with a note.

I hope you get better soon—perhaps we might meet at the gallery?

Having told the lie, she felt trapped in her house, for fear that he or one of his henchmen might be outside, spying on her. But after a couple of days with only her mother, aunt and grandmother for company, she decided to risk leaving the villa, in order to seek out the one person who always gave her solace.

It was a hot, humid afternoon in August when she set off for Vicenzo's house wearing a cap-sleeved gingham dress and gold sandals. When she was halfway across the park, it occurred to her that he might not even be there. His family usually spent the summer on their estate on the coast, and she knew he had already sent on most of the staff. So she was relieved, as she walked up the drive, to see the dogs lying as usual in the cool of the porch. If they were there, so must be Vicenzo. The dogs stood up as she approached, and gently nuzzled her hand.

"Good boys," she said gently. "Where's your master?"

The dogs lay back down with a sigh and closed their eyes.

Isabella knocked on the door, but there was no reply. She walked around the side of the house, surprised at her boldness. Perhaps he had fallen asleep in the garden, she thought.

The house appeared silent, but as she approached the back terrace, she heard a woman's laughter—his sister, Luciana, perhaps. As she turned the corner, she saw Vicenzo sitting on a cane sofa next to a young woman. She had blond hair and wore a white figure-hugging dress. Isabella recognized her immediately as a young actress, recently contracted by Cinecittà. Vicenzo was in full flow, clearly in the middle of an amusing anecdote, and the girl was laughing gaily—gazing up at him enraptured.

Isabella stood for a few moments observing the pair jealously, but the blonde soon noticed Isabella out of the corner of her eye; she nudged Vicenzo who leapt to his feet.

"Isabella, darling. I didn't know you were here."

"I did knock," she said nervously, "but there was no answer. The dogs were lying on the doorstep, so I presumed you were at home. I'm sorry, I didn't mean to interrupt. I should go."

"No, stay. You know Miranda, don't you?"

"We haven't yet been introduced." Isabella smiled frostily at the girl. "But it's nice to meet you."

The girl smirked.

"Miranda and I were talking about a possible part in my next film," Vicenzo said disarmingly, "although when I will have a chance to make it, I don't know."

The girl was young—no more than eighteen or nineteen. Her skin was fresh, her eyes clear and very blue. She was delicate and gamine.

"I'm interrupting, I should go." Isabella suddenly felt uncomfortable. She retreated, hurrying around the side of the house, but Vicenzo followed her.

"Isabella cara, wait." He grabbed her arm and swung her round to face him. She had tears in her eyes. "It's not what you think," he said.

"No? I think perhaps it's very much what I think."

"It's not," he insisted.

"So you don't like that girl?" she asked. "She's very beautiful."

"She's pretty enough, yes, but no prettier than you. And yes, I like her, but no more than that."

"There has to be some reason," Isabella said, fighting back the tears, "why you don't love me."

"But I do love you." He took her face in his hands, wiping her tears away. "Surely you know that."

"Just not the way I want." Her voice was breaking with emotion as she took his hands in her own and kissed them.

They were interrupted by the sound of coughing. They turned around to find Miranda staring at them.

"I should go," said Isabella quietly.

"I'll call you," he promised.

She backed away, until just their fingertips were touching. Finally, as they parted, he blew her a kiss and she turned and walked hurriedly out of the garden, down the drive and home.

A large basket of red roses was delivered to Isabella's house the following morning. She knew who they were from but took comfort from the card in the basket, nevertheless.

Cara Bella, with all my love, Vicenzo.

Two days later, he phoned her. "Come over tonight. I have some friends staying with me—writers, directors, musicians and so on."

"Are you sure? Isn't there someone else you'd rather have?" she asked sulkily.

"Don't be silly," he said firmly. "I'll see you at eight."

The sound of male laughter floated down the drive, as Isabella walked toward Vicenzo's front door. The maid took her evening coat and showed her into the drawing room.

"Bella, at last, here you are," said Vicenzo cheerfully. "I've been waiting for you." Taking her by the arm, he introduced her to everyone. "Lino, this is my friend Bella, the actress I was telling you about. Isabella darling, meet Lino. He's a brilliant man, trust me—a superlative writer as well as a talented philosopher."

"He's too kind," said Lino, bowing slightly.

All the guests were "intellectual polymaths," in Vicenzo's opinion. Although they were mainly connected with the cinema and publishing, the discussion soon turned to politics.

"Badoglio is an idiot," declared a journalist called Salvato. "And the King is no better. There's a vacuum at the top. No one is taking a lead. We need to involve the unions in the north more, and bring the country together. If we're not careful, the Germans will take control of Rome and then everything will be lost."

"Vicenzo, have you had a chance to canvas the other anti-Fascist groups?" asked Lino.

"Yes, I have an old friend who's a founding member of the Pd'A—a lawyer in Florence. He's a good man, a liberal, you know?"

"Will he help us?" Lino asked.

"I believe so, yes," Vicenzo said. "I have arranged to meet him later this month. He has a wonderful daughter called Livia—very bright. I've known her since she was a child. She is a student, and a fiery little thing, and I'm pretty sure that she and her father are both on our side."

Vicenzo had never mentioned this girl before. Isabella took a cocktail from the tray and leaned forward, listening intently.

Sensing her interest, Vicenzo casually changed the subject. "I hear the actress Luisa Ferida has been shouting her hatred of Mussolini from the rooftops."

"Really?" said a young man on the edge of the group.

"Yes—she and that boyfriend of hers, Osvaldo Valenti. I don't believe them for a moment; he's a snake in the grass."

"You think they are pretending?" asked Lino.

"Of course. The pair of them are Fascist to the core. They're just trying to work out which way the wind is blowing." Vicenzo looked pointedly at Isabella. "What do you think? Is Osvaldo a convert to the anti-Fascist cause?"

"You're asking me?" She blushed, embarrassed at being challenged. "I don't really know. Osvaldo is such an egotistical man. I've never really liked him. But it's hard for actors like us. The State has controlled our business for so long, people don't know who to trust anymore."

"Isabella thinks there is an indulgent, paternalistic side to the Fascist authorities," said Vicenzo sarcastically. "They've looked after her so handsomely since she was a child, she can't believe 'Daddy' has abandoned her."

There was a ripple of laughter. Isabella, wounded by Vicenzo's comment, sensed his friends' contempt. He had been so kind and sympathetic when they had last met, encouraging her to expose her fears. Now she was just the butt of his joke. She felt herself flushing with embarrassment and anger. "I really ought to be going."

"Oh, really?" Vicenzo looked surprised. "Don't go just yet."

"I really think I should. Thank you, though—it's been most enlightening."

Vicenzo followed her out into the hall.

"Why did you say that—about me and the Fascists?" she asked him, as he helped her on with her coat.

"Well it's true, isn't it? You were friends with Ciano, everyone knows that."

"Not friends—he took over the club, it was impossible to avoid him."

"You could have left," he said simply.

"Why should I? I like it there."

"What, that awful place? A bourgeois collection of old ladies and stupid young men playing cards."

"They've been very kind to me," she replied coldly. She turned to leave, her hand on the door handle, but he grasped her shoulders and turned her round to face him. "Don't go like this," he implored her. "I was only teasing."

"You're showing off to that court of yours," she snapped. "All those men who adore you."

"They're my friends."

"I thought *I* was your friend."

"You are," he insisted. "How could you think anything different?"

"Prove it to me." She took his face in her hands, and spontaneously kissed him on the mouth. She felt him recoil slightly.

"Don't," he said, moving her hands away. "Please don't."

"But why? You must know that I love you. I adore you. I want you, Vicenzo."

"Isabella..." He closed his eyes for a moment, and ran his hand through his hair.

"What? What is it?" she asked desperately. "*Is* there someone else? Someone you have never told me about?"

"Don't be ridiculous." His tone was suddenly dismissive, as if he was bored, even irritated. He stepped away from her. "You know I love you and only you," he said gently. "Now, I must get back to my guests, and you should go—it's late."

Isabella walked through the park, fighting back the tears. Vicenzo could be so quixotic and confusing: in an instant he could turn from being cruel to loving. Perhaps that was why she loved him so much—she never quite knew where she stood. It was like torture, the way he pulled her toward him, only to push her away.

As she lay in bed, she ran over the evening in her mind, trying to decipher his feelings for her. "I love you and only you," he had said. And yet he had laughed at her and humiliated her in front of his friends. That wasn't the behavior of a lover—it was cruel. She remembered the filming in Ferrara, and how he had encouraged Girotti to hit Clara. Was that Vicenzo's idea of love? Cruelty mixed with affection? He had recoiled from her as she kissed him. And yet he often told her how beautiful she was. Why wouldn't he make love to her?

She began to weep, imagining his hands on her body, him kissing her deeply. Why did he continue to resist her? The only logical explanation, the only reason he continued to push her away, was that he loved someone else. As she lay in the dark, tossing and turning, she agonized about who it could be. Clara Calamai perhaps? She was certainly beautiful and exotic. Isabella wondered if she had been invited to join them that evening in Ferrara to make Clara jealous? Or had Vicenzo fallen in love with Miranda—the fresh-faced and innocent young actress. Or maybe it was the girl he had mentioned that evening to his friends—the girl he spoke so enthusiastically about, someone he obviously admired. Livia from Florence. Had this girl stirred a passion in him Isabella had been unable to ignite? Could it be that all this time he had been in love with Livia?

Isabella was still weeping when the sun rose and streamed through her bedroom window. Hot and damp, she wrestled with the sheets, finally throwing them off and getting out of bed. She stood in the bathroom staring at herself in the mirror. She looked old, she thought—her skin gray and dull, her eyes bloodshot. No longer the beauty she had once been. This girl was taking away the one man she had ever really loved. The one man she had set her heart on. She rinsed her face in cold water and ran a bath. She lay in the warm water, watching the steam rise. Somehow, she must find a way to make Vicenzo love her again. She would not, she could not, give him up.

Chapter Fourteen

The hills above Florence
August 1943

Livia and Elena lay under the shade of a large fig tree in the garden, two baskets filled with fruit by their side. Bees and wasps buzzed above their heads, lazily sucking the juice that oozed from the ripe fruit.

"We must not waste anything," Luisa had said at breakfast. "If you want to spend the morning in the garden, then do something useful and pick as many figs as you can. I shall make a preserve which might see us through the winter."

"I know we should give them all to Mamma," said Livia, sucking the juice from a fig, "but I love them fresh."

"Me too, they're delicious," agreed Elena, waving away an angry wasp. "You're so lucky to have this garden. We don't even have a terrace in Florence."

"It used to be very beautiful," Livia mused, leaning against the trunk of the fig tree. "But we've had to turn a lot of it into vegetables now. Still, at least it means we eat a bit better up here in the hills."

"Have you heard from Cosimo?" Elena asked.

"Yes," Livia replied. "I had a letter this morning."

"And...?"

Livia rolled over onto her stomach and began pulling blades of grass out of the rough lawn.

"Oh do tell me, Livia."

"He's much better. They've fitted his new prosthetic foot, and he's getting used to it."

"That's wonderful. He couldn't have done that if he'd come away with us, could he?" Elena still felt guilty that she had been secretly relieved Cosimo had been unable to join them.

"No, I suppose you're right. He needs to be in Florence in order to visit the hospital."

"Besides," Elena went on, "I'm not sure your mother would have liked him being here—she's finding it hard enough to put up with me."

"That's not true," Livia insisted. "She likes you, really."

"And I like her, but she's very protective of you. And I'm not sure she thinks Cosimo is good enough for you, a nice middle-class boy with one foot." She laughed, but Livia frowned.

"Don't say that, it's not kind—either to my mother or to Cosimo. Mamma's just old-fashioned, that's all."

"I'm sorry," said Elena. "But whenever he's mentioned she changes the subject, as if she doesn't really approve."

Livia sighed and stood up. She picked the last few ripe figs and dropped them into her basket. "Mamma's got it into her head that I'm going to marry an old family friend."

"Who?" asked Elena.

"Count Vicenzo Lucchese," Livia replied with mock grandeur. "It's ridiculous, really. Our families have been friends for generations. Our grandfathers were in the army together and we used to spend our holidays with them. They're very rich. They have a lovely house on the coast in Forte dei Marmi. Do you know it?"

Elena shook her head.

"Anyway, Vicenzo is their oldest son. He's much older than me—ten years or more. He's very handsome and charming and all the women are in love with him. I mean *really* in love with him." She laughed.

"Would it be so bad to marry him?" asked Elena slightly enviously.

"And become 'La Contessa'!" Livia curtseyed theatrically. "No, it's too absurd. Besides, he's never shown the least interest in me, so my mother's fantasy will remain just that. And let's not forget, I'm already in love...with Cosimo." She picked up the basket of figs. "Let's take these to the kitchen before the wasps get them all. Then we can go for a walk, I'm bored here."

*

At lunchtime, the family assembled in the dining room. Angela brought a pot of soup and laid it out on the table.

"Where's Nonno?" asked Livia.

"I don't know," said Luisa, arranging plates. "I've not seen him all morning."

Livia went upstairs to her grandfather's room. Alberto was still in bed, apparently asleep. She crossed over to him and listened to his breathing—it was slow and deep with an unusual gurgling sound at the back of his throat.

"Nonno, Nonno..." She gently touched his hand. "Nonno, are you all right?"

He opened his eyes and tried to smile, but one side of his face seemed curiously fixed.

"Nonno, are you all right?" she asked again.

The old man mumbled something incoherent.

"Wait a minute." She rushed downstairs to her mother. "Mamma, it's Nonno. Something's happened to him. He can't speak properly."

Luisa ran upstairs, followed by Angela and Livia. She sat by the old man's bed and took his hand. "Nonno, Alberto, it's Luisa."

He turned his head slowly and smiled lopsidedly.

"He's had a stroke," Luisa said softly. "Livia, run into the village and fetch the doctor. Ask him to come immediately."

The family gathered in the sitting room, waiting for the doctor's verdict.

"You're quite right," he said when he came downstairs. "It's a stroke. Alberto will recover over time, but he will need rest and constant nursing. Can you manage, do you think?"

"We will have to," Luisa replied phlegmatically, glancing at Livia.

"Good. Well, I shall return tomorrow to check on him."

After the doctor had left, Luisa sat down heavily on the sofa. She looked pale and shocked. "We haven't had our soup yet," she said distractedly. "It will be cold now."

"Don't worry, Mamma." Livia picked up the tureen. "I'll go to the kitchen and heat it up again."

Back in the dining room, Luisa spooned the soup into their bowls and they all ate silently.

"We will have to stay here now," Luisa said eventually. "We cannot go back to Florence. Even your father must see that. We will tell him tonight, when he comes for the weekend."

Livia wanted to tell her mother that she couldn't abandon her degree, that she couldn't bear to be parted any longer from Cosimo, that she had her duty to the Pd'A. But she felt unable to argue. "Let's see what Papa thinks," she murmured.

That evening, Livia leaned out of her bedroom window listening for her father's car. He was due to arrive in time for supper and she was desperate to seek his support before her mother had a chance to persuade him that they should all stay in the country. She heard his car before she saw it, the gears grinding as he negotiated the hairpin bends leading to the village. Eventually she caught sight of his familiar black Lancia coming down their narrow lane.

She ran downstairs and threw herself at him as he walked through the door. "Papa, you're here at last, thank God."

"I am, darling, what a welcome! And it's wonderful to be here. Florence is so very hot, too hot even for me."

"We have to talk," she said urgently.

"What about?" he asked, putting down his bag and removing his Panama hat.

"It's Nonno, he's had a stroke, Papa."

Luisa came into the hall. "Giacomo, thank God you're back. Has Livia told you?"

"Yes," he said uncertainly, sinking down onto the settle. "I can hardly believe it."

"Well I'm afraid it's true," she replied. "It happened this morning, we think, or maybe during the night."

"I must go to him."

Livia and Elena waited with Luisa outside on the moonlit terrace while Giacomo went to see his father. Luisa and Angela had laid out a cold supper on the long table and cicadas buzzed insistently while mosquitoes whined overhead.

"Eat your supper, girls," Luisa instructed them. "Giacomo might be some time."

Livia ate nervously, wondering what her father's reaction might be to Alberto's condition. Perhaps he would agree with her mother that they should all remain in the villa and care for the old man.

After half an hour, Giacomo joined them. He poured himself a glass of wine and sat down in one of the cane chairs.

"How was he?" asked Livia.

"Much as before, I suspect. It looks quite serious, doesn't it? He cannot move his right side. What are we to do?" He seemed uncharacteristically indecisive.

Livia sat down next to him. "He'll improve, Papa, I'm sure of it."

"How do you know?" asked her father.

"Elena told me." She looked at her friend for support. "Her father's a doctor," Livia added.

"My grandmother also had a stroke several years ago," explained Elena, "but she's quite well now."

Giacomo nodded. "Well, that's good to hear."

"I'm sure you'll agree that we must all remain in the villa," said Luisa. "And Giacomo, you can move your practice up here."

Livia exchanged worried glances with Elena. "But Mamma," she began, "I have to go back to Florence in September for the start of term."

"But I need you with me," her mother insisted.

Her father sipped his drink thoughtfully.

"No, Livia's right," he said eventually. "She can stay for another couple of weeks, but in September she must go back. There's really no need for her to miss out on her degree."

"Giacomo!" Luisa exclaimed. "Have you no sense of duty? Who is going to nurse your father? I can't manage on my own."

"We have Angela and Gino—they will help. Besides, my father wouldn't want his granddaughter to nurse him. I'm sure you'll cope."

"Will I?" Luisa was indignant. "And what about you? Are you deserting him as well?"

"I'm afraid I must return to Florence after the weekend—I have work to do."

Luisa stood up furiously. "Well, I really cannot believe it. I'm going to bed. And if your father needs anything in the night, I presume it will be me getting up for him?"

"Of course not," said Giacomo wearily. "I'll get up. And tomorrow I'll start looking for a nurse, I promise."

Elena, sensing that Livia wanted time alone with her father, made her excuses. "I ought to go to bed too," she said, kissing Livia's cheek. "See you in the morning."

When they were alone, Giacomo beckoned to his daughter. "Come into my study. I want to talk privately." Once inside, he closed the door behind them. "I will get you back to Florence, don't worry."

"Mamma will never forgive me."

"She will, in time. But things are getting complicated—politically—and I need to be back in the city."

"What do you mean, complicated?" Livia asked.

"From what I can gather, the government is making a terrible mess of an armistice. I fear that by the time one is actually signed, we will effectively have been invaded. I think war with Germany is now inevitable."

"What can we do?"

"If we are to defeat Fascism, we must join forces with the other parties."

"The liberals and the communists, you mean?"

"Indeed. The Pd'A have a conference planned in early September—it will be held in Florence. I have to be there. But more than that, I am arranging various meetings with senior figures in the other left-wing parties. One of them is coming here tomorrow, in fact."

"Really?" Livia was surprised. "But you hardly ever meet people here."

"I know, and with your grandfather falling ill, I wish I had made a different arrangement, but my guest is already on his way."

"Who is it?" she asked.

"Someone you know—Vicenzo."

"Vicenzo? But he's a film director—how can he help?"

"He is also a leading member of the Communist Party."

"I remember he told me he was 'on the left' when we stayed with them last summer. But I had no idea he was so influential."

"He's developing a network of partisans in Rome."

"The Resistance, you mean?" she asked.

Her father nodded. "My problem, Livia, is how to explain his arrival at this terrible time—with my father's illness and so on. Your mother is already anxious enough, but if she thinks we are plotting partisan activity with a leading communist she'll never forgive me." He sat down heavily behind his desk and sighed audibly.

"Couldn't Vicenzo just be passing by—visiting old family friends?"

Giacomo looked at her. "Even your mother is not that stupid. He's never visited us before."

Livia wandered around her father's study, examining the books and legal texts. "How about..." she began. "No, it's too ridiculous."

"Tell me," he said.

"You know that Mamma has long had this mad idea that I might one day marry Vicenzo?"

Giacomo stared at her open-mouthed. "You are joking, of course."

"No, not really. Last year, when we stayed with the Luccheses on the coast, she told me it had been a dream of hers for years—uniting the two families."

"Your mother is unbelievable. So what is your idea?"

"Could Vicenzo not come here—to see me? Perhaps to explore the idea of marriage, to sound you out?"

Giacomo sat at his desk, his chin propped up on his hands. "It is a preposterous idea," he said at last. "You hardly know each other."

"Well, we got on when we were together last year. I think Mamma would believe it."

"Really?" Her father sounded unconvinced. "Well, it might work, but I don't want to overcomplicate things. There should be no talk of an engagement—we don't want announcements in the newspapers."

"Of course not," said Livia. "But if you could convince her he wanted to explore the possibility, I really think it could work."

*

Over breakfast the following morning, Giacomo casually mentioned Vicenzo's visit.

"He's coming to lunch?" Luisa exclaimed. "Today?! But I have nothing prepared, and your father is upstairs ill in bed, or have you already forgotten?"

"No, my dear, I've not forgotten. But it seemed important to Vicenzo. He wrote to me and asked if he could come. The arrangement has been made. It's not a real problem, is it?"

"What am I supposed to feed him on?" Luisa asked plaintively.

"I don't know. We have to eat lunch anyway—can't we just lay another place?"

"Oh really!" Luisa threw her napkin down on the table. "I cannot give the young Count nothing but a bowl of soup. You know how wonderful his mother's meals are. What on earth am I supposed to do?"

"I'm sure you'll think of something," Giacomo said encouragingly. "The girls will help you, won't you?" He looked across at Elena and Livia, who nodded earnestly.

"Of course we will," they chorused.

"And what is so urgent that he has to come today, anyway?" asked Luisa.

Giacomo glanced across the table at Livia. "He mentioned something about Livia," he replied innocently.

"Livia? What about her?" Luisa exclaimed.

"I'm not sure, just that it would be lovely to see her again."

Elena nudged her friend, who looked at her sideways and winked conspiratorially.

Luisa's expression changed from fury to excitement. "Did you know anything about this, Livia?"

"Me? No! I had no idea he was even coming."

"Well, never mind," said Luisa excitedly. "I told you he liked you. Now, what do we have in the cupboard that I can turn into something edible?" She left the dining room muttering, heading for the kitchen.

Moments later, Livia heard cupboard doors slamming and pans being put onto the stove. "Oh, poor Mamma," she said sympathetically.

"It's good for her," replied Giacomo. "It will take her mind off my sick father."

Vicenzo arrived at midday, carrying a large bunch of roses which he handed theatrically to Luisa. She blushed and started to make polite conversation about his family.

Giacomo quickly interrupted her. "Luisa my dear, Vicenzo has something important to discuss with me in private. I think we should get on."

"Of course, of course," she replied. "The girls and I will get lunch ready. Will two o'clock be all right?"

Lunch was laid out on the terrace. Livia and Elena had gathered fresh vegetables from the garden, and Luisa had prepared as many dishes as their rationing allowed. Wild flowers were placed in small vases all down the long table, shaded by a Russian vine scrambling over a pergola above.

By two o'clock, Luisa had put on her best dress, and was waiting expectantly on the terrace with Livia and Elena. Vicenzo, who by then had been informed of the little deception, emerged from Giacomo's study and everyone sat down for lunch. He began to chat animatedly with the two girls, paying particular attention to Livia—complimenting her on her dress, asking about her studies and occasionally openly flirting with her.

Sitting at the head of the table, Luisa looked on approvingly.

When lunch was over, Vicenzo finally made his excuses. "Well, I'm afraid I really must get going," he said. "It's been a wonderful day, but I have to get to Forte dei Marmi tonight."

The family stood outside the villa to say their goodbyes. Vicenzo shook Giacomo's hand and kissed Elena on the cheek. "Look after your friend—Livia's a special girl," he murmured. He took Luisa's hand and kissed it theatrically. "Thank you for a wonderful lunch. I hope to see you in Forte dei Marmi very soon—you're welcome at any time."

"Oh, Vicenzo!" Luisa blushed, fanning herself. "We'd love to come. Give my love to your parents."

Vicenzo finally turned to Livia and whispered into her ear: "I think we convinced your mother."

He climbed into his open-topped Alfa Romeo, and drove away in a cloud of dust.

Luisa took Livia by the arm and steered her back into the house. "Well, what do you think?" she asked conspiratorially.

Livia feigned innocence. "Of what?"

"Of Vicenzo, of course! Has he asked you?"

"If you mean what I think you mean, then no, he has not proposed—which is a relief, as I would have had to refuse him."

"Refuse him? Are you mad?" cried Luisa. "Refuse a Count who's an old family friend? Why, what objections could you possibly have? He's handsome, rich, charming, talented, artistic—"

"I don't love him," Livia interjected simply.

That evening, once the table had been cleared, and Livia had helped to feed and settle her grandfather, she and Elena sat together in the garden, watching the sun sinking over the trees.

"I was thinking," Elena began, "that I might go back to Florence tomorrow with your father."

"Don't you want to stay?" Livia asked, slightly hurt.

"It's not that," replied Elena quickly, "and I feel terrible leaving you, but I'm worried about my mother. She's by herself all day, while my father's at work. As your father is driving back to Florence tomorrow, it would be sensible to go with him. Otherwise I'll have to wait till September."

"I'll be lonely without you." Livia felt suddenly dejected. "I wish I was going back too."

"Why don't you?" Elena asked.

"I have to stay and help with Nonno. But hopefully we'll find a nurse soon, and I'll be able to get back."

*

Livia felt bereft as she waved goodbye to Elena and her father the following morning. It was unbearable to have been left up in the hills with her mother, out of harm's way, while down on the plain in Florence, the Resistance was forging ahead. She would never be content with an ordinary life, she realized. The business of running a home, loving a husband, raising a child, would never be enough for her. She yearned for danger, for challenges and excitement, and she was determined to get back to her real existence as soon as possible.

PART THREE

CIVIL WAR

"When women take up a cause you can assume it has been won!"

Italian proverb

Chapter Fifteen

Rome
September 1943

It had been several weeks since Vicenzo's party, and Isabella hadn't received either flowers or even a phone call from him. Normally, if they parted on bad terms, he would make it up to her within days. His silence worried her, and she yearned for reassurance. If she could just speak to him and hear his voice, she would know whether he still loved her. But each time she picked up the phone to call him, she hesitated, eventually replacing the receiver. Better perhaps to live in ignorance than to have your fears confirmed, she thought to herself.

Eventually, driven mad by curiosity and jealousy, she decided to confront him in person. Every day she would walk to his house, but her nerve always failed her. Rather than going boldly to the front door, she would hide just out of sight on the pavement, waiting behind a hedge. What she was watching for, she couldn't really explain—a glimpse of an unfamiliar woman...the girl from Florence perhaps?

On one occasion, the dogs nearly gave her away. Vicenzo emerged one morning, the dogs following closely behind. Suddenly, they caught Isabella's scent and ran down the drive, barking, heading straight toward her. She stood frozen, hidden from view, wanting to run, but she knew the dogs would only follow her if she did. Still hiding on the pavement, she let them nuzzle against her legs, sniff her hands and lick her fingers. She heard Vicenzo's footsteps as he walked down the drive toward them. Terrified she would be discovered, she flapped her hands at the dogs. "Go home," she whispered. "Good boys, go home." They looked up at her, questioningly. To her relief, Vicenzo called their names and whistled to them. The dogs pricked up their ears, and bounded back to the house. Filled with shame, and desperate to get away, she ran into the park, only stopping to catch her breath when she was out of sight.

Isabella had never chased a man like this before, nor ever spied on anyone. She thought she had felt true love for the soldier aristocrat, Ludovico, but that was nothing compared to the intensity of her feelings for Vicenzo. Now she was tortured by the realization that Livia was exactly the sort of girl a man like Vicenzo would be expected to marry—a girl he had known all his life, who was from a good family. She remembered her final meeting with Ludovico's mother, when the Baroness had made it quite clear that Isabella would never be good enough for her son. Now she felt the same humiliation and disappointment she had felt then—like a stab through the heart.

"Did you have a nice walk?" her mother asked, when she got home. "Where do you go every day?"

"Just around," Isabella replied guardedly.

"Well, if you have nothing better to do, why don't you come and help us? Housework doesn't do itself, you know." Giovanna was making pasta with her sister Ariana. They were rolling out the dough with white floury hands.

"Oh no!" exclaimed Isabella, "I'm no good at making pasta."

"Only because you don't practice," replied her mother, pushing a small round of dough toward her. "Don't waste it...it was hard enough getting hold of the flour."

Isabella joined the two women at the table, and began to roll out the dough, sighing repeatedly.

"What's the matter, Isabella?" Giovanna asked impatiently. "Is it work?"

"No, not particularly," replied Isabella. "There is no work, of course, and that makes me a bit miserable."

"Is it money, then?"

"No," said Isabella firmly. "We have enough. The house is paid for, we're no longer paying the staff, and I have a few savings."

"Well, what is it then?" her mother asked.

Isabella glanced uneasily toward her aunt. Giovanna whispered to her sister, who wiped her floury fingers on her apron and left the room.

"Now, we're alone. So tell me—what's the matter?" asked Giovanna. "Is it that director?"

Isabella slumped down on a chair and began to cry.

"Crying won't help," Giovanna said coolly. "Are you in love with him?"

Isabella nodded.

"But he doesn't love you, is that it?"

"He says he does," said Isabella, wiping away her tears, "but something always holds him back. He won't commit to me in any way. He says he cares about me, but then he ignores me for weeks on end."

"Perhaps there's someone else?" Her mother had an uncanny ability to read her mind. It was almost a relief to hear her worst fears articulated.

"Do you really think so?" Isabella asked.

"I don't know," said Giovanna, "but it seems the most logical explanation. What sort of man is he? Does he play the field?"

"No, not really," Isabella replied uncertainly. "Lots of actresses are in love with him, but he is aloof from everyone. Oh Mamma, I really love him! He is my soulmate."

"Well, he's handsome, I know that—I met him once, remember? He's the best-looking man I've ever seen."

"I know he's beautiful, but that's not why I love him."

Giovanna snorted in disbelief.

"Really!" Isabella insisted. "His looks are irrelevant."

Her mother rolled her eyes heavenwards.

"Believe me, Mamma. I fell in love with him because he was so attentive. But recently, he's begun to change—he was quite cruel to me at a party recently, humiliating me in front of other people. Everyone laughed at me. I felt ridiculous and very hurt. He's never been like that before. I worry..." She paused, rolling the dough rhythmically between her fingers.

"Worry about what?" her mother asked impatiently. "Tell me?"

"That he's found someone else," Isabella finally blurted out.

"Who? Another actress?"

"No. Someone from a good family—someone he's known all her life. He mentioned he was visiting her family over the summer. I keep thinking, what if he's planning to marry her? What if it's like Ludovico all over again? A man who did love me but was never going to marry me, because I wasn't..." She trailed off, angrily punching the dough with her fingers.

Her mother took the dough away from her and sat down. "Because you weren't good enough?"

Isabella nodded, sobbing.

"You won't achieve anything by crying, my girl."

Isabella wiped her eyes with the back of her hand. "I know, you're right."

"So what are you going to do about it?"

"I don't know. Vicenzo's never actually said I'm not good enough, but perhaps he's being pressured by his family."

"By that bitch of a sister, you mean? I remember you telling me how controlling she was at their dinner party."

"Maybe," Isabella agreed. "It's just like Ludovico's mother all over again, isn't it?"

Giovanna stood up and began to knead the two piles of pasta dough together. "What do you know about this other girl?"

"Only that she's a university student in Florence. Her father is a lawyer—a liberal."

"Mmm—a liberal..." mused her mother. "And what makes you think she may be the one?"

"He spoke about her with such...passion. He described her as 'fiery.'"

Giovanna raised her eyebrows. "Passion, eh?"

"He's had other women friends before," replied Isabella, "other actresses, but I've never heard him expressing such *admiration* for a woman before."

"Well..." said her mother, choosing her words carefully, "...perhaps you could make her disappear?"

"What on earth do you mean?"

"We live in complicated times, Isabella. Maybe this girl isn't all she seems. You said her father is a liberal, so I presume he's anti-Fascist. Does she share his feelings?"

"I don't know, Mamma."

"What are Vicenzo's political views?"

"He's left-wing, like a lot of artistic people—but the last thing I want is to get him into trouble."

"Of course not, but have you thought that perhaps this girl is bewitching him, encouraging him to believe things that are dangerous?" suggested Giovanna knowingly.

"Do you think so?"

"Perhaps he needs protecting... from himself."

"I don't know." Isabella sounded doubtful. "I have no evidence that's what is going on."

"Well, Vicenzo must have said something to make you think this girl and her father are involved with anti-government activities," Giovanna persisted.

"All he said was that he was meeting with them over the summer, and that they might agree to help him in some way. I had the impression they were part of some kind of political movement."

"There you are then," said Giovanna firmly. "She is dragging him down a dangerous path. I think he needs you to help him, to protect him."

"How on earth could I do that?"

"By discouraging their relationship."

"But how?" Isabella insisted.

Her mother sighed, set aside the dough and crossed her arms. "You have friends in high places, don't you, Isabella?"

"I used to," replied Isabella, thinking of Ciano.

"You still do. For example, you're friends with Princess Agnelli. You told me yourself she is involved with negotiations between the German High Command and the Vatican—I don't know how much more influential you could get."

"I suppose so," said Isabella anxiously.

"And what about that German officer you met?" Giovanna suggested.

"Wolff?" Isabella said with surprise. "I hardly know him."

"But he asked you out, didn't he? You must learn to use your femininity and your charms, Isabella. You have great beauty. You're a star. Stop behaving like a downtrodden woman. Grab what you want with both hands. Stop being such a victim."

Isabella, chastened, sat up at the table, wiping her eyes.

"All it would take," her mother went on, "would be a word from you that this girl is not all she seems . . . that she may be involved with some anti-Fascist organization—"

"I couldn't do that!" Isabella was appalled. "For one thing, I don't know if it's true."

"You don't know that it's a lie either," replied her mother. "Just think about it."

Isabella was due at the Acquasanta Golf Club that evening. As she dressed for dinner, she thought about her mother's advice and began to convince herself that Livia could indeed be a dangerous influence. The more she thought about what her mother had said, the more likely an explanation it seemed. If this girl was an anti-Fascist, she could be manipulating Vicenzo and putting him in serious danger.

Driving toward the club, she turned on the car radio. The announcer suddenly interrupted the music and introduced the Prime Minister, Marshal Badoglio: *The Italian government, recognizing the impossibility of continuing the unequal struggle against an overwhelming enemy force, in order to avoid further and graver disasters for the nation, has sought an armistice from General Eisenhower, Commander-in-Chief of the Allied forces. The request was granted. Consequently, all acts of hostility against the Anglo-American forces by Italian forces must cease everywhere. However, our armed services will react to attacks from any other source.*

Isabella pulled over at the side of the road, trying to make sense of the announcement. What did it mean? Did "any other source" mean Italy was now at war with Germany?

*

"Darling, there you are," said Stefano, when Isabella arrived at the golf club. "Have you heard the latest news?"

"Yes, I heard the announcement on my car radio. What does it mean? Are we no longer at war with the Anglo-Americans?" She lowered her voice, aware that the room was peppered with the black uniforms of senior Nazi officers. "Are the Germans now our enemy?"

"Lord knows," said Stefano, winking. "But it strikes me that we need to start looking both ways now... make friends wherever we can, darling."

Isabella scanned the room, looking for people she knew. On the opposite side of the drawing room, leaning against the fireplace, was Karl Wolff, the SS commander she had met in the summer. It seemed as if fate had brought them together.

He crossed the room toward her. "Isabella, how wonderful to see you again." He clicked his heels, and raised her hand to his lips. "I trust you are quite recovered?"

"Oh yes, that was a long time ago—I'm much better, thank you."

"Let me get you a drink—and you will join us at dinner, I hope?"

He ordered her a cocktail from the bar, and insisted on sitting next to her at dinner. As the wine flowed, she began to relax. He was the model of good manners and erudition. They discussed art, opera and films.

"I saw you in *La Bohème*," he told her, "I thought you were wonderful. You have a great talent." He gazed at her. "You appear so young and innocent, but I suspect beating beneath that tender breast is the heart of a lion."

She blushed, genuinely pleased. It was good to feel valued and made to feel special. Inevitably, the conversation turned to the latest political news.

"I have to confess, I don't really understand what's happening," Isabella said. "I heard the Prime Minister on the radio as I drove over, and am quite confused."

"I wouldn't worry about it," Wolff reassured her, refilling her glass. "I think you'll find that announcement was rather premature."

"I see." Isabella tried to sound unconcerned. "So we are not at war with our German friends, then?" She looked at him and smiled, trying to keep the conversation light-hearted.

"It's complicated, I agree," he replied gently, "but a beautiful woman like you shouldn't have to worry about such things. You'll be all right."

"The problem is," she persisted, "we all feel we're in limbo, caught between one world and another. It's very confusing."

"It must be." He sounded genuinely sympathetic.

"One doesn't really know who one's friends are anymore," Isabella went on. "I miss the old days when Mussolini was firmly in charge and we all knew where we stood."

Wolff nodded supportively.

"There's a sense that one doesn't know who to trust anymore," she continued. "There's so much secrecy and confusion. I hate it."

"Secrecy?" he asked gently. "In what sense?"

"Oh you know, people who are working against the government behind the scenes. Anti-Fascists, I suppose you'd call them."

"Partisans you mean?"

"I suppose so," she said uncertainly. "I'm not really sure I know what a partisan is."

"Someone who is fighting against the government," he explained calmly, "someone who seeks to overthrow legal authority."

"I see. Well, yes, I suppose partisan is the word. I don't understand why people are so anti-Mussolini. He's done such a lot for this country and supported my industry. I wish we could just go back to the way we were."

"It must be very difficult for you," he said. "Very frustrating—as an artist."

"It is!" She was warming to her sense of injustice.

"Now, these partisans…" he began, refilling her glass, "…have you met any? Here in Rome, perhaps?"

"Oh no, I don't think so." She took another mouthful of wine. She knew Vicenzo was on the left and was therefore anti-Fascist. Did that make him a partisan? She realized she must say nothing that might endanger him. Her head began to spin. "As you say, I'm just an actress, what do I know about it?"

"Oh, I think you know more than you realize." Wolff looked deeply into her eyes. "I sense there is something you wish to tell me—am I right?"

Her mother's advice came back to her: "… all it would take would be a word from you…"

"It's only that," she faltered, "I'd hate to be responsible for getting someone into trouble."

"Of course you would," he said kindly. "But think of it this way—if someone is innocent, they will come to no harm. On the other hand, if people are trying to cause trouble, they need to be stopped—or you get anarchy. You wouldn't want that, would you?"

She shook her head. "There may be someone in Florence." The words tumbled out of her.

"Ah, Florence! Another beautiful city," Karl's voice took on a dreamy quality. "One of my favorites, although it's not as beautiful as Rome." He poured more wine into her glass.

"I don't know Florence at all," said Isabella. "I've never been there, can you believe it?"

"Oh you should go. We could go together and visit the museums and art galleries." Wolff leaned forward. "Now you must tell me, who in Florence might be working against us? I can assure you that if they are innocent no harm will come to them."

Isabella felt a flicker of anxiety, but her head was spinning and she just wanted the questions to stop. "I don't know any names or anything."

He paused, waiting for her to fill the silence.

"She's a student I think," she went on tentatively. "Students, they're not living in the real world, are they? I could have been a student—I was very academic at school. But I had to go to work in the film industry at sixteen. I don't think students understand what it is to work hard all your life to make something of yourself."

"I agree," he said. "It's obvious to anyone how intelligent you are. It must be very frustrating to feel that one's work is not appreciated anymore, particularly when you have worked so hard."

"It is!" replied Isabella, relieved to get the conversation back onto neutral ground. "I feel completely redundant, if I'm honest. There's no work here anymore. I don't know what I'm going to do."

"Just indulge me a moment longer," Wolff cajoled. "This student in Florence, do you have a name?"

Isabella felt light-headed, as if she might faint. She thought about Vicenzo and how he had laughed at her that night in front of his friends; of how he had told them about the bright, fiery young girl called Livia.

"Livia," she murmured, not sure if she had actually said the name out loud.

"Livia," Wolff repeated gently. "Do you have a surname?"

"No, but I think her father is a lawyer—a liberal lawyer. He's an old friend of someone I know...someone who is completely innocent."

"And who is that?"

"Vicenzo Lucchese..." The name was out before Isabella realized what she had said. She felt mortified.

"Well done," Wolff said, patting her hand. "Your loyalty does you credit. It will not be forgotten."

The following morning, Isabella woke with a terrible headache. As she hauled herself up in bed, she noticed her dress lying abandoned on the floor. She had no memory of either taking it off, nor of getting home. Someone had presumably driven her, but she couldn't remember who it was. Stefano perhaps?

Isabella's mouth was dry. Reaching out to her bedside table, she fumbled for a glass of water and took a sip. Slowly the details of the evening filtered back to her. She remembered sitting next to Wolff at dinner, but what had they talked about? He had suggested they visit Florence together...something she would have to extricate herself from, she thought.

Climbing out of bed, she walked unsteadily to the bathroom. Catching sight of herself in the mirror, she suddenly remembered the conversation about Livia. "Oh what have I done," she muttered to herself. Overcome by nausea, she retched and vomited violently into the basin. She wiped her mouth and splashed her face with water. Stumbling back to bed, she pulled the covers over her head and tried desperately to reassure herself she had done nothing wrong. After all, there must be hundreds of girls in Florence called Livia. It would be impossible to trace her from just her Christian name.

Isabella finally dozed off, only waking when her mother opened the curtains. Light streamed into the room.

"What are you still doing in bed? It's nearly lunchtime. Don't you have any work to do?"

"No, Mamma," Isabella said, rolling over and covering her eyes with her hands. "I've told you, there are no films being made."

"Well, there are plenty of jobs to do in the house. You should get up, Isabella. Oh, and you just missed a phone call. Your friend Vicenzo rang." Her mother smiled. "If I were you, I'd get up and ring him back."

"What did he want?" Isabella asked, her heart suddenly racing. Her mother winked. "He's invited you to lunch tomorrow."

Isabella was overwhelmed with relief. If Vicenzo had rung her, obviously nothing terrible had happened to Livia. And more importantly, if Vicenzo had invited her to lunch, perhaps he did still love her after all.

Giovanna was reading the newspaper in the kitchen when Isabella came down for breakfast the following day.

"Look at this," cried her mother, throwing the newspaper across the table. "That man's a disgrace."

Isabella saw the headline on the front page.

King Deserts Capital

Reading the article, it appeared that the King and Queen had fled Rome and gone into hiding, along with the Prime Minister, Marshal Badoglio.

"The old rogue has run away and deserted his people," said Giovanna, going over to the stove and stirring a pot of soup.

"There's another headline, Mamma," Isabella went on. " 'Italian forces have been defending the capital against German troops.' " She looked at her mother fearfully. "They say in the article, there was fighting in Rome last night. 'The situation is perilous,' it says. I didn't hear anything last night, did you?"

Giovanna shook her head. "So, it seems the Germans will be in charge soon enough. Lucky for us that you have so many useful German friends."

"Do you think so?" Isabella said anxiously.

"Of course, they know you're a loyal Fascist."

"Am I?" asked Isabella. "Is that what you think?"

"Yes," said her mother. "And very sensible too. You're on the right side."

As Isabella skirted Villa Borghese, on her way to have lunch with Vicenzo, German troops were setting up a military encampment in the park. Clearly her mother was right—the Germans had taken over.

Walking up the drive of Vicenzo's villa, she felt nervous and excited. The dogs were lying on the porch steps as usual and rose to greet her.

Vicenzo answered the door wearing a dark shirt, open at the neck. He looked tanned but tired, she thought. He kissed her on both cheeks.

"I've missed you," she said.

"I've missed you too," he replied automatically. He took her coat and led her through to the sitting room. It felt like old times and gradually she began to relax. She convinced herself that nothing bad could have happened to Livia. She almost began to believe that the whole experience had been a terrible dream.

"Have you heard the news?" she asked.

"Of course," he replied gloomily, handing her a cocktail. He slumped on the sofa opposite her.

"There are German troops in the park. What are they doing there?"

"They're not just in Rome, they're massing all over Italy." He appeared angry, his tone sarcastic. "Rome is an 'open city,' apparently—that's a joke. Basically, we've been overrun."

"But the Germans have no quarrel with us, surely? We were their allies until a day or so ago."

Vicenzo looked at her wide-eyed. "I don't understand you sometimes," he said. "Do you know nothing? Our government is in tatters. The King and Prime Minister have run away. The Anglo-Americans have demanded our capitulation, in return for which they will deal more sympathetically with us when this is over. But in the meantime, we are at war with the Germans, Isabella. War. And believe me, it's only just begun."

Unnerved, she changed the subject. She tried to amuse him with funny stories about fellow actors, and indiscretions of colleagues, anything to avoid mentioning the war. But he seemed distracted, uninterested. Eventually, she decided to broach the one subject she had been avoiding.

"Did you have a good time in Florence over the summer?"

"Why do you ask?"

"The night of your party, you mentioned you were going to meet a girl called Livia in Florence."

"Did I? Well, yes, it was her father I went to meet, not the girl. In the end I saw them at their villa in the country. Why, what's it to you?" He sounded defensive, irritable.

"I just remember you saying how much you liked her, how bright and 'fiery' she was." Isabella stared deep into his eyes, looking for some kind of clue about his feelings.

"I have no memory of that." He looked at her, bewildered. "I suppose she is quite bright. I've never thought about it. I've known her since she was a child. She's very sweet, but just an ordinary girl."

Isabella blushed. "Really? I thought perhaps…" She ground to a halt suddenly realizing she had made a terrible mistake. "No, I'm sorry, it's nothing," she said. "So what did you do after Florence? Did you visit your family as you'd planned?"

While Vicenzo told her about his trip to Forte dei Marmi, Isabella's mind was a blur. It seemed that she had been completely wrong about Livia. She had put a young woman in danger for no reason. More importantly, she had given Vicenzo's name to a top German officer. She tried desperately to convince herself that no harm would come to either of them—especially if, as Wolff had said, Livia was innocent.

"Isabella?" Vicenzo touched her arm. "Isabella? Are you listening to me?"

"Yes, yes of course. You were telling me about Forte dei Marmi."

"Yes, I spent a few days there with my parents, although how long they will be able to keep that house open, I don't know. It's bizarre, the place goes on as if nothing is happening, but it can't last. I wish they would just leave and go abroad, to America maybe."

"But why?"

"Because nowhere in Italy is safe anymore, Isabella, and it's getting harder to know who can be trusted. What is certain is that the Germans are in charge now and we can't sit on the fence anymore. It's time to take sides."

Chapter Sixteen

The hills above Florence
September 1943

Livia had spent the morning sitting in the shade of the fig tree. Coming inside, her bare feet padded silently across the cold stone floors. She knocked on her father's study door. "It's me, Papa."

Giacomo had driven up from Florence the day before, arriving at sunset. Since then, he had been closeted in his study and she had hardly seen him.

"Come in," he called out, "and lock the door behind you."

Unusually, the windows were wide open, allowing a cool breeze to blow through the room. As she sat down on the chair opposite his desk, she could hear Luisa outside, calling for Angela.

"I'm glad you're here," said Giacomo softly, shuffling a pile of papers on his desk. "Can you close the window? I've got something to tell you and I don't want your mother to hear what I'm about to say."

Livia shut the window and drew the curtains. The room suddenly felt heavy and airless.

"I need to get back to the city as soon as possible," he said. "Tomorrow, ideally."

"Can I come with you?" Livia asked.

Giacomo looked at his daughter over the top of his spectacles. "Are you sure you want to?"

She nodded.

"I didn't tell your mother last night, but there are German troops in the city already, and there's a curfew in place."

"Troops? But I thought you said Florence would be of no interest to them."

"I was wrong," he admitted. "Would you rather stay here?"

"No," she said quickly. "I want to help. I can't just do nothing. Besides, Elena and Cosimo are there. I ought to be with them."

He studied her for a few moments. "Your mother would argue that your place is with her."

"I know, and I'm sorry about that. But I must go back... please take me with you."

"I will, don't worry. I thought you'd want to—and I'm very pleased, if I'm honest. We're going to need you, as the Pd'A is expanding its role. We need to be more than just a political party. We are organizing ourselves into a proper fighting force."

"Good," she said. "I've long thought we need to do more than argue our point intellectually."

"There's nothing wrong with making sure people know the truth—in fact it's vital if we are to bring the general population with us. But we must do more than publish a paper. The time has come to fight back." Giacomo looked into her eyes. "Listen Livia, I've been authorized by my colleagues to recruit you, along with other young people, to work as a staffetta."

"They only carry messages, don't they?" Livia sounded disappointed.

"They do carry messages, yes, but also guns and arms, and spare parts for printing presses, and they distribute the party newspaper of course. More importantly, I've arranged for you to take on a special job."

"What sort of job?"

"To monitor coded messages on the radio."

"Whose messages?" Livia asked, wide-eyed.

"The British Secret Service. They want to communicate information to the partisans about things like arms drops and sabotage attacks. The instructions will come in the form of random meaningless sentences. These are codes which only a few key people will understand and then act upon. But the sentences need to be transcribed exactly. I know you'd do it well."

Livia felt thrilled to be asked to do something so important. "Of course, Papa," she assured him.

"Before the coded message, they will play the opening bars of Beethoven's Fifth Symphony. Do you remember the tune?"

"Yes, I think so." She hummed a few notes. "*Da da da, daaaa.* Is that it?"

"Yes. It's an idea of Churchill's, the British Prime Minister, I'm told. Those notes represent the Morse code for the letter 'V.' Dot, dot, dot, dash."

Livia looked confused.

"V for Victory."

She smiled. "That's quite clever. When do I start?"

"As soon as we're back in Florence."

Livia left Giacomo's study suddenly full of energy. The days of living quietly in the country were over. She was going back to the city, with all the associated dangers and intrigue. It was everything she had hoped for.

Luisa, predictably, was against the whole idea of her husband and daughter returning to the city. She berated him that evening. "You must be mad, Giacomo. I can't believe you're going back—and taking Livia too. Apart from the risks to her safety, I need her here to help me with Alberto. I can't manage him by myself."

"I know that," replied Giacomo. "But I've found you a nurse."

"A nurse? I don't want a stranger here," she protested.

"So you would rather cope by yourself?"

"No, but..." She leaned back in her chair, sensing she would not win this particular argument.

"Good," he said firmly. "I'm glad that's settled."

Livia and Giacomo arrived back in Florence the next afternoon. As they drove into the center of the city, they had to stop the car to allow columns of German troops to march past. As their boots hit the cobbles, Livia felt an almost visceral hatred for them.

"Stare straight ahead," her father advised her. "Don't catch their eye."

"I can't bear it," she murmured.

"I know," he said, patting her knee affectionately. Livia squeezed her father's hand until the soldiers had finally disappeared, strutting round the corner toward the Duomo. "Let's get moving," he said. "The curfew begins soon."

Back at the apartment building, Livia opened the family postbox and was thrilled to find a letter from Cosimo.

My darling Livia,

Hopefully you will get this when you return from the country. I hear from Elena you had a wonderful time together. You'll be glad to hear I have not been idle over the summer. There have been improvements in my condition, which I am keen to share with you. The one advantage of my injuries is that I have been officially discharged from the army and I can return to university to complete my studies. Shall we meet on the first day of term—in the main entrance hall?
I can't wait to see you.

With all my love,
Cosimo.

Livia kissed the letter and slipped it into her pocket. She unpacked her clothes and began to cook the food they had brought with them for supper. The apartment felt strangely quiet without her mother there—although it was a relief not to have to conceal her radio activity. After she and her father had eaten, she went up to the attic to monitor the BBC broadcast. The roof of the Duomo was lit by a brilliant red-ochre sky, with starlings performing their evening ritual, swooping and diving over the rooftops. Livia found it hard to believe Florence had been overrun by such a hostile enemy. Down below, the streets were silent, as Florentines retreated to their houses, fearful of the German soldiers policing their beautiful city.

Livia switched on the attic radio and tuned into Radio Londra, making notes from the news bulletin as usual. The news was followed by the "V" signal of Beethoven's Fifth Symphony, announcing that evening's coded messages. "The hen has laid an egg," "The cow does not give milk." She carefully noted them, handing them to her father along with her news summary for the partisan paper.

"That's very good," said Giacomo. "I'll put it in the paper on the second page. It's going to press tomorrow. Could you take the text to the printer first thing in the morning?"

"But you always go to the printer," she replied.

"I do normally. But I have so much to do before the conference next week. Can you do it?"

"Of course," she said, "I won't let you down."

"I know," he replied.

The following morning, Livia woke early and hurried to the printer's offices, checking constantly that she was not being followed. The office was in an unobtrusive building down a small side street. When she was confident there was no one else around, she knocked on the door.

"I'm coming, I'm coming." The disembodied voice from inside was deep and gruff. "Who's there?" he asked warily.

"Livia," she said. "My father, Giacomo, sent me."

She heard bolts being slid back, and the door swung open to reveal a short stocky man, his hands covered with printer's ink.

"Come in," he said, peering out into the street. "You weren't followed?"

"No...no one saw me," she reassured him.

The tiny room was dominated by a black metal printing press. There was a large table at one end covered in blocks of type.

"I hope I'm not too late for *L'Italia Libera*," she said hurriedly. "I've got one more story for the paper."

The printer sighed. "I've got the layout all organized," he said irritably, nodding toward the letterpress blocks. "And I've got another job coming in at lunchtime."

"I'm so sorry, but my father was rather insistent."

"All right. Give me the text then."

"He told me to tell you it's for the second page," she said, handing over her typescript.

"It's the latest news, I presume."

"Yes, from Radio Londra."

"I'll have five hundred papers printed by lunchtime. Will you be back to collect them?"

"Yes."

"Do you know where to take them?"

"I do—28, Via Paganini."

The printer nodded. "Bring a pram, or something you can hide them in."

Livia spent the afternoon in the tiny apartment on Via Paganini with two other members of the Pd'A. Their task was to find ways of disguising the newssheets, so they could be safely distributed—putting them into innocent-looking envelopes, slipping them inside regular newspapers, or even hidden within the covers of Fascist hand-outs. These would then be delivered over the next few days to prearranged drop-off points. She returned home to find her father working, as usual, in the dining room.

"Did it go all right?" he asked.

"Yes," she replied. "I didn't run into any soldiers, fortunately, and the papers are all ready for distribution."

"Well done." Giacomo smiled at her. "I think it would be useful if you took the copy to the printer every week for me, from now on. I can get others to collect them and organize the distribution."

"I don't mind doing it," Livia said.

"No, I have something else in mind for you."

Livia was intrigued.

"Tomorrow afternoon there's a meeting of the Pd'A staffettas. I'd like you to go and meet them all." He handed her a piece of paper with the address.

The meeting was held in a tall ornate building near the railway station. Livia knocked on the impressive double doors. They were opened by a girl with striking red hair. "Come in," she said, peering outside into the street. "You're alone?"

"Yes." Livia thought she looked familiar. "I know you, don't I?"

"Yes, I'm in the year below you at university. I'm Rosa."

She led Livia down a stone staircase, lit only by oil lamps. The smell of burning oil was soon overwhelmed by the stench of damp. The basement was a large gloomy space, with an arched ceiling. Between the arches were wide bays lined with shelves, holding elaborate-looking gilded jars, glinting in the glow of the lamps.

"What is this place?" whispered Livia. "And what is in those jars?"

"It's the Society for the Cremation of Cadavers," said Rosa, winking. "And those jars are urns..."

"Seriously?" Livia shuddered.

"The president of the society is a leading member of our organization," Rosa continued. "That coffin there"—she pointed to a vast ornate oak coffin in the center of the room—"is filled with ammunition and weapons. Now, follow me—the meeting is being held in the next room."

Rosa pushed open a door and Livia heard female chatter. Through the gloom she could see twenty or so other young women—looking just like schoolgirls waiting to go on into class.

"Who are all these girls?" Livia asked.

"All sorts," Rosa explained. "Students like us, but also secretaries, shop girls, housewives..."

"I had no idea," said Livia. "I thought there might be a couple of us at most."

"Oh no! I suspect there are hundreds of us in little groups around the city. All desperate to do something to support the Resistance."

Rosa took Livia's arm and led her to a woman with short dark curly hair, dressed in trousers and a cream shirt. She looked strong and capable, Livia thought.

"Adreana," said Rosa, "this is Livia."

"Ah good, we've been expecting you, thanks for coming."

Adreana grabbed a chair and stood up on it in the center of the room. "Hello everyone," she announced. "My name is Adreana and

I'm delighted to see so many of you here today. You're all here because you want to support the Resistance movement."

The young women smiled and nodded.

"Many of you have brothers or husbands fighting in the war—young men who are disillusioned and angry. Now it's your turn to do something about it. The Germans are working alongside the Fascist Italian police to control us. Our job is to fight back—disrupt where we can. But secrecy is paramount; no one can be trusted. Already we are hearing stories of cells of partisans being infiltrated and betrayed by spies." The girls looked at each other disbelievingly. "I know it seems incredible," said Adreana, "but trust no one—only each other."

Livia's life was suddenly filled with urgent, adrenaline-fueled work. It was everything she had hoped for over the summer, as she sat up in the peaceful hills fearing life was passing her by. She monitored broadcasts and coded messages. She wrote for the Pd'A newspaper. From time to time, she was assigned the job of delivering caches of weapons, and even bombs and grenades. The safest method of concealing such illegal cargo was in a pram, hidden under a toy baby wrapped in blankets. But one of Livia's colleagues—a young mother named Maria—was happy to put her own baby, a charming one-year-old named Francesco, on top of the weapons.

One day, Livia and Maria were delivering a pramful of grenades to some Resistance fighters in a hideout near the Arno. As they walked toward the drop-off point, they were approached by a pair of German soldiers.

Livia touched Maria's arm anxiously.

"Don't worry," said Maria calmly. "Francesco will deal with them."

The young men stopped, leaned into the pram and admired the baby, who gurgled appreciatively.

"What else do you have in there?" one of the soldiers asked.

"Only bombs," Maria said coolly, winking at him.

The soldiers laughed and moved on.

Livia and Maria safely delivered their cargo, hugging each other afterward, delighted by their daring and luck.

It was the first day of the winter term, and Livia approached the university building with mixed feelings. She was excited at the prospect of seeing Elena and Cosimo again, but less enthusiastic about the prospect of attending lectures and writing essays. Her life in the Resistance had superseded everything else. The entrance hall echoed with the voices of hundreds of young people arriving for their first day of term. She recognized several of her fellow *staffettas*, but they had all been briefed to behave normally, ignoring each other in public. Rosa walked past her and briefly touched her hand, glancing sideways and smiling at their shared secrets.

Looking around her, Livia finally spotted Cosimo leaning against a marble column and ran over to him.

"Livia darling," he said, embracing her. "I'm so happy to see you."

"And I you, it's been far too long. You look different somehow," she said playfully, standing back and admiring him. "I know what it is, you aren't using your crutches."

He laughed and raised his trouser leg, revealing a wooden foot inserted into his shoe, and above it the beginnings of a jointed metal ankle. Livia bent down and touched it. "Can you really walk on it?" she asked, gazing up at him.

"Of course." He walked a few faltering steps with the aid of his stick.

"Well done," she said, applauding him. "I'm so proud of you."

"I'm lucky to have a father who is a doctor and could pull some strings, otherwise I don't know how long I'd have had to wait."

"Let's go and make use of it. We could go to our favorite place for coffee. I want to hear all your news."

They went to Café Paskowski and sat at a table outside in the sunshine.

"So," she began, "what's been happening?"

"To me, very little. I've been stuck here getting my foot fitted, nothing else. What about you? How did you and Elena get on?"

"Most of the time we lay in the garden or went for walks. And my mother got us making jam. If I'm honest, I think Elena was a bit bored. She went home after a couple of weeks."

"I hear you had an interesting visitor." Cosimo smiled playfully.

"Who do you mean?" Livia had sworn Elena to secrecy about Vicenzo's visit and was irritated that she had obviously broken her promise.

"A famous film director?" prompted Cosimo casually.

"Oh him, well, he's just an old family friend. Nothing more. I don't know why she bothered to mention it." There was an awkward silence as the waiter put down their coffees. Livia decided to change the subject. "My grandfather had a stroke."

"I'm sorry." Cosimo took her hand. "Is he all right?"

"He's getting better. My mother tried to convince me I should stay with her to care for him. Fortunately, my father found a professional nurse."

"That was lucky—I can't imagine you as a nurse, somehow..."

"No." She sipped her coffee, unable to think of anything else to say. It was as if there was suddenly a barrier between them. It wasn't only her annoyance that he knew about Vicenzo's visit, it was also that she couldn't share the main focus of her life—her work for the Pd'A.

"Look," she said, squeezing his hand, "I can't stay much longer. I've got a lecture in ten minutes, but let's meet for lunch."

"Of course," he replied cheerfully, but Livia could see he was disappointed.

A dog barked nearby. Livia looked up and noticed a group of men dressed in black on the other side of the piazza. She recognized the uniform of the Banda Carità, a local unit of the Italian Fascist police, headed by Mario Carità, a man with a reputation as a sadistic torturer. They were walking purposefully toward the café.

Unnerved, Livia drained her coffee cup, and stood up. "Let's go." She put a couple of coins onto the little saucer with the bill.

Cosimo struggled to his feet, clutching his stick.

Suddenly the policemen were upon them. "Livia Moretti?"

"Yes," she said, turning to face them.

"You are under arrest. Come with us."

Her arms were pinioned behind her. Cosimo tried to pull her away, but one of the policemen shoved him, and he fell awkwardly onto the ground, revealing his prosthetic foot.

"Keep out of this," said the officer. "Were you injured fighting for the Fatherland?"

"I was in Russia, yes," said Cosimo.

"Then our argument is not with you," said the officer, helping him to his feet. "Go on your way."

They began to drag Livia, kicking and screaming, across the square.

"Go to my father, Cosimo," she yelled over her shoulder, "and tell him what's happened."

Livia was bundled into a police car and driven through the streets of Florence, finally arriving at an anonymous cream stone building on Via Bolognese. Known locally as "Villa Triste"—the sad house—it had at one time been used by the army, but was now the headquarters of the Fascist police. She had heard rumors from colleagues in the Pd'A about what might happen if you were picked up by the police and taken there.

She was pushed into a featureless waiting room, with off-white walls and a tiled floor. There was an officer behind a wooden desk, but he scarcely looked up from his work, as she sat down nervously on one of the wooden chairs. Looking around, she noticed an ill-lit corridor leading off the waiting room, with doors on either side. She assumed they were the infamous interrogation rooms, as she could hear occasional cries of pain. Now her mind began to race with frightening scenarios. If she were interrogated, would they torture her and could she resist? What would she say to stop the pain?

The man at the desk appeared unconcerned by the noises down the corridor; it was as if he was in a soundproofed box. As Livia waited, and the minutes turned to hours, she agonized about why she had been arrested. Could it be her membership of the Pd'A, or her involvement with the newspaper? Perhaps the printer had been arrested and given her away? Or had they somehow discovered she was monitoring foreign broadcasts—an illegal activity punishable with prison and a costly fine. She resolved to deny everything, and hoped that if they searched the apartment, they would not find the radio. It was well hidden in the attic.

"Livia Moretti, come with me!" She looked up to see a short, pudgy-faced man dressed in a black uniform. He led her down the corridor. He stopped outside a metal door and unlocked it, revealing a small room with a tiny barred window high up on one wall. She glimpsed blue sky and a cloud scudding across, invitingly. There were two chairs in the center of the room, and a table to one side, on which lay a set of electric cables and a block of wood studded with vicious-looking nails flecked with blood.

Livia began to sweat.

"Sit there," the officer said, indicating one of the chairs.

She sat down, her legs primly together, her sweating hands clasped in her lap. Her mouth was very dry. She wanted a drink, she wanted her mother, her father, anyone.

"We have received some information," he said, sitting down opposite her, brandishing a typewritten document. He lolled—his legs apart, sweat marks spreading around his waistband and shirt. "It concerns you," he went on.

"Really?" she asked calmly.

"Shall I tell you what it's about?" he said, glancing at the paper.

"I wish you would," she replied boldly.

"That you are involved in the partisan movement."

She felt light-headed, dizzy, her heart racing. She tried to calm herself.

"That's absurd," she replied. "I'm just a student."

"We have been given information from a very authoritative source that you are involved in partisan activities, and that you are working with a group in Rome."

"That's nonsense," she said firmly. "I don't know anyone in Rome."

He raised one eyebrow quizzically.

Somewhere in the distance, she thought she could hear her father's voice, shouting. But it could have been her imagination.

"Your father is a lawyer, I understand."

"Yes," she replied.

"A *liberal* lawyer," he said accusingly.

"He is kind, if that's what you mean. He looks after those who cannot defend themselves."

"He is also political, I think?" The officer looked down at his notes.

"Not especially," she replied, wondering what evidence they could have found against her father. "He tries to remain above politics." She paused. "Who told you these lies about me?"

"You are brave," he said curtly, "but a little too bold for someone in your position. I would try harder to be more helpful if I were you. Wait here."

He left the room, but a guard remained standing by the door. He had a fleshy neck that protruded from his shirt collar, and thick lips that he licked from time to time like a lizard. Livia tried not to look at him.

"I need to go to the bathroom," she said eventually.

He looked over her head and smiled. "Go on then." He made it sound like a challenge.

"Here?" she asked, appalled.

He shrugged.

She squeezed her legs together, regretting the coffee she had drunk a couple of hours earlier.

The short officer with the pudgy face returned. He sat down opposite her and leaned back in his chair. "You will stay here until you have told us what we want to hear," he said simply.

"But I don't know what you want to hear. I haven't done anything," she cried out. "I'm innocent. How can I tell you something that isn't true?"

"Think about it," he said, as he left the room.

The thick-lipped guard returned, clutching a china pot which he put in the corner of the room with a smirk. He walked out, locking the door behind him.

When night came, Livia lay down on the hard, tiled floor. She curled into a ball, her arms wrapped protectively around her knees,

as she had done as a child. Through the thick walls of her cell came
the screams of men and women, mingled with sadistic male laughter.

Livia must have fallen asleep, for she woke as the door was
thrown open with a clang, and a bowl was deposited on the floor.
Feeling hungry, she crawled over to the bowl which was filled with
a watery gray slop. She took a mouthful, but it tasted so disgusting,
her stomach heaved. Sitting back down on the floor, she tried to
calm herself by counting the number of tiles on the wall.

Two days passed, with the sweaty policeman continuing to question
her. She responded defiantly, protesting her innocence and demanding to see her father.

On the third morning, she heard the sound of keys in the lock.
She braced herself for another grilling. The policeman was now
accompanied by a man wearing the uniform of the Gestapo. It was
clear from his manner that the German would be leading that day's
interrogation. He spoke adequate Italian, but his questioning of her
simply went over old ground. When they had finished, the two men
stood in the doorway for a few moments, talking quietly together,
before leaving and locking the door behind them.

The following day, she once again woke to hear the keys in the
lock.

"Stand up," demanded the guard with the fleshy neck.

Her heart racing, her legs shaky, Livia followed him down the
corridor toward the waiting room. To her relief, her father was
standing by the desk. She ran to him and he embraced her, kissing
her hair. "It's all right, my darling, it's all right," he whispered.

The German officer emerged from the corridor. "Fortunately for
you, we have received new information that changes the situation,"
he said. "But you will report here every morning at nine o'clock
until further notice. Do you understand?"

"But I have lectures to go to," she protested.

Her father touched her arm. "She understands—she'll be here,
thank you."

Outside on the pavement, he guided her hurriedly across the road until they were out of sight of the building.

"What did he mean about 'new information'?" she whispered.

"Let's get home," her father said, "and I'll explain everything."

Back in the apartment, Livia ran a bath and lay soaking in the hot water. She washed her hair and brushed her teeth. She changed her clothes and put a little scent behind her ears to dispel the sour stench of Villa Triste. Her father was waiting for her in the sitting room.

"You must be hungry," he said. He pushed a plate of bread and a small piece of ham toward her.

"Ham? Where did you get this?"

"A contact of mine. I wanted something nice for you."

She smiled. "Black-market food, Papa? I'm surprised at you! And grateful." She tore at the bread and devoured the ham greedily.

"Do you want a drink?" He handed her a glass of grappa. "You must need it. I know I do." He poured himself a large tumblerful, took a swig, and settled into his armchair.

"So tell me," she said. "Why did they arrest me? Was it the radio? The newspaper?"

"No, neither of them. It's Vicenzo."

"Vicenzo? Why?"

"It's complicated, but I will try to explain," Giacomo said wearily. He looked tired, she thought, older than his years. Suddenly, his hair seemed to have grown whiter. "It seems that an actress is in love with him. She heard him mention you, just in passing, and jumped to the wrong conclusion. She thought he was in love with you. Filled with jealousy, she decided to denounce you—she has connections with the German SS."

Livia sipped her drink. "Is it because we pretended to Mamma that he had a romantic interest in me?"

"No, I don't think so. But it helped to get you out."

"How?" She was confused.

"The police contacted Vicenzo in Rome—thank God he was still at his house. They asked about you and whether he knew you, and he told them you were an old friend. They asked if there was anything more to it—a more 'personal' relationship. He said that he was fond of you and had recently visited you. He was asked if you were in the partisan movement, which of course he said was nonsense. Eventually he was ordered to come to Florence, where he was interrogated by Carità himself. He managed to convince Carità that this actress was jealous of your relationship with him, and simply wanted you out of the way. Before he returned to Rome, he came to see me and told me the whole story, and asked me to convey his sincere apologies to you. He is desperately sorry, Livia—'distraught' was the word he used—that you should be dragged into this. To end up in the hands of a sadist like Mario Carità...it doesn't bear thinking about."

"Is that who interrogated me?" asked Livia. "Carità himself?"

"Yes. I don't understand why he didn't torture you. He has a terrible reputation."

"So I've heard," said Livia, sipping her drink.

"Your arrest will make life more difficult for everyone, particularly now you have to report to Villa Triste each day. You must be very careful. They will be watching us all, including Vicenzo. I think you should withdraw from the Pd'A for your own safety."

"No, Papa," Livia said immediately. "I still want to help."

"Livia—" Her father reached across and took her hand, his eyes filled with tears. "When you were locked up in that terrible place, I thought it would break my heart. The realization that I had brought you into danger was unbearable."

"But it wasn't your fault," Livia protested, "it was this crazy woman, whoever she is."

"As it turned out, yes. You were lucky—but it might just as well have been your work for the Pd'A. You must stay out of it now. If anything happened to you, I could never forgive myself—and your mother would never forgive *me*. Thank God she's not in Florence and doesn't need to know what's happened."

Livia knew it was pointless arguing with her father. A better strategy would be to comply and wait for his attitude to soften over time.

"Have you seen Cosimo?" she asked, changing the subject. "He looked so frightened when I was arrested."

"Yes, he came to find me straight away. I'm sure you'd like to see him."

She nodded.

"We'll go and see him now—would you like that?"

"Thank you, Papa."

"And tomorrow we will try to get back to normal. I have a lot of work to do, preparing for our first Pd'A conference here in Florence."

"I'd like to come," said Livia.

"No, you will not come," he said firmly. "You will report to the police and go to your lectures. For the next few weeks, or months, you will be the perfect student and the perfect citizen, do you understand?"

Chapter Seventeen

Rome
September 1943

The Germans had taken over Rome. Their troops were permanently billeted in the park surrounding Villa Borghese, and their military high command now occupied the luxury hotels nearby on the Via Veneto. The senior officers began to host glamorous receptions, inviting leading Italian Fascists and their supporters.

One morning, Isabella received an invitation to a dinner dance to be held that evening at Hotel Flora.

"I'm not going," she said to her mother, throwing the invitation down on the breakfast table. "It would be a betrayal."

"Of whom, exactly?" asked Giovanna.

"Vicenzo, and the people of Rome," she replied grandly.

"Don't be ridiculous," her mother said. "Look, the Germans are running things now, Isabella. You need to keep them on your side. You must go."

Early that evening, Isabella was lying upstairs on her bed, idly listening to the radio when her mother bustled into her bedroom.

"It's six o'clock already," Giovanna said. "That reception starts in an hour and a half."

"I already told you, I'm not going," Isabella replied petulantly.

"You are going," her mother insisted, selecting three evening dresses from Isabella's wardrobe. "And, more importantly, you're going to look like a movie star."

She draped the dresses over the sofa.

"Say what you like," said Isabella, swinging her legs out of bed, "I'm not going." She walked through to the bathroom and slammed the door. Fifteen minutes later she emerged, her hair arranged and her makeup immaculate.

"You've changed your mind then?" her mother muttered smugly.

Sighing, Isabella picked up one of the dresses—a full-length silver sheath.

As she slid into it, she admired her reflection in the cheval mirror. She had lost weight in the previous few months, and the dress, cut on the cross, skimmed across her hip bones elegantly.

"I won't enjoy it," she said gloomily to her mother.

"Don't be ridiculous!" Giovanna rummaged in Isabella's wardrobe. "There will be food and drink and dancing. Why shouldn't you enjoy it?" She turned and gazed at her daughter. "You look wonderful in that dress. Wear these." She threw a pair of silver sandals onto the bed alongside Isabella's white fox-fur wrap.

The lobby of the hotel, only recently an elegant meeting place for well-to-do Romans, was now packed with Germans in uniform. They stared at Isabella admiringly as she walked toward the ballroom. The last time she had been there was to audition for Vicenzo. She had avoided the hotel ever since, as it brought back memories that she preferred to bury—the embarrassing effects of the drug she took, her sense of failure at not getting the part. It was also, of course, the place where she had first met the man she loved.

At the entrance to the ballroom, she handed her invitation to a soldier on the door, who announced her as "Fräulein Isabella Bellucci." She was startled to hear herself referred to as "fräulein" rather than "signorina." It was dramatic evidence that Rome had been completely taken over by a foreign power.

As Isabella's name was called, the other guests turned to stare at her—intrigued, she supposed, by her past fame. Mingling with the high-powered German officers were a sprinkling of other Cinecittà actors—like her, she presumed, doing their best to keep on the right side of the new regime. She spotted Doris Duranti, striking in a scarlet gown, hanging on the arm of her lover, Alessandro Pavolini. When she saw Isabella, she plunged through the crowd to meet her.

"Isabella," she said, kissing the air on either side of her face. "How lovely to see you. It's been far too long. I didn't realize you were part of this crowd."

Isabella, who had never liked Doris, was uncertain how to respond. She didn't consider herself "part of this crowd" and was unclear why she had been invited at all. Before she could respond, she found Karl Wolff suddenly at her side.

He bowed and kissed her hand. "Isabella, how delightful you look."

Suddenly her invitation made sense.

"How nice to see you again," she replied uncertainly.

Doris smiled knowingly and drifted back to her group who gathered excitedly around her to hear the latest gossip.

Wolff began to chat animatedly, but out of the corner of her eye, Isabella noticed Doris's friends staring at her. Clearly they were fascinated to see the woman who had caught the eye of the Supreme Commander of SS Forces in Italy.

Isabella was seated next to Wolff at dinner. Their table included a number of other leading German and Fascist figures, including Pavolini. The talk was all of the imminent release of Mussolini.

"He'll be set up in the north," Pavolini said, "on Lake Garda. The situation in Rome is a little too unpredictable, but we'll soon have it under control. Our distinguished friend here," he continued, turning toward Karl Wolff, "will be escorting him on his journey, isn't that right?"

"I have that honor," Wolff nodded. "I hear you've been promoted?"

Pavolini preened slightly. "Yes, I am now Secretary of the Fascist Republic." Doris kissed his cheek, then turned to Isabella.

"Have you heard the news about Count Ciano?" she asked pointedly. "I know you're a friend of his."

"Not a friend exactly," replied Isabella, "and no, I haven't heard anything recently."

"He's been arrested. All that bitchy talk of his about Il Duce has come back to bite him. Mussolini is out for his blood."

Isabella was genuinely shocked. She had never like Ciano much, and being forced to be part of his little court at the golf club hadn't been easy, but she didn't wish ill on the man. "But he's Mussolini's son-in-law. Can't his wife help him? Surely, Il Duce couldn't harm the husband of his own daughter?" she asked earnestly.

"Oh, of course she's begging her father for mercy, but Il Duce doesn't take disloyalty lightly," Doris said with relish.

"What disloyalty? I know Ciano could be a bit cruel and mocking sometimes—he had a wicked tongue—but he always had Il Duce's, and the country's, best interests at heart," insisted Isabella.

"You really are the most silly girl," said Doris. "Ciano was one of the ringleaders of the coup against Mussolini! The King asked his ministers to vote—kick Mussolini out or keep him in position. The majority, including Ciano, voted out. Now the King's run away, Mussolini is back and Ciano can't survive. His execution is certain—at least, that's what Alessandro says."

Isabella sat back in her chair, bewildered; her world was imploding.

"And have you heard about Cinecittà studios?" Doris went on.

Isabella looked at her blankly.

"The technicians have stolen all the equipment and costumes—isn't that disgraceful?"

"Well, they have no work anymore," said Isabella. "Perhaps they needed the money."

"What an extraordinary attitude!" declared Doris. "There's a plan for the studios to be turned into a camp for the displaced, isn't there Alessandro?" She gazed at him, picking a piece of thread off his sleeve.

He nodded. "It seems the sensible thing to do," he murmured.

"But, excitingly," Doris continued, "there's talk of Cinecittà being revived in the north! Freddi is working on it, isn't he Alessandro?"

"Give him time, my dear," said Pavolini. "There is much to be done first."

*

After dinner, the band struck up, playing a medley of classical German waltzes. Wolff invited Isabella to dance and, although reluctant, she realized she couldn't refuse him in front of Doris and the other guests. Isabella had to admit he was a good dancer, firm and decisive, but he held her too close and his hand strayed a little too much from her waist as he guided her around the floor. She yearned to be released.

Finally, at midnight, she made her excuses. "I'm sorry, I have the most terrible headache and really must go."

"So soon?" Wolff was clearly disappointed. "I insist that my driver takes you home, and tomorrow we will visit the Cranach exhibition at Villa Borghese. Those are the only terms on which I will allow you to leave."

"Then I accept," she said weakly.

"Tomorrow at the Villa Borghese then? One o'clock... will that suit?"

Isabella arrived at the gallery a little early. She was wearing a pale-gray linen suit. It was flattering without being provocative.

In the entrance hall, she was surprised to see someone she recognized sitting on a bench. It was a good friend of hers, Gianni Cini. He had his head in his hands and appeared to be weeping.

"Gianni!" she said, sitting down next to him. "What's the matter?"

"Oh Isabella, it's you. Such terrible, terrible news."

"Tell me," she said gently. "What's happened?"

"My father, Vittorio, he's been sent to Dachau."

Isabella put her arm around her friend's shoulders. "I don't understand," she said. "What is Dachau?"

"It's a camp... a terrible prison camp in Germany."

"That's awful, but why?" she asked. "What has he done?"

"No one will tell us," wailed Gianni.

"But wasn't he one of Mussolini's ministers?"

"Yes, the Minister of Communications, but Mussolini always hated him. Now that Il Duce has been reestablished by the Germans in the north, they've decided to get rid of him." He began to sob. "He'll never survive a place like that, he's an old man, Isabella."

Isabella remembered her conversation the previous evening with Doris about Count Ciano's arrest. So, now two of Mussolini's ex-ministers were potentially at risk of death.

"Let me see what I can do," she said soothingly.

"How could you possibly help?" asked Gianni, looking up at her with surprise.

"I'm not sure exactly, but I know someone who might have some influence."

After Gianni had left, Isabella waited nervously in the lobby for Karl Wolff. She would charm him, she decided, and persuade him to save her friend's father. He swept in on the dot of one o'clock, walking briskly over to her. He clicked his heels, bowed his head and kissed her hand. His lips lingered slightly before he straightened up.

"How lovely you look," he said.

"Thank you," she replied politely. "Shall we go in? I'm looking forward to seeing the exhibition through the eyes of such an expert."

They spent the next hour exploring the gallery's ground-floor rooms, before Wolff suggested they move upstairs.

"The Cranachs are on display up there and I'm anxious to show them to you."

They climbed the grand staircase to the upstairs galleries, their footsteps echoing on the wooden floors. They stopped in front of Cranach's painting of the Crucifixion.

"Ah," said Wolff, "this is Cranach's 'Centurion at the Cross.' A starkly realistic representation of Christ's final moments."

"One can't fail to be moved by it," said Isabella appreciatively.

"It's always useful, I think, to be reminded of our Lord's suffering," Wolff continued. "Have you seen Cranach's 'The Arrest of Christ'? It's not here sadly, but in a gallery in Austria."

She shook her head.

"It's a wonderful work, a profound representation of betrayal, of course."

"Judas's betrayal, you mean?"

The word betrayal hung in the air. She sensed he was waiting for her to ask about Livia, but her guilt made her too frightened to bring it up.

"We tracked down that girl by the way," he said suddenly. "The girl you told us about in Florence."

"Really?" Isabella replied, her heart racing.

"She denied everything of course, as you'd expect." He glanced down at Isabella and took her arm. "Shall we take a look at the 'Venus'?" He steered her toward a painting of a slender naked woman gazing down at Cupid. "The child," began Wolff, "is holding a honeycomb, while being stung by bees, do you see? The painting is an allegory on the pains and pleasures of love, or perhaps a warning about the perils of venereal disease... the temptress and the innocent child."

Isabella blushed. Was he implying that she was the temptress, and poor Livia the innocent child?

"You seem remarkably uninterested," he went on, "in our findings about this girl."

"Not at all," she said nervously. "It's just that I... well, I may have been too hasty."

"Too hasty?" He looked at her quizzically. "I thought you were doing your patriotic duty."

"That too, of course," she replied weakly.

"Well, as it happens, the other party came to her rescue."

"The other party?" asked Isabella uncertainly.

"The film director you mentioned. Although he is thought to have left-leaning tendencies, he is also a member of the aristocracy—a Count apparently. The family have a home not too far from Florence and are highly respected locally. He maintained that the girl is an old family friend with no interest in politics, and certainly not a partisan. He was merely visiting her over the summer for personal reasons."

"I see," said Isabella weakly.

He paused, still studying the painting. "He mentioned, during the course of his own interrogation, that an actress had become, what was the word he used?" He tapped his mouth rhythmically with his fingers. "Ah yes, that was it, 'infatuated' with him." He emphasized the word, as he turned to look at her. "He said that she was a fantasist. Basically, she made it all up." He smiled at Isabella, who looked away, embarrassed. "Anyway," he went on, "the girl was released, but we are keeping an eye on her—and that director friend of yours, of course, just in case."

Isabella nodded politely, while pretending to study the picture of Venus and Cupid. But her mind was not on the art. She had betrayed an innocent girl for the basest of motives—an unjustified jealousy—and now it seemed she had endangered the life of the person she loved most in the world. What must Vicenzo think of her? He had called her a fantasist. He would now surely despise her and never speak to her again. She felt light-headed, almost giddy with guilt and regret.

"Well," she said at last, "I'm sorry if I wasted your time. As I said, I must have been misinformed." She wanted to get out of the building there and then—to run across the park, and throw herself on Vicenzo's mercy.

"She may still be guilty, of course," Wolff mused, his gray eyes sparkling. "No smoke without fire, isn't that what they say? So don't worry, if she is up to something, we'll find out."

Wolff guided her to the next painting—a pastoral scene featuring naked men and women dancing around a tree.

"'Primitive Man'—another Cranach," said Wolff. "It's charming, isn't it? I like the way the adults are almost childlike in their innocence."

He stood so close to her, she was aware of his soft breathing, of the rough texture of his wool jacket pressing against her linen sleeve. She wished then that she could go back to an age of innocence. A time before she had committed her own venal sins. Suddenly, she remembered the promise she had made to her friend Gianni. She had an opportunity, if she was brave enough, to make amends by helping her old friend, even if it brought her into danger.

"I wonder," she began nervously, "if I might ask a small favor."

"Another one?" Wolff replied, raising his eyebrows in surprise.

She ignored his sarcasm. "I have an old friend, Gianni Cini. His father, Vittorio was one of Mussolini's ministers. He has been arrested, and worse still, sent to somewhere called Dachau."

"Oh dear," said Wolff. "I'm afraid I know nothing about that."

"Of course, I wasn't implying it was your decision in any way. I simply wondered . . . if a mistake had been made. He is a loyal Fascist, you see—surely it can't be right. They're a very good family, wealthy and well-connected."

He turned to look at her, studying her heart-shaped face and clear blue eyes. "That makes two favors I've granted you," he said, laughing. "I shall expect a favor in return."

She felt a rising sense of panic, as she imagined the sort of "favor" he might have in mind.

"I will make some inquiries," he said.

"I'd be so grateful," she replied. "Thank you so much, Herr Wolff."

"Call me Karl... please."

Isabella spent the next couple of days in a turmoil of indecision. She reproached herself for the arrest of Vicenzo's friend—an innocent girl, as it turned out. That she had also inadvertently brought *him* into danger made it worse still. She walked past Vicenzo's house several times, intending to go in, to confess her sin, to beg his forgiveness. But her nerve failed her on each occasion, and she returned home and shut herself away in her bedroom, refusing even to come out for meals.

On the third day, Giovanna grew impatient with her daughter. Instead of leaving her food on a tray outside the door as she had been doing, she barged in and found Isabella lying on her bed in the half-light, her face streaked with tears.

"What is the matter with you?" she demanded, putting a cup of coffee on her bedside table. "You go out, you come back, you don't speak, you hardly eat—I'm worried about you."

"You shouldn't be," said Isabella self-pityingly. "I don't deserve your sympathy."

"Don't be ridiculous!" Her mother opened the curtains. "It's a beautiful autumn day out there. Get up, get dressed. Go to the club," she urged. "See your friends."

"No," Isabella said gloomily, rolling over away from the bright light. "I only get into trouble when I go there."

"I don't know what you're talking about," said her mother briskly. "Put on a dress and some lipstick and go!"

The following afternoon, Isabella finally relented and drove to the Acquasanta.

Nothing at the club seemed to have changed. As usual, the tennis pros sat around the bar, chatting with their clients. A bridge game was going on in one corner.

Isabella settled herself on a bar stool and was soon joined by Stefano.

"Isabella darling," he began eagerly. "Have you heard the latest?"

"No," she said, "but I'm sure you're going to tell me, anyway."

"Well," he began, ignoring her barbed comment, "I'm not sure if it was that chap we met the other day—Wolff was it? But someone high up in the SS has made a grab for all the Jewish gold in Rome."

"What on earth do you mean?" asked Isabella.

"The heads of all the Jewish families have had to cough up their gold—fifty kilos of the stuff, I hear. It was either that or..." He made a swiping gesture across his neck. "Drink, darling?"

Isabella thought it unlikely it was an initiative of Wolff's. He was a senior SS officer, of course, but he had seemed so cultured and charming, honorable even. Surely, she thought, he couldn't be guilty of common theft.

She joined a game of bridge with a group of elderly women who, to her relief, avoided discussing politics—but she struggled to keep her mind on the game. Life had become a series of complexities, in which no one was as they seemed. Count Ciano, until recently the king of this particular court, and a relative of Mussolini himself, had been banished and was soon, apparently, to be executed. Vittorio Cini, a loyal government minister, had been sent to Dachau. And now, ordinary, good people had been robbed, simply because they were Jewish. No one, it appeared, was safe.

Toward the end of the afternoon, as the sun was setting over the greens, and the golf players began to assemble in the bar, Gianni

Cini rushed excitedly into the club lounge. "Isabella," he called out, "I must speak with you."

"I'm so sorry," she said to her bridge partners, "perhaps you could just play three-handed for a moment?" She took Gianni's arm and guided him to a quiet corner of the room where they could talk privately.

"I'm so glad to see you," he said. "I don't know what you did, or who you spoke to, but thank you, thank you." He kissed her on both cheeks.

"Why?" she asked. "What's happened?"

"He's been released! My father is on his way back to Italy now. We had to pay quite a lot of course—family jewels, some artworks—but he's a free man. And it's all thanks to you."

"Oh I'm so relieved, Gianni. All I did was have a word with a senior German officer I knew."

"Thank you," he repeated, taking her hands in his and kissing them. "And don't be so modest. You were prepared to stand up for something you believed in, to help a friend. I know what a risk you took, speaking out. Thank you from the bottom of my heart."

Isabella drove home that evening feeling she had redeemed herself in some small way. Nothing could make up for what she had done to Vicenzo or Livia, but at least she had helped Gianni. What was disturbing was the idea that Wolff appeared to be implicated not only in the theft of the Jewish gold, but of artworks too. Perhaps she had been wrong about him. He was not an honorable man after all, just an opportunistic thief. She had been wrong about so many things and it seemed that her faith in the SS Commander had been misplaced. She may have rescued Gianni's father and she was glad, but had she "supped with the devil"?

Chapter Eighteen

Florence
November 1943

The air was crisp and cold, the sky a cloudless blue, as Livia stepped out of Villa Triste into the autumn sunshine. Her registration at the offices of the Fascist police that morning had gone without a hitch, and instead of forcing her to wait, she had been able to sign the book and leave after just ten minutes. In spite of the pressures of the war, and the burden of having to report to the Fascist headquarters each day, she felt a momentary lightening of her soul as she walked past the Duomo, its cupola glowing in the morning sunlight. The doors to the cathedral were open and she could hear the priest intoning to the congregation. Outside, passers-by chatted, people stood at polished bars in cafés ordering their morning coffee, and all around her, men and women hurried through the streets on their way to work, or to queue up in shops.

Suddenly, over the everyday hubbub of people's voices, came the sound of engines. Rumbling at first, but growing louder and louder. She looked up instinctively, and within minutes the sky was filled with planes. Moments later, hundreds of paratroopers floated down toward the city. Shopkeepers, waiters, housewives and businessmen ran excitedly into the streets, thinking it was the Anglo-Americans. But as the first troops crashed to the ground, it soon became clear to everyone that these were German soldiers occupying their beautiful city and not Americans coming to their rescue.

Within hours, German tanks and armored cars were rumbling down the streets. Florence had been taken over.

*

Over the coming days, people became used to being stopped and interrogated at random by German troops, while their officers monopolized the best cafés and restaurants, forcing out the regular customers.

"We'll have to find somewhere else to go," Livia said gloomily to Elena one afternoon, as they walked toward Café Paskowski and found it filled with senior members of the Gestapo.

"I don't see why we should have to move." Elena glared at the officers behind the windows. "It's our place, not theirs. I hate them."

"We all hate them," Livia replied pragmatically. "But I'd rather not sit next to them."

Livia took Elena's arm, and led the way to a smaller, less grand restaurant on the other side of the square, and ordered coffee. They sat outside and stared glumly at their favorite meeting place. Small talk suddenly seemed irrelevant when face to face with the enemy. Besides, Livia had no small talk. Her thoughts were dominated by her work with the Resistance.

Two months after her arrest by the Fascist police, and her father's admonition that she should steer clear of any work for the Pd'A, Livia had slowly reintegrated herself. She was, once again, monitoring Radio Londra broadcasts and writing articles for the paper. She had even persuaded her father that she should be allowed to go out on patrol with her fellow *staffettas*.

"They need me, Papa," she had pleaded. "And I can't help them by staying at home."

He had finally relented, and she was now happily immersed in her important work, fitting in her university course when she could. But, inevitably, this had led to a sense of distance from both Cosimo and Elena.

Now, sitting opposite each other at the café table, neither Elena nor Livia felt like making conversation. They sat in silence, sipping their coffee and glowering at the Gestapo officers on the other side of the square.

"I found a copy of the underground paper, *L'Italia Libera*, this morning," whispered Elena eventually. "It was wrapped inside a Fascist leaflet—just left on a doorstep."

"Really? Was it interesting?" Livia asked innocently, for she had never mentioned her involvement with the paper to her friend.

"Very," said Elena.

"I hope no one saw you reading it."

"Of course not," Elena replied irritably. "I'm not stupid."

"No, of course you're not…sorry." Livia reached across the table and squeezed her hand.

"Anyway," Elena continued, "the point is, there was an awful story in the paper about Jewish citizens in Rome being rounded up and sent to a death camp in Poland—a place called Auschwitz."

Livia, who had actually written the piece herself, feigned surprise and horror. "That's terrible," she said.

"A couple of girls in our year are Jewish," Elena went on. "They must be worried, don't you think?"

"It must be very frightening," Livia agreed.

"Do you know Rebecca?" Elena asked.

"Not well, she's doing history, isn't she?"

"That's right. I knew her from school—she's such a nice girl. Her parents are terrified the same thing will happen in Florence. They've told her she's not allowed to come to university anymore. They're all in hiding at home."

"I'm so sorry," said Livia earnestly. "It's a tragedy. I just wish there was something we could do to help."

The two girls sipped their coffee, an awkward silence developing between them once more. It would have been natural to discuss how to rescue Rebecca and her family, but both held back, nervous of saying anything that could get them into trouble.

That evening, Livia mentioned Rebecca's plight to her father.

"There are so many Jewish people in the same position," he said. "And it's pointless them trying to hide in their homes. The authorities already know where they live. They will be rounded up sooner or later."

"Can't we do something?" Livia asked. "What's the point of the Resistance if we can't help these people?"

Livia arrived at Villa Triste the following morning as usual to sign the register. To her surprise she found a German soldier manning the desk. She had heard rumors that the SS were now operating out of Villa Triste, working alongside Carità's men. Clearly it was true.

She sat down on a wooden chair and waited. The guard deliberately ignored her, and by half past nine she was frustrated, angry and anxious to get to her lecture.

"Excuse me," she said to the soldier. "I've come to sign in." He ignored her. "Ich habe seit neun Uhr gewartet," she said, tapping her watch impatiently.

The soldier, startled by her use of German, looked up. "Du sprichst Deutsch?" he asked.

"Ja," she replied.

He stood up. "Warte dort." He left the waiting room, returning a few moments later with a senior German officer.

"Fräulein Moretti?" The officer spoke softly.

"Jawohl," she replied.

"Komm mit mir," he said, beckoning her toward him.

She was taken to a room that looked exactly like the one she had been incarcerated in a couple of months before. She felt a sickening sense of déjà vu as she was invited to sit down on a chair opposite the officer.

"I understand you speak good German, Fräulein," he said.

"Yes—what of it?"

"How did you learn our language?" he asked.

"I had a German governess when I was a child."

He nodded approvingly. "You will do something for us—to prove your loyalty to the Fatherland."

"What?" she asked nervously.

"You will act as an interpreter when we need one."

"Oh, I'm sorry, I couldn't do that," she apologized. "I'm a student—I have lectures to attend."

"That is not my concern," he replied dismissively. "Besides, we won't require you to work every day, but from time to time we will need your services. When you report here each morning, we will tell you what is needed."

Her mouth felt dry; perspiration was breaking out on her forehead.

"You may go," he said.

She stood up, and walked unsteadily across the room.

"And Fräulein," he called out, "perhaps now we will find out whose side you're on."

Somehow, Livia got through the rest of the day, but that evening, back at the apartment, she broke down. "Oh Papa, it was so frightening. I cannot work for them. It's impossible."

"I think you must. There is no alternative. Anything else would alert them to your true allegiances." Her father slumped down on a chair in the kitchen. "This is all my fault," he said dejectedly.

"How?" she asked gently.

"I should have left you in the countryside with your mother. Now I have brought you into terrible danger."

"I would have been no safer there, Papa. After what that actress told the Germans, they would have arrested me in the villa, which would have brought Mamma and Nonno into danger as well. At least here, Mamma need never know."

She sat down next to her father at the kitchen table, and put her arm around his shoulders. He looked helpless suddenly, his gray eyes filled with fear. "I'll make us some supper, shall I?" she asked cheerfully.

He smiled faintly. "Is there any food?"

"A little...not much." She had been saving a small ration of flour, which she began to mix with an egg to make dough, rolling it out and cutting it into strips.

"I didn't know you could make pasta," he said appreciatively.

"I haven't had to bother before, but I've watched Mamma for years."

Their meager supper over, they sat together in the sitting room—she on the sofa, a rug over her knees, a book open on her lap, and he in his favorite armchair nursing a glass of grappa.

He turned to her. "I need to ask you something," he began. "It's difficult..."

"Papa," she urged, "just ask me."

"We had a meeting of the Pd'A council yesterday. There's a feeling that we must do something for our Jewish neighbors here in Florence. We cannot allow what happened in Rome to happen here. Jewish people are in danger of being rounded up, herded onto trains and sent...God knows where."

"I agree," said Livia. "I wrote about it a couple of weeks ago."

"Yes, of course—I was forgetting." Her father continued: "We passed a resolution that our members would be asked to hide Jewish families in their homes. Not everyone can be protected, of course, but we must do what we can. I told the meeting you and I would be glad to consider sheltering a couple or even a family. But, after what happened to you today, I fear the authorities will be watching you. It would be a risk at any time, but the risk may now be too high."

"I see what you mean, but on the other hand, if I do as they ask and translate for them, they might begin to trust me."

"I don't know." He shook his head, sipping his drink.

"Papa," she said, coming over and kneeling next to him. "Our whole lives involve risk. You can't go about in a state of fear, otherwise you'd never step outside the door. We have a moral duty to help these people."

He looked down at her and stroked her hair. "You're a good girl." He reached over to the drinks tray next to his chair and refilled his glass. "Let's have a think," he began. "Practically speaking, where could we put a family? We have so little room here."

"It depends how many there are, but I'd suggest the attic."

"But it's full of old files and furniture."

"We can move all of that, surely."

"You really think we can make it work?" he asked. "What about the radio? You use the attic to monitor the broadcasts—it's the only place you can get a clear signal. How could you hide it from the family? What would happen if they were arrested? They might talk."

"Well," said Livia, standing up and pacing the room, "now Mamma is not here, I could try and make the radio work downstairs. But if the signal is bad and we have to move it back to the attic, we'll just have to tell them."

"But it's supposed to be a secret," he insisted.

"Papa, it will be all right." She leaned down and took his hand. "Just think, if we don't take in a family, they risk being sent to prison or even killed. We must make it work."

Giacomo sent word the following day that he and Livia could provide sanctuary for a family of up to four, and Livia began clearing out the attic. The first job was to free up the space by removing her father's work files, which were stored in tea chests. They would have to be moved downstairs to her father's bedroom, but to get them down the steep attic staircase involved dragging them along the attic landing and bumping them, stair by stair, to the bottom.

Livia was hauling the last chest noisily across the hall floor of the apartment when there was an insistent knocking at the front door.

"Yes?" she asked pleasantly, when she opened the door. "Can I help you?"

It was a neighbor called Lombardi who lived across the landing. An elderly man, he had a habit of lurking on the stairs whenever they had a visitor.

"Signorina Moretti," he said, "what is that terrible noise? I'm trying to listen to music and I simply can't concentrate." He peered behind her, noting the line of tea chests filling the corridor.

"I'm so sorry, Signor Lombardi," she replied politely, half-closing the door behind her. "Do forgive me. I'm just tidying up my father's office. I'll be finished soon, I promise."

She retreated inside and closed the apartment door in his face. They would have to be more careful in the future—Signor Lombardi would be watching their every move.

The attic rooms, now cleared of their contents, were ready for cleaning. To her surprise, Livia discovered that the smaller of the two was, in fact, a disused bathroom, consisting of a rather grubby lavatory and an old washbasin, which clearly hadn't been used for decades. She turned on the rusty taps; at first they rattled and wheezed, but eventually brownish water spurted out. Then, armed with bleach, polish and cloths, she scrubbed the attic clean.

"You've made a fine job of it," said Giacomo, when he went upstairs that evening. "And just in time too."

Livia looked at him expectantly.

"Yes," he said smiling, "we've been assigned a family."

"Who? What are their names?" Livia asked excitedly.

"I don't know yet, but they're a young couple with a child."

"How old is the child?"

"Three or four, I think." Giacomo looked around him and shivered. "I'm worried it will be too cold. The wind whistles through that roof—that's why I stopped using it as an office."

"Well, they only need to sleep up here," Livia suggested. "They can come downstairs for meals and a hot bath. Have you had any luck finding camp beds?"

"Yes, someone in the Pd'A has two spare camp beds, and a little mattress we can borrow for the child. Where did you hide the radio?"

"It's over there in the corner in that little cupboard. But I'll take it to my room after this evening's bulletin."

They went back downstairs, closing the door to the apartment behind them. Livia stopped and frowned, looking at the door.

"There's one problem," she began. "How can we conceal this door? If the authorities searched the apartment, they'd easily find the family upstairs."

Giacomo nodded. "We could hide the door to the attic," he suggested. "Perhaps put some furniture in front of it."

They looked around them.

"What about this?" Livia pointed to the coat rack opposite the front door. "Covered with coats and hats, it would conceal it completely."

"Perfect," said her father, "let's drag it into position."

Within a couple of days, Giacomo had made the arrangements to collect the Jewish family. "They're sheltering temporarily in a church. I'll pick them up as late as possible before the curfew, just before it gets dark."

"You must be careful when you bring them into the building," said Livia. "Signor Lombardi has ears and eyes everywhere."

"Don't worry," her father said calmly. "Lombardi's not such a bad old man."

That afternoon, a dense fog descended on the city, and visibility was down to a meter.

"The conditions are perfect," said Giacomo, as he peered out the kitchen window. "No one will see anything in this weather. I'll fetch them now."

Livia began to prepare a simple soup with some meat bones she had found at the market that morning. She laid a small fire in the sitting room using the last of their firewood. But she was nervous and kept darting to the window every few minutes, keeping a watchful eye on the road below. She jumped when she heard her father's key in the lock, and ran into the hall.

"Thank God you're back," she whispered as she hugged him, "I was beginning to worry."

"We're fine, we're fine," Giacomo said calmly, closing the apartment door behind him. "Jacob, Sara, this is my daughter, Livia."

The couple smiled politely, but Livia could see they were terrified and exhausted, with dark rings around their eyes and anxious looks on their faces.

"Let me take your coats," she said gently, "you must be tired."

The man smiled, and put down their suitcases. He removed his trilby hat, which he handed to Livia. He was tall and bearded, with dark hair and a gentle expression. His wife was small, with curly fair hair framing her round face. When she removed her coat, Livia could see she was already some months pregnant. A small boy with a crop of blond hair peeped out from behind his mother's skirts.

"And who is this?" Livia asked, crouching down to him.

"I'm Matteo," he said shyly.

"It's lovely to meet you, Matteo," Livia replied, standing up. "Now, please come into the sitting room. We managed to find a little firewood, so it'll soon be nice and warm."

The woman eased herself slowly into an armchair. Her son leaned against her legs, his head in her lap.

"When is your baby due?" Livia asked.

"March," Sara replied.

"How exciting," said Livia. "Is Matteo looking forward to having a brother or sister?"

The little boy removed the thumb from his mouth. "I'm having a baby," he said proudly.

They all laughed, and Sara ruffled the boy's hair.

"So, tell me, Jacob," asked Giacomo, "what do you do for a living?"

"I am an engineer."

"Do your employers know where you are?"

Jacob shook his head. "We've been in hiding for a while. They think we left the city a few weeks ago. Now I wish we had." He glanced uneasily at his wife. "But it was difficult to obtain papers and so on."

"I'm sure it was," said Giacomo. "And not without risk, either. Don't worry, you'll be safe here with us." He turned to his daughter. "Shall we eat?"

Livia had laid the dining table earlier in the afternoon. She and her father had got used to eating in the kitchen, but the arrival of the family called for a celebration, so she had cleared away her father's work papers, and laid the table with a white linen cloth, and her mother's "best" crystal glasses and china. She had even decanted a bottle of wine. Livia realized the elegance was at odds with the simple meal that she served—a tureen of weak soup and a small portion of bread for each of them.

Over dinner, they chatted about the war, and their aspirations once it was over, but when the food and wine were finished, Matteo was yawning and Sara was white-faced with exhaustion.

"I think maybe you'd like to go to bed now?" Livia suggested.

The woman nodded gratefully.

"I hope you'll be warm enough," Livia said, as she showed them their room. "I've put a lot of blankets on the beds. They're only camp beds, but they're quite comfortable. Will Matteo be all right on that little mattress?"

Sara nodded and sat down heavily on the bed.

"If you get really cold, you must tell me," Livia went on. "You can sleep downstairs—although we have no heating either, apart from the fire in the sitting room. But I could always share my father's room and you could have mine."

"Thank you," said Jacob. "But it's better if we stay up here. This is all we need. You're very kind."

Back downstairs, Livia closed the attic door, and dragged the coat rack across it. She checked her watch. It was ten minutes to nine. She went down the corridor to her bedroom and turned on the radio. The signal from Radio Londra was not as clear as it had been up in the attic, but she managed to hear most of the broadcast.

At a meeting of the Italian Social Republic in Verona, the party reversed Italy's previous policy toward Jews within its borders. Its manifesto declared: "All those who belong to the Jewish race are foreigners. During this war they belong to an enemy nationality. All Jews living within the borders of the Italian Socialist Republic will be arrested."

Livia sat back in shock. It seemed they had rescued Jacob and Sara just in time. She hurriedly wrote up the story for the paper, before hiding the radio behind some of her father's weightier legal textbooks.

Early the next morning, she went up onto the roof terrace with a pile of laundry. The fog had lifted, and it was a crisp winter's day. The terra-cotta roofs looked beautiful against the clear blue sky.

As she hung the laundry from the line, little Matteo appeared at her side.

"Hello," he said.

"Hello, Matteo, are you hungry?"

"Yes."

"Well, if you help me hang this up, we'll go down to the kitchen together, and get some breakfast—all right?"

She watched him as he struggled with a pillowcase, standing on a chair to reach the line. He was such a sweet child, she thought, his tongue slightly protruding as he concentrated on pinning up the laundry. The thought of Matteo being sent to a prison camp was unimaginable. She picked him up and held him closely, kissing his hair. When she put him down, Jacob was standing in the doorway watching them.

"Let me help you," said Jacob. He hung up a couple of sheets, pinning them carefully onto the line. "You are very kind," he said, "we appreciate what you and your father are doing."

"It's nothing," she replied. "I'm just glad we can help."

After a breakfast of toast, scraped with a little fig jam, Livia went to the sitting room where her father was already working at the dining-room table. The article she had written the night before lay to one side. He was writing a pamphlet for distribution, but he covered the work with his hand. "For your own safety," he said, "it's better if you don't know what it's about. Good article by the way—excellent."

"Thank you." She blushed slightly, touched by her father's praise. "Now, I must go, or I'll be late for Villa Triste. Can you look after the family?"

"Of course." He was already scribbling on a notepad.

"Papa, will you promise me not to get too bogged down in your work? I know what you're like. A bomb could go off around you and you'd have no idea."

"We'll all be fine. You take care. Off you go."

Livia hurried through the streets, arriving at Villa Triste just before nine o'clock. The waiting room was empty, the reception desk unmanned. Relieved that she wasn't late, she sat down.

Half an hour went by, before the German officer she had met during her interrogation appeared in the waiting room. "Fräulein...come with me."

She followed him anxiously down the corridor.

"You are to go with our soldiers today," he said.

"Why?" she asked warily.

"We have reason to believe a number of Jews are being hidden somewhere, and I need you to be there when they are arrested."

Her heart began to race. Had they discovered Sara and Jacob already? "Jews?" she asked. "Where?"

"The Church of Santa Maria Novella," he replied, "near the station."

"I'm not sure I can come now," she said feebly, "I have a lecture."

"Du musst," he insisted.

"How do you know the Jews are in there?" Livia asked the soldiers as they crossed the piazza toward an impressive gray marble church.

The soldiers ignored her question, pushing her ahead of them.

As they passed a group of market stallholders, one of the women called out to Livia in the local Florentine patois. "What are these soldiers doing here?"

Livia, desperate to get a message to the Jews, replied in the same dialect: "To arrest some Jews hiding in the church. Go and warn them."

The soldiers stopped in their tracks and one of them grabbed her by the arm demanding to know what she had said. "Was hast du zu diesen Frauen gesagt?"

Out of the corner of her eye, Livia noticed one of the women had slipped away and was running toward the church. She was desperate to keep the soldier occupied while she gave them some kind of explanation. Perhaps they would believe she was asking if there was a back door—some way of escape. It would convince them she was on their side.

"Ich habe sehn gesacht—'es eine Hintertür?'" she told them.

"Und ist da?" asked the soldier.

"Nein," she replied.

When they arrived at the church, the soldiers barged through the main doors, dragging Livia along with them. The church was almost empty with just a handful of parishioners kneeling in the pews, their heads bowed. They turned round in alarm at the sound of steel-tipped boots clattering on the marble floor and raised German voices. Livia could see there was a Mass in progress—at the high altar a priest in colored vestments stood with his back to the congregation, his hands raised, as if calling on God for help. The soldiers ran up the aisle shouting, "Wo sind die Juden?"

The priest continued with his prayers, but the parishioners began to stand up, muttering amongst themselves and shuffling up the aisle toward the main doors.

"Wo sind die Juden?" one of the soldiers shouted again. He grabbed Livia, pulled her up the altar steps and thrust her bodily against the priest. He made the sign of the cross and turned to face her, smiling beatifically.

"Please," she whispered, "I'm sorry, but they're here to arrest the Jews. I tried to warn you; did they get out in time?"

"Bless you," he said. "Take them to the crypt—they will find nothing. It's the door over there."

She beckoned to the soldiers and led them to a small arched doorway in the corner, standing aside as the men ran down the stone stairs, shouting loudly. She heard the sound of metal ornaments crashing to the ground.

The priest joined her and put his hand on her shoulder. She found his presence comforting. The soldiers ran back up the stairs. They pushed Livia aside, and hurled the priest up against the wall. He grimaced in pain.

"Wo sind die Juden?" they screamed at him.

He shook his head in a bemused fashion, looking from one soldier to another.

"Where are the Jews?" Livia asked the priest, although it was obvious that he had understood.

Once again, he shook his head and shrugged. The soldiers dragged him outside into the square, where a small crowd was gathering. Livia pushed her way through. One of the soldiers slapped the priest's face.

"Bitte," she begged, grabbing the soldier's arm, "tu ihm nicht weh... *don't hurt him.*"

He shook his arm free and scowled at her.

"Please," she said to the priest, "we must tell them you don't know anything about Jews. Deny they were ever here."

He looked fearful for a second. "Will they believe that?"

"I don't know," she said desperately. "But I'll try..."

As she explained the priest's innocence to the soldiers, they glared at him, their fingers twitching over the triggers of their guns.

"Es ist die Wahrheit," she insisted nervously. "*It's the truth.*"

"Er kommt mit uns," they shouted, pointing at the priest.

"They insist you go with them." Livia took his hand again and murmured into his ear, "You must say you knew nothing about it, that your duty is to the Catholics, they might believe you."

The soldiers dragged the priest across the piazza, while the crowd looked on helplessly.

At Villa Triste, the priest was pushed roughly into the waiting room. He tripped and fell onto the tiled floor.

Livia helped him back onto his feet. "I'm sorry," was all she could say.

He took her hand and kissed it. "Bless you for saving them," he whispered.

"But what about you?" she asked, fighting back tears.

"I have the Lord," he replied.

As the priest was pushed aggressively down the corridor toward the interrogation rooms, an officer turned to Livia. "You may go," he told her.

She stumbled tearfully out of the building into the street and joined the crowds walking toward the Duomo.

Chapter Nineteen

Rome
November 1943

In the days that followed Isabella's meeting with Karl Wolff, she was haunted by the words Vicenzo had used to describe her: "fantasist," "infatuated." She squirmed at the memory, cursing her weakness. Not only had she put Vicenzo's young friend in danger, but she had brought *him* to the attention of the authorities. Even saving Gianni's father gave her no comfort—it could not make up for the damage she had done to the person she cared for most in the world.

Every morning she resolved to visit Vicenzo and admit her sin, to warn him of the danger she had placed him in. Each time she drew back, fearful of his reaction. He must hate her, she realized. But finally, one cold day in November, she could put it off no longer. She dressed hurriedly, and left the house before either her mother or aunt were awake.

Arriving at his villa, she was surprised to find the dogs snoozing on the porch. Vicenzo normally kept them inside in the winter months. She knelt down and stroked their soft fur, taking comfort from the way they rubbed the tops of their heads against her palm.

"Good boys," she murmured. She cradled them in her arms, realizing this might be the last time she ever saw them. Once Vicenzo knew what she had done, he would never want to see her again.

Her heart pounding, she knocked on the door. Unusually, he opened it himself. He was barefoot, and wearing just a robe. His face fell as soon as he saw her. "Oh it's you," he said harshly. "You'd better come in."

The dogs followed her inside and nuzzled her hand as he led her through to the sitting room. She sat down nervously on the sofa, the dogs lying peacefully at her feet. Vicenzo stood in front of the fireplace, glaring at her.

"I've come here to apologize," she said eventually.

"Have you?"

"I have done something terrible. I hardly know how to tell you."

"Go on." His black eyes were flashing.

Her mouth was dry; she stroked the dogs' heads, desperately trying to find the words.

"I'll help you, shall I?" He spoke so softly, she could hardly hear him. "For some inexplicable reason, you informed on a young woman I have known all my life—an innocent girl, just twenty years old—and told inexcusable lies about her."

Isabella's eyes filled with tears; she began to sob.

"Is that all you can do?" he asked. "Cry like a child? Do you really have nothing to say?"

"I thought you loved her," she mumbled. "I was mad with jealousy. I met someone at a dinner, a German officer. I didn't say anything terrible, I just mentioned that she might..." She paused uncertain how to go on. Whatever she said, it was inexcusable.

"Might what? What exactly did you say?"

"That she might be a partisan," she blurted out miserably, "that she might be influencing you."

He put his head in his hands, and exhaled deeply. He walked across the room and stared out of the window. His shoulders were hunched, his back taut with tension. The dogs followed him with their eyes and whined.

"Do you have any idea what you have done?" he asked.

She began to weep. The dogs pricked up their ears and laid their heads in her lap, as if to comfort her.

"A girl of just twenty," he said icily, "spent nearly a week in a torture cell!" He swung round suddenly and glared at her. "Can you begin to imagine what that must have felt like?"

She shook her head, tears spilling down her cheeks.

"The poor child was terrified, fearing she would be tortured, or killed at any moment."

"I'm sorry, I'm so sorry…forgive me," she begged. "I didn't mean her any harm. I wasn't thinking properly. I didn't think anything bad would happen to her. I see now it was a terrible thing to do, so foolish."

"Foolish!" He marched toward her, his fists raised.

She shrank into the sofa, fearing he would hit her. "I'm sorry," she said, "that was the wrong word. Not foolish—sinful, terrible, evil."

He came to a halt, and sank down exhausted onto the sofa opposite her. The dogs lay back down, their heads resting on Isabella's shoes.

"Is she all right?" Isabella asked tentatively.

"What do you care?" he snapped.

"Please, Vicenzo," she pleaded.

"Yes, she's all right," he said impatiently. "She's very strong, fortunately. But I had to go to Florence and speak up for her. They told me what you had said, so I'm glad you didn't lie. I could never have forgiven that."

Here, she thought, was a glimmer of hope; he spoke of forgiveness. She closed her eyes, as if praying.

"I told them you were a madwoman—jealous of her for no reason. Fortunately, because you are an actress, they believed me. But she is now under suspicion—as is her father, as am I."

"You? Why you?"

"Why do you think?" He stood up again and leaned against the mantelpiece, irritably kicking the brass fender with his naked foot. Suddenly he swung round to face her. "I have been accused of being a partisan. I will spend the rest of the war looking over my shoulder. I will never be safe again."

Isabella began to sob.

"I think you should go now," he said coldly. "I never want to see you again."

"No, no…I beg you—please don't say that." She fell to her knees and crawled on all fours across the room to him, her hands grasping for him. "I'll do anything, anything you ask. Just say you forgive me."

"How can I?" he asked. Her fingers were wrapped round his naked ankle, but he shook himself free and walked back to the window. The dogs followed him.

"I could be useful," she suggested. "This officer I met, he's already helped me get someone out of Dachau."

Vicenzo turned around and stared at her intently. "Why would he do that for you?"

"I don't know. He likes me, I suppose. But it's not what you think—I'm not having an affair with him, honestly."

"I really don't care who you have an affair with, but a German? Really, Isabella, how low can you go?" He turned his back on her, and stared out at the garden.

"I'm not having an affair, I promise. You know it's you I love, Vicenzo, and only you. You must know that. I would never deliberately hurt you, never."

"How can I believe that after what you've done?"

"You must believe me," she begged.

He paced the room, as if considering how to proceed.

"I don't know if I can ever trust you again," he said at last, "that's the problem."

"Of course you can trust me...with your life. Let me prove it to you."

"Get up off the floor. You look pathetic." He walked toward her, and held out his hand, helping her up. He looked deeply into her eyes, and for a moment she sensed him weakening.

"I love you," she whispered.

"Don't." He led her back to the sofa and she sat down, gazing up at him. "You really are like a child sometimes, Bella," he said gently. "You must learn to think before you act."

She nodded eagerly, relieved at the use of her nickname.

"Your connections with these Fascists might be useful, but I need to know whose side you are on."

"I'm on your side," she insisted.

"You understand that I am opposed to everything they stand for?"

"Yes, of course."

"If you betray me again, it will almost certainly result in my death. Do you understand?"

"I will never betray you...never."

He sat for a moment staring at her, as if trying to see into her soul.

"I think you should go now," he said eventually. "Don't tell anyone you've seen me, do you understand?"

She nodded.

"I'll be in touch. I may need a favor soon."

"Anything," she said, "anything at all."

A few days later, Isabella came downstairs in the morning to find a handwritten note had been slipped beneath her front door.

Come and see me as soon as possible, it's urgent. Vicenzo.

Wearing her fur coat to keep out the chill, she hurried across the park, past the rows of tents set up for the German troops. As she turned into Vicenzo's quiet road, a German tank rolled noisily by. The tank commander was peering over the top of the gun turret, barking orders to his team. Isabella pulled her coat tightly around herself, and hurried on.

Walking up the drive to Vicenzo's house, she felt her heart racing with anticipation. She knocked on the door, and the maid opened it almost immediately. Isabella noticed a suitcase in the hall, as Constanza took her coat.

The maid took her through to the sitting room. Vicenzo was at his desk by the window, overlooking the garden. He looked tired, Isabella thought.

"Ah, Bella...Good, you're here."

The dogs, lying by the fireplace, stood up wagging their tails. They sniffed her legs and stood waiting for her to stroke their soft heads.

"They like you," he observed.

"I love them," she replied. "They are faithful, as well as beautiful."

"Sit down, please. I asked you here to seek a favor of you."

"Of course, anything," she replied, sitting on one of the sofas.

"I am going away," he said simply.

"Where?" she asked.

"I can't say, but I feel compelled to save my country. I have serious war work to do. Needless to say, if anyone found out what I was doing, it would certainly lead to my death."

"You can trust me, Vicenzo, I promise."

"I hope so." He sat down opposite her. "Now, this is what I need you to do. I want you to move in here, to make it look as if I'm still in Rome—and look after my dogs. Will you do that?"

She nodded.

"And hide some valuables for me—family jewels and so on—they are all there in that box." He pointed to a carved box on the sofa table. "Can you keep them somewhere at your house?"

"Yes, of course."

He handed her a check. "Cash this—you'll need money."

"You don't need to do that," she said blushing. "Besides, I have money."

"No, I know you are not working anymore, Isabella. You will need money to feed the dogs, and to pay Constanza and the gardener."

"Vicenzo—" she began.

"Don't say it," he murmured.

"You don't know what I'm going to say yet."

"Your face says it all. You love me, I know that. That is why I am asking you. There is no one else I can turn to. No one else I can trust."

"I'm frightened for you."

"Don't be, I'll be all right. One other thing—they're listening to our phones. If I need to contact you, I'll do so through Constanza, or I'll send a note. Now, I think that's everything. I should go."

He snapped his fingers and the dogs ran across the room to him; he knelt down and kissed them. When he looked up at Isabella, he had tears in his eyes.

"They will need meat, can you try to find them some?"

"Of course I will—anything they need."

He stood up and walked across to her. He took her in his arms and kissed the top of her head. "I'll be in touch," he whispered.

When he had gone, Isabella wandered through the house in a daze, the dogs following at her heels. She felt a huge surge of relief that he had forgiven her. She could make a new start—prove to him how reliable she was, and how much she loved him. She went upstairs, something she had never done before. At the back of the house, overlooking the garden, was a large bedroom decorated in shades of blue. This, she realized, must be Vicenzo's room. There were photographs of his family on the chest of drawers, alongside photographs of him on location with his crew and some of his stars. On the wall between the two windows was a watercolor of a beautiful house set amongst pine groves. Signed by Vicenzo, it was entitled simply "Forte dei Marmi."

She sat down on his bed and was amazed to find that, among the various portraits of friends and family, he had a photograph of her on his bedside table. Lying down on his bed, she wept, inhaling the scent that lingered on the pillows. The dogs lay down on the floor next to her, whining.

"It's all right," she said, reaching down and stroking their heads. "He'll be back soon. I'm here now."

She must have slept, for when she woke, it was late in the afternoon and almost dark outside. She got up hurriedly, aware there was much to be done. Leaving the dogs with the maid, she took the box of jewels, and promised to return that evening before the curfew. At her house, she went straight to her dressing room. There was a hole in the wall behind her evening dresses, which she assumed had once contained a small safe. She slid the box into the hole, concealing it with her dresses.

Isabella packed enough clothes to last a couple of weeks and took her suitcase downstairs. Her mother was in the kitchen.

"I have to go away for a while," Isabella said.

"Where?" her mother asked.

"I can't say, but I won't be far away. Please don't worry about me. I'll come back from time to time to make sure you're all right. But I'll take the car."

"How long will you be away for?"

"I don't know . . . as long as it takes."

Giovanna looked at her quizzically.

"As for money," Isabella went on, "you must take what you need from the bank account—for food and so on."

"I don't understand," said her mother.

"Please...I can't explain. If anyone comes here and asks for me—just say I'm out somewhere. I'll drop in regularly so you can give me any messages. And don't trust the phone—they're listening." She kissed her mother's cheek.

"You are a strange girl."

"Perhaps," said Isabella. "But I am doing the right thing at last."

Chapter Twenty

Florence
December 1943

Every morning, as Livia signed the register at Villa Triste, she thought about the priest who had been arrested, wondering whether he was still there. Had he ever been charged with anything? After all, the soldiers never found the Jewish people who were supposedly hiding at the church, so technically he was innocent. But she knew enough about the methods at the Fascist HQ to know that innocence did not result in automatic release. The Gestapo must have had intelligence that the church was being used as a refuge, and they would be sure to use all means necessary to extract the truth from the gentle priest. As she waited, she considered asking the desk clerk about him, but fear held her back. She could hear such terrible things coming from the interrogation rooms: the screams of people as they were tortured and, more terrible even than that, the laughter of their torturers echoing down the corridor. There was even a rumor that Mario Carità invited his mistress to watch these torture sessions. The thought of the priest being tortured for someone's entertainment, in one of those basement prison cells, was terrifying.

Once or twice, Livia went back to the church, hoping to find him there. But by the beginning of December, a younger priest had taken his place, and she had to accept that the old man had either died under torture, or had been sent away to a prison camp. It grieved her that a man of God could be so badly treated. But it angered her too, and that anger seeped into her soul and made her more determined to fight back.

The Germans at Villa Triste were increasingly making demands of her. Once or twice a week, she had to accompany soldiers as they attempted to intercept a partisan, or search for a Jewish family hiding in a barn or a church. By now, many of the Germans had begun to understand basic Italian, so the Resistance increasingly communicated using the local patois. Women, acting as lookouts, would call out to her as she passed by: "Who are they looking for?" While she pretended to the soldiers she was seeking information, one of the women would run ahead and warn the intended victims. When Livia arrived with the soldiers, they would discover the partisans had disappeared.

Her main concern was that eventually the Germans would become suspicious that they never found their quarry when they went out with her. She knew they needed the occasional success, and wrestled with her conscience every time she was sent out, wondering if this should be the day she didn't alert someone to danger. If not, one day, she feared it would be her who was being tortured. But that fear was soon superseded by rage, and a sense of defiance that she would not give in. And every time she was sent out with the guards, she found a way to save another life, at whatever cost to her own safety.

Back at the apartment, Sara, Jacob and Matteo had settled in well, and a routine had been established. Each morning they would creep down the staircase from the attic, and knock gently on the door leading to the apartment. Livia would move the coat rack as quietly as possible, and once inside the apartment they would gather in the kitchen. While Sara made breakfast—a little weak coffee and a scrap of bread for each of them—Jacob sat and read quietly with his son. The family had arrived with few possessions of their own, but Livia had unearthed a selection of her childhood books buried behind a stack of her father's legal textbooks. *Pinocchio* seemed a particular favorite, and she relished hearing Matteo laughing as his father read to him.

Inevitably, rations were short. It was already hard enough for two people to live on what was allocated. But to stretch it to five was near impossible. Everyone was hungry, but no one complained. They could not have survived without the help of local partisans, who would occasionally deliver emergency rations. Livia, going upstairs to hang out washing, would find food parcels dropped off by some nimble-footed young member of the Resistance. Bringing the parcel downstairs, she would discover a rabbit shot in the fields, or a fresh fish caught in the River Arno.

As she left the apartment each morning, it cheered Livia that somewhere out there, people were prepared to support them, to face danger in order to bring them food. Signing the register at Villa Triste, she would think about Sara and Jacob, safely ensconced in the attic; it gave her a sense of rebellion that glowed deeply and satisfyingly within her. While the authorities thought they had her under their control, she was fooling them every minute of the day.

She and her father were in no doubt that by harboring a Jewish family they were putting themselves in terrible danger. Giacomo reminded her constantly of the need for absolute secrecy. "No one must know about the family—not your Mamma, not your best friend, nor Cosimo. Do you understand?"

"But surely Cosimo is part of the Pd'A now? Can't even he be trusted?"

"No," replied Giacomo firmly. "He's a good boy, and you love him, I understand that. But the rules of the Pd'A are strict for a reason. All our work is done on the principle that people must know as little as possible. We operate with small cells of people who know something but not everything. I have no idea, for example, who else in the organization is sheltering a Jewish family. That way, if I were arrested, I would be unable to reveal their secret. Try to keep a wall between you." He peered at her over his glasses. "It's hard, I know. I have to keep everything from your mother, remember."

"What about the people who bring our food?" Livia persisted. "They must know something about the family."

"They may simply have been told that people are in need in this building. They probably have no idea who it's for. Believe me Livia, it's the best way."

Livia acquiesced to her father. But she also knew that while the Partito d'Azione might consider themselves in charge of the Resistance effort, all over Florence little breakaway partisan groups were springing up, working in isolation from one another. While the Pd'A were busy writing and delivering leaflets, encouraging people to stand up against Fascism, people in separate organizations were prepared to risk their lives to defy the occupying forces of Nazi Germany. Cosimo told her as much when they had met one cold afternoon in a small café near the Duomo.

"I've joined another Resistance group." He spoke quietly in case they were overheard. "They're called Gruppi di Azione Patriottica—GAP for short."

"But you're part of the Pd'A," Livia insisted.

"Yes, I know. But GAP are prepared to fight for what we believe in, not just distribute leaflets."

"Oh Cosimo." Livia looked around anxiously. "Please, you must take care."

"I'm all right." He sounded defensive. "Just because I've lost my foot doesn't mean I'm weak, or frightened."

"I know that," she replied. "No one could ever accuse you of that."

"I have to do something, Livia. I can't bear watching these soldiers marching around the streets as if they own them."

"This group—are you sure you can trust them?" Livia asked him.

"Yes. Your father will know of them. They have cells all over the country. Our aim is to make the Germans feel unsafe everywhere—on the streets, in their cars, in restaurants, even in Villa Triste itself." He stabbed his fork into the wooden table.

"How?" she asked, lowering her voice.

"I can't say, but you will hear about what we've done after it's happened. We have weapons and will attack soon."

"Cosimo, please be careful."

"I'm a soldier remember. I know how to fight. And fight I will."

Walking back to the apartment, Livia wondered if she should tell her father of Cosimo's plans. As Giacomo had himself said, everyone needed to operate in secrecy. And were the plans of GAP any less important than those of the Pd'A? She felt her loyalties were divided. Her father had insisted on a wall of silence between her and Cosimo. Was there now also a wall between herself and her father? Still wrestling with this conundrum, she let herself into the apartment. Her father was standing in the hallway speaking on the telephone.

"Darling Luisa," he said, "we can't come this weekend... Yes, I know it's been weeks." He glanced at Livia, a pained expression on his face. "It's your mother," he whispered, his hand over the receiver. Livia smiled supportively. "I know my father would love to see me," he went on, "but Livia has exams... she needs to review."

Livia went into the kitchen to prepare supper. She was chopping an onion when her father came in, and sat down heavily at the kitchen table.

"I don't know how much longer I can put your mother off. She wants us home for Christmas."

"How can we?" asked Livia. "The Germans will never release me. They're using me more and more."

"I didn't tell you," her father began, "but I wrote a letter to the Villa Triste commander, asking if you could have a few days to visit your mother over Christmas."

"You shouldn't have done that without telling me first." Livia was irritated that her father should have done something so risky without warning her.

"I'm sorry," Giacomo replied uncertainly. "Perhaps it wasn't the right thing to do..."

"It's all right," Livia said gently, "I know you were acting in my best interests, but this relationship with the Germans is complex. It takes all my ingenuity to navigate it. You have to remember—they don't care about me or my mother, or Christmas, for that matter. They tortured a priest who they suspected of harboring Jews; they've probably killed him by now—a priest, for God's sake. These people are vicious brutes. They have no heart, Papa."

Her father's eyes filled with tears.

"Out of interest, have they bothered to reply?" she asked.

"Yes," he said weakly, "with Teutonic efficiency. You are not allowed to leave the city for any reason."

"There you are then. I could have told you that. I think perhaps we have to tell Mamma the truth—get it over and done with."

"Don't you know your mother at all?" Giacomo said, his head in his hands. "If we tell her that you are working for the Gestapo, she will panic and insist on returning to Florence. Then she will discover the family in the attic. The whole edifice that we have constructed will come tumbling down over our heads. No, we must keep her in the countryside, for everyone's sake."

"I suppose you're right," Livia agreed. "Let's sleep on it, and call her tomorrow evening. I'm sure we'll think of some innocent explanation." She walked round the table and kissed the top of Giacomo's head. "Don't worry, Papa."

The following day, when Livia woke, large flakes of snow fell from a dark sky. It continued to snow all day, and by late in the afternoon, as Livia walked back home, it was drifting against the buildings, reaching almost to the windowsills of the ground-floor windows. By the time she reached the apartment, her boots were soaking wet, her coat and hat covered with snow. As usual, her father was working at the dining table.

"Oh good," he said, "you're back. I've been waiting for you before telephoning your mother. We can use the weather as an excuse." He nodded toward the window, where snow was piling up on the windowsills.

"I had the same thought. I've never been so happy to see snow." Livia smiled encouragingly at her father.

Standing in the hall, Livia nervously dialed the villa. The telephone line crackled as she tried to explain to her mother that they would not be back for Christmas.

"It's snowing very heavily here," Livia explained. "We're worried that the roads will be impassable. I'm so sorry, Mamma."

She could hear her mother weeping on the other end of the phone. Riddled with guilt, she tried to comfort her, but Luisa continued to sob.

"Perhaps you should speak to Papa," Livia said helplessly, handing her father the receiver.

Giacomo spoke to Luisa for some time. Judging by his responses, Luisa wasn't giving in without a fight. But Giacomo was immovable. Finally, when he put the phone down, he had tears in his eyes.

"Oh Papa...I'm so sorry." Livia wrapped him in her arms. "Was she very upset?"

"We've never been apart at Christmas before," he explained. "In twenty-eight years—can you believe it?"

"It's for the best," Livia said encouragingly. "I know it's hard, but what else can we do? Besides...she'll manage. And so will we."

"The worst part," her father said, blowing his nose on a large white handkerchief, "is not being able to tell her the truth. The thought that she must feel we don't really care...that we'd rather stay here, that's what upsets me." He looked up at his daughter and kissed her. "If she only knew..." he said sadly, as he walked through to the sitting room.

Chapter Twenty-One

Rome
December 1943

Throughout the last few days of December, rain fell day and night. The roads ran with water, the gardens became waterlogged, and the park around Villa Borghese became a sea of mud, as the troops marched back and forth to their rain-sodden tents. The day before Christmas Eve, the temperature dropped below freezing, and when Isabella opened the curtains in Vicenzo's bedroom, the garden was covered in a carpet of virgin white snow. As she came downstairs, the villa was silent except for the ticking of clocks and the faint sounds of the maid in the kitchen. A fire already crackled in the drawing-room grate. Outside the villa, Isabella knew German troops had taken over the streets of Rome, but here, in Vicenzo's house, she was the mistress of all she surveyed, enveloped in its opulent embrace.

Hearing her come downstairs, the dogs padded through to the sitting room, followed by Constanza. "This was delivered for you this morning," she said, handing Isabella an envelope. The handwriting was familiar, and Isabella felt a surge of excitement.

"Thank you, Constanza," she said, "you may go." She tore open the envelope and read the note.

> *Meet me at the crypt of the Church of Santa Maria della Concezione dei Cappuccini at two o'clock. Burn this. Vicenzo.*

Dressed in her best fur coat and thick winter boots, Isabella walked through the park surrounding Villa Borghese. It had stopped snowing and the sun had come out. The arching pines were weighed down with snow, and the neat hedges lining the paths were covered with white. Everything seemed renewed, and the cream stucco paintwork of Villa Borghese glowed against a bright-blue sky.

She left the park and began to walk down Via Veneto. Three German tanks rumbled by, noisily churning the snow into gray slush. As she passed Hotel Flora, a gaggle of German officers stood on the pavement outside the hotel. They looked cheerful, she thought, as if they had just enjoyed a good lunch. They parted as she approached, allowing her to walk between them. She smiled politely, and nodded her head left and right, not wishing to provoke them in any way. One officer tipped his hat at her.

When she arrived at the church, Isabella checked she had not been followed, before climbing the staircase up to the impressive entrance. She stamped her boots to knock off the snow and pushed open the heavy oak door. Uncertain where the entrance to the crypt was, she began to walk slowly down the aisle. Although only a mile or so from her home, she had never visited the church before, and was impressed by the baroque architecture and magnificent painted ceiling.

She noticed an elderly verger arranging candles on a side altar. He glanced up at Isabella, who nodded politely, and crossed herself. Sensing she was being watched, she slipped silently into a pew, where she knelt, her eyes closed, pretending to pray. After a few moments, she heard the verger walk to the back of the church, and felt a cold draft as he left by the main entrance.

Now alone, Isabella set about looking for the entrance to the crypt. She tried one door after another before opening one to the right of the main altar. Pushing it open, she was almost overcome with the stench of damp and decay. In front of her were steep steps leading down into the dark. She covered her face with her gloved hand and, clinging to the cold iron handrail, descended to what she hoped was the crypt.

The walls flickered in the candlelight, and as her eyes became accustomed to the gloom, she gasped at what she saw. An underground chamber, its walls bizarrely decorated with hundreds of human skulls, arranged in complex designs. A coat of arms on one wall looked like a pair of crossed swords, before she realized with horror that they were in fact a pair of dismembered arms.

Suddenly, she sensed a presence and swung round. She knew it had to be Vicenzo, but he was almost unrecognizable. Dressed in a tatty coat and a crumpled hat, he looked like a tramp, as if he was in costume for a play.

"Thank God you're here," he said. "But how did you get in?"

"Down the staircase."

"You should have used the separate street entrance; it's next to the main doors. Did anyone see you come down here?"

"No. There was a verger in the church, but I pretended to pray until he left."

"Good, well we'd better be quick."

"This place is bizarre," she said, looking around. Every wall, even the vaulted ceiling, was decorated with skulls arranged in complex patterns.

"I know," he said, smiling. "I think it's rather wonderful, if somewhat macabre." He threw his arms out and bowed theatrically. "Welcome to the crypt of skulls." Isabella sensed he was enjoying her discomfort.

"Who are all these dead people?"

"They are the remains of Franciscan monks, the order of the Capuchin," explained Vicenzo. "They brought the bones here when they moved to Italy from Lebanon in the seventeenth century. Three hundred cartloads of skeletons—can you imagine?"

She grimaced.

"There are several rooms, all featuring different parts of the body." He took her hand, leading her further into the gloom. Isabella could dimly make out yet more bones on the walls. "This is the crypt of pelvises," said Vicenzo. "It's my favorite."

"Oh my God—it's disgusting!" Isabella suddenly realized what she was looking at. Hundreds of individual pelvic bones were stacked on top of each other to create complex designs. On either side of the central display entire skeletons dressed in monks' habits had been propped up in the curved recesses. "I feel as if they're watching us," she said nervously.

"Well, fortunately they're not," he replied. "That's why I chose it for a meeting place. No one comes in here—it's too scary."

She glanced at him. "So why did you want to meet?"

"To check if you were all right and that my dogs were happy."

"The dogs are fine. I managed to find some meat for them. Someone at the golf club knew someone...you know how it is. So they're eating well. They sleep on the bed with me—it makes me feel less alone."

"You have Constanza for company."

"Yes I know, but it still feels odd being in your house, without you."

"I'm sorry," he said gently, "but I'm grateful that you're there."

"I don't really understand why you need me there," she said. "Constanza could feed the dogs."

"She's only a young girl and not very bright. Besides, I need it to look as if I am still there, with lights going on, comings and goings. Why, don't you like living in my house?" He smiled at her. He was more like the old Vicenzo, soft and loving.

"Of course I like it," she said. "It's your house, so how could I not? I feel close to you when I'm there."

He stroked her cheek. "You're very sweet."

"You have my picture by your bed," she said shyly.

"I know."

"Why?"

"You know why."

"No," she said, searching his face for some hint that he might love her. "Explain it to me."

"I care for you," he said, gazing down at her, his dark eyes glittering in the candlelight. She felt the familiar longing deep inside. She desperately wanted him to kiss her, to hold her.

"Do you love me?" she asked quietly.

"Yes, in my own way."

"What does that mean?"

"Have you seen your German officer?" he asked, changing the subject.

"Wolff? No. He seems to have disappeared."

"He's gone up north," Vicenzo said. "He's been replaced—by a man named Kappler; he's the new Gestapo Chief. He works in tandem with an evil little bastard called Pietro Koch."

"That's an odd name."

"Yes. He's Italian, but he has a German father, I gather. He runs a special Fascist police unit, with orders from Kappler to root out partisans."

"You must be careful."

"I am," he replied. "They raided a seminary last night in the Vatican City."

"A religious building. Why?" asked Isabella.

"It was a partisan hideout—so they must have had good intelligence."

"Did everyone get away?" she asked.

"Some did. Kappler's decided to increase the SS police forces in Rome—they're going to be making house-to-house searches, looking for every able-bodied man."

"You too?" she asked, her eyes widening in fear.

"Why do you think I went into hiding?"

"I see. But you're safe...wherever you are?"

"For the time being, yes. But if they come looking for me, you must just say I'm away, do you understand?"

"Of course. You can rely on me," she reassured him.

"Isabella, little Bella." He held her firmly by the arms and looked down at her with dark thunderous eyes. She felt herself once again under his spell. "There is something you need to know."

It sounded ominous. Was he about to confess to loving someone else—Livia perhaps? He looked away awkwardly as if he was embarrassed suddenly.

"Tell me," she insisted, her heart racing.

His grip on her arms weakened and his hands fell limply to his side. "I cannot love women," he said flatly, before turning away from her.

"What do you mean?" Isabella replied, genuinely puzzled.

"Unlike other men, I don't find women attractive, do you see?"

"Who *do* you find attractive then?" she asked.

He laughed quietly. "Men, of course."

She felt a curious sense of relief. "So you don't love another woman?"

"No!" He swung round and held her face between his hands. "If I love any woman at all, it is you, little Bella, and only you."

She smiled and stroked his cheek with her gloved hand.

They were interrupted by the noise of the crypt door being opened and footsteps on the staircase.

"We should get out of here," he whispered. "Quickly, follow me."

He led her through a series of small rooms, each more macabre than the last, before finally they reached a door. Moments later, they were outside on the street. He pulled her into a side street, turning up the collar of his coat and tugging his hat down over his eyes. It made him look like a street vendor, she thought.

"I won't be around for a while," he said. "All I can tell you is that I am working for the Resistance. You will only hear from me again when it's safe."

"Don't go yet," she implored him. "Please."

"I must, carissima Bella." He kissed her on the cheek and was gone.

Walking back through the snow to Vicenzo's villa, Isabella mused on what he had told her. She had heard of men who loved each other, although she was not exactly sure what it meant. He had told her he loved her, and if that love couldn't be quite as she would have liked, she could learn to live with that. To be loved by him was all that mattered. She would care for his home, care for his beloved dogs. They would share their love of art and of cinema. They were soulmates, after all. They belonged together. She would do anything for him, anything at all. That, after all, was what real love was all about.

Chapter Twenty-Two

Florence
January 1944

It was late in the afternoon, and almost dark as Livia hurried home. Letting herself into the apartment, it seemed strangely quiet.

Unusually, her father was not working at the dining table. Nor was he in his bedroom, nor the kitchen. She called his name, but no answer came. She could hear the muted voices of Sara and Jacob up in the attic. They had come to an arrangement with Giacomo when they had first arrived, that it would be safer if they stayed upstairs as much as possible—particularly if both Giacomo and Livia were out. That way, as Giacomo said, if they were raided and the apartment searched, there was a chance they would escape detection. And so, as soon as breakfast was finished, they went back upstairs, only re-emerging in the evening to help with dinner. When the meal was over, they returned to the attic and all evidence of their presence was erased. The extra dinner plates and glasses were washed and put away and the coat rack was placed back in front of the secret door.

With an hour or more until supper time, Livia pottered in the kitchen. She jointed a hare that had been left for them on the roof that morning, and began to fry it on the stove. Periodically she peered out into the darkening gloom, looking anxiously for her father, but the street below was deserted. He had said nothing about being home late, and to be out after the curfew was completely out of character.

She was just laying the table, when she heard Jacob's gentle knocking on the attic door. As soon as she opened it, Matteo ran to her and buried his head against her legs.

"Hello there," she said, stroking his blond head affectionately. "Have you had a good day?"

"Yes," he nodded. "Papa and me did a jigsaw."

"Oh, that was clever. Where did you find that?"

"I hope you don't mind," Jacob said, joining them in the hall. "Your father told me he thought there was one in your room."

"Of course I don't mind. We have a few things from when I used to visit Papa as a child. There may be some more buried away... I'll look out for them."

"Is your father not home?" Jacob asked, peering into the sitting room.

"No." Livia caught Jacob's eye. His face mirrored her own anxiety. "He's probably just caught up at his office," she suggested reassuringly. "Let's eat. We can leave him some food."

They ate their supper in relative silence—each of them worrying about Giacomo.

"It's not like him to be so late," Jacob said eventually. "He said nothing about going out after breakfast. Perhaps I should go and look for him."

Sara, alarmed at this suggestion, grabbed his hand.

"That's very kind," interjected Livia. "But you know it would be madness for you to risk going out. We don't need to worry just yet. You'd better go back upstairs. I'll clear up here and wait for him."

Livia knew that to be out after the curfew was a risk. Partisans did it all the time, but they were usually young and fit, and could run if spotted by the enemy, whereas her father was an old man. She tried to think of logical reasons for him to be so late, but her mind kept wandering to more frightening scenarios—that he might have been arrested and detained, even tortured.

When it was time for the Radio Londra broadcast, she went to her room and listened to Colonel Stephens. His gentle voice calmed her a little. She made her notes, as usual, and began to start work on her weekly round-up of news stories for the paper, but she found it hard to concentrate. Eventually, she abandoned her work and began to pace frantically around the apartment.

To her immense relief, Livia heard her father's key in the lock at last. She ran into the hallway and found him stamping the snow off his feet, forming a little pool of water on the parquet floor.

"Papa," she said, hugging him, "thank God you're back. I've been so worried. Where have you been?"

"Let me come in first." He took off his coat and shook it, before hanging it on the coat rack in front of the secret door.

"We kept you some supper," she said.

"Thank you. I'm very hungry and could do with a drink."

While he opened a bottle of wine, she laid out his food on the table. When he'd finished eating, he pushed his plate away and poured himself another glass of wine. "There's something I need to tell you."

"Go on," Livia urged.

"Someone will be coming here shortly—a member of the British Intelligence Service."

"Coming here, but why? What do we have to do with British Intelligence?"

"You'll find out," he said, refilling his glass again. "Let's go into the sitting room and wait."

He settled down at the dining table with his papers and the half-drunk bottle of wine. Livia marveled at his calm exterior. He had an ability to concentrate on his work, whatever the circumstances.

After an hour or so, he checked his watch and stood up, draining his glass. "I arranged to wait for him downstairs—so he doesn't need to knock or alert the household."

"Shall I come with you?" asked Livia.

"No," said her father. "Stay here. I won't be long."

As he opened the front door of the apartment, Signor Lombardi opened his door a crack.

"Buonasera, Signor Lombardi," said Giacomo cheerfully. "Are you well?"

"Thank you, yes," the old man replied gruffly, before shutting the door again.

Ten minutes later, Giacomo returned, accompanied by a man dressed in a shabby overcoat and trilby hat. Livia stood up as her father brought the visitor into the sitting room.

"Livia, my darling," said Giacomo, "can I introduce you to Lieutenant Marshall of the British Army."

"Good evening." The man spoke Italian, but with an interesting southern Italian accent.

"Do sit down," Livia replied.

"Grappa, Lieutenant?" asked Giacomo.

"Thank you, and do please call me David." He sat down on the sofa and looked around him. "What a lovely room."

"I'm sorry it's so cold," Livia said. "We can't get any firewood."

"Please don't worry on my account. I was brought up in Britain, where you break the ice off the water in the bowl before you wash every morning. Besides, it's warmer in here than outside." He smiled cheerfully, and rubbed his hands together.

"I've not told my daughter anything yet." Giacomo handed him a drink. "Apart from the fact that you are part of British Intelligence."

"Delicious," said David, sipping his drink. "Well, I'd better explain why I'm here. Our job in military intelligence is primarily sabotage, but we also support the Resistance, both here and in France. The Allied army is moving slowly up from the south, as you probably know, but we've got a bit stuck down in Naples. The Germans see Italy as an essential part of their defense, and to that end have created certain defensive lines—a couple to the south of Rome and two more to the west of the Apennines. The weather is proving a bit of an obstacle to the Allied advance too—who knew you had snow this deep?" He looked out at the blizzard that was now swirling around the building.

"The good news," he went on, "is that the Resistance here in Italy is getting stronger every day and will prove to be an impressive adversary to the Nazis. Our unit's job is liaison and support—by disrupting the enemy, of course, but also supplying groups like yours with vital information and equipment."

"What sort of equipment?" Livia asked.

"Weapons, and technical support of all kinds. We get airdrops from Allied planes from time to time. In fact, we have one planned for tomorrow night. But I'm rather worried about the weather; finding canisters filled with guns in deep snow is no joke." He laughed, and

Giacomo refilled his glass. "Your father tells me that you are the Pd'A's radio operator, here in Florence."

"Yes," Livia replied uncertainly. "That makes it sound more impressive than it really is. I only have a short-wave radio, but it's good quality and we can pick up Radio Londra. I pass on information to the group, and also turn that information into articles for our newspaper—so the wider public know what's going on."

"Excellent," said the Lieutenant. "Well I wonder if you might extend your role a little?"

She nodded.

"I have with me a rather special radio." He pointed to a black leather case he had deposited on the dining table when he came in. "If you are willing, I'd like to show you how to use it."

Livia looked up at her father questioningly, while the British officer unlocked the case, revealing a metal unit festooned with knobs and dials.

"At our last Pd'A council meeting," Giacomo explained to his daughter, "it was agreed that we should work with British Intelligence in this matter. We pass information to them and they in turn can assist us. We both benefit. In the process, we gather more information that we can send out to partisans around Florence. To support this work, we've decided to create our own radio station."

"The idea," said the Lieutenant, "is that you transmit, once, or even twice a day, if you can manage it—information about what the Germans are up to here in Florence—troop movements, armaments, anything really. That information will be picked up by us and will help our troops understand the lay of the land here in this area. It will be vital to our being able to rescue the city from the grip of the Nazis. Does that seem clear?"

"Yes, very clear," she replied solemnly.

"In particular," he went on, "we need help with establishing safe places for our Allied airdrops. Without that information, the arms we drop will fall into enemy hands. So knowing where it's going to be safe is absolutely crucial. The truth is, Florence is looking like it's going to be critical to victory. Whoever wins Florence wins Italy."

"I'm ready to help in any way," Livia said with conviction.

"Good. Now the Germans will eventually work out what's going on, of course, so we suggest that you keep on the move."

Livia looked at him blankly. "I don't understand."

"What I mean is that the Germans will be able to trace the origin of your signal, so it's essential you move to a different place each day to avoid discovery."

"I see." Livia looked up at her father. "So we'll need a series of safe houses."

"Exactly." David glanced nervously at them both. "There is inevitably great danger associated with this operation."

"I appreciate that," said Livia. "I also appreciate my father's faith in me."

Giacomo smiled at Livia. "It will be called Radio Cora. It stands for Commission Radio."

"And I need hardly tell you," David went on gravely, "it may well prove an indispensable link in our defeat of the enemy."

Chapter Twenty-Three

Rome
January 1944

One cold afternoon in January, Isabella was at the golf club, idly playing a round of bridge with three middle-aged friends, when Stefano rushed in ashen-faced and collapsed onto a bar stool.

Isabella put her cards face down on the table. "Would you excuse me for a moment?" she asked her fellow players.

She hurried across the club room and sat down next to him. "Stefano darling, what on earth is the matter?"

"Have you heard the news?" he asked.

"What news? There is so much of it, and none of it's good."

"About Ciano, of course."

She shook her head.

"He's been executed—a week, or so ago—I only just heard. Shot in the back, strapped to a chair."

"Oh my God," she said. "I mean, I never liked him much, but I wouldn't wish that on him."

"Mussolini's own son-in-law!" exclaimed Stefano. "How could a father do that to his own daughter, killing her husband?" He ordered a large whisky from the bartender.

"Is she all right?" asked Isabella.

"Rumor has it she's gone to Switzerland."

"Well I never met her, but I can't help feeling sorry for her," Isabella said. "Was there a trial?"

"If you can call it that. Two days of a tribunal, and finally found guilty of treason. Bit of a foregone conclusion, if you ask me. Ciano argued he was merely seeking to support the regime during the crisis, but the court saw it differently. What was it they said?" Stefano took a gulp of his drink. "That Ciano 'tended toward the elimination of Fascism and its Duce.' I tell you, Isabella, between the Allies in the south and the mad Fascists in the north, we're doomed." He drank the remains of his whisky and demanded another.

That evening, back at the villa, Isabella sat at Vicenzo's desk in the window of the sitting room. Outside, it was snowing heavily. The dogs lay at her feet and a fire crackled comfortingly in the grate. Ciano's death had unnerved her. She had never liked him—had found him insufferable in many ways—but the idea that a loyal Fascist could be dispensed with so summarily was alarming. Although she had moved in Fascist circles, she did not consider herself to be one of them. If anything, she was apolitical. She had merely gone along with the way things were, in order to work—to survive. Now it occurred to her that if the Fascist authorities could turn on their own previously loyal ministers, what would they do to someone like Vicenzo—a man who opposed them completely?

Unnerved, and desperate to get news of events, she turned on the radio. She knew there was a British radio station, Radio Londra, but had never looked for it, partly because it was illegal to listen to it, and it was against her nature to break the law. But after that day's events she decided to risk it. She turned the dial until she found the station. There was an interesting discussion program in which a well-known liberal was challenging the Fascist orthodoxy. This was followed by a news broadcast, delivered in Italian by a man with a soft, calm English voice.

Allied troops have moved up from their stronghold in Sicily, landing virtually unopposed at the coastal town of Anzio as part of "Operation Shingle." British and American infantry divisions were supported by both tank and airborne battalions. By the end of the day, 36,000 troops were landed ashore.

Anzio was just fifty kilometers away from Rome. Isabella was exhilarated by the closeness of the Anglo-American armies. Maybe this awful war would be over soon, Vicenzo could return, and their life together could begin in earnest.

When the broadcast was finished, she retuned to a music station, and picked up one of a stack of letters she had collected that afternoon from her house. It was from the director of a film she had shot a couple of years earlier. It had been mothballed for some time but was now to get a cinema release. Isabella felt conflicted about it. She was happy, of course, that her work would be shown at last. But it seemed inappropriate somehow to get pleasure from something quite so superficial, when all around her was death and destruction.

She slipped a knife beneath the flap of another envelope. The handwriting seemed familiar. As she removed the letter, she saw it was from her friend Mimi in Genoa and was dated December.

> *Dear Isabella,*
>
> *I write to bring you terrible news. Daniele, my darling husband, was arrested five days ago. He was picked up at the hospital by German soldiers. He has not returned home since. I have been quite desperate, as you can imagine. I went to the hospital, then to the police station, and initially no one could tell me anything. Finally, I have discovered he has been sent to a prison camp. I had hoped at first that it would be here in Italy, but it seems he is on his way to a camp in Poland called Auschwitz.*
>
> *Isabella, I know you are close to the authorities. I beg you to help us. Please, is there anyone you could speak to? Our happiness, our lives, are in your hands.*
>
> *Your friend,*
> *Mimi*

Isabella stood up and walked across the room to the fire, suddenly needing its warmth. Mimi was under the impression that she had friends in high places. Little did she know that one of Isabella's contacts had recently been executed. The only high-ranking official she still knew was Karl Wolff. Would he help her friend? There was no art or jewelry to bribe him with; Daniele and Mimi were not rich, and, most significantly, Daniele was Jewish.

Isabella agonized all evening about how she could help him. All she could offer Wolff was her body, but would that be enough? He might sleep with her and then betray her.

She slept fitfully, but as she watched the dawn, she made a decision—she must at least try to help her friend.

That morning, Isabella took great care over her appearance, doing her hair and makeup meticulously, as if preparing for a part. She put on an elegant woolen dress and, because it was still so cold and snowy outside, wore her best fur coat and matching hat with warm boots. Walking briskly through the parkland surrounding Villa Borghese, she stopped at the gallery hoping Wolff might be there. Negotiating with him there would be easier than in his hotel, but she checked in all the rooms, and he was nowhere to be seen.

She continued down Via Veneto to Hotel Flora. She knew he'd had a room there when they had last met. She paused on the pavement outside the hotel, considering the step she was about to take. Perhaps, she reasoned, Wolff would be away, and she would be able to write to her friend and explain that she had tried to help Daniele but there was nothing she could do.

Isabella took a deep breath and pushed through the glass revolving doors. The lobby was filled with German officers; they stared at her lasciviously as she walked toward the reception desk.

"Is Karl Wolff staying here?" she asked.

The young man inspected the hotel register. "Yes, signorina. The General arrived a couple of days ago."

Isabella's heart began to race. "Would you call him, please?" she said nervously. "Tell him that Isabella Bellucci is in reception." Perhaps, she hoped, he would come downstairs, and suggest they have coffee, and then she could ask her favor. She waited nervously while the reception clerk dialed his number.

"He has asked that you go up to his suite."

Isabella felt a wave of nausea. For a second, she contemplated leaving, there and then. But instead, she breathed deeply, and crossed the lobby to the lifts. On the third floor she walked along the silent carpeted corridors toward Wolff's room. She stood outside his door, feeling sick and light-headed, her mouth dry, her heart thumping. If she went inside she knew what he would expect. Would sacrificing herself to him really save Daniele's life? Or would he sleep with her first, and betray her later? As sweat broke out on her forehead, she removed her fur hat and backed away from the door.

She began to walk rapidly down the corridor toward the lift. She pressed the button and waited impatiently until it arrived. Stepping inside, she turned to face the corridor and saw Wolff come out of his room. He looked left and right, finally spotting her in the lift.

"Isabella," he shouted, "come back."

She pushed the ground-floor button frantically, but he was already walking purposefully down the corridor toward her. The doors closed in his face and she sank against the mirrored walls.

Back in the lobby, she ran, pushing her way between crowds of officers, out into the street. She stood for a moment on the pavement, wondering where she could hide. Then she remembered the Capuchin church.

She sprinted down Via Veneto and turned onto the side street. Her heart was pounding as she pushed the door that led to the crypt, and to her relief, it opened. Once inside, she stood silently, listening to her own breathing, her heart beating, praying she had not been followed.

Eventually, her heart slowed, her breathing calmed and she began to go over the episode in her mind—her fear about trading her body for Daniele's life, and her realization that Wolff would be bound to betray her. Her sacrifice would almost certainly have been for nothing, and yet, as she knelt at the altar in a small chapel in the damp basement crypt, she felt a profound sense of shame.

"My child, how did you get in here?" It was a young priest, standing in the doorway to the chapel.

"I'm sorry," she said, struggling to her feet, "I came through the door from the street."

"That door should have been locked," he replied kindly. "Never mind, come up into the church with me."

Hesitantly, she followed him.

"Sit down please," he said, indicating a pew. "You seem troubled."

Tears filled her eyes. "I am. I have sinned, Father, in so many ways. I have been weak."

"Do you seek absolution?" he asked.

"I cannot confess," she cried, "it's been too long."

"It's never too late," the priest said kindly, "to wash yourself free of sin."

Isabella walked the streets after her confession, filled with an overwhelming sense of failure and remorse. Sitting in the darkness of the confessional, she had been too ashamed to admit the worst of her sins—her betrayal of Livia, and her terror as she stood outside Wolff's door. How could she explain that to a priest? She had spoken instead in generalizations, of not doing as much as she could, of her fear. The priest told her that it was normal to be fearful—understandable even—and that God would forgive her. But when she came out into the street, she did not feel cleansed or absolved of her sins. Quite the reverse. She had failed her friend, and Daniele would almost certainly die. It was her fault.

It was almost dark when she got back to Vicenzo's villa. She crept silently upstairs, crawled into bed, comforted only by the dogs lying at her side, and wept.

Chapter Twenty-Four

Florence
February 1944

It was the coldest winter anyone could remember. When Livia went up onto the roof terrace, she marveled at the transformation of the city. Instead of shades of apricot and burnt siena, Florence had taken on an almost ghostly appearance, with its roads, parks, roofs and cupolas blanketed with snow. For Livia, who not only had to shop for the family, but also had duties as a *staffetta*, it made everyday life more difficult, with icy pavements and deep drifts of gray slush piled up at the edges of roads.

Leaving the apartment one morning, Livia headed toward Villa Triste. Relieved to discover there was no translation work to be done, she signed the register and left the building, heading toward the Arno. Her task that morning was to check out the movement of tanks near the river—information that would be transmitted later that day on Radio Cora.

The river was an expanse of gray-blue, reflecting the sky overhead. Livia skidded on the frozen pavements as she tried to avoid pairs of German soldiers patrolling the Lungarno. When she got as far as Piazza Ognissanti, she found it filled with tanks. German troops were lining up in the large square, and their senior officers were gathering outside the grand Hotel Excelsior which dominated one side of the piazza.

Livia was familiar with the hotel. When she had been at boarding school, her mother used to take her there for lunch. Boldly, she pushed through the revolving doors and walked confidently into the dark paneled lobby. It was just as she'd remembered, smelling of beeswax polish and cigar smoke, except it was no longer filled with elegant couples meeting for coffee and drinks. Now the plumped sofas were occupied by leading Italian Fascists and German officers. She walked calmly through the lobby, as if heading for the ladies' room. She recognized a couple of Fascist leaders as she passed through, Alessandro Pavolini among them.

In the ladies' room she made notes of everything she'd seen; she brushed her hair, and walked confidently back through the lobby and out into the piazza, before hurrying toward the Ponte Vecchio to finalize the arrangements for her transmission that afternoon.

The premises she would use that day belonged to Signor Casoni, a wealthy merchant who owned a row of shops along the Lungarno selling luxury clothing and jewelry. He was an old friend of her father's, and did his best to support the work of the Pd'A. When she arrived, she was shown to his office on the first floor. He was sitting at his desk, filling in the pages of a leather ledger.

"Livia!" he said, standing up and greeting her. "How are you? How is your father?"

"He's well, thank you. We're very grateful to you for allowing us to use your office today. I'll be back with the radio transmitter about two o'clock," she told him. "Will that be all right?"

"Of course. We close at one o'clock for lunch, so there'll be no one about. Come to the side entrance and knock three times. I'll let you in."

Leaving his office, she hurried past the Uffizi, heading toward the university. She slipped breathlessly into her seat in the lecture theater.

"Where have you been?" whispered Elena urgently. "You're late."

"I had things I had to do for my father," Livia replied evasively.

Elena shrugged. "You're always busy these days."

"Please don't be like that," Livia whispered, trying to placate her friend.

They sat in silence for the rest of the lecture. When it was over, they stood up and filed out of the theater.

"I'm meeting Cosimo in a moment," Elena said as they walked down the grand staircase with the other students.

"Really?" Livia replied. "Can I come? I've not seen him for days."

"I know...he told me."

Livia sensed her friend's resentment. She wondered if Cosimo shared Elena's feelings. Livia knew he would have liked to see her more often, but they were both so busy, so involved with their work.

The two girls waited in the large marble-floored hall for him to arrive. Livia checked her watch anxiously. It was already one o'clock. She still had to get back to the apartment, collect the radio and get to Signor Casoni's by two.

Eventually Cosimo arrived, loping along unevenly. He looked genuinely delighted to see her. "Shall we all go and have a coffee?" he asked eagerly.

"I'm really sorry," said Livia. "I'd love to, but I can't stay."

"You always have to be somewhere else these days." Elena sulked.

Cosimo touched her arm. "Don't be like that," he chided. "I'm sure she'd stay if she could..."

Elena turned away impatiently.

"I really am sorry," Livia said again to Cosimo. "But I'll see you both soon—yes?"

Cosimo kissed her on the cheek. "Take care," he murmured.

When she got to the doorway, she looked around. Cosimo and Elena were standing with their heads close together, deep in conversation.

Back at the apartment, Livia collected the transmitter that was hidden in her room. She packed it into a raffia shopping basket and covered it with a cloth, hoping she looked like an ordinary girl on her way to the market. As she opened the door, Lombardi was waiting, predictably, on the landing.

"Good afternoon, Signor Lombardi," Livia said cheerfully, "it's very cold today...better to stay indoors, I think."

"Yes, I suppose so," he replied gruffly and retreated inside, closing the door reluctantly.

Livia ran downstairs and out into the street, heading toward the safe house. Her route took her past Café Paskowski. It had now become the meeting place not only for Carità and his band of followers, but also for the Gestapo. In the summer months, the café's tables and chairs spilled out onto the piazza, but in the depths of winter, the customers were crammed together inside.

As she hurried past, Livia noticed Cosimo and Elena sitting at a table in the corner. She was about to stop and knock on the window to attract their attention, but then noticed they were holding hands and gazing into one another's eyes. Half an hour earlier, they had been begging her to join them. Now it seemed they only had eyes for one another. She was tempted to stop and confront them, but she knew the café would be filled with members of the Fascist police. She couldn't afford a scene and risk discovery. Besides, it would make her late for her transmission. So instead, she walked briskly on to Signor Casoni's office, and once she was finished, headed home. Her route took her past the café again, and she was relieved to see Cosimo and Elena had gone.

That afternoon, as Livia sat in the lecture theater, she felt a rising sense of indignation. Elena and Cosimo were the two people she loved most in the world, apart from her family, and they had apparently betrayed her.

Unusually, Elena was late. When she finally arrived, she looked nervously at Livia as she slid into her seat.

As they filed out an hour later, Livia grabbed her by the arm. "I need to speak to you." Her tone was firm, challenging.

"What about?" asked Elena. "I can't stay long. I have a meeting with my tutor in five minutes."

"It won't take long," Livia said.

She pulled her friend into a small anteroom off the main entrance. There was nowhere to sit but a cold stone seat.

"So, what do you want?" Elena asked impatiently.

"I saw you, with Cosimo at the café."

Elena blushed.

"So you admit it?"

Elena turned her face away.

"I saw you holding hands," Livia said accusingly. "You should have told me."

Elena stood up suddenly. "I have to go."

"Don't you have anything to say?" Livia asked furiously.

"You have your secrets and we have ours," Elena replied.

Livia remained in the anteroom for some moments after her friend had left. She was stunned. It seemed extraordinary that Elena had not denied her relationship with Cosimo, but neither had she admitted it. And what did she mean about "having secrets"?

As she walked slowly home, she struggled to understand how Cosimo, her own beloved Cosimo, could betray her in this way.

That evening Elena's mother telephoned Livia. "Elena has a terrible cold, poor thing. She has quite lost her voice and has a bad chest; her father says she must stay at home. Will you tell the lecturers she won't be in for several days?"

"I see." Livia was furious that her friend seemed to be avoiding her. "Has Elena seen Cosimo at all?"

"Cosimo? Not as far as I know. He's certainly not been here, why?"

"Oh, nothing," said Livia. "I hope she gets better soon."

A few days later, Livia was still smarting from her friends' betrayal. She had seen neither Cosimo nor Elena since that day, and felt desperately hurt and confused. She tried to bury herself in her responsibilities, but the memory of them holding hands and gazing into each other's eyes disturbed her concentration. It seemed incredible that they could be so disingenuous, declaring their affection for her while meeting behind her back. Perhaps it was her fault for being so secretive, and yet what else could she do? She was forced to behave secretly for her own and everyone else's protection.

That evening, after the family had retired to the attic, Livia monitored the broadcast from Radio Londra while her father worked at the dining table. She wrote up her notes as usual, and was just tidying the kitchen when a ball of snow hit the kitchen window. She opened it and peered outside into the street. Cosimo was standing outside, hammering on the oak door with his walking stick.

"Cosimo!" she called out. "What are you doing here?"

He looked up at her. "I have to speak to you...please, it's urgent."

"Wait there," she shouted, "I'm coming."

As she opened the door of the apartment, Lombardi appeared on the landing. "Who is that making such a racket at this time of night?" he asked irritably. "I presume it's a visitor for you?"

"Excuse me, Signor Lombardi, but a friend has an emergency. I must go down and let him in."

"It's after curfew," he said grumpily. "I could report you."

She took his hand in her own. "Please don't do that," she begged. "He's a war hero, injured on the front in Russia. He lost part of his leg, and he wouldn't be here if it wasn't urgent." She gazed into the old man's eyes, willing him to agree.

"Well," he replied, "all right...but don't make a habit of it."

She rushed down the five flights of stairs and opened the door. Cosimo staggered inside and leaned against the wall, breathing deeply. He had obviously been running and appeared distraught.

"Cosimo," she asked tenderly, "what on earth is the matter?"

On the floor above, a door opened. Livia held her fingers up to her mouth. They heard muffled voices on the landing. Cosimo held his breath, as tears streamed silently down his face. When they finally heard the door close above them, Livia led Cosimo upstairs. Once inside the apartment, he collapsed onto the floor.

Giacomo rushed out into the hall and helped him into the sitting room.

"Dear boy, what on earth has happened?"

"It's Elena," he said tearfully, sitting on the sofa.

Livia sat next to him and held his hand. "What's happened to her?"

"She's been arrested—by Carità. We think she's been taken to Villa Triste."

Livia blanched. "Why? What on earth has she done?"

Cosimo began to sob uncontrollably. "Here, drink this," urged Giacomo, handing him a tumblerful of grappa.

Cosimo upended the glass, knocking back the liquid so fast he began to choke.

"Take your time," Livia suggested gently, handing him a glass of water.

He sipped it, trying to slow his breathing. "She's accused of being a member of the Resistance," he said eventually.

"The Resistance! But she's got nothing to do with the Resistance...has she?" asked Livia.

"She joined GAP with me," Cosimo explained. "She wanted to help."

"Why didn't she tell me?" asked Livia, aghast.

"For the same reason you don't tell her anything," said Cosimo pointedly. "We are all operating in secret, aren't we?" He put his glass down and picked up his stick. "I shouldn't have come here. I'm sorry, I panicked and I couldn't think where else to go. I'll only bring you both into danger and that's the last thing I want. I ought to leave; I need to go and help her...now." He struggled to get to his feet.

"We will help her," said Giacomo, his hand on the boy's shoulder. "And of course you were right to come to us. But first, you must tell us what happened."

Cosimo sank gratefully back in the chair. "I hardly know where to begin."

"At the beginning," said Giacomo.

"GAP had a plan...to blow up Mario Carità." He paused, looking between Livia and Giacomo, allowing the full force of this audacious idea to sink in.

"Were they mad?" asked Livia.

"Maybe," said Cosimo. "But it seemed a good idea. Carità goes to Café Paskowski every day at lunchtime, regular as clockwork. It gave us the perfect opportunity. Elena and I volunteered for the job." He glanced up at Giacomo, who raised his eyebrows quizzically. "We were to go to the café, as often as possible, and behave as if we were a newly engaged couple, in love." He looked across at Livia and blushed. "We weren't in love—you must believe that."

"It's all right." Livia took his hand and squeezed it. "Go on."

"So the idea was that we should be recognized by everyone—you know, the young girl and the damaged, heroic soldier."

"My God," said Livia, astonished.

"Today was the day we were going to act. We positioned ourselves at the corner table; Carità arrived and sat at the neighboring table, his usual one. Today, he actually smiled at us. Our instructions were to put a bomb under our table, and when it went off he would be killed instantly."

Giacomo caught Livia's eye and shook his head in disbelief.

Cosimo began to get agitated. "I really must go and help Elena," he said.

"We will, I promise," said Livia, "but first, tell us the whole story. What went wrong?"

"There's a waiter at the café who is in the Resistance. He had screwed a hook beneath our table. We were to finish our drinks, I was to light the fuse, Elena would fix the bomb on the hook, and we would leave. A few moments later—Boom! Carità would be dead."

"So, what happened?" asked Livia.

"We sat at our table and ordered a vermouth—to make it look like we were relaxed, celebrating. As always, we chatted, held hands, and so on." He glanced anxiously at Livia, who smiled.

"It's all right, I understand," she reassured him.

"Elena had the bomb in her handbag, wrapped in tissue paper, like a little present. She put the bag onto her lap, and took the bomb out and laid it on the table. I lit a cigarette casually, and used the match to light the fuse on the bomb. She slipped it under the table, but she couldn't attach it to the hook—it was too big, or wide, or something. She was panicking, the fuse burning away. So she dropped her napkin and, while she pretended to pick it up, pinched the fuse out with her fingers. Then she calmly put the bomb back into her bag. She was incredible, so brave. We took another sip of our drinks, and asked for the bill. We thought we'd got away with it—no harm done. We'd come back in a few days and try again." He wiped his face with his hands.

"Go on," said Livia.

"As we stood up, a German officer at another table came over. He asked Elena what was in her bag. He must have seen what she was doing. 'Nothing,' she replied, taking my arm and kissing me. We began to leave, intending to cross the piazza. Once we were outside, she began to walk very fast, but with my foot, I couldn't keep up. Suddenly, I was surrounded by Germans. When she got to the other side of the piazza, Elena turned around to check where I was. When she saw me, she started to walk back. I screamed at her to run, but she came back anyway. She grabbed the officer and she said to him: 'What are you doing? This man is a war hero! How dare you accuse him of anything?' Some of the customers came outside and cheered her on. The soldiers got distracted and started shouting and pushing the customers back into the café. They let go of my arm, and I backed slowly away, hoping she would follow. But when I got around the corner, she was the one surrounded by Germans." He began to weep, his head in his hands. "I left her, Livia. I betrayed her, she saved my life, and I let them take her."

Livia wrapped her arms around him. "You didn't, you didn't," she whispered.

He pulled away, desperate to finish his story. "I waited out of sight and watched as they marched her across the piazza. I should have gone after her."

"No," said Livia. "You did the right thing. She made a mistake coming back. She should have left you."

Cosimo stared at her. "How can you be so unfeeling?"

"We all know the risks when we join, don't we?" She looked up at her father, who nodded. "You must believe me, Cosimo, you did the right thing. There was no sense in both of you being arrested." She put her arm around him, but he shrugged her off.

"I will go and tell them to take me instead," Cosimo said.

"No." Giacomo put his hand firmly on Cosimo's shoulder. "They will just arrest you both. I will go to Villa Triste in the morning and see what can be done to rescue her."

"But Papa, you shouldn't get involved," urged Livia. "Let me speak to them—they trust me."

"No," Giacomo was emphatic. "You're too important to us now. The last thing we need is for you to get involved. They will believe me, I'm a lawyer, and a friend of the family. Of course it would be quite understandable that I should go." He turned to Cosimo, and took the boy's hands in his own. "You will stay with us tonight. Tomorrow we will find you a safe house. You can't go home, I'm afraid. If Elena breaks down under pressure, she will identify you, and then you, your family and everyone in your cell will be in serious danger."

Chapter Twenty-Five

Rome
March 1944

Through the cold, dark winter months of February and into March, Isabella remained at Vicenzo's villa. Alone, with just the dogs and Constanza for company, she spent her days reading or drawing, cocooned from the rest of the world, only venturing out occasionally for supplies. Snow continued to fall, and they were low on firewood. Eventually, the gardener felled an old pine tree. Because it wasn't properly seasoned, the wood burned slowly, but it created enough heat for Isabella to be able to settle down in the drawing room, and sit listening to the wood crackling, the dogs at her feet. At five o'clock, when the curfew was in place and the streets fell dark and silent, she would light the lamps, imagining some future life after the war, living with Vicenzo as the chatelaine of this house. If they were ever to marry, their relationship would be different from other couples', but she was prepared for that. Their love was unique; it was a spiritual thing, based on a shared appreciation of art and mutual respect.

The one dark spot on her horizon was her failure to help her friend Mimi and her Jewish husband, Daniele. Mimi's letter begging for help lay unanswered on Vicenzo's desk, a nagging reminder of her failure. One evening, unable to bear the guilt any longer, she picked up the letter and threw it onto the fire. As she watched it burn, her shame evaporated while Mimi's words of desperation curled and were reduced to ashes.

In the evenings, the radio was her companion. Although it was illegal to listen to foreign broadcasts, she and Constanza listened to the nine o'clock news on Radio Londra. After all, who would reveal their secret? One evening, the announcer brought news of the Allies' struggle to broach the Germans' defensive line reaching from coast to coast across the country south of Rome.

"It doesn't sound very positive, does it?" said Constanza.

"No," replied Isabella. "I fear the chances of the Allies coming to our rescue anytime soon appear rather remote." She looked up and smiled encouragingly at the maid. "Don't worry, we'll survive."

But as she lay in bed that night, the distant rumbling of guns broke through the silence and she thought of the men battling for a position not far away.

She was woken the following morning by the maid. The dogs stood up from their night's sleep by Isabella's bed, wagging their tails.

"Buongiorno, signorina," Constanza said, pulling open the curtains, revealing a clear blue sky. "The Count has written and asked me to tell you that he has some friends who are coming to stay here today. He thanks you very much for caring for the dogs and the house but suggests that you return to your own home now."

Isabella sat up in bed, her mind still fuzzy with sleep. "He wants me to go?" She was confused.

"Yes, signorina. He tells me to say thank you and that he will be in touch soon. But it would be safer for you not to be here today."

The maid left, followed by the dogs. Isabella dressed and packed her things. Half an hour later, she came downstairs carrying a small suitcase. In the kitchen, Constanza had laid out some coffee on the table.

"Constanza, is he angry with me?" she asked.

"No, signorina, not at all! He just said that, as others are expected, it would be safer for you to go."

"I see, and the dogs?"

"I will manage, thank you. I think maybe in a few days, his sister may come here and take them to the country. They will miss you though, they really do love you."

"And I love them." Isabella held out her hand and the dogs ran toward her, snaking their heads beneath her fingers. "Did he say whether he wants me to come back?" Isabella asked.

Constanza handed her a cup of coffee.

"No, madame." The maid picked up the letter and read his instructions. "He said to tell you that he would be honored if you could continue to care for the house, but from a distance. That it would be safer for you not to live here anymore."

Isabella was hurt he had chosen to write to Constanza and not her. Surely a personal note, explaining the situation, would have been better?

"Well, I'd better be going then," she said, putting the cup back on the table.

Constanza smiled, picked up the cup and took it to the sink to wash. Isabella felt as if her presence was being erased from the house.

"I'll see you soon," said Isabella, retreating to the hall, followed by the dogs. She put on her fur coat and picked up her suitcase. She walked to the doorway of the sitting room and took a last lingering look at the house she had hoped, one day, to call home. Only the evening before, she had been imagining that her place was at Vicenzo's side forever. Now it seemed she was no longer necessary—that she was being dismissed, like a superfluous servant. She leaned down to kiss the dogs goodbye, before loading her suitcase into her car and driving home.

Isabella let herself back into the villa just as her mother was coming down the stairs.

"You're back then?" Giovanna said. "I thought you'd left us forever."

"I was just staying at a friend's house," Isabella replied defensively, hanging up her coat. "They were away and needed me to look after it." She felt deflated and humiliated, and was not in the mood to justify herself to her mother.

"Well at least that man hasn't been back here," Giovanna said.

"What man?" Isabella asked warily.

"That German officer, what was his name—Wolff? He's obviously given up on you now." Her mother made it sound as if this was something to be regretted.

Isabella ignored her mother's barbed comment. She went upstairs and crawled into her bed exhausted, pulling the covers over her head.

She spent the next few days miserably at home, rising late, going to bed early. Living at Vicenzo's house had given her life purpose. But now she realized she had been deluding herself. Her life no longer revolved around his. Back home, in the company of her mother, aunt and grandmother, she felt empty and hopeless.

"You're like a lovelorn teenager," her mother snapped late one morning when Isabella finally got up. "Why don't you go out? Try to get some food from the market, flash your beautiful smile at the stallholders and see if they can find something for a famous actress to eat."

Reluctantly, Isabella got dressed, pulling on trousers and a sweater. Although still smarting from her "dismissal," she was curious about who Vicenzo's mysterious guests might be, and so decided first to go to the villa. After all, Vicenzo had said she should continue to care for the house, even from a distance, and it would give her a chance to check on the dogs.

As she approached the front door, she put her hand out to ring the bell, but instead let herself silently into the villa, using the set of keys Vicenzo had given her. The dogs, lying in the hall, trotted happily toward her. She called out for Constanza, but there was no reply, so she walked into the drawing room and was surprised to see a man she didn't recognize sitting at Vicenzo's desk. He looked up startled when she came in.

"Hello," he said.

"Hello, my name is Isabella. Vicenzo left me in charge of the house. I just came over to check everything was all right."

The man stood up and held out his hand. "How nice to meet you. My name is Pietro Mocci, I'm also a friend of Vicenzo's." He didn't look like a friend, Isabella thought—his clothes were too shabby. "He's asked me to do some gardening for him while I'm here," Pietro said, as if reading her mind.

"I see," she replied. "Well, please don't let me stop you."

She left the house sensing she had been lied to. Vicenzo already had a gardener. He had no need of extra help, particularly in the winter months. Besides, this man didn't have the hands of a gardener, they were too soft and manicured, and he seemed educated and refined. And what was he doing sitting at Vicenzo's desk?

Isabella set off for the center of the city, walking through the park surrounding Villa Borghese. The snow that had lain for so long had finally begun to melt and snowdrops poked their way through the brown earth. The sun felt warm against her skin, and she tried to put her questions about Vicenzo to the back of her mind. It was good to be outside at last in the sunshine. She made her way through the back streets toward the food market and bought a few vegetables. She put them in her basket and walked on toward the Trevi Fountain, where she sat in a café, drank coffee and read a newspaper. There was a story about a volcanic eruption at Vesuvius near Naples. She sat quietly, her face in the sun, imagining the horror of being engulfed by molten lava. Perhaps there were even worse things than war, and they should all be grateful for what they had. Her coffee finished, she headed for home, taking a shortcut up a narrow side street, Via Rasella. As she hurried along, she was surprised by how deserted it seemed.

Suddenly, a street cleaner grabbed her by the arm. "Signora," he said quietly. "Get out of here now."

"Why?" she asked, shaking her arm free.

"Trust me," he said firmly. "Do as I say, run away fast."

Instinctively she obeyed, sprinting up Via Rasella and around the corner, hiding in the nearest shop doorway, uncertain where to go next. She became aware of the sound of marching boots, and a ragged chorus of German voices singing in time to their footsteps. The marching men's voices came closer.

Moments later, she noticed the street cleaner racing past her. A second man, who had been waiting on the opposite side of the road, grabbed him and draped him with a raincoat, covering his clothes and together they ran away up the main road. Sensing danger, Isabella chased after them. Suddenly there was a huge explosion, followed by a violent gust of air that pushed her onto the ground. A bus traveling up the road was blown over onto the pavement. All around her, people were screaming, men and women scattering in all directions. There was a second explosion and then the sound of gunfire, as bullets ricocheted off the buildings.

Stumbling along, Isabella felt her face and body being assaulted by shards of stucco and stone. Her ears ringing, blood trickling down her face, she staggered away toward Via Veneto, past Hotel Flora and the Excelsior Hotel, as German officers spilled out onto the street, racing toward the sound of the explosion.

When she arrived home she was still shaken and weeping.

"Isabella!" her mother exclaimed, coming into the hall. "What's happened to you?" Blood was pouring from a wound on Isabella's cheek onto her fur collar.

"Didn't you hear it?" Isabella asked.

Her mother shook her head, mopping at Isabella's cheek with a handkerchief.

"It was a bomb I think...on Via Rasella," said Isabella, dazed. "People must have been killed—German troops, I suspect. Someone warned me or I would have been killed too."

The following day, Isabella received a phone call from Constanza. "Signorina, signorina, something terrible has happened." The maid sounded hysterical.

"What is it?" asked Isabella. "Tell me."

"The police came here last night. They arrested that man who was staying here, Signor Mocci."

"Arrested him?" Isabella asked. "Why?"

"They think he has something to do with the bomb." Constanza began to sob.

Isabella was stunned. "Are you all right?" she asked. "Do you want me to come over?"

"No, no, signorina. The Count said to tell you to stay away. It's better for you."

Isabella put the phone down in a state of shock. Could Mocci be working for the Resistance alongside Vicenzo? Were they responsible for the bomb in Via Rasella? If she had still been living at the villa, she would probably have been arrested too. Perhaps Vicenzo was trying to protect her by asking her to leave—perhaps he did love her after all.

*

Isabella, unnerved and desperate for news, went to the Acquasanta club for lunch the following day. People were gathering by the bar, deep in conversation.

"They say the local GAP cell in Rome planted the bomb," said one of the golfers. "It was in a street sweeper's cart."

Isabella remembered the street cleaner grabbing her arm and telling her to get out. "I was there! Someone told me to get out, or I might have been killed too."

"You were lucky," said Stefano. "The target was the German troops. They use that road every day as a shortcut, apparently. Thirty-three of them died in the end. Kappler, the new man in Rome, wanted to blow the whole road sky-high when he heard about it."

His audience listened in stunned silence.

"Someone stopped him though," Stefano went on. "Now Hitler's demanded that ten Italian men should die for every German."

"Ten times as many?" Isabella was shocked. "That means three hundred and thirty men. Surely that can't be true?"

"I'm afraid it is." Stefano took a sip of his drink. "My cousin is a clerk at the German interrogation center at Via Tasso. They've already started pulling together a list of the prisoners who are going to die."

Isabella suddenly remembered about Mocci. "I know someone who was just arrested. Would he be on the list?"

"Possibly. Every suspected partisan, every communist and Jew—however innocent—they're all doomed."

She began to panic. Perhaps Vicenzo had been arrested too?

Rumors swirled around for days as to what had happened to the men. People spoke of seeing trucks driving through Rome, heading north down the old Appian Way. Members of the golf club had heard explosions at dusk coming from the other side of the Parco della Caffarella.

Finally, a gardener who worked for the club revealed the grisly truth. He had been walking near the Ardeatine Caves when the trucks were driven in. He had hidden in some bushes high above the caves, and watched as men of all ages, some only in their teens, along with a priest, and many Jews, were taken in groups of five into the caves. He'd heard shots—single pistol shots—one for every victim. The German soldiers, he said, looked scared. Some of them even refused to shoot. Their commanding officer was encouraging them, shouting sometimes, giving them brandy to drink. By the end, they were so drunk they couldn't shoot straight and instead of five shots, there were ten or twenty for each group of five. At dusk, the engineers moved in and set explosives; they blew up the entrances to the caves, blocking the bodies inside.

Isabella—like everyone else who knew the truth—was reeling at the wanton cruelty of it. Any hope she had ever had that the Germans in their midst were capable of humanity evaporated.

She saw Wolff one last time. She was walking down Via Veneto a few days after the massacre. A German staff car pulled up in front of the Excelsior Hotel, and Wolff got out carrying a slim bricfcase. He walked toward the hotel, flanked on either side by junior officers. Kappler, the man who had overseen the massacre, was waiting for him outside. He shook Wolff's hand warmly, and led him through the revolving doors into the hotel. Perhaps, Isabella thought, he was there to be briefed on the massacre. She was about to carry on up the road, when, to her surprise, Wolff emerged and came back onto the pavement to speak to his driver. For a moment, she thought he had seen her. She shrank back into the shadows of a shop doorway. But his gray eyes looked right through her. There was no recognition, no empathy. Just a cold, grim, unfeeling expression.

Chapter Twenty-Six

Florence
March 1944

For weeks Giacomo had tried to intervene on behalf of Elena. He had gone to Villa Triste and offered to represent her in court. But Carità was insistent that she was a partisan, and would stay behind bars until he was finished with her.

"I'm not surprised," said Livia, when Giacomo gave her the bad news. "He's an evil man. Did he let you see her?"

"No, not even that. I argued of course. I told him it's against the law to deny her representation, but he just laughed. I went to see her parents afterward. They're frantic with worry. I wanted to give them hope—but I didn't know what to say."

"I just keep thinking of her there. I remember my own time spent in that terrible place. The things I heard, the things I saw..." Tears welled up in her eyes. "Oh Papa, I'm so frightened for her. Elena's not strong. She's courageous certainly, but I can't believe she'll withstand Carità's methods."

Her father held her, kissing her hair. "We won't give up."

"Maybe I should go and see Benedetta," Livia suggested. "I don't know what I can say to comfort her, but I must at least try. She has always been so kind to me."

"I'm sure she'd appreciate that," said Giacomo.

Cosimo, who was in hiding in a basement room belonging to one of the Pd'A, was desperate to get Elena released. "Maybe we could break in and rescue her?" he suggested to Livia, when she went to visit him later that afternoon.

"Cosimo, don't be ridiculous. The place is guarded day and night. Remember, I go there every day, so I know."

He got up and stared gloomily through the basement window. "Livia, I have to do something; I'm going mad here. Give me a job, please?"

"There may be something you can do," Livia suggested. "Let me talk to my father."

That evening, after dinner, Livia broached the subject with her father.

"Can I talk to you about Cosimo?"

"Of course."

"He's going crazy with worry and frustration. He wants to help, he needs to keep busy, to focus on something."

"I understand. I'm sure we can find something for him to do."

"He's good with technology," Livia said. "He worked as a radio operator in the army. I was thinking...he could help me with Radio Cora. It's getting to be too much for one person, monitoring the Germans' movements, finding a safe location for the transmission every day. I could do with the help."

"Can we trust him?" asked Giacomo.

"How could you even ask that? You know we can."

"It's just..." Giacomo paused, wandering over to the window, staring out at the snow which had begun to fall once again. "That scheme of his and Elena's at the café, it was too high risk. I worry he's too volatile, overly emotional. Our work with Radio Cora needs precision. We must all be calm under pressure."

"He knows that. He's very intelligent, Papa. I agree their scheme was crazy, but that wasn't his fault. It was a GAP idea, he just volunteered."

"There's something else," Giacomo said, turning to look at her. "We are hearing rumors of organizations like ours being infiltrated by the enemy."

"Cosimo is not the enemy," said Livia aghast. "How could you even think that? Please give him a chance, Papa."

*

The following night, the Allies planned to drop canisters to the partisans containing machine guns, grenades, ammunition, incendiary bombs, food and clothing. Livia had already scoped out a suitable location just outside Florence, and that afternoon there was to be a briefing to discuss the last-minute arrangements. Livia introduced Cosimo to the team leader, Paulo.

"I was wondering," Livia asked when they arrived, "if Cosimo could be of help tonight?"

Paulo looked at Cosimo, noting the walking stick. "You've been injured, I presume?"

"Yes," Cosimo replied. "I lost my foot in Russia. I have a prosthetic."

"I'm sorry," said Paulo, "but I think you'd be a liability. I can't risk it."

Livia, sensing Cosimo's disappointment, interjected. "Surely we could find something for him to do—please, Paulo?"

Paulo stared at Cosimo's foot, as if musing on the problem. "I'll think about it. All right, everyone, gather round. The weather forecast tonight is bad, I'm afraid; heavy snow is forecast, which will make collecting the canisters harder than ever. But we have to go ahead—the plans have all been made, and we need this equipment."

"How do we get everything back to town?" asked Cosimo.

"We have my father's car," Livia said, "and a charcoal hauler's cart that Paulo borrowed yesterday. We load the stuff up and bring it back in the middle of the night."

"There will be roadblocks of course, but we can avoid them," said Paulo. "Once we're back in the city we'll store the stuff in a house on Via Guicciardini near the Ponte Vecchio. Livia," he went on, "you've done your part liaising with the Allies on the radio, so you stay behind tonight." He looked pointedly at Cosimo. "You can drive a cart, I presume?"

Cosimo nodded.

"Right, meet back here at midnight. And remember, anyone who gets into trouble will be left behind. Understood?"

*

Livia had a sleepless night, waiting anxiously for news of the operation. She was on edge the following morning, and distracted herself by making coffee and toasting the remains of a stale loaf on the ancient grill.

When the family came downstairs from the attic, they gathered in the kitchen. While Jacob entertained Matteo, Sara sat down heavily at the table. Now eight months pregnant, her ankles were swollen and it was clear she felt uncomfortable. After breakfast, Jacob took Matteo back upstairs to tidy their little flat.

"I think the baby might come any day now," Sara said, after they'd gone. She sipped her cup of weak coffee and nibbled her tiny square of bread.

Livia pushed her plate toward Sara. "You must have mine," she insisted. "You and the baby need it more than I do."

Sara shook her head. "I can't do that."

"Please," said Livia. "Eat it for me."

"If you're sure?"

"Of course. Are you excited about the baby?" Livia asked. She was trying to sound optimistic, but the truth was she was worried about the birth. Finding a midwife they could trust was proving difficult, and she had no idea how to deliver a baby herself.

Sara smiled encouragingly. "Not excited exactly. I'm anxious, if I'm honest."

"We'll manage." Livia squeezed her hand. "Don't worry."

There was a sound of the front door being opened, and boots stamping in the hall. It was Giacomo, who had gone out very early that morning to collect his car after the airdrop.

"Papa, at last," Livia said, taking his coat.

He pulled her into the sitting room, closing the door behind them, and kissed her fervently on both cheeks. "I have exciting news," he whispered. "Thanks to you and Radio Cora, the drop last night was a huge success. We picked up a massive haul of weapons. Added to what we already have, there's quite an arsenal now. And look," he said, putting down a shopping basket on the table, "one of the canisters was filled with provisions. We have food!" He opened the basket, revealing a large bag of flour, along with some salt and sugar—neither of which Livia had seen for over a year.

"Oh Papa, that's wonderful. I'll take this flour to Sara now. With the baby coming, she really needs it." As she reached the door, she asked: "How did Cosimo do?"

"All right, I think. He drove the cart and acted as lookout. He was even able to help loading up the vehicles."

"I knew he wouldn't let us down. It will be good for him; he needs to have his mind taken off Elena. He still feels so guilty."

The flour and other provisions made a big difference to their daily life. For a few days at least, the family went to bed with relatively full stomachs. But one evening, Giacomo returned to the apartment, just as Sara was feeding her family in the kitchen. "Is my daughter here?" he asked. He looked wild and panicky, beads of sweat breaking out on his forehead.

"She's in her room," Sara replied.

Giacomo hurried down the corridor and flung open Livia's door. She was sitting at the desk, working.

"Thank God you're here," he said.

"Why, what's happened?"

"The Fascist police have found the hideouts." He sank down on the edge of her bed.

Livia sat down next to her father and put her arms around him.

"The house where we had the weapons stored has been discovered. They got everything—all the new supplies, plus the rest of the weapons we've been storing for some time. They even took the printing press."

"Was anyone arrested?" she asked.

"Yes, everyone there was rounded up. Five or six people." He put his head in his hands and groaned.

"How did you get away?"

"I wasn't there; I had a meeting with a client this morning. Someone found me just now and told me what had happened."

"How did they know where we were keeping everything?" asked Livia.

"I can only assume that we've been infiltrated." He looked up at her, tears in his eyes. "Someone has betrayed us, Livia."

"Who would do that?" she asked. "Do you know?"

"I've been asking myself that question ever since I found out. Who among our recruits is working against us? I just don't know. But no one is safe anymore. I wonder if we should get out of Florence."

"And go where?" she demanded.

"We could go home—you and me."

"Papa, this is not like you. You never give up. Besides, how could we leave now? I have to report to Villa Triste every day and if I don't turn up, they'll come here and search for me. Then they would find the family. I can't do that to them. We must stay here, and carry on with our work."

"No, please stop your work, and lie low for a while," Giacomo implored her.

"Well," she said calmly, "we can stop planning operations, limit the number of airdrops perhaps, but surely I must go on transmitting and sending information. It's needed now more than ever."

He shook his head. "I think we must stop everything."

"No, Papa," she insisted, "I won't do that. I'll be all right. Why don't you go home and see Mamma, and leave me here?"

"No, Livia, if you stay, I must stay with you. But if they associate me with the weapons haul and come searching for me, you're to give me up, you understand? You must say you know nothing."

"How could I do that?"

"What did you say to Cosimo? What's the sense in both of us being arrested?"

The following morning, Livia reported, as usual, to Villa Triste. She felt slightly anxious when she signed the register. As always, she thought of Elena and whether she was still there...somewhere in the building.

"May I leave now?" she asked the guard.

He nodded mechanically and she began to relax slightly. Perhaps they hadn't yet connected her with the haul of weapons. Just then, a man in black uniform came into the waiting room. Livia recognized him instantly—the slightly squashed face, the mean dark eyes. It was Mario Carità himself.

"Signorina, come with me please."

She followed him down the dark corridor, her heart pumping. She was shown into a small room, similar to the one she had been interrogated in before.

"Sit there," he said, pointing to a hard chair in the middle of the room.

She sat down uneasily. "I can't be too long," she said boldly. "I have to get to university."

His thin mouth formed itself into a sneer, as he dragged another chair across the floor. It sounded like chalk being scraped on a blackboard. He sat down opposite her, his legs apart, and leaned forward.

"I thought we should have a little chat," he said. "I think we have a friend of yours in here."

Livia's heart thudded so loudly she was convinced he would be able to hear it. "Really?" She tried to sound relaxed.

"Oh come now, you know we do. Your friend Elena."

"I wasn't sure where she was," replied Livia casually.

"Oh yes, she's here, although she is not very well."

"What do you mean?" she asked, frightened now.

"She is not very strong. I will show you, if you like."

He stood up, opened the door and gestured her to follow him. They walked down the corridor, pushing through a door at one end that led to a staircase. At the bottom of the staircase were another series of rooms with iron-barred observation-panels on the doors. Every cell contained either a man or a woman, lying on the floor in pools of blood, moaning and crying. Some appeared to have terrible wounds on their arms and legs. The awful stench of excrement caught in Livia's throat. Carità stopped at the last cell.

Peering into the darkness, Livia could just make out Elena, lying on a dirty mattress on the floor, her eyes closed. It was impossible to tell if she was asleep or unconscious, and her face had been battered so badly, she was almost unrecognizable. Only her golden hair identified her.

"Elena," Livia called out. "Elena darling…"

Elena didn't move.

"What a shame," said Carità, "she was such a pretty girl."

"What have you done to her?"

"She must tell us what she knows; did you know what she was planning?"

"No!" Livia swallowed hard. "Of course not! I have no idea why she's here."

He stared at her, musing, a smile playing on his lips. "She tried to kill me."

"I really can't believe that," Livia said bravely. "She's just a sweet, ordinary girl—clever, but not political. She'd never kill anybody. It's just not in her nature."

"She's part of a Resistance group called GAP," he went on.

"I'm sure that can't be true," Livia insisted.

"Oh it's quite true," replied Carità. "And she is either very brave, or very stubborn. She refuses to tell us anything."

"Maybe there's nothing to tell," she said defiantly.

"Ha!" he shouted, pushing her so violently that her head hit the brick wall with a crack. He grabbed her by the neck. "You people—you think you can outwit us." Livia could smell his sour breath and felt his spittle on her cheek. "But we will find every partisan, every disloyal, traitorous bastard and we will kill them all."

"I don't know why you're telling me this," she said, trying to placate him. "I am a loyal Italian. I work for the Germans as a translator. I'm doing everything I can to support you."

"I hope so," said Carità, eyeing her suspiciously. "Because we will be watching you. Get upstairs."

She took a last look at her friend lying motionless on the floor, and walked unsteadily down the corridor, hardly daring to breathe. Back upstairs, as she approached the main door, glimpsing the sunshine outside, Carità called her back. "Signorina!"

"Yes?" Livia's heart lurched.

"What do you know about arms?" he asked.

"Nothing. I don't know what you mean."

"Don't insult me. You know exactly what I mean. I'm talking about secret caches of weapons, hidden in a building near the Ponte Vecchio."

Livia exhaled quietly, trying to get control of her racing heartbeat. "Nothing," she replied. "I know nothing about anything like that."

He narrowed his eyes, studying her. "Get out," he said suddenly.

She rushed out into the street and walked briskly down the road before darting down a side street, where she collapsed onto the pavement in tears.

Chapter Twenty-Seven

Rome
March 1944

Isabella had opened the garden gates, and was just getting into her car, intending to go to the Acquasanta Golf Club for a game of bridge, when a policeman walked into the garden.

"Buongiorno, signora," he said politely.

"Buongiorno," she replied. "How can I help you?"

"Would you come with me please?"

"I beg your pardon," she said. "Where to?"

"To the police headquarters at San Vitale."

"What on earth for?" Isabella was confused.

"I cannot say, signora," he replied.

Her heart began to race. "I need to just tell my mother where I'm going, is that all right?"

"Of course," he said. "I'll wait in the car."

During the short drive to the police station, Isabella's mind was whirring with questions. Why did they want to speak to her? Was it something to do with Vicenzo? She resolved to behave with polite indifference. She would make it clear she was an honest, upright citizen. It was a part she knew she could play.

She sat anxiously in the waiting room until a tall, overweight man introduced himself as Commissario Guarnotta. "Come with me please," he said, leading the way to his private office.

The room was unremarkable. One wall was lined with shelves filled with books and files. A map of Rome was pinned to the opposite wall, marked with small red flags.

"Please," he said, "do sit down." He pointed to a leather chair while he remained standing, leaning casually against his desk. "You are an actress?" he began.

"I am. Well, at least I was. There is less work now, unfortunately—but once the war is over, I hope to return to it." Isabella pulled her fur coat tightly around her shoulders, comforted by its softness.

"You are a friend of many interesting people," he observed.

"I have many friends from all walks of life, yes."

"Influential people," he continued.

"I wouldn't necessarily describe them in that way. I suppose some of them are," she admitted.

"You know that Rome is full of people working against the government?" he asked.

"No, no, I didn't know that. I'm not involved with anything like that."

"I'm talking about partisans," he persevered. "Surely you have heard of the Resistance."

"I've heard of it, yes, but what has that to do with me?"

He picked up a folder from his desk and flicked through it. "You are a friend of a well-known communist, I think."

"Am I?" she asked innocently.

"Do not play games with me, signorina. I am not a big fan of fairy tales." He put the folder down and began to pace the room.

"I really don't know what you mean," she said.

"Vicenzo Lucchese. You were staying in his house for many weeks; you aren't going to deny it, I hope?"

"No, of course not. I stayed there. He's a friend from the film industry. He was going away for a while and asked that I take care of his house, make sure his dogs were fed, that sort of thing."

Guarnotta laughed sardonically. He walked round the other side of his desk, and sat down arranging his papers. "We have conducted a search of the Luccheses' house."

"Have you?" she asked indignantly. "I hope you didn't make a mess."

He ignored her question. "Would you like to know what we found?"

"I'm sure I really don't know," she said.

"Guns, bombs—weapons of all kinds."

She gasped.

"You seem surprised. Are you really telling me that you didn't know?"

"Absolutely! I had no idea," she said. "I'm quite shocked. I don't understand."

"You are an actress—perhaps you are giving a fine performance?"

"No!" she protested.

"Not only is Lucchese a communist, signorina, and so an enemy of the State, but we found evidence that he is running a partisan cell. He is part of a Resistance group in Rome called GAP. Have you heard of it?"

"No," she lied. "I've never heard of it."

"I'm surprised," he said, "I thought everyone knew GAP was responsible for the deaths of thirty-two German soldiers in Via Rasella. Are you still sure you knew nothing about it?"

"Yes, I mean, no . . . I mean, I knew about the bombing of course. In fact, I was nearly killed myself that day. I was about to go down Via Rasella when the bomb went off. I wouldn't have done that if I'd known about it beforehand, would I? You can ask my mother—she'll tell you, I came home in a terrible state."

He stared at her, his dark eyes unblinking. "Signorina, are you asking me to believe that you were in charge of his house, a house filled with weapons and bombs, and you knew nothing?"

"Absolutely," she replied firmly. "I was just there to mind the house and feed the dogs."

"We arrested one of his fellow cell members there—you must have lived alongside him."

"I certainly did not," she replied indignantly. "I was quite alone when I lived there, apart from the maid."

"So you never met a man named Pietro Mocci?" Guarnotta asked.

Isabella thought frantically. If she denied meeting him, and he had already implicated her, they would punish her. If she admitted to meeting him, it might implicate Vicenzo. She decided she had no other option than to simply tell the truth.

"I only met him once. I'd already left the house by the time he moved in. I went over to check everything was all right, and he was there in the sitting room. He told me he was the gardener. I thought it was odd, because Vicenzo already has a gardener. Besides," she said, her voice trailing off, "he didn't look like a gardener. His hands were too soft."

The policeman narrowed his eyes, exhaling through pursed lips. "If you are lying to me, I will make you suffer, do you understand?"

Her mouth was dry, her heart racing, but as an actress she was used to concealing her fear. "Of course I'm not lying," she replied indignantly. "That would be stupid."

He stood up and gestured toward the door. "You may go, but we will be watching you."

In the entrance hall were two men, presumably waiting to be interviewed. As Isabella walked past, she realized she knew one of them.

"It's Mario Chiari, isn't it?" she said.

He looked up at her, his eyes wide with fear.

"I thought I recognized you," she went on. "I met you once at a party at Vicenzo's house—do you remember?"

"Maybe," he replied distractedly.

"What are you doing here?" she asked, lowering her voice so the officer behind the desk couldn't hear.

"I don't know," he replied desperately. "We were picked up an hour ago but no one will tell us anything."

"Well, whatever you do," she whispered, "be careful of the Commissario—he's a most unpleasant man."

The following day, Isabella found a handwritten note in her postbox at the end of the drive.

   Meet me at twelve o'clock in the usual place, Vicenzo.

He was waiting for her in the crypt. He kissed her on both cheeks when she arrived, holding her to him briefly.

"I'm so glad you're all right," he murmured, before releasing her. "I heard you'd been arrested."

"Yes. A horrid man named Guarnotta accused me of knowing you were in the Resistance. He told me your house was full of weapons."

"I'm sorry. That's why I had to get you out of there; it was getting too dangerous for you to stay."

"So it was true—about the weapons?"

He nodded.

"And that man they arrested—the 'gardener.' He was no gardener, was he?"

"You met him?"

"I did. I came back briefly to check everything was all right, and he was there."

Vicenzo looked down, ashen-faced. "And now he's dead," he said. "He was put in prison, and after the Via Rasella bombing he was one of the three hundred and thirty-five prisoners taken to the caves and murdered."

"I heard about the killings—it's just unbelievable. I'm sorry about your friend." She touched his arm.

"It's a risk we all take. You too, now."

She looked at him nervously. "Why me? I'm not part of the Resistance."

"But you are...don't you see? By helping me, you have shown me whose side you're really on."

She felt uneasy suddenly. His assumption that she was part of his group unnerved her. "I saw Mario Chiari, by the way, at San Vitale. He's a friend of yours, isn't he? A film designer, I seem to remember. What on earth was he doing there?"

"We have been working together—getting Anglo-American prisoners out of Italy."

Isabella was stunned. It seemed everyone associated with Vicenzo was at risk. "I had no idea," she said.

He took her hands in his and kissed them. "Little Bella, I need you to do one more thing for me. There really is no one else I can trust."

She knew she should say no. He was involved in dangerous work, and now he was drawing her in even further, and it frightened her.

But her love for him, her lingering sense of guilt about the girl Livia, made her feel she couldn't refuse him. She gazed into his dark eyes, and said softly, "I suppose I could help."

"Go back to my house; upstairs in my bedroom is a list of names—members of the cell. It's nailed beneath a section of carpet, near the chest of drawers. They will find it if they search the house. Go and get it and bring it to me, please?"

Isabella felt frightened, but exhilarated. "If the house is being watched, it will be dangerous. Do you really think I can do it?" she asked anxiously.

"I know you can," he said, kissing her cheek. "You are braver than you think."

Isabella was jolted awake early the following morning by a surge of adrenaline, as if she was about to attend an important audition. She put on her makeup and an elegant figure-hugging dress, topped with her best fur coat. As she checked her reflection in the mirror, she looked like a movie star.

Vicenzo's house and gardens were swarming with policemen when she arrived. She had a moment's hesitation as she stood outside on the pavement. Should she leave now, walk away and save herself? Or go in and risk arrest? She drew on Vicenzo's faith in her—this surely was a role she could play. She pulled her coat around her and marched boldly through the gates.

The policemen started when they saw her. They clearly recognized her and tipped their caps.

"Good morning," she said politely.

She walked confidently up to the front door and rang the bell. Constanza opened the door. "Signorina Bellucci, what are you doing here?" Constanza asked nervously.

"I think I may have left something behind from when I was living here," Isabella replied boldly. "I just need to look for it."

As she stepped into the hall, Amadeo, Vicenzo's cousin, walked through from the kitchen, followed by a couple of policemen—one tall, the other short and squat.

"Amadeo, darling," Isabella said grandly, embracing him. Holding him to her, she whispered: "Vicenzo wants me to fetch something for him from upstairs. Pretend we're old friends, and while I'm upstairs, distract the police... It's so lovely to see you again," she said loudly, releasing him. "Shall we have coffee in a moment? There is so much to discuss. But before we do, I think I left a ring here a few weeks ago... I'll just go up and get it and then we'll chat, yes?"

The policemen watched her walking calmly upstairs. The taller of the two looked as if he was about to follow her, but Amadeo clicked his fingers and the dogs ran into the hall from the sitting room. They wound themselves around the policemen's legs.

"They are beautiful dogs," said the short policeman.

"They are very easy to train," Amadeo replied. "They can do tricks; shall I show you?"

In Vicenzo's bedroom, Isabella closed the door quietly and wedged a chair against it. She searched under the Turkish rugs, and eventually found the piece of nailed-down carpet. She took a pair of scissors from the dressing table and prised up the nails. Between the joists, there was the list of names Vicenzo wanted. She folded the paper until it was no larger than a book of matches, and slipped it inside her bra. Then she smoothed out the carpet, covered it with the rug and went back downstairs.

"Did you find it?" asked Amadeo.

"No, it's so annoying. It was a little pearl ring my mother gave me when I was young. I can't find it anywhere. I thought perhaps I'd left it here, but it wasn't in the bedroom, or the bathroom."

"I'll ask Constanza to look for it, shall I?" said Amadeo.

"Oh please don't bother," said Isabella. "I'll ask her myself. Shall we have that coffee?"

Outside in the street, Isabella put her hand to her chest, checking the folded paper was safely tucked away, and began to walk quickly toward the church where she had arranged to meet Vicenzo. He was waiting for her in the crypt of skulls and was staring at the altar, flickering in the candlelight.

"You are amazing," he said when she handed him the list. "I knew you could do it. I'm so grateful."

She felt proud of herself, she realized, as if she had achieved something remarkable.

"They didn't suspect anything?" he asked.

"I don't think so," she replied. "I did my 'grande dame of the cinema' act. They seemed quite charmed, in fact."

He slipped the paper inside his coat pocket and took her in his arms. "I am in your debt," he said, kissing her lightly on the lips.

"I would do anything for you," she murmured.

"I know," he replied.

"Will I see you again?" she asked.

"Yes of course. Not tomorrow but the day after, here in the church, at two o'clock."

"Good," she said. "Until two o'clock then." And she kissed him.

Chapter Twenty-Eight

Florence
April 1944

It was still dark when Livia was woken by a soft knocking sound. She stumbled sleepily along the corridor. "Jacob, is that you?" she asked through the secret door.

"Yes, I'm sorry, but it's Sara—she's started."

A rush of energy jolted Livia properly awake. They had been unable to find a midwife and now that the moment was upon them, she realized there was no alternative—she would have to deliver Sara's baby. She moved the coat rack as quietly as she could and opened the door. Jacob looked exhausted.

"I'll get some things," said Livia, "and see you up there."

She put the kettle on the gas to boil, and then went to her room to dress. In her father's room, she searched for sheets and towels in the linen cupboard. He stirred in his sleep.

"It's only me, Papa," she said quietly. "Sara's having her baby. Go back to sleep."

He rolled over and was soon snoring.

Upstairs in the little bedroom, Matteo was standing at the foot of the bed, wide-eyed, as his mother moaned and panted.

"Jacob," said Livia, "take Matteo downstairs. There's a jigsaw puzzle on the table. He needs distracting."

"Can you really manage?" he asked.

"Yes," she replied bravely. "I'm sure we'll be fine; off you go." Turning to Sara, she said, "I know it's hard, but you must be as quiet as you can. People in the building might hear you, and then all will be lost."

Sara's eyes were filled with fear, but she nodded uncertainly.

Livia found a small piece of wood that had been used to steady a table leg. She washed it in the basin and handed it to Sara. "Bite down on that when you want to scream. I'm sorry, but you must."

Back in the kitchen, she poured the boiling water into a bowl, and brought it back up to the attic, with some soap. She wasn't really sure what else would be required, but sat next to the bed, mopping Sara's forehead. When the contractions grew more intense, Sara grabbed Livia's hand, and dug her nails into her palm.

The hours slowly ticked by, and as the contractions got closer together, Livia steeled herself to look between Sara's legs. "Sara," she whispered. "You've done this before. I don't really know what to do. You must tell me what you need."

Sweating and panting, Sara nodded. "In a moment," she gasped, "I'll be ready to push. I'll try not to scream." She began to strain, her face screwed up with agony. She squeezed Livia's hand and clamped her jaws down on the piece of wood.

"I can see it," Livia said excitedly. "I can see its head."

Sara gasped, panted and pushed again. She let out a solitary cry as the child's head was expelled.

"The head's out, it's there. Oh God!" whispered Livia. "It's amazing. Can you push some more?"

Sara pushed again, her face once more screwed up in agony, and the child's body slithered into Livia's waiting hands.

"It's a girl," Livia announced, "a beautiful girl."

The baby took a gasp and cried out. Livia laid the child on Sara's stomach. "Thank you . . . thank you, Livia," Sara whispered, stroking the baby's head. "You must cut the cord—do you see? Not too close to the baby—and tie it off."

Livia looked at her, appalled. "What do you mean—cut it?"

"With some scissors," Sara said.

Livia ran downstairs. She was rummaging in a drawer when Jacob came into the kitchen. "Is she all right?" he asked nervously.

"Yes, you have a daughter, Jacob. Come and see—in fact, you can help. We have to cut the cord, and I don't know how to do it."

"I do," said Jacob, "I saw the midwife do it last time."

Livia found a pair of scissors, which she washed under a tap, and then went upstairs with Jacob and Matteo.

When the cord had been cut, Livia washed the baby in a bowl of water, wrapped it in a towel, and laid it on her mother's breast.

"I'll leave you now, Sara. I'll bring up some coffee, would you like that?"

"And some food?" Sara asked weakly.

"I'll see what I can find."

Downstairs in the kitchen, Livia was opening the cupboards, searching for something to eat, when her father ambled in, wearing his dressing gown. "Has the baby come?" he asked.

"Yes, a lovely little girl. But Sara needs food and there's nothing left."

"Is there no bread?"

"No. I was going to try and get some today. I'll go out quickly and get it now."

"It's nearly eight o'clock," her father said. "You mustn't be late for Villa Triste—I'll go."

"It's all right," Livia replied, already slipping on her coat. "I'll be back in time."

At the baker's, Livia joined a line of women queuing for bread. The line moved slowly, and she checked her watch anxiously. By the time she arrived at the front of the queue, it was already half past eight and she was due at Villa Triste at nine.

She raced back to the apartment. Her father was working at the dining table, as Livia threw the bread down in front of him. "Papa, please can you take this up to Sara. I have to go now."

She ran all the way to Villa Triste, arriving five minutes late. The guard glared at her. "I'm sorry," she apologized breathlessly. "I had an accident. But I'm here now."

The guard told her to wait and left the room. A few moments later, he returned, accompanied by a German officer. "You are late, Fräulein," said the officer irritably.

"I'm sorry. As I was explaining, I had an accident. It won't happen again."

"Come with me," he ordered.

Livia followed the officer down the corridor, her heart racing. He led her into one of the interrogation rooms and closed the door behind him.

"Sit here," he instructed, pointing to a wooden chair.

She sat down nervously. The last time she had been in one of these offices, the evil Fascist Mario Carità had taken her to see Elena, bloodied and bruised in the basement.

The officer stood leaning against the doorframe, his arms folded, looking almost relaxed. "We heard a radio transmission last night," the officer said, "from the BBC in London. It's called Radio Londra. Do you know it?"

"I've heard of it," she replied. "But I've not listened to it—it's illegal, isn't it?"

"Yes, it is illegal. We listened to a very interesting broadcast from the American General Alexander. Have you heard of him?"

"No," she lied.

"He is the commander of the Allied forces here in Italy. He was praising the work of an underground radio service... now what was it called?" He looked at her through narrowed eyes.

Her face remained impassive, blank.

"Radio Cora," he said at last, "that's it."

She swallowed anxiously.

"He was saying what a wonderful job they were doing."

"I don't know anything about it," she replied.

"Someone is running this radio service; do you know who they are?" he pressed.

"No. Why should I?"

"Are you really sure? Because if you are lying, you will end up like your friend, Elena."

"I'm not lying," she said defiantly, before adding tentatively: "Is Elena still here?"

"No," he replied, "she has been transferred."

"Where to?" she asked. "May I visit her?" She realized it was a stupid thing to say, and yet, Elena was, after all, her friend; he might think it stranger if she didn't ask about her.

"Of course not!" He laughed. "She is still our prisoner, but we have sent her to recuperate in the women's prison at Santa Verdiana. As soon as she is well enough, she will be brought back here for further questioning. Signor Carità has taken a personal interest in her case—especially as he was the target of her bomb attack."

"I understand," said Livia. "May I go now?"

"Yes, I suppose so." The officer sounded almost bored. "But if you hear anything—anything at all about Radio Cora, you must tell me, do you understand? You work for us now, remember?"

"Yes," Livia replied. "Of course I understand."

At lunchtime, Livia had arranged to meet Cosimo at a safe house and make a transmission about German troop movements outside Florence. He had spent the morning gathering information.

"I have news of Elena," she said when he arrived. "She's been transferred to the convent prison called Santa Verdiana. It's about thirty kilometers away, on the road to Pisa."

"Why have they moved her?" he asked.

Livia's eyes filled with tears.

"Tell me," he insisted.

"She was too injured for them to interrogate anymore. Oh Cosimo, what have they done to her?"

"Bastards," he said.

"It must mean she has told them nothing. But they are threatening to bring her back when she's well enough."

"Not if I get to her first," Cosimo said.

"What do you mean?"

"We can't leave her there, can we? I owe it to her, more than anyone, to get her out. And I will, if it's the last thing I do."

Chapter Twenty-Nine

Rome
April 1944

Isabella arrived at the crypt of the Capuchin church just before two o'clock for her meeting with Vicenzo. While she waited, she wandered the various rooms, studying the shapes of the skulls, the arrangement of the bones. They no longer appalled her; in fact, she had begun to find them almost beautiful in the candlelight.

Sitting quietly in the crypt, she heard a sudden noise on the stairs. It was unlikely to be Vicenzo as he always used the street entrance. Fearing it was the priest, Isabella hurried through the various chambers until she reached the exit.

Outside, she continued to wait for Vicenzo. Three o'clock came, with no sign of him. It was unlike Vicenzo to miss an appointment—he was nothing if not punctual. Concerned for him, she hurried to his villa, praying he was there.

Unusually for such a warm day, there was no sign of the dogs on the porch. Perhaps Luciana had collected them after all.

Isabella knocked frantically, and was relieved when Constanza opened the door. "Thank God you're here," she said. "I had an appointment to meet Vicenzo earlier, but he never arrived. Is he here?"

"No," said Constanza. "I've not seen him for days."

"I'm terribly worried that something's happened to him." Isabella grabbed Constanza's hand. "If you hear anything—promise me, you'll let me know."

*

Back home, Isabella paced the house for the rest of the afternoon. Something was wrong. Finally at half past four the doorbell went. Standing outside was Vicenzo's cousin, Amadeo.

"Come in," she said, looking anxiously around in case they were being observed.

Amadeo looked pale and drawn. "Vicenzo's been arrested."

Isabella felt a jolt of fear, like an electric shock, running through her body.

"I knew something bad had happened," she exclaimed tearfully. "I waited for him for over an hour at our meeting place today, but he never turned up."

"We're all very worried."

"Of course. Do you know where he is?"

"No, not yet. We have people trying to find out."

"Please let me know as soon as you hear anything, won't you? I would do anything for him, anything at all."

"I know that." Amadeo held her to him. "We'll find him," he said gently, "don't worry."

That night, try as she might, Isabella was unable to sleep. She eventually dozed off, but a little after midnight woke with a start; her mother was screaming.

"Mamma?" she called out, alarmed, as she hauled herself up in bed.

Suddenly three policemen burst into her room, brandishing machine guns. "Come with us," one of them demanded.

Her mother followed them into the room. "I'm sorry," she cried to Isabella. "I let them in. I was just going to bed, and they were knocking on the door."

"It's all right, Mamma. I'll handle this." Isabella, though terrified, was determined to stay calm. She climbed out of bed and pulled a robe around her. "I presume I am allowed to get dressed first?" she asked the policemen imperiously, before picking up a pair of trousers and a shirt and sweeping into the bathroom. A few moments later, she emerged fully dressed.

"Where are you taking her?" Giovanna demanded, grabbing one of the policemen by the arm, as they frogmarched Isabella down the corridor.

He shrugged her off.

"She's a good girl," Giovanna shouted after them, "a famous actress. She knows Mussolini!"

"Don't worry, Mamma," Isabella called back, "I'll be all right."

The men bundled Isabella down the stairs to the hall, where she was blindfolded and pushed out of the door into a waiting car.

They drove around for what felt like twenty minutes, before she heard the crunch of tires on gravel and angry voices. The car stopped. She was pulled roughly out of the car and led into a building, where her blindfold was removed. Squinting, her eyes gradually adapted to the light and her surroundings.

"Give me your papers and any jewelry you are wearing," demanded a woman in a curious black apron.

Isabella handed over her handbag and watch—all she had with her.

The woman led her down the corridor to a tiled room furnished only with a table and two chairs. High up on the wall was a window protected by iron bars.

"You will be interrogated by Commissario Koch," the woman said as she locked the door behind her.

Isabella waited. There was something familiar about the name. She wracked her brains, before finally recalling Vicenzo had mentioned a man named Pietro Koch who was working hand in hand with the Germans. He was a sadistic creature, Vicenzo had said. She began to feel nervous—frightened even.

Without her watch, it was hard to know exactly how long she waited, but she observed the moon drifting across the night sky through the barred window, and reasoned that an hour or more had gone by. Eventually, a tall, slender young man entered the room. He wore a smart double-breasted blue suit with a high-collared white silk shirt. In the circumstances, it looked incongruous, as if he was dressed for dinner. He was tanned, with brown eyes and, despite a slightly bulbous nose, was almost handsome. There was something about him that reminded her of her first love, the army officer Ludovico Albani—perhaps it was the mustache, or the wavy hair smothered in brilliantine. He had the same upright bearing and slightly imperious manner, but his footsteps, as he walked delicately across the room, were quite different from Ludovico's. This man's were soft, almost velvety, like a dancer. He removed a pair of suede gloves and placed them on the table. Isabella stood up nervously.

"Please, do sit down," he said. His voice was gentle and educated.

He laid a notepad and pen on the table next to his gloves. She could see he had already written out some questions, leaving spaces for her answers beneath. He was obviously a meticulous man.

"You are a friend of the director, Vicenzo Lucchese?" he began.

"I am yes."

"You have been staying in his house, I understand?"

"Yes."

"Are you lovers?"

Isabella blushed—something her interrogator noted on his pad.

"No," she replied firmly. "We are friends, that's all."

She saw him write down the word "friends," pick up another pen and underline the word in red.

He looked up. "Does he work for you?"

"What on earth do you mean?" she asked, genuinely confused now.

"I think perhaps you are the ringleader of his Resistance cell."

"What an absurd idea!" Isabella said boldly. "I don't have the faintest idea what you're talking about. What Resistance cell?"

"First, you live in his house, a house where we found caches of arms. Then, you are in Via Rasella on the day of the bombing. I think perhaps you are the mastermind behind this bombing."

"That's ridiculous! I was on my way home, if you must know, from the market. Fortunately I stopped to look in a shop window when the bomb went off, or I'd have been blown up as well."

He laughed. "You expect me to believe that? No civilians were killed in Via Rasella. Everyone was prevented from entering the area, you included."

"I knew nothing about the bombing," Isabella retorted. "The fact that I wasn't badly injured can't be used against me—if it wasn't so ludicrous it would be laughable."

He flushed slightly, pursing his lips, as if considering his response. "It would be better for you," he said, "if you admitted your part in it, admit you are a partisan, and if not the leader, at least a member of the GAP cell here in Rome."

She shook her head defiantly. "I will not admit to something that is totally untrue."

He stood up and walked behind her. It was unnerving. She sensed his eyes examining her. His tone softened. "If you admit it now, things will be easier for you." He moved round in front of her, his thin mouth curling itself into a smile.

"There is nothing to admit to," Isabella said, drawing herself up in her chair. "How dare you accuse me of these things?"

He sat down again. "You live with your mother?" he asked.

"Yes, and my aunt and my grandmother—what of it?"

"They are partisans too?"

"Don't be ridiculous!" she exclaimed in disbelief.

"You have had other lovers, before the director?"

"No. And I've already told you, he's not my lover. My only other friend was an officer in the Italian army, if you must know—Baron Ludovico Albani—a loyal member of the Fascist forces. He is the only man I've ever..." she paused, blushing slightly, "ever had a relationship with."

He wrote down Ludovico's name in his notebook, underlining the words "Baron" and "Fascist" twice.

"You spend time at the Acquasanta Golf Club. You were a friend of the traitor Count Ciano."

"I knew him, yes. But he was not a friend. Most definitely not."

"And Mario Chiari? You were seen talking to him at the police station. He is a communist and a partisan. What were you discussing?"

"Nothing, I scarcely know him. He's a film-set designer. I had met him once at a party, I think. I merely wondered what he was doing there."

Koch continued to make notes, glancing up at her from time to time.

"How can you be so distant and cold?" he asked her eventually.

"I don't know what you mean."

"I have seen many people crack under pressure, strong men drop to their knees begging me for mercy. You seem almost relaxed. What is wrong with you?"

"There is nothing wrong with me. I am simply innocent of everything you accuse me of."

He took a piece of writing paper from his inside jacket pocket and laid it on the table in front of her. Vicenzo's signature leapt out at her.

"You should know... we have your friend."

Isabella, who until now had remained calm throughout the long and exhausting interrogation, felt her resolve crumbling. Tears welled up at the thought of what might be happening to Vicenzo.

Her interrogator leapt up suddenly and came around the desk, pulling her roughly up onto her feet. "Why do you care about this man?" he shouted, shaking her, his face close to hers. "How can you be mixed up with a man like this? Don't you know who he is? He is a pervert, of the worst kind. Italy doesn't want people like him."

"You're wrong," Isabella said bravely, staring him in the face. "He's an artist, like me. We speak a different language from people like you, we live in a different world."

He released her suddenly, shoving her back down onto her chair. "We will put an end to your 'different world.' It's over." He sat down behind the desk once again and smoothed his delicate hands across his brilliantined hair. He picked up his gloves, putting them neatly together next to his notepad, and adjusted the collar of his silk shirt. Clearly order was important to him.

He looked tired, Isabella thought, pale-faced with dark rings around his eyes. "I will ensure you are given special treatment while you are here, given who you are." He looked up at her with his brown eyes, and she saw a glimmer of something unexpected—affection maybe.

"I don't want any special treatment," she said defiantly.

"Trust me, you will. I will have you put into a private room upstairs, and not in the quarters with the other prisoners."

"No," she replied sternly. "I will go with the others. I don't want any favors from you. But I want it noted that I am completely innocent of all the charges."

He gazed at her, with something like admiration.

"My life is in your hands," she went on. "And I suggest that you either charge me, or send me home."

He stared at her wide-eyed, then suddenly rose from his chair. "All right, you can go. But you're to remain in your house at all times. You may not leave it without my permission, is that understood?"

In reception, she was blindfolded again and shepherded roughly into the back seat of the car. A few moments later, someone—a policeman, she assumed—climbed into the driver's seat, and they set off.

After a few miles, the car suddenly came to a halt. The engine stopped and the driver's door opened and shut again. Isabella felt someone climbing into the back seat next to her. She smelled brilliantine hair oil, and felt soft suede gloved hands removing her blindfold. It was Koch himself, and they were now quite alone. Outside the car was the Colosseum, lit by a huge full moon hanging low in the sky. In any other circumstances it would have been romantic.

"It's a beautiful sight, isn't it?" he asked softly.

She nodded nervously.

"It seems such a tragedy that the Italian people are so divided," he began.

She realized he simply wanted to chat with her, as if she was a friend. Sensing he wanted something more from her, she was aware of his breath on her cheek. It made her feel uneasy.

He turned to look at her. "You are very beautiful."

She remained impassive, determined not to give him any encouragement. Then, without warning, he got out of the car and climbed back into the driving seat. He drove her home silently and parked outside her house.

"Well, you're home," he said, turning round. "I meant what I said about not leaving your house—do you understand?"

She nodded mutely.

"I have the power to bring you back in at any time, and I will, if I suspect you of any kind of involvement with the Resistance."

Climbing out of the car, she noticed him watching her in the car's mirror. As she unlocked her front door, she glanced back. He raised his hand slightly before driving away.

Chapter Thirty

Florence
May 1944

The phone rang early in the morning. Livia, befuddled with sleep, stumbled along the hallway and picked up the receiver.

"Livia, Livia, you must help me...save me!" Her mother was hysterical.

"What is it, Mamma?" she asked, alarmed.

Giacomo, ambling into the hall, mouthed, "Who is it?"

"It's Mamma. Something terrible has happened." She passed the receiver to her father. Livia could hear her mother screaming at the other end of the phone, and saw her father's face turning white. "I'm coming, Luisa," he said finally. "I'm coming right now." He was shaking as he put the phone down.

"Papa, what's happened?"

"The village has been occupied by German troops retreating north from the Allies. They've arrested all the men and taken them to the village square. There has been gunfire—lots of it."

"What about Nonno and Gino?" Livia asked.

"They've taken Gino, but not Nonno, thank God. They tried to get him out of bed, but he couldn't stand up. Mamma thought they would shoot him there and then. But in the end they left him. Perhaps some of these young men do have a heart."

Livia stared at her father in disbelief. "I can't take it in. So Mamma is alone in the house with Nonno and Angela and surrounded by German troops?"

Giacomo nodded.

"If you go there, and they're rounding up the men, they'll take you too and shoot you."

"I can't leave her in the house alone, Livia," he said, his voice trembling.

"No, no of course not," she replied gently. "But maybe I should go instead."

"No! You must stay here—keep on reporting to Villa Triste, carry on our work with the Resistance, and look after Sara. I'll leave right now and try to work out how to get them out."

Standing forlornly by the sitting-room window, Livia watched her father's car disappear down the road. She had a terrible sense of foreboding. His chances of coming back alive—of her family surviving what was clearly an appalling massacre—seemed utterly remote. The support system of her family seemed to be collapsing beneath her, and she felt her world crumbling. She was responsible to so many and yet felt utterly alone.

Livia went about her tasks that day in a daze. She queued for bread and milk, and signed in at the offices of the Fascist police. At lunchtime, she met up with Cosimo outside the Uffizi to pool information for their transmission later that day for Radio Cora.

"I know how worried you must be, but I'm sure Giacomo will be all right," he reassured her, when she told him what had happened. "He's a wily old soul, your father." He put his arm comfortingly around her shoulders, and kissed her hair.

"I wish I shared your faith," she replied. "He looked so broken when he left the apartment. I worry that he'll do something foolish."

Livia heard nothing from her father for several days and began to fear the worst. And yet she could not cry—it seemed too defeatist. She thought of his last words to her as he left: "You have your work to do." Now, she was determined to live up to them.

One lunchtime, she was at home collecting the radio transmitter, when the phone rang. Was it her father? She picked up the phone; it was a member of their Resistance cell. German tanks had been spotted heading south along the Arno river. Could she go and count them and urgently radio the information to the Allies?

She picked up the transmitter, hid it in her shopping basket and arrived at the Ponte Vecchio just in time to see the German column. She counted over thirty tanks. She then ran to one of the safe houses nearby and made her transmission. On her way home an hour later, Allied planes flew low over the city, presumably strafing the column. She had a brief moment of elation as she climbed the stairs to the apartment. That day, at least, they'd had a small victory.

The phone was ringing again when she let herself into the hall. Presuming it would be a member of the Resistance congratulating her on her work, she picked it up.

"Livia…" Although faint, it was clearly her father's voice.

"Papa, thank God. Where are you?"

"I'm in the villa." He sounded exhausted.

"Is Mamma safe?"

"Yes. But Livia, it's been so terrible." He began to weep—loud wracking sobs of desperation. "Gino is dead," he sobbed, "along with every able-bodied man in the village—all slaughtered like cattle, even the priest."

Livia felt sick. She stood for a few seconds swallowing back the bile, trying to calm herself. Her father needed her to be strong.

"Why would they do such a thing?" she asked eventually.

"I don't know," he said weakly. "It was probably a reprisal for something trivial. The Germans are capable of such cruelty. They are on the run and are destroying everything in their wake." Giacomo began to weep again. Livia's mind was full of questions.

"Papa, tell me what happened. How did you survive?" she asked quietly.

"It's a very long story," he said wearily. She heard him take a deep breath, trying to calm himself. "When I drove up to the village," he began falteringly, "I saw flames leaping into the sky and troops everywhere. I hid the car in the woods a few kilometers away, and spent the night in an old cave where I used to play as a boy—the entrance is hidden in a copse. The next morning, I hid in the undergrowth on the outskirts of the village, and once I realized the tanks and troop carriers had left, I walked in. Almost half of it has been destroyed, Livia—burned to the ground. When I reached our villa I could hardly believe it was untouched. Your mother was distraught, but alive—and even Nonno has survived." His voice cracked as he began to weep again. "We've spent the last few days trying to look after all the widows and orphans left abandoned in the village. The house is full of women and children with nowhere else to go."

"Thank God you're alive," was all Livia could say, as tears poured down her face.

In order to avoid the Germans locating the transmitter's signal, Livia was under orders to move it to a new location every day. But with many buildings destroyed by Allied bombing, there was a shortage of suitable safe houses—in particular, buildings with an attic where she could get a good signal. And every time she approached someone to borrow a room, she risked being betrayed—so many partisan cells were being infiltrated by the enemy.

Radio Cora had received a message from General Alexander requesting some urgent information—details of German fortifications, map references of the mined areas south of Florence, as well as possible airdrop positions. They also needed information about the numbers of partisans operating in the area. Running out of transmission locations, Livia decided she would have no option but to use her apartment. It was completely against the rules of the cell, but if she kept the transmission short, she reasoned she would probably get away with it. She met with Cosimo later that day at the university and told him her plan.

"It's far too dangerous," he said. "We should find somewhere neutral."

"I can't," she replied, "not in the time. I've got to transmit tomorrow afternoon. That gives us only twenty-four hours to pull the information together. There's just one problem . . . one thing you ought to know." She paused. She had sworn to her father a year before that she would never reveal the family's existence, but now she felt she had no choice. "We are hiding a family in the apartment."

"A family?" He looked puzzled.

"A Jewish family. They've been with us for months. In fact, they've just had a baby."

"Is that why you won't ever let me come over?"

She nodded.

"You are a truly wonderful person," he said, putting his arms around her and kissing her. "More wonderful than I had ever realized."

She blushed, enjoying the sensation of being held. He made her feel safe, if only for a few seconds.

"But seriously, Livia," he went on, "surely that's another reason not to transmit from your apartment. You are risking more lives than just your own."

"Yes, I realize that. The problem is, General Alexander's request is urgent. They want the information by tomorrow. We have to do this now. The faster we act, the sooner we can bring this whole nightmare to an end, don't you see?"

"I don't know," he said doubtfully. "It's too risky."

"You should meet the family," Livia suggested, "they're lovely."

"I'm sure they are," Cosimo began, "but really, Livia—"

"Come back with me now, before the curfew," she urged him. "Please?"

The family were initially reluctant to leave the attic to meet Cosimo, but Livia persuaded them. "He's in the Resistance with me; he's on our side."

Over supper, they all gradually relaxed, drinking the last of Giacomo's grappa and a bottle of red wine Livia found in her father's wardrobe. "He was obviously saving it for something special, but I think this is an occasion he would approve of. Here's to the end of the war," she declared, raising her glass with an optimistic flourish.

"And to a kinder world," answered Jacob softly.

After dinner, Livia went to her room to monitor Radio Londra, leaving Cosimo amusing Matteo. When she came back into the sitting room she found him performing card tricks, Matteo sitting, fascinated, at his feet.

"I didn't know you could do that," Livia said, impressed.

"Every boy knows how to do card tricks," Cosimo replied, flipping the cards onto the table. "Here," he said to Matteo, "you have a go."

Livia watched Cosimo explaining the trick to the little boy, and tried to imagine him with a child of their own.

Later that evening, after the family had retreated to their attic eyrie, Livia took Cosimo by the hand and led him to her bedroom. They lay down together in her narrow bed and held one another. Sometime, in the deep dark of the night, they made love. For both of them it was the first time. It was tender and yet urgent, a chance to lose themselves in a moment's ecstasy.

The following morning, they lay wrapped in each other's arms.

"I love you so much," Cosimo said, kissing her mouth, her eyes, her forehead. "I had thought maybe we had lost each other."

"Never," she said. "I just couldn't show you my love. The war has taken all my strength, all my concentration; and there have been so many secrets between us."

"I know," he replied, stroking her cheek.

She pushed herself up on her elbow and gazed at him. "I wish we could stay like this forever."

He pulled her toward him and they made love again, more slowly this time. As she climaxed, she whispered his name over and over again.

When she finally pulled away from him, he clung to her hand. "Don't go yet," he said gently.

"I must." She climbed out of bed and began to dress hurriedly. "I have to be at Villa Triste at nine. And we need bread—if I don't go out now, it will be too late. When you leave, try to avoid our neighbor, Signor Lombardi. Open the door of the apartment, just a crack, and wait. He will almost certainly come out onto the landing to see what's going on. Wait until he gets bored and goes back in, then leave. Can you tell everyone from Radio Cora to meet us here at five o'clock. We'll pool everyone's information to give to the Americans. And ask them to bring maps of Florence and the surrounding area."

"Do you really think it's safe to meet here?"

"We have no choice, Cosimo."

"But I still worry we're breaking all the rules. What would your father say?"

"Well, my father's not here, so it's my decision," said Livia, picking up her keys. "Come on—let's get going."

The sun was slowly sinking in the sky, casting deep shadows in the streets, as Livia hurried home for her evening meeting. Up in the attic, she explained to the family what was about to happen.

"I have some people coming here shortly," she told Sara. "We might have to come up to the roof terrace. It's important that you keep out of sight."

"Shall we stay in our room?" Sara asked.

"Yes, that would be best. It won't be for long—half an hour at the most. When they've all gone, I'll come and get you and we can make supper." Livia smiled encouragingly.

As the time of the Radio Cora meeting approached, she positioned herself by the window overlooking the street. Cosimo arrived just before five o'clock, accompanied by three other members of the Radio Cora team. Livia hurried downstairs in stockinged feet to let them in.

They held their meeting in the sitting room—spreading out maps of Florence and the surrounding area on the floor. They had a long list of questions from General Alexander, and as they worked through the answers together, one of the team converted them into code for the transmission.

"He wants to know how many partisans there are in each cell," Paulo said. "That's an impossible question to answer—none of us know. We all work in total isolation from each other."

"Just put in a rough figure then," suggested Livia.

Eventually, the answers assembled, Cosimo and Livia climbed up to the terrace to make the transmission. They set up the radio out of sight beneath the wall, attaching the aerial to the hook where Livia normally hung the washing line. Cosimo put on his headphones and began the transmission, sending coded messages to the Americans.

Livia knocked on the attic door to check on the family. She found Sara propped up on the bed, the baby sucking greedily on her breast. "It keeps her quiet," Sara explained.

"It won't be long now," Livia said. "I'll come and get you when we're finished."

Livia ran downstairs to find the team packing up. "Where's Paulo?" she asked.

"He had to leave," Sergio explained. "He had another meeting, I think."

Moments later, there was a pounding on the apartment door, as if a metal object was being hammered against the solid chestnut paneling, accompanied by German voices.

Livia rushed into the hall and raced back upstairs to the attic. She ripped off Cosimo's headphones. "It's the Germans! You have to escape across the roofs, and take the family with you."

"What?" he asked. "How? We can't possibly get away—not with a child and a baby!"

"You can. You must." She pulled him to his feet and pushed him toward the metal fire escape.

"I can't leave without you," he said desperately. "Come with us."

"No! I'll keep them occupied downstairs, and give you a chance to escape. Get up the ladder onto the top terrace—from there you can cross over to the neighboring roof. I'll send the family after you. Be quick."

She rushed to the family's room, and threw open the door. "You have to get out," she whispered. "There are Germans downstairs, banging on the apartment door."

Jacob picked up Matteo, and the family ran outside onto the terrace. Livia pointed to the fire escape.

"Go up there—Cosimo is waiting for you." She took the baby from Sara, and Jacob clambered up the ladder, pulling Matteo and Sara up behind him. As Livia handed the baby up to him, she whispered: "Good luck, all of you."

She ran back down the stairs, shutting the secret door behind her. As she pulled the coat rack in front of it, the apartment door gave way and three men wearing tan raincoats burst in, carrying pistols.

"You have a radio transmitter here," one of them shouted in Italian, with a strong German accent. "Where is it?"

"I don't know what you're talking about," Livia replied calmly. She could hear her colleagues in the sitting room whispering, presumably concealing the folded maps and messages.

"Don't lie to me, we have been monitoring you. We know there's a transmitter here. Show me!" the German demanded.

Livia looked him in the eye and shrugged her shoulders. "I still don't know what you're talking about."

She felt a slap across her face. It was so hard, she almost blacked out. She was pushed into the sitting room, where her colleagues were already standing with their hands on their heads. Livia raised her arms, and while one German stood guard, the other two ransacked the apartment.

A minute went by, then two. She thought of Cosimo and how far he and the family might have got in that time. Had they escaped? Suddenly she heard the coat rack being dragged across the hall floor and the sound of boots clattering upstairs.

Moments later, they were back in the hall, brandishing the transmitter. "Who does this belong to?" demanded the policeman.

"I have no idea," she said defiantly. "I've never seen it before."

He slapped her face again. "This apartment is owned by Giacomo Moretti. Is it his?"

"No."

"Where is he?"

"He's not here," she replied.

"Who were you transmitting to?"

"I don't know what you're talking about." She was determined to keep them talking as long as possible.

"We found evidence of people living upstairs—where are they?"

"They left."

"Without their clothes?" one of them asked, incredulous.

"They took what they needed."

"What are their names?"

Livia hesitated, desperate not to give any clue to the heritage of her erstwhile house guests.

"Maria and Angelo," she said. "They're cousins of mine. Their flat was bombed, so they came to stay with me."

The officer shook his head in disbelief. "Take them to Gestapo headquarters," he instructed his two companions.

The group were bundled into two cars, and as they drove toward Via Cavour, Livia was in no doubt what lay ahead.

Chapter Thirty-One

Rome
May 1944

Isabella woke early, the sun streaming through her bedroom window. She had slept fitfully after her interrogation, in spite of being exhausted. Her immediate thought was of Vicenzo. He was being held captive by the Fascist police and she had to do everything she could to save him. Although she was aware that her phone was probably being monitored, she decided to risk a call to Salvato Cappelli, a journalist friend of Vicenzo's. He was also a communist and a member of the Resistance.

"Salvato, I must speak with you—it's urgent. Can you come to my house?"

"Yes," he said, "I'll be there in an hour."

It was the first day of May, and very warm. They sat outside in the garden, in the shade of a large pine tree, as Isabella recounted her experience of being interrogated by Pietro Koch.

"I can't believe you got out of there in one piece," said Salvato. "That man is very high up in the Fascist Police—he's got the most appalling reputation for cruelty. Are you sure you're all right?"

"Yes, I'm fine. He didn't hurt me. He was almost pleasant at times. I think, perhaps, he's a fan?"

"Ha, well you were lucky. Few people get out of Pensione Jaccarino without being tortured—either mentally or physically."

"Is that where he took me? I was blindfolded for the journey, so I really have no idea."

"I'm sure it must have been there. Pensione Jaccarino is a run-down hotel, requisitioned by Koch—four floors of hell, or so I'm told. People herded together in rooms with no windows, and just mattresses on the floor, if they're lucky. In the basement are the interrogation rooms—a fetid space, with straw on the floor to mop up the blood."

Isabella shuddered.

"Then there are the isolation cells," Salvato went on. "Imagine being alone in a cell for months on end, in a room no larger than a meat safe."

"I didn't see any of that," she said weakly. "He did mention not putting me with the others, though. Now I think I understand why."

"He obviously likes you. I've not heard of him showing anyone else such mercy."

"Salvato, I asked to see you today not to discuss my own experience, but because I want to know how I can help Vicenzo. Koch told me they have him locked up. The thought of him in that place is too terrible." She looked up at Salvato with tears in her eyes. "We have to get him out."

"Look, Isabella," said Salvato, "you had a lucky escape last night. Don't get involved. You're not even a member of the Resistance. Besides, what Vicenzo needs is a good lawyer, not a friend."

Shortly after Salvato had left, the phone rang.

"Isabella Bellucci?" It was a man's voice she didn't recognize.

"Yes, that's me."

"Commissario Koch will be at your house at twelve o'clock."

The phone went dead before she had a chance to ask why. Had he listened to her earlier phone call? Was he going to arrest her again? Or maybe, given his "interest" in her, he was going to proposition her. She went upstairs and changed, putting on a modest summer dress and flat shoes.

A blue open-topped car drew up outside at twelve o'clock precisely, with Koch at the wheel. He opened the passenger door for her and Isabella climbed into the seat next to him.

"Where are we going?" she asked nervously.

"Nowhere," he replied evasively. He looked tired, she thought, his eyes red-rimmed.

They drove around for a while.

"The Germans are pressuring me," he said at last, "to interrogate 'your friend.'" He spat out the word "friend" venomously.

Uncertain how she should respond, and remembering Salvato's words of advice that she should not get involved, she decided to remain silent.

"They think he will give up the names of his fellow partisans," Koch went on, "if I can use my..." he paused and flicked a look in her direction, "...my methods on him."

The prospect of Vicenzo being tortured was so appalling that Isabella forgot Salvato's advice. She could not abandon Vicenzo. "Please do not hurt him. He is not strong," she pleaded.

"What is that to me?" Koch said, his gloved hands gripping the steering wheel.

"I ask nothing for myself, just for him," she continued. "You have already been kind to me and I'm so grateful." She paused, hoping his attitude would soften.

"Well," he said, "it is not you we are interested in." He glanced at her. "I have admired you very much in the past. At least, I've admired your films." He blushed slightly, she noticed.

"Really?" If he could believe she liked him a little, perhaps she could persuade him to release Vicenzo. "Tell me," she added sweetly, "which was your favorite?"

"The one where you played a blind orphan girl." His red-rimmed eyes, she noticed, had taken on a misty look.

"Oh yes," she said encouragingly, "I loved that part. She was so noble and kind to those around her."

"Was it autobiographical?" It was such a naïve question, he sounded like a shy fan, rather than a sadistic policeman.

"Not really," she replied smiling. "I'm not blind, after all, but I hope I always treat people with respect, and I believe that we get what we deserve in life. If you are kind, you should get kindness back, no?"

He frowned. Perhaps she had gone too far. She tried to bring the conversation back to Vicenzo. "Will you promise me something?" she asked.

He turned to look at her.

"Don't let the Germans take Vicenzo," she pleaded. "He will not survive."

"It's nothing to do with you," Koch replied curtly. "You should stay out of it. He doesn't deserve your loyalty."

Suddenly, the mood had changed. He was no longer the shy fan, but a harsh policeman. They drove around in silence for half an hour, before finally arriving back at her road.

"Well," Koch said, "it's time for my lunch." He looked straight ahead, as if slightly impatient.

Isabella climbed out of the car feeling confused, aware that nothing had really been achieved.

A few days later, Vicenzo's sister, Luciana, phoned. "Isabella, I'm in Rome. I've come up from the country. I want to talk to you about getting Vicenzo out of prison. Can I come and see you?"

They met the following morning. A storm had been brewing overnight; it hung out to sea threatening rain, and the air was heavy and uncomfortable. Isabella showed Luciana into the garden, where she served iced tea under the shade of a tree.

"Now," Luciana began, "I understand from Salvato that you've been interrogated by that awful man Koch. Tell me everything."

"It was very odd," said Isabella. "I was arrested and interviewed most of the night—which was awful, obviously. But some of the time Koch was quite sweet, behaving like a movie fan."

"That's good. He obviously likes you."

"Then we had this odd car journey," Isabella went on. "He picked me up and we just drove around Rome, with him talking about my films, and me trying to bring the conversation back to Vicenzo. But every time I mentioned him, Koch got really angry."

"It sounds like he just wanted to take you out for lunch, but couldn't pluck up the courage," said Luciana. "I suspect the last thing on his mind was discussing my brother."

"Do you really think so?"

"Oh Isabella, don't be so naïve," said Luciana impatiently, sipping her tea. "The man is obviously in love with you. Can't you give him what he wants."

Isabella recoiled. "I don't really know what you're suggesting, but if it's what I think it is, then no. I couldn't do that...I just couldn't."

Luciana sighed, and fanned herself irritably with a napkin. "God this weather, I wish it would break, we need rain." She looked up toward the sky.

"The thing is, Luciana," Isabella went on nervously, "and not to put too fine a point on it, I won't sleep with Koch. I just can't. Besides, I'm not even sure that's what he wants. I think he's in love with my characters, not me—it's a fantasy."

"I suppose you know what you're talking about," Luciana said irascibly, "but his affection for you might be our best chance. If you invited him to lunch—suggesting you want to see him, I'm sure he'd come. Then we could send a lawyer to interrupt the lunch and bribe him to release Vicenzo."

"Do you really think that could work?" asked Isabella.

"Well it might. We've discussed it in the family, and you really are our best chance to get my brother out." Luciana leaned forward, touching Isabella's hand with her diamond-ringed fingers. "We would be forever in your debt if you would do this for us," she said softly. "Will you?"

Isabella was torn. Inviting Koch to lunch would only encourage him, but as always, she was desperate to help the man she loved.

"If I do this for you, will you tell Vicenzo how I helped him?"

Luciana looked slightly surprised. "If you really want me to," she said curtly.

"I just think he should know what I'm prepared to do for him, to show my love for him."

"He has that effect on so many women. Even I am powerless to refuse him, Isabella." Luciana smiled and stood up. Clearly the meeting was at an end. "Ring us when you've arranged the lunch, and let us know where it's going to be. Then we'll send the lawyer."

After Luciana left, a clap of thunder broke over the city, and rain poured down out of a black sky. Isabella ran into the sitting room, watching the garden being deluged with water. Eventually, she picked up the phone, and with a beating heart, dialed Koch's number.

"Hello, I'd like to speak to Commissario Koch, please. Tell him it's Isabella Bellucci."

Koch sounded excited when he came on the line. "Hello . . . is it you—Isabella?"

"Yes, it's me. Hello."

"How lovely to hear from you. How can I help you?"

"I . . . I was wondering," she began falteringly, "if you might have lunch with me—tomorrow maybe?"

"Yes," he said instantly. "Of course. I'll collect you at twelve, all right?"

"Good. See you then."

The following day was cooler, the air fresher and Rome appeared washed and clean. Isabella, keen not to appear too flashy or provocative, dressed modestly in a patterned summer frock. She stood waiting for Koch outside her house, and watched nervously as he drove into her road in his blue open-topped car.

"Thanks for agreeing to meet me," she said, climbing in beside him. "I didn't book anywhere for lunch. I thought I'd leave the choice to you."

"Of course," he said, a hint of a blush spreading up his smooth cheeks. In some lights, Isabella thought, he was almost handsome.

He pulled up and parked outside an elegant restaurant called The Belvedere. Isabella had been there before the war, but these days it was filled with senior German officers. Anxious that Karl Wolff might be there, she scanned the restaurant as they walked in. To her relief, he was not there, but she was aware of the officers' eyes following her lasciviously, as she sidled past them on her way to the table.

They studied the menu, and Koch ordered white wine. Isabella took a sip before asking if she could make a phone call. "I promised I'd let Mamma know where I was," she said.

"If you must." He was clearly irritated.

She went to the back of the restaurant where a pay phone hung on the wall. To her surprise, Koch followed her. She dialed Vicenzo's number, knowing Luciana would be there. "Mamma," she said, looking nervously over her shoulder at Koch, who was staring glumly at her.

"Yes, Isabella," Luciana replied.

"I promised to let you know I was here safely. We're at The Belvedere," she went on cheerfully, "it's lovely."

"Thank you," replied Luciana, putting down the phone.

"I know," Isabella said, pretending to continue the conversation. "I'll be good, see you later."

The lunch was excellent. Restaurants serving senior military personnel always had the best of the rations. Isabella, waiting nervously for the lawyer, made polite conversation.

"Have you always been a policeman?" she asked.

"No, I joined the army originally."

"Why did you leave?"

"It wasn't political enough. I joined the Fascist movement—I admired its coherence."

"Its coherence? I suppose I understand what you mean," she said, looking constantly toward the door, hoping for the arrival of the promised lawyer. "In my world—the world of art," she went on, "we try not to think about politics."

Koch snorted derisively. "Everything is about politics," he said.

"Perhaps, although the films I made were not political. What I mean is that there are 'higher' things than politics. Where would the world be without painting, or film for that matter? Vicenzo, for example, is a great artist on film. Far more talented than I."

"Why do you insist on continuously bringing this man into our conversation," he interrupted. "He's beneath contempt; I despise him."

"Then why not release him?" she asked, leaning toward him over the table. "You know that if the Germans take him and torture him, he will never get out alive." She reached across the table and took his hand. Koch trembled visibly at her touch. Isabella lowered her voice until it was seductive, sweet and gentle. "Please, Pietro...for me?"

He studied her heart-shaped face, her white skin, her soft red mouth. He withdrew his hand slowly, and swilled back his wine.

"I'll think about it," he said.

Isabella rang Luciana as soon as she got home. "What went wrong?" she asked. "I kept Koch talking as long as I could, but the lawyer never turned up."

"I'm sorry," Luciana said matter-of-factly, "we changed our minds about bribing Koch. It might have inflamed him and made matters worse for Vicenzo."

"I see," said Isabella, repressing her fury at being left in the lurch.

"What did he say, anyway?" Luciana asked. "Will he help us?"

"I don't know," Isabella replied. "I begged him to release Vicenzo and he said he would think about it."

"I suppose that's something," Luciana said curtly, and rang off.

Isabella felt both betrayed and deflated. Luciana clearly thought she had failed. It was as if all her efforts had come to nothing.

Chapter Thirty-Two

Northern Italy
June 1944

Livia was sitting at the back of the bus with her eyes closed, still wearing the summer dress she had been arrested in a few weeks before. The bus suddenly lurched, wedging her up against the wheel arch, and sending a sharp pain through her body.

A girl seated next to her touched her arm gently.

"Are you all right?" she asked. "You've been so quiet on the journey."

"Yes," replied Livia weakly. "I'm OK."

"I noticed you keep your eyes closed all the time."

Livia turned her face away, as tears trickled down her cheeks.

"I'm sorry," said the girl, "I don't mean to pry."

"No, it's all right," Livia replied. "It's nice of you to ask. My eyes hurt. When I was being interrogated, they shone a bright light in them for so long, my eyesight's been damaged. For ages, I could only see flashing lights. That's passed now, thank God, but I still can't see very well and my eyes ache if they're exposed to light for too long." She turned toward the girl and tried to smile. She half-opened her eyes, scrunching them up against the light, wincing as she did so.

The girl squeezed her hand. "Close them again. I'm Valentina by the way."

"And I'm Livia."

"You have blood on your dress," Valentina said gently, touching Livia's skirt.

"Yes," replied Livia. "They beat me quite badly."

"Me too. I was arrested in Siena two weeks ago."

"Why?"

"For being a member of the Pd'A."

"So was I—in Florence!" exclaimed Livia. "What happened to you?"

"We were scouting airdrop locations, and we got intercepted. I think we were betrayed."

"I'm sorry," said Livia. "Was it really bad—the interrogation?"

"Of course," Valentina answered, "but I wouldn't tell them anything."

"Do you know where we're going?" Livia asked.

"Yes, I think we're all being sent to a camp somewhere in Emilia Romagna. I have cousins up here in the north, and before the war we used to drive up here and visit them. So I know the road."

They arrived late at night. The signpost hanging outside said: Fossoli Internment Camp.

"I've heard of this place," Valentina murmured in Livia's ear, as they were herded off the bus. "They've been sending Jews here since forty-two. It's got a terrible reputation."

The girls were registered and assigned a number, which was printed on a triangle of colored cloth. Livia and Valentina's triangles were red, indicating they were political prisoners. The triangles were attached to their clothing with a few stitches, and they were then shown to their barracks—a set of bare wooden huts with a basic lavatory that was just a hole in the floor. The beds, Livia discovered as she lay down exhausted, were crawling with insects.

Over the following weeks, Livia and Valentina got used to the routine in the camp. Because of her poor eyesight, Livia was sent to work in the kitchens, washing pots and pans for the officers' mess. It was a kind of torture, smelling the well-cooked food, knowing that her only meal that day would be a bowl of hot water with a piece of vegetable floating in it, served with the occasional slice of bread made of rice flour.

Sometimes, as she washed up pots and pans, Livia would scrape off a morsel of meat stew or potatoes from the inside of the pan, and surreptitiously lick her fingers. From the empty plates, she would steal twists of salt and sugar, hiding them in her bra. She shared the salt with Valentina, sprinkling it on their tasteless broth, but she found her body heat often melted the sugar, creating a sticky crust on her breast, which she wiped off with a damp finger and sucked.

Livia's only respite from work was half an hour of exercise in a large central yard each evening. Here, the women were allowed to mix with the male prisoners and, to her amazement, she discovered two of her fellow members of Radio Cora—Sergio and Paulo, the man who had left their meeting early on that fateful evening when they were all arrested.

"Do you know much about this place?" Livia asked as they walked around the perimeter fence.

"Only that it's a transit camp," said Paulo.

"What does that mean?"

Paulo hesitated.

"Tell me," Livia urged. "What do you know?"

"From here we may be moved to a camp in Germany—that's if we're not executed first."

"Might they do that?" Livia stopped in her tracks.

"I think it's a possibility." Paulo glanced up at the guards, guns in hand, standing in their observation towers. "Keep walking," he said, taking her arm and propelling her forward. "I feel so guilty. If it wasn't for me, you wouldn't be here."

"Why do you say that?" Livia asked.

"I think I led the Germans to your apartment."

"How?"

"When I left your building that afternoon, there was a man waiting on the doorstep. He was wearing a raincoat, which I thought was odd at the time, because it was such a hot day. But he nodded politely, and before I could close the door behind me, he slipped in—it was as simple as that. I should have gone straight to a café and rung you, to warn you all, but I was in a hurry. I can't believe I was so stupid, so naïve."

Livia took Paulo's hand. "That's how these people work—they wait for one of us to make a simple mistake. I suppose that once he was in the building, he just let the others in. But I wonder how they found us in the first place."

"Obviously, they were tracking the signal. We knew it would happen one day. I just can't believe I was so foolish; I made it so easy for them."

"Look," said Livia, "they'd have got in somehow. They'd have rung the bell to another apartment and forced the owner to open up; we were just unlucky."

Livia thought back to that night, and wondered if Cosimo and the family had got away. She hoped they had, and that one day, she would escape too and see them again.

One evening, after they had all been counted into the barracks for the night, Livia and Valentina lay on their beds watching the sun setting over the woods. In the soft light, her eyes ached less, and she was able to make out the shapes of trees in the distance. She was imagining how wonderful it would be to be in those woods, smelling the pine, feeling the leaves beneath her feet, when she heard shouting.

"Valentina," Livia whispered. "What's happening out there?"

Valentina looked out of the window. "Oh my God," she said.

"What?" asked Livia anxiously.

"The guards are herding men into lorries. I can see Paulo and Sergio—did they mention they were being moved on?"

"No," said Livia. "They would have told me if they were going."

There was more shouting from outside.

"What's happening now?" Livia asked frantically.

"They're resisting. Sergio is shouting at the guard. Oh! The guard's hit him with the butt of his machine gun."

"Valentina, I don't think they're going to another camp," said Livia nervously. "Someone in the kitchen told me that before they move you, they give you papers. Paulo and Sergio didn't have any papers."

"So what do you think is going to happen to them?" asked Valentina.

"I don't know, but I think we should pray for them."

*

The following morning, the camp was alive with rumors. One of the prisoners who served in the officers' mess, had overheard two soldiers talking over breakfast. About thirty men had been taken to a clearing a few miles from the camp and machine-gunned to death. It was a reprisal for a partisan attack on a train leaving Genoa filled with German troops. It was rumored that two partisans had managed to escape.

"Do you think it could be Paulo and Sergio?" asked Valentina that evening.

"I don't know," replied Livia, "but if anyone could escape, it would be those two."

Over the following days, lorryloads of prisoners were removed from the camp. Most were destined for camps in Germany—a guaranteed death sentence in itself. One evening after exercise, the women in Livia's barracks were all handed their transfer papers.

"I'm being sent to Brandenburg, in Germany," Valentina said, opening the envelope. "What about you?"

"The same place... do you think we'll survive?" Livia asked uncertainly.

"Of course," said Valentina, putting her arms around her. "We will, Livia, you'll see."

The women piled into a lorry the following morning. From the camp, they were to travel first to Verona, where they would spend the night before being put on a train and sent to Germany.

Arriving in Verona late in the afternoon, they were herded into an empty school and marched to the gymnasium, where they were instructed to sleep on the floor, watched over by guards.

"I told you I have relatives up here, didn't I?" Valentina whispered to Livia as they lay down on the floor. "Well, I have a cousin who lives here, in Verona. I've not seen him for years, but he works for the railway, I think. If we can get away, I'm sure he will help us."

Livia reached over and squeezed her friend's hand. A guard patrolling the gymnasium noticed the women whispering and hit Livia on the back with the butt of his gun. "Sleep, bitch!"

She closed her eyes, but lay awake most of the night, her mind racing. Could they possibly escape? And if so how?

The following morning, the women joined hundreds of other prisoners being herded at gunpoint toward the railway station. SS guards frogmarched them three abreast in a long column of people snaking through the streets of Verona. The sight of so many of their countrymen being treated in this way brought out the crowds, who lined the streets muttering their distaste.

As the column neared the station, a group of men at the front tried to make an escape, rushing off into the side streets. Many of the SS guards gave chase, leaving the women at the back of the column unguarded.

"Come on, let's make a break for it," whispered Valentina.

Livia felt her right arm being pulled hard as she was dragged out of the column and into the waiting crowd of bystanders. They quickly parted to let the women through, one man pressing a few coins into Valentina's hand, before closing ranks again to conceal the two women's escape. As they ran through the streets, Livia and Valentina tore off the red triangles—the only thing identifying them as prisoners.

Verona was the regional headquarters of the Fascist Party, and was crawling with Italian and German patrols.

"We need to find some false papers quickly," Valentina whispered, as they lurked in front of a café. "And we have to get off the streets before curfew."

Coming toward them they suddenly noticed two SS guards returning from the railway station, laughing and joking with one another.

"Quick," said Valentina, "in here." She shepherded Livia into the café. To her dismay, she realized the two SS men were following them.

The waitress saw the panic on the girls' faces. "There's a ladies' room at the back," she told them. "I'll distract them. Go!"

Valentina grabbed Livia, found the toilet, and locked the door behind them. After a few minutes, Livia heard one of the guards shouting to the other.

"One of them needs a pee," whispered Livia.

"You speak German?" asked Valentina.

Livia nodded. They heard the cubicle next to them being locked, the sound of flushing and then the boots of the soldier retreating.

A few minutes later, the waitress knocked on the door. "You can come out now," she murmured. "They've gone."

Back in the café, she offered them a coffee. "Here," she said, pushing it across the bar. "You look as if you could do with it."

"Thank you." Livia gratefully sipped the coffee. "It tastes divine."

"We only have a little money," said Valentina, offering the few lire she had.

"Keep it, you'll need it," said the girl. "You're escaping?"

The girls nodded.

"Partisans?" she asked quietly. "Do you need somewhere to stay?"

"Yes, desperately," whispered Valentina.

"Go to San Girolamo convent. They support the Resistance. Good luck."

The convent stood on the shores of the river. Surrounded by tall columns of yew, the pale-stone building glowed welcomingly in the sunshine. The girls knocked on the large oak doors and were ushered inside by a kindly nun who showed them to a small room with a pair of comfortable-looking beds and a basin with running water.

Valentina sank down onto the bed. "It's so soft and clean."

"And look," said Livia, ripping off her dress, "soap and water!"

She washed every part of herself, soaping her hair, scraping her nails, scrubbing her skin clean, until the basin was black with dirt.

There was a knock at the door. Livia opened it, wrapped in a small towel.

A nun stood outside carrying a pile of clothes. "I thought you'd like something clean to wear," she said. "Let me take yours—I can wash and mend them for you. When you are dressed, join us in the refectory for some food; supper is about to be served."

It was a simple meal of vegetable soup and bread, but so tasty that the girls ate greedily. For the first time in months, their stomachs felt full, almost bloated. They slept deeply and woke the following morning feeling refreshed and optimistic.

They wandered through the cloisters to the refectory, where they breakfasted on eggs laid by the convent hens, which clucked contentedly round the garden. Afterward, they sat on a bench in the sun warming their faces, listening to the birds singing.

A young nun approached them. "Reverend Mother would like to see you, can you follow me please?"

The Mother Superior was a tall elegant woman with violet-colored eyes. Her office was very simple, with plain white walls decorated only with a large crucifix which hung behind her Victorian desk.

"Please, sit down." She pointed to a pair of comfortable chairs. "I imagine you have been through a great deal." Her voice was gentle but firm.

"We have," replied Livia. "We were both arrested and then imprisoned because of our work with the Resistance."

"Well, we can give you sanctuary here for as long as you like," she told them. "You are welcome to work in the gardens."

"You're very kind," replied Livia. "But we feel we have a duty to carry on our work."

Valentina nodded encouragingly.

"I understand." The Reverend Mother smiled gently. "How can I help you?"

"We need false identity cards," said Valentina, "so we can get back to Florence."

"Getting false papers will be hard. I have no contacts, I'm afraid," Reverend Mother replied. "Is there no one else you can ask for help?"

"I have a cousin who lives here," Valentina went on. "But I've not seen him for years. I think he would help."

Valentina's cousin Mauro was a shy and retiring man who had never married. He came to the convent the following day. He had last seen Valentina when she was a child, and seemed genuinely pleased to see her.

"I have a spare ration book, and here are a few lire. At least then you can eat in a restaurant."

"Thank you Mauro, you're very kind," said Valentina.

"The thing is," Livia interjected, "we need to get back to Florence if we can, but we have no papers."

Mauro mused on the problem. "Getting papers in Verona would be risky, because the Germans will be looking for you, and watching the Town Hall. You'll need to go somewhere else. I have an old college friend called Dario who lives in Milan. We did engineering together. I will buy you two train tickets to Milan, where he will meet you and help you get papers. But you should leave straight away."

The two girls said their goodbyes to the nuns and the Reverend Mother, and Mauro walked them to the railway station. There were SS men at all the entrances, questioning people at random. But the girls aroused no suspicion. Dressed in new clothes, their hair washed, their faces scrubbed clean, they looked just like two local girls on their way to visit family.

"You will have to make up a story about why you have no papers," Mauro said, as he handed them their tickets. "Can you manage that?"

"Of course," said Valentina. "We'll think of something, and thank you, Mauro, we're in your debt."

The train journey to Milan would take several hours, passing through Brescia, Parma and Bergamo. At each stop, the train filled up, as more and more people climbed aboard.

As it pulled out of Parma station, Valentina whispered, "Bergamo is the next stop, then Milan. With luck, no one will ever check our papers."

They gazed at the passing countryside, and both began to relax a little.

"Papers, papers...have your papers ready." It was two Fascist policemen, accompanied by the guard. Slowly and meticulously, the men began to work their way down the carriage, checking every set of papers as they went.

"How are we going to get away with it?" Livia whispered to Valentina, grabbing her arm nervously. "Perhaps we should walk back down the train and try to keep one step ahead of them."

"We could," agreed Valentina. "But they'd find us eventually."

"Or we could hide in the toilet?" Livia suggested.

"That might work," agreed Valentina.

They stood up, smiling at the couple opposite, trying to look nonchalant.

"Will you save our seats?" Valentina asked. "We just need to go to the ladies' room." The couple nodded.

"You two," shouted one of the policemen, "stay where you are!" He fixed them with a determined stare and marched up the carriage.

"Damn," whispered Livia. "Now all we've done is draw attention to ourselves."

"Keep calm," said Valentina. "I've got an idea."

"Papers," the policeman demanded, holding out his hand.

Valentina began to cry theatrically. "I'm so sorry, officer, but we have no papers, we were traveling from Florence to Milan when our train was bombed, and we lost everything."

"We made our way to Verona," Livia continued, "where my friend's cousin bought us some new tickets." They held their tickets out for inspection.

The guard, who had now joined the policeman, took the tickets and checked them.

"So you have no papers," said the policeman.

The two girls looked at one another and then at the guard. "No," said Livia. "Oh dear, what can we do?"

At that moment, the train pulled into Bergamo station, lurching violently as the driver applied the brakes. The girls were thrown back against their seats, and the guard and policeman stumbled, just as the doors opened. Men, women and children—many of them refugees, carrying baggage and boxes—rushed onto the train. It was chaos.

"Oh come on, forget the girls," said the guard impatiently to the policeman, "it happens a lot—people who've lost their papers. We'd better get on, the train is filling up, and I've got a lot of tickets to check." He moved away and waited at the door to the next carriage for the policeman, who hovered for a moment, before grudgingly moving on.

When they arrived in Milan, they went straight to Mauro's friend, Dario.

"I think we should go immediately to City Hall," he explained as they hurried along the street. "The authorities may already be looking for you. Come up with some new names and I'll vouch for you. There are so many displaced people, the clerks don't really bother to check."

"What name will you choose?" Livia whispered to Valentina as they sat in the waiting room of the grandiose hall.

"I've always rather liked the name of Paola, Paola Ricci. What about you?"

"I could be Laura, that's a nice name."

"What about a new surname?" asked Valentina.

"De Luca," said Livia. "It's the name of my boyfriend, Cosimo."

Chapter Thirty-Three

Rome
June 1944

Isabella woke with a knot in her stomach. Koch had taken to calling her every morning at half past ten, and she dreaded it.

"How are you today?" he would ask, like a fond lover. It was both inappropriate and disconcerting. A few chaste meetings did not constitute a love affair, and yet he treated her, at times, as if she were his mistress.

She would reply as dispassionately as she could, "I'm fine thank you, and you?"

"I'd be happier if I could see you," he purred one particular morning. "Perhaps we could have lunch again?"

"I don't know, maybe," she said, hoping to discourage him.

"I've still got your director friend locked up in Pensione Jaccarino, you know. The Germans keep demanding I send him for questioning at their headquarters at Via Tasso, but I've managed to fend them off—up till now. I'm only doing it to please you."

"Thank you," she said, "you know how grateful I am."

"Grateful enough to have lunch with me?" he pressed.

She realized she had no option but to agree if she was to keep Vicenzo out of the hands of the SS.

"I'll send a car at twelve-thirty—be ready."

The car took her not to a restaurant but to Pensione Jaccarino, Koch's own headquarters. Isabella was horrified at the idea that Koch thought it was a suitable place for them to have lunch. She knew that somewhere in the building people were being interrogated and tortured. It was possible that Vicenzo himself was suffering at that very moment. Isabella resolved that when she saw Koch she would beg him, on her knees if necessary, to release Vicenzo.

She pushed through the shabby half-glazed doors into the lobby. The receptionist looked up as Isabella came in. "Wait here please, signora," she instructed.

Isabella sat on the hard chair in the waiting room, feeling irritated and uncomfortable. She gazed out into the sunny street, wishing she was anywhere else in the world but there. Suddenly, there was a piercing female scream, followed by a man's agonized roar. The sounds were repeated, echoing from somewhere in the building—the basement, Isabella thought. She leapt to her feet.

"Sit down please, signora," said the receptionist.

Isabella did as she was told, but it was impossible to ignore the terrible agonized sounds coming from the bowels of the building. The receptionist, on the other hand, appeared unconcerned.

Eventually the screams ceased, and were replaced by an eerie silence. What had happened? Isabella wondered. Were the unfortunate people unconscious, or dead?

Finally Koch appeared. He looked flushed, fine beads of sweat breaking out on his forehead. There was a speck of blood on his white silk shirt.

"I'm afraid we'll have to postpone lunch to another day," he said coldly. "But I will take you home."

Koch drove in silence, apparently brooding on something. Isabella was relieved when he drew up outside her house. She climbed hurriedly out of his car.

Early the following morning, Isabella received a phone call from a man with a German accent. "You are required to report to Via Tasso this morning at ten o'clock."

Via Tasso was the headquarters of the SS in Rome. Isabella was terrified, wondering who she could turn to for help. The obvious person was Koch, and she was on the verge of dialing his number when the phone rang.

"I've just heard," Koch said. "Kappler, Head of the SS, wants to see you. You have to go, I'm afraid, but go alone and keep calm. I'll be there, waiting for you in the car outside. Your fate," he added wistfully, "is in God's hands now."

Isabella was shown into a squalid windowless room. Just a desk separated her from her interrogator. Plump and balding, Kappler had large sweat marks spreading from his armpits. He motioned her to a chair opposite him. There was a lamp on the desk, and as she sat down, he swung the head round until it was shining directly into her eyes.

"That's too bright," she said, raising her hand to shield her face.

"That's rather the point," he said, drawing on his cigarette and forcibly exhaling into her face.

Just out of her eyeline sat a junior officer, who appeared to be taking notes of their conversation on a typewriter. The noise of the keys and the clash of the return bar was disorienting.

The questions, predictably, were all about Vicenzo. When did they meet? When did she realize he was part of the Resistance? Why did she not report him? Was she part of his cell? Did she really not know about the cache of arms in the house on Via Salaria? And as for the attack in Via Rasella, did she really expect him to believe she knew nothing about it?

It was old ground, questions she had answered before and deep down, she felt in a strong position. She could reply honestly to almost every question. No, she was not part of the cell. She knew nothing of the arms, or the planned attack on German troops on Via Rasella—she had nearly died herself, after all. When asked if she knew Vicenzo was part of the Resistance, she was forced to lie. "Of course I didn't know," she replied fiercely. "To be honest, I can't believe it. I think a terrible mistake has been made. He's an aristocrat, for heaven's sake."

Kappler drew deeply on his cigarette, and studied her for some minutes. Suddenly, he stood up. "That's enough for today," he said and left the room.

*

Koch was waiting for her outside in his car. Isabella climbed in and sat alongside him, still trembling slightly. He reached out and took her hand in his. He lifted it to his lips and kissed it. She wanted to snatch it away, but she resisted the temptation. His passion for her was the only card she held, and she was determined to make use of it. Nevertheless, as she thought about the previous couple of hours, she couldn't resist a moment of moral superiority.

"It must be terrible to be in the clutches of people like that," she said haughtily.

Koch looked away, embarrassed, and started the car.

For two days, Isabella heard nothing from either Koch or the SS. Part of her was relieved. She was exhausted by Koch's passion for her, and fearful of being summoned back to SS HQ and another round of questioning. Although the odious Kappler had let her go, she sensed he had not finished with her yet, and unlike Koch, he appeared impervious to her charms.

One afternoon, Luciana rang her, asking for an update on her brother's possible release.

"I'm afraid I have nothing to tell you yet," Isabella said truthfully. She had begun to find Luciana's single-minded approach rather upsetting, and felt a little used by Vicenzo's family. They appeared to show no concern for her; it was him, and only him, who was the focus of their interest.

"Oh, and before I go, Salvato wants to see you tomorrow," Luciana said.

"Why?" asked Isabella.

"You'll find out," replied Luciana.

Salvato Cappelli arrived just before lunch. Isabella showed him into the sitting room. Her mother was sewing quietly in one corner.

"Mamma, would you mind?" Isabella asked. "This gentleman has some private business with me."

Her mother looked irritated. "It seems to me, Isabella, that everyone has something to ask of you, and yet—what do you get from it?"

"Mamma, please?"

Her mother left the room; Isabella listened to her disappearing footsteps down the corridor toward the kitchen.

"Thank you for seeing me," Salvato began.

"What do you want to ask?"

"It's not I who want to ask, but we, the Resistance."

"Go on," she said.

"You appear to be in a good position with this man Koch."

"I wouldn't describe it as 'good' exactly," she replied. "It's complicated and rather exhausting, if you must know."

"Oh, come on," he said, "Luciana has told me. He's obviously mad about you."

Isabella blushed. "He is a fan of my work," she said grandly. "But as for his passion—well, I hate it; it's most unwelcome and completely unrequited, I assure you."

"I realize it's difficult," Salvato went on, "but it puts you in a very strong position to help us, don't you see?"

"What do you mean?" she asked.

"We'd like you to arrange a meeting with him—at a restaurant or café—somewhere we could," he paused, choosing his words carefully, "somewhere we could assassinate him."

As the full force of his words sank in, Isabella blanched visibly. However much she hated Koch, the thought of having his blood on her hands was unbearable. She stood up and began to pace the sitting room nervously. "I couldn't do that," she said.

"You could," Salvato urged. "It would be easy enough. Suggest a meeting place, and we'll be waiting for him."

"You have no idea how hard it would be," she protested. "Sometimes, he does come here alone, I admit, but I couldn't guarantee he wouldn't be guarded."

"But you have met him alone in restaurants before. Luciana told me. Please, Isabella."

"I've only ever met him once before in a restaurant. Since that time, he just seems to want to drive around talking to me. It's very complicated, Salvato. I'm already taking so many risks. Besides, to murder him in cold blood like that—it would be wrong."

"And how many people has *he* murdered, Isabella?" he asked aggressively.

"I know, but it still can't be right to kill someone, it can't be."

Salvato stood up angrily. "You're obviously not on our side."

"That's not fair," she protested. "All along, my only aim has been to get Vicenzo out of prison, that's why I'm doing this, and Koch is my only hope of succeeding. If he dies, Vicenzo's chance might die with him."

"If Koch dies, so does a branch of the Fascist police in Rome. It would set them back for weeks, months maybe," Salvato replied.

"I'm sorry," said Isabella, walking toward the door. "I can see how it would help you, but the answer has to be no."

Chapter Thirty-Four

Milan
June 1944

Livia and Valentina, armed with their new identities as Laura and Paola, stayed with Dario in his apartment in Milan for a few days. He gave them some money to buy a change of clothes and a few basic supplies. In the evenings, they crowded round his old radio and listened to Radio Londra, desperate for news. In the first days of June, it came thick and fast—firstly with the liberation of Rome. They were guided through it all in the calm tones of Colonel Stephens.

The Allies are poised to enter Rome. General Maitland Wilson, Supreme Allied Commander in the Mediterranean, said he is determined that Rome's cultural significance should be protected. "It is the Allies' intention," he said, "to ensure that the military take all measures to protect the people of Rome, alongside their historical and religious monuments in the city."

"It sounds like the Germans are being squeezed between the Allied forces in the north and south," said Livia. "My fear is that Florence will be caught in the middle. It will become the Germans' most important defensive position. The Resistance will need all the fighters they can get. I think I should go back."

"You'd be mad to do that," said Dario. "People are fleeing Florence and coming north."

"I know," she replied, "but everything I love is there. I have to go back."

That evening, Livia rang her parents at the villa. It had been weeks since she had spoken to her father and she was desperate to hear his voice. Part of her dreaded the call. To discover he was dead, or that her mother had not survived, was almost more than she could bear. So, with a trembling hand, she dialed their number. The phone rang for a long time and she was about to give up, when it was answered by a faint voice at the other end.

"Hello?" In spite of the crackling phone line, she recognized her father's voice immediately.

"Papa! It's me, Livia."

"Livia, is that really you, darling?"

"Yes, Papa, it's really me."

"Where are you?" he asked desperately.

"Somewhere in the north—but I'm safe."

"In the north—what are you doing there?"

"It's a very long story. Tell me, how are all of you?"

There was a moment's silence on the other end.

"Papa, what's happened?"

"Mamma and I are both fine, but I'm sorry to tell you that Nonno died a couple of weeks ago."

"Oh no," said Livia tearfully.

"I'm so sorry, but he was a very old man and in poor health. It was a blessing really, he'd been bedridden for months, and his end was peaceful—Mamma and I were both here holding his hand."

Livia composed herself. "And how is Angela?" she asked. "She must be so upset about Gino."

"Well, it was very hard for her at the beginning. But we keep her busy and that helps. The house is now a refuge for women and children displaced by the war. Your mother complains a lot, but secretly I think she likes it."

"Have you been back to Florence?"

"No, not yet. Mamma won't let me out of her sight, and for once I'm doing as I'm told. But I'm supporting the Pd'A in any way I can from here. Although Radio Cora has been disbanded, we are getting together with the other liberal parties to form a coalition, preparing for government."

"But aren't the Germans still in charge?"

"Yes, they are for now, but the writing is on the wall," her father went on. "The Allies are very close, and we intend to negotiate some sort of peace as soon as possible. Whether we'll manage it, I don't know. Oh Livia," her father said, his voice sounding old suddenly. "I can hardly believe you're alive. When I heard from our colleagues in the Pd'A that you'd been arrested... when they told me you'd been sent away, I thought I'd never see you again." Giacomo began to sob.

"I know, Papa, but I'm all right, really."

"For so long I feared the worst, Livia. I felt so helpless. I should have been able to get you out of prison—that's my job as a lawyer, as your father."

She heard the pain in his voice.

"I understand, and I'm sorry I couldn't get in touch sooner to tell you that I was all right. But I'm coming back to Florence tomorrow."

"No! You mustn't do that! They might still be looking for you. It's not safe there."

"It's not safe anywhere, Papa. And as for them looking for me, there must be hundreds of partisans on the run. Besides, I have a new identity, and new papers—they'll never track me down."

"You'll go back to the apartment?" he asked.

"Yes. I've not been back since the day I was arrested. God knows what I'll find."

"If the phone is working, will you ring me when you get there?"

"I will."

The following day, Livia and Valentina stood on the concourse at Milan railway station. Valentina was heading for Bologna and a job working for the local Pd'A. Livia clutched a ticket for Florence.

"I will miss you," Valentina said tearfully, hugging her friend.

"And I you," replied Livia.

"Why don't you change your mind and come with me?" Valentina suggested. "We can work together in Bologna. I can look after you."

"I don't need looking after."

"But your eyes..." Valentina said, concern in her voice.

"They're improving every day," Livia reassured her. "Besides, I must go back to Florence, you can see that can't you?"

Valentina nodded; they hugged for a final time.

As the train pulled out of Milan station heading for Florence, Livia had a brief moment of panic that she had made the wrong decision. She hung out of the window and waved to Valentina standing on the platform, until her outline merged with the darkness of the station. Sitting back in her seat, sunlight streamed in through the window, Livia put on a newly acquired pair of sunglasses to ease the pain in her eyes, and breathed deeply. She was heading back into the maelstrom. The struggle to save Florence had begun.

Florence's Santa Maria Novella station was swarming with people, most of them fleeing the city. German soldiers were patrolling the concourse, but Livia managed to slip unchallenged through the crowds, clutching her small suitcase, with her new papers in her dress pocket. Once outside, she walked quickly to the apartment. She had no key, as all her personal possessions had been left inside the apartment when she was arrested. She loitered in the street, waiting for someone to come out of the building and let her in. But after half an hour she gave up and rang everyone's bell, hoping to find anyone at home. To her dismay, the only apartment to respond was Signor Lombardi's.

"Who's that?" shouted the old man, hanging out of the window five stories up.

"It's me Signor Lombardi, Livia."

"Why are you ringing my bell?" he asked irritably.

"I've lost my key," she explained.

He disappeared from the window and a few minutes later, slightly to her surprise, the front door opened.

"You'd better come in," he said.

She followed him up the five flights of stairs. On their shared landing, he nodded toward the door. "I fixed it as well as I could," he said. The beautiful chestnut paneled door, destroyed by the German secret agents, had been boarded up with cheap pine. "You can make a better job of it after the war. I have a spare key if you need it—your father left one with me." He retreated inside his apartment and emerged brandishing the key.

"Thank you so much for mending it," said Livia, nodding at the door, "that was kind."

"Well, we don't want people breaking in, do we? The commune has always looked after each other and even the war won't stop that." A glimmer of a smile played on his thin bluish lips.

As Livia slotted the key in the lock, and opened the door, she inhaled the familiar scent of the chestnut flooring and beeswax furniture polish. Hesitating at the doorway, she turned round and beamed at him.

"I'm so grateful to you, signore."

"You're welcome," he said. "I know you think I'm not to be trusted, but I'm on your side. I admire you—you're prepared to give your life for what you believe in. And it's time you stopped calling me Signor Lombardi," he added. "My name is Massimo."

Livia was surprised by this little speech. For years she had assumed he was pro-Fascist. She had feared and mistrusted him, he was right about that. Now she almost felt warm toward him.

Inside, she wandered the apartment, delighting in its permanence. Everything was just as she had left it, even the armchairs upended by the Germans during their raid. She went from room to room putting things back into their place—chairs were righted, books replaced on shelves, cups put back into cupboards. In the kitchen, she found a couple of tins of beans and opened one for her supper. There was a small tin of coffee; she unscrewed the lid and inhaled, reveling in its scent. In a cupboard in the hall, she found a couple of bottles of wine. She poured some into a crystal glass and gazed at its ruby color glinting in the sunshine. It seemed unimaginably indulgent.

She ran a bath. The water was cold. Signor Lombardi must have turned off the water heater. She switched it on, and while it heated up, boiled a few kettles of water on the stove, which she poured into the bath until steam filled the bathroom. She lay, floating in the warm water, her hair fanning out around her head. Finally, she climbed out, wrapped herself in a towel and brushed her teeth.

In her bedroom she searched for clean clothes. Only then did she pick up the phone, and her heart racing with excitement, dialed Cosimo's number.

Washing up in the kitchen the following day, she waited eagerly for him to arrive, willing the bell to ring. When it did, she leaned out of the window and threw down the key.

He climbed the stairs as fast as he could, arriving breathless at her apartment. As usual, Lombardi half-opened his door when he heard the noise outside on the landing.

"It's just my friend, Signor... I mean Massimo—nothing for you to worry about," she reassured him.

The old man raised his hand to his head in a little salute and retreated inside. Livia suddenly realized he hadn't been spying on them, but had merely been keeping a watchful protective eye.

Alone together, Cosimo and Livia clung to one another for what seemed an eternity, reluctant to let each other go. Eventually, Livia looked up at him with love in her eyes. "I'm here, and we're both safe," she said. "Let's go to bed."

They made love, and afterward lay in each other's arms. It was only then that Livia felt able to tell him everything that had happened to her since they had last met. When she finished her story, Cosimo leaned over her, tracing her face with his fingers. "I can hardly believe what they did to you and your poor beautiful eyes." He kissed her eyelids, then her lips, and her forehead.

"I can't pretend it wasn't awful," she said. "But my eyesight is improving. I'll get some glasses—that will help."

"And I am honored that you took my name for your new identity." He smiled down at her. "Laura de Luca—it sounds good. Almost as good as Livia de Luca, don't you think?"

She blushed. "That does sound good... very good."

"Well, I think, when this is over, we should make it official, don't you?" he said, smothering her face with kisses.

"Yes, maybe," she replied playfully. "Now, tell me everything that happened to you—from the moment I left you on the roof terrace."

Cosimo rolled over and lay with his hands behind his head. "I hardly know where to start," he said.

"What about...how you and the family got away?"

"Well," he began, "we made our escape over the roofs, as you suggested, although it was not easy. Fortunately Jacob and Matteo were both very nimble and brave. I know I was a terrible burden to them all, with my bad leg and my stick. Jacob had to help me more than once. Poor Sara was struggling with the baby, but Matteo was very grown up, and guided his mother through some scary moments. We managed to get onto the roof of a house in the street behind this one. It also had a roof terrace, so we climbed down onto it. The door to the house was unlocked. We crept down the stairs and opened the door into the apartment. By a miracle it was empty. We simply opened the front door and ran downstairs, or limped in my case, and then up the road, and away. I knew of another safe house nearby and we went there at first. The next day, I arranged for the family to move to the crypt of a church. They were quite safe there, I promise, and the priest and others from the Resistance brought them food each day."

"Where are they now?" Livia asked.

"Another safe house, south of the river. They're doing well, as far as I know."

Livia's eyes misted with tears. "I'm so relieved, I was very fond of them."

"They were very fond of you too," he said.

"And I hardly dare ask, what of Elena? How is she?"

"Well therein lies a tale," he said, lying on his side and gazing at her. "I told you I would not abandon her, and I didn't. A group of us went to the convent where she was being held, dressed in Nazi uniforms. You would have laughed to see us. We showed the guard on duty a forged release document for Elena, and demanded she was released on the spot. He, of course, was suspicious and picked up the phone to check with his superior officer. Gianni, one of our group—I don't think you know him—pulled his pistol on the guard, forcing him to drop the phone. He began to shout for help, so Gianni had to kill him. I felt bad about that, but we had no option, did we?"

Livia nodded. "What happened next?"

"In the meantime, the Mother Superior heard the noise and discovered us. I was worried that all would be lost, but it turned out that she was a remarkable old lady, who hated the Fascists as much as we do. She helped us dispose of the guard, then she released Elena. Poor Elena—she was so overjoyed to see us, she couldn't stop crying. Then, as we were leaving, the Mother Superior called us back frantically, warning us that if Carità heard one woman had escaped, he would kill all the others. In the end we released the lot—over twenty women came running out of the prison, scattering far and wide. I was worried Carità would work out that the nuns had helped us, and punish them. So before we left, we tied them all up and locked them in a cell."

"And how is Elena?" asked Livia.

"She was very weak at the beginning, but she is doing all right now. She wants so much to see you."

"And I want so much to see her. I'll go tomorrow."

Eventually, their stories told, they closed their eyes. As Livia slipped into unconsciousness, she heard Cosimo whispering, "Goodnight Signora de Luca." And he kissed her on the forehead and they slept.

Chapter Thirty-Five

Rome
June 1944

The day after her meeting with Salvato, Isabella received an early-morning phone call from Koch.

"Good morning," he said gently. "I have something important to tell you."

"What?" she asked, her heart suddenly racing.

"I can't tell you now, on the phone. I'll send a car—be ready."

She dressed hurriedly, fearful of what might be about to happen. Was she to be interrogated again, or worse? Perhaps Salvato had been right and she should help the Resistance get rid of Koch once and for all.

The car brought her to Pensione Jaccarino and she was escorted to Koch's main office.

"Ah good, you're here," he said, emerging from his private office next door, "do sit down. I have some news," he began. He was interrupted by a knock on the door. "What is it?" he asked the guard irritably.

"You are needed, sir. Please come quickly."

He looked across at Isabella. "Wait here, I won't be long."

She waited for some minutes, but when he didn't return, she grew restless and wandered around the room. It held no interest, as it was almost completely bare, with only a single desk and two chairs. So she plucked up the courage to peep into Koch's private office. She tried the door and, to her surprise, found it was unlocked.

As she opened the door, she was amazed by what confronted her: almost an entire wall covered with pictures of herself. Publicity shots, magazine covers, film posters—her whole career was laid out, neatly pinned onto a huge cork board. It was both flattering and disconcerting. Koch had obviously been obsessed with her for years. Suddenly all his behavior made sense: his indulgent treatment of her, his unexpected agreement to her request to help Vicenzo, his studied politeness. It was all at odds with his reputation as a torturer and murderer of her countrymen.

Remembering Salvato's admonishment of her, she wondered if there was anything in Koch's office that might assist the Resistance—something that would clearly demonstrate her loyalty. The surface of Koch's desk was predictably tidy—there was only a fountain pen and a leather-bound notebook. She flicked through the notebook, and found it disappointingly empty, but at the back was a leather pocket, in which he had hidden a small key. Her heart racing, she tried the key in the desk's top drawer, and it opened. The first thing she saw was a typed list of over thirty names, under the heading: "Partisan suspects—to be arrested." Some of the names were people that she knew—aristocrats and famous industrialists among them. Realizing its importance, she removed the document and hid it in her handbag. Breathlessly, she closed the drawer, locked it and replaced the key. She had only resumed her seat moments before Koch returned.

"Please," he said, "come with me."

"Where are you taking me?" she asked nervously, as he led her down the stairs. She was struck by a terrible thought. Had he been spying on her, and seen her rifling through his desk?

"You'll see," he said calmly, as they reached reception. He held open the main doors for her and escorted her outside to his car.

He drove off at high speed, taking a route past Villa Borghese and toward Parioli. Was he taking her home? she wondered. No. To her surprise, he drove into Via Salaria and pulled up outside Vicenzo's villa. He switched off the engine and turned to look at her.

"I've let Vicenzo go," he said simply.

She gasped, scarcely able to believe it.

"I have transferred him to a prison for VIPs called San Gregorio; it's an old convent and quite comfortable. He can receive food from outside and occasional visits. He has been given a false name, Guidi, so the Germans can't track him down."

He remained quite impassive as he spoke, but Isabella was overcome with emotion. Almost involuntarily, she took his hand and squeezed it. Then, on impulse, she lifted it to her lips and kissed it.

"Thank you, Pietro. From the bottom of my heart, thank you."

He blushed. "I have brought you here to collect some things for him. You know what he will need?"

"Yes, of course."

Koch waited in the car while she ran to the house.

Constanza opened the door and Isabella threw her arms around her. "Vicenzo's been released!" she said excitedly. "I've come for some clothes for him."

Isabella went upstairs and packed a bag with clothes, bed linen and a few toiletries. Downstairs, she went to the sitting room and took a couple of bottles of his favorite whisky from the drinks tray and slipped them beneath the clothing. Then, waving Constanza goodbye, she ran back to Koch's car and they drove to San Gregorio.

Vicenzo met them in a communal room. He looked tired and scruffy. He was unshaven, his hair long and unkempt, his black eyes hollow from lack of sleep. He was wearing an old pair of trousers that she didn't recognize, and a tattered shirt. He smiled faintly when he saw her, but something seemed to hold him back. Perhaps it was the sight of Koch lurking in the shadows at one side of the room, studying his enemy.

"Aren't you happy?" Isabella asked, kissing Vicenzo on the cheek. She had dreamed of this moment for so long, of him being out of danger, of his gratitude, and how he might tell her he loved her. "Look," she said, handing him the bag, "I've brought you some clean clothes, sheets and whisky."

Vicenzo glanced angrily toward Koch. "Send him away," he muttered.

She took his hand in hers; it felt frail and thin. "I can't do that," she whispered, "not after what he's done for you. He's the one who got you out of prison and into here."

Vicenzo shook his hand free. "Get him out of my sight," he said angrily.

Isabella glanced over at Koch and smiled. "I'm sorry," she mouthed.

His small black eyes looked back at her impassively.

"Please, Vicenzo," she urged, "stay calm. It's been so hard to get you released, don't spoil it now."

"Thank you for bringing my things," he said coldly.

"I think we should go," said Koch suddenly.

Isabella gazed at Vicenzo, wanting him desperately to say something intimate, something loving, but he simply turned toward the door and knocked, requesting the guard return him to his cell.

Back home, Isabella felt deflated. Vicenzo had seemed angry rather than grateful. And far from feeling relieved that her role was over, she knew Vicenzo's continued safety depended on Koch not revealing his whereabouts. He'd made it quite clear that the Germans were still looking for Vicenzo, and it was up to her, and only her, to keep Koch onside. She called Luciana, hoping for some words of thanks and encouragement.

"Have you heard?" she said excitedly. "Vicenzo's out! He's been moved to the prison at San Gregorio—it's really quite comfortable. I took him some clothes and linen and so on."

"How did he seem?" Luciana asked coldly.

"Tired, irritable, but I think he's going to be OK."

"I'd like to see him," said Luciana, "can you get me in?"

"I can try, but it will mean asking Koch for another favor."

"Well you can do that, can't you?" Luciana replied icily.

Koch seemed delighted when she rang the following morning.

"I've really missed you," he purred.

Isabella was determined to keep the conversation as businesslike as possible. "Vicenzo's sister would like to see him."

"I see," Koch replied. "The Count's sister, eh? How funny, the aristocracy asking me for favors." He laughed. "I'm sure it can be arranged," he went on, "they are, after all, an important family. Perhaps you and I could meet too?" he suggested hopefully.

"If you like," Isabella replied, with a sinking heart.

"How about dinner, tomorrow, at Albergo dell'Orso? Meet me there at seven o'clock."

A dinner invitation was a worrying development. It was too romantic a gesture, and one which Isabella was loath to accept, but once again she felt she had no option other than to agree. She began to feel as if she would never be free of Koch, and went to bed that night filled with foreboding. She would be trapped forever in this unenviable triangle—caught between two men, one whom she loved and the other who loved her.

The following morning, a letter arrived from Vicenzo.

> *My dearest Bella,*
>
> *I must write to thank you for all you've done for me. I can imagine how difficult it must have been to befriend that monster. I'm sorry I was unable to be more effusive when we met, but I hate him. I hate everything he and his Fascist cohort stand for—the betrayal of our country and its values, the moral destruction of our people. To see him standing there, gloating, was agony for me.*
>
> *But you, little Bella, have been kindness itself and I want you to know how much I appreciate it.*
>
> *Thank you again.*
>
> *With love,*
> *Your friend,*
> *Vicenzo*

Isabella read and reread his note, weeping as she did so. To receive Vicenzo's thanks and expressions of love made her feel it had all been worth it.

She dressed carefully for her meeting with Koch. Determined to look smart, but not seductive, she chose an elegant, demure blue dress that matched her eyes. She would be friendly and polite, but no more. The restaurant Koch had suggested was a fashionable meeting place for the Roman elite. It had a garden outside, filled with intimate little tables, lit by candlelight, and was the perfect location for a romantic evening.

The restaurant was within walking distance, and her route took her past Salvato Cappelli's office, so Isabella decided to drop in on him. She had not spoken to him since refusing his suggestion of luring Koch into a trap, and was anxious to redeem herself in his eyes.

"Have you heard?" she asked, as she sat down in his office. "Vicenzo's out of that terrible place. He's in the prison at San Gregorio. He now has his own clothes and bed linen—even whisky."

"Yes, I heard," Salvato said. "Luciana rang me."

"Without Koch, you know, it could never have happened," she continued. "I was right, I think, to befriend him. It really was the only way." She looked at him expectantly, waiting for him to congratulate her, but instead he was offhand, tapping his fingers on his desk. She was perplexed. "I've brought you something," she said eagerly, handing him the list she had taken from Koch's office. "It's a list of people they want to arrest. I stole it from Koch's desk. I thought it might be useful."

He studied it. "Yes it might be," he said. "There are some key names on here, thank you. I shall be able to warn them."

"Good," Isabella stood up and smoothed her skirt. "I'm really glad I could help. I just wanted to show that I...I am on your side."

"Are you really?" Salvato looked at her intently.

"Yes, yes of course—why do you ask?"

"You've been spotted all over Rome with that man Koch. People are saying that you are having an affair, and that you have been passing information to him. That you are a collaborator."

She stared at him in disbelief. "You are joking, surely?"

"Not at all," he replied, stony-faced.

"I am not having an affair!" she said angrily. "I am not! How dare people say that? After all I've done for Vicenzo, how can people think that?"

"I'm just warning you, that's all. It's what I've heard."

She left Salvato's office in a state of shock. Surely, she thought, everyone must realize how much she despised Koch. Everything she had ever done was to save Vicenzo—the only man she had ever truly loved.

She wandered aimlessly through the streets in a daze, weeping at the unfairness of it all, and considered going home. But she realized Vicenzo's very existence still depended on Koch. He might have been moved to a more congenial prison, but he could be taken by the Germans at any time and tortured or executed. Whatever she did, she must keep Koch onside and not make him angry.

She arrived at the restaurant slightly late. Standing on the pavement outside, she took out her powder compact and studied her face in the mirror. Her eyes were red from crying, her complexion blotchy. She patted powder on her face, wiped beneath her eyes and touched up her lipstick.

Koch stood up eagerly as she walked toward his table, and held out his hands to her. He was dressed as usual in his smart blue suit and white silk shirt. He took her hands in his and kissed her on both cheeks.

"You look lovely." He pulled out a chair for her and as she sat down, she noticed a large bunch of red roses lying on the table. "These are for you," he said, handing them to her theatrically. "Do you like cocktails, by the way?" he asked.

"Yes... I suppose so," she replied.

He snapped his fingers at the waiter. "Two champagne cocktails," he barked.

As Koch studied the menu, discussing what they might eat, Isabella's mind was elsewhere. Salvato's warning about Rome's wagging tongues worried her. Might these elegant people, also dining à deux, misconstrue this meeting between an actress and Rome's most notorious Fascist police chief? At neighboring tables, she became aware that people were staring and whispering. She suddenly realized how compromising this dinner looked.

Their drinks arrived, and Koch ordered their meal. He looked nervous, she thought—fingering his silk tie, fussing over her every need. She got the impression that there was something he wasn't telling her.

"Pietro," she said eventually. "Why did you ask me here this evening?"

He paused, fingering his glass. "I have some important news," he began. "I am leaving Rome. The Americans will be here soon. I'm going up north where the Fascists are still in control. Freddi has set up a cinematic operation in Venice—other actors like Osvaldo Valenti and Luisa Ferida are both coming. We need people like you. Come with me, please?" His tone was urgent, passionate.

She was appalled—Valenti and Ferida were well known for their Fascist sympathies. "I couldn't," she protested. "I simply couldn't. My family are here, my friends, everyone I know. I couldn't leave them all."

"I can't leave without you," he said, reaching across the table and grabbing her hand.

"Look, Pietro..." She was desperate to make him understand. "I'm grateful for everything you've done, you must know that. But I have to stay here. You do understand, don't you?"

"But I'll be so lonely without you." He looked at her, his lower lip trembling.

Aware that they were being watched by their fellow diners, she removed her hand from his. "I'm sure we'll see each other again," she said encouragingly.

"Are you?" he entreated, leaning forward over the table. "I wish I could believe that."

She could think of nothing to say. She wanted to run away, but Vicenzo was always there at the back of her mind. She was still afraid of what Koch might do if she rejected him. Eventually, as they sat in silence, she could bear it no longer. "I think I ought to go," she said quietly.

"You really won't come with me?" he pleaded disbelievingly.

"I can't," she said. "I've explained why—please don't ask me again."

He looked away, his face flushed—with anger, she assumed. He clicked his fingers impatiently and asked for the bill.

"There is something else," he murmured, almost inaudibly.

She leaned forward to hear him better.

"It's something I must tell you before I leave," he went on.

Her heart began to race. She should have been nicer to him, she realized. He was going to punish her now—tell her that Vicenzo would be handed over to the Germans. "Go on," she said nervously.

"Vicenzo is being released from prison."

"What?" Isabella was incredulous.

"Yes, this evening."

She reached across the table, took his hand and kissed it. "I can hardly believe it. Thank you, Pietro."

He stood up abruptly and threw some money onto the table. "I'll drive you home now," he said.

She would have liked to refuse him. All she wanted was to leave the restaurant and take a taxi to Vicenzo's house and be there when he got home. But Koch stood waiting for her by his car. And while she hated the idea of being alone with him, after all he had done for Vicenzo, the least she could do was accept a lift from him, she thought.

Driving through the quiet streets, she glanced across at him. He looked broken. "Will you be safe in the north?" she asked.

He shrugged. "What do you care?"

"I worry for you," she went on. "You think you're a hero of the Fascist cause, but people will say you're a traitor. Surely, it's not too late to give yourself up, to fight for the other side."

He laughed ironically as he pulled up outside her house. He turned to look at her. "I don't think you understand how the real world works, Isabella." He gazed at her and touched her cheek. "You have lived in the world of make-believe for so long, you can't see the truth in front of your eyes."

She smiled nervously, struggling to follow his train of thought.

"I may be many things, Isabella," he went on, "but I am loyal to a cause and would never go back on my word. I can't turn my back on Fascism now. What I have done, I did for the love of my country, and I will go on doing so—even if it costs me my life."

She stared into his black eyes. He really believed it, she realized.

"Well, goodbye," she said, feeling for the door handle.

"One more thing before you go," he said, reaching across her and covering her hand with his. "I want you to promise me something."

"Yes?"

"That you will be careful."

"Me?" she asked. "Why?"

"You have been denounced as a collaborator. I think you should go into hiding, or I fear you'll be in trouble." He took her hand in his and kissed it delicately. "I wonder if your friend Vicenzo will help you, as you have helped him?"

"I don't understand," she said.

He smiled ruefully. "It has been an honor to know you, Isabella Bellucci." He bowed his head, and kissed her hand again.

As she climbed out of the car, she looked back at him. He was gazing up at her with tears in his eyes. She slammed the car door shut, and watched as he drove away.

The following day, Isabella woke with a sense of relief and anticipation. Vicenzo had been released, the Allies would soon be in Rome and Koch was gone, at last.

At home, she paced the house, waiting for Vicenzo to call. Surely, now he had been released, he would ring to tell her how grateful he was. But there was no word from him.

By six o'clock, she could wait no longer, so she took a taxi to his villa in Via Salaria. To her surprise, the gate was open, and as she walked up the familiar drive, she could hear a party in full swing. In the drawing room, people from the world of cinema and Roman high society were all gathered together—laughing, drinking and dancing to music. She spotted Vicenzo standing by the window; he was immaculately dressed in his favorite black shirt and trousers. He looked thin, she thought, but happy.

When he spotted her, he walked toward her and took her hands in his.

"Little Bella," he said affectionately. "It's so good to see you."

She yearned to hold him but sensed his reluctance. She hadn't asked for his thanks, and yet it seemed strange that he offered none.

A waiter handed her a glass of champagne and feeling nervous, she drank it down in one draft.

"So tell me?" he began, drawing her to one side, toward a window seat overlooking the garden. "How did you manage to avoid being taken up north? I heard he'd asked you."

That was disconcerting. How could he know about her conversation with Koch the previous evening? "Oh," she said dismissively, "that was ridiculous. I have no idea why he asked me. I suppose he had a crush on me. Of course I would never have gone with him. I made it quite clear I couldn't leave Rome—and my family and friends."

"Still," he persisted, "it seems remarkable that you have escaped so unscathed. You obviously have friends in high places."

She stared at him, incredulous. "I'm sorry?" she said. "Friends who got *you* out of prison. How else do you think you got out?" she asked.

"My sister has been marvelous," he observed, turning to look at Luciana, who was holding forth amongst a group of admirers, hanging on her every word. She noticed his glance, and raised her glass to him. He mouthed, "I love you" and raised his drink back to her. Isabella was reminded of how the brother and sister had played the tower game. It seemed there was still only room on the top of the tower for two people, Luciana and Vicenzo. "Well," he said casually, "I really must circulate; it's been great to see you again. Enjoy the party."

Isabella was dumbfounded. Instead of a fulsome appreciation for everything she had done for him, she was being dismissed, like a casual acquaintance. She felt faint, her heart thumping.

A passing waiter refilled her glass and she drank the champagne swiftly, trying to obliterate her feelings of emptiness. It hit her now, like a hammer to her chest, that Vicenzo didn't need her. She had served her purpose and now she was irrelevant.

She put her glass down on a table and stumbled out of the room, into the hall. Vicenzo's two greyhounds ambled over to her and snaked their heads beneath her hand. She stroked them affectionately and knelt down, burying her face in their soft fur. The dogs whined, as tears cascaded down her cheeks.

Isabella stood up, straightened her back, and walked down the drive. She hailed a taxi and clambered into the back seat, where she wept openly. It seemed that, finally, the bond between her and Vicenzo, a bond she had thought unbreakable, had dissolved.

At home, she went to her bedroom and retrieved the letter he had sent her after her visit to the prison of San Gregorio, a letter that had seemed, on the face of it, to be so full of love. Now, as she read it again, she realized how much he had changed. Gone was the affection and the gratitude. Instead all that was left was cold disdain. She thought of the way he and his sister had looked at one another at the party—their relationship had always been exclusive, she realized. Had Luciana poisoned Vicenzo against her? If so, why?

Angrily she tore the letter into pieces and threw them onto the smoldering logs in her bedroom fireplace. As she watched them burn, Isabella realized it was the end of her dream—a dream of being united with Vicenzo. It was over, and she would have to learn to live without him, forever.

Chapter Thirty-Six

Florence
July 1944

Although in Rome the war was effectively over, in Florence the battle was reaching its peak. The Allied army were ten miles away, approaching from the south. The Germans meanwhile were dug in, preparing to battle street by street, buying time to allow the bulk of their troops to retreat to the hills north of the city.

Livia and Cosimo had joined with three thousand other Resistance fighters, all prepared to fight to the death if necessary. They had been organized into four divisions by the Tuscan Committee for Liberation—the CTLN—a temporary government made up of all the anti-Fascist parties, which had divided the city into four sections. Each group had established a first-aid point, a food supply and a weapons cache. Between them, they had nine hundred shotguns, one thousand pistols and hand grenades, but only enough ammunition to last for one hour.

With her new identity as "Laura de Luca," Livia had effectively disappeared—as far as the authorities who ran Villa Triste were concerned. But still, when she went out on patrol, she worried that she might be recognized by one of her torturers from Carità's vicious gang. Fortunately, her appearance had changed radically in the two months since her arrest. She was no longer the fresh-faced student. Her face, though still striking, had lost its youthful bloom, and its angularity was emphasized by a pair of round wire-framed glasses. She had lost weight, and her once willowy figure was now emaciated.

There was little food to eat, and when the Germans turned off the gas supply, cooking became impossible. Livia and Cosimo set up a small brazier on the roof terrace and in the evenings, as the sun set over the Duomo, they barbecued whatever they had foraged that day, sometimes sharing their meal with Massimo Lombardi.

"It's good of you to invite me again," the old man said as he struggled up the steep staircase to the attic.

"It's our pleasure, Massimo," Livia replied, pulling out an old metal chair for him to sit on and pouring him a glass of wine.

"What's that cooking?" he asked expectantly.

"Rabbit." Cosimo turned the pieces on the grill. "It was donated by a friend."

"Delicious," said Massimo, rubbing his hands. "My wife used to make a very good rabbit dish." He smiled at Livia.

"What happened to your wife?" Livia asked. "If you don't mind me asking?"

"She died over twenty years ago," he answered, sipping the wine.

"I'm so sorry," said Livia. "I had no idea."

"I still miss her," he went on, "and my son..."

"Your son?" Livia asked. "I didn't know you had any children."

"Oh yes, Antonio. He was a lovely boy—clever, very intellectual. I thought he would become a lawyer like your father, but before he went to university, he went off to fight against the Fascists in Spain." He mopped his eyes with an old handkerchief. "Tragically, he never came back."

"You must miss him terribly," Livia said, taking his hand.

"I do, I do..."

"Livia!" Cosimo interrupted their conversation. "I'm sorry, but you must come over here. Look."

Down below, a pair of German soldiers were patrolling Livia's narrow cobbled street. They were being followed by two partisans.

"They're stalking them," Cosimo whispered.

They watched, fascinated, as the partisans shadowed the soldiers, ducking into doorways whenever the soldiers stopped.

"They're going to take them," Cosimo said excitedly.

Over the next few minutes, the partisans drew closer and closer to the two soldiers, before suddenly launching their attack. One plunged his knife into a soldier's back, who collapsed dramatically to the ground, before rolling over and reaching for his gun. The partisan swiftly kicked the weapon out of his hand, and stabbed him again in the chest. Meanwhile, the other partisan had grabbed the second soldier from behind and efficiently slit his throat. In a few brief minutes the two Germans lay dead on the pavement.

"Yes!" said Cosimo triumphantly.

Suddenly two other fighters appeared—a girl and a man. They ran toward their colleagues, pushing a stallholder's cart partially filled with onions. While the men kept a lookout, the girl quickly stripped the soldiers of their uniforms and stuffed them into a large holdall. She then picked up their guns and ran away up the street. The remaining three fighters hauled the men's bodies into the cart, covered them with a blanket, redistributed the onions, and headed off toward the Arno.

"They'll dump the bodies in the river," said Cosimo with satisfaction.

The following morning, Livia and Cosimo set off to make their usual patrol. They had been assigned a section of the city that ran from the Ponte Vecchio, west along the north bank of the Arno, back up past Santa Maria Novella and the market, and east via Piazza San Marco. Their job was to note the positions of sharpshooters, military hardware and possible explosives—information they would pass on to the Allies.

As they crossed over Via Cavour, Livia glanced up the street toward the Gestapo headquarters, where she had been interrogated. She was keen, as always, to get away from the area as soon as possible. But that morning, she stood transfixed, watching as Mario Carità walked purposefully out of the building, surrounded by his henchmen. They climbed into a fleet of cars and drove toward them, passing Livia and Cosimo on the pavement.

For a second, Livia feared Carità had recognized her and might even stop and arrest her. She grabbed Cosimo's arm.

"What's the matter?"

"I think he saw me," Livia replied, looking frantically around for somewhere to hide.

Cosimo pulled her into a shop doorway and waited until the cars had driven away. "It's all right," he said, putting his arm around her, "it looks like he's gone now. Come on, we'd better get going."

Later that day, rumors flew among the partisans that the Fascist chief had left Florence for good.

When Livia and Cosimo returned from their patrol later that afternoon, Livia was amazed to find her father installed in the apartment.

"Papa!" she cried, hugging him. "Why didn't you tell me you were coming? And how did you manage to get back to Florence—weren't there German patrols on the roads?"

"I'm sorry. I should have rung you but I only made the decision this morning. I've been trying to persuade your mother for weeks that I needed to come back. This morning she finally gave in. As for getting here, I thought it would be more difficult than it was, but apparently an old man driving an old car is not considered a threat. It was as if I was invisible." He smiled cheerfully.

"I'm so happy to see you," Livia said, "but I hope you won't expect me to look after you. I have my work to do, you know." She kissed him affectionately on the cheek.

"I do realize that," he said. "When have I ever asked for anything?"

"Papa, one thing you ought to know…" she blushed slightly.

Giacomo looked up at her expectantly.

"Cosimo has moved in here. It seemed easier as we are on patrol together—I hope that's all right."

"You think I will disapprove?" he asked.

"I was worried you might," she said anxiously. "I know what Mamma would say."

"Well, Mamma is not here, fortunately. As for me, I'm just glad you have found each other and that you're not alone when you're out there on duty."

For the next few days, her father was busy attending meetings about the possible handover from the Fascist authorities to the CTLN.

"Pavolini is trying to bargain with us," he told Livia and Cosimo one evening, as they sat on the roof terrace.

"You're not going along with it, are you?" Livia asked.

"I'm not inclined to, no. But one or two of my colleagues are considering it."

"What does he want?" asked Cosimo.

"He's offered to free all political prisoners if we agree to allow the Germans to withdraw and promise not to take reprisals against the Fascists."

"My God," said Livia. "Surely, we'd never agree to that?"

"I hope not," interjected Cosimo. "We've got them on the run, surely?"

Giacomo inhaled deeply on his cigarette, admiring the view across the roofs to the Duomo. "I think," he said, "that Pavolini hoped we might agree, in order to avoid unnecessary bloodshed." He turned to his daughter and Cosimo. "But I suspect it's too late for that now, isn't it?"

Livia nodded.

"We'll fight to the death," Cosimo said earnestly.

The negotiations between Pavolini and the local government continued for a few days. Giacomo was tight-lipped about their progress. But one afternoon, as Livia and Cosimo were patrolling the Arno, they made a detour past the Excelsior Hotel. As they walked into the piazza, they noticed a fleet of cars lining up outside the hotel.

"Something's going on," said Cosimo, pulling Livia into the shadows. "This is Pavolini's headquarters. I think we should just wait here, out of sight, and watch."

An hour later, two men in Fascist uniforms came out of the hotel and looked left and right, as if checking all was safe, before beckoning to a senior officer, who emerged blinking into the sunlight.

"That's Pavolini!" Cosimo whispered excitedly. "Where are they taking him?"

Pavolini climbed into the first car, followed by his bodyguards and assistants. As the convoy of cars drove out of the piazza, a column of bellboys filed out of the hotel carrying leather suitcases and boxes of papers and files, which they loaded into the last car in the cavalcade.

"It looks like Pavolini's leaving for good," Cosimo suggested. "Negotiations have obviously collapsed."

"But why leave?" Livia asked. "Unless they're planning something, and it's not safe for him here anymore."

As they hurried back toward the apartment, they observed Nazi sharpshooters taking up positions on top of buildings. At a meeting of the partisans later that afternoon, Cosimo reported on what they had seen.

"It makes sense," said Marco, an ex-soldier who had been appointed the partisan leader. "We're hearing rumors that they intend to blow the bridges."

"Oh, that can't be right, surely?" Livia said, looking at her fellow partisans in alarm. "Not our beautiful old bridges?"

"Think about it," Marco went on. "The only thing stopping the Allies breaking through now is the river. The harder the Germans make it for the Allies to cross, the more time they have to allow their troops to retreat to the hills north of the city. Presumably they intend to make battle from there. Either way, the bridges are the last line of defense."

"We have to stop them," urged Livia.

Others in the group shouted out their agreement.

Marco held up his hands, asking for quiet. "I understand your anger. It's unimaginable that Florence might lose such a vital part of its history. The trouble is, how do we stop them? All we can do is keep watch day and night and report back to the Allies. We need to know everything the Germans are doing—if and when they wire the bridges, where the dynamite is—any information we can radio to General Alexander and his troops. But it's going to mean a team of us working round the clock. Let me know who's interested in helping."

A forest of hands flew up.

"Good," said Marco. "Sort yourselves out into a rota—two hours each round the clock. Livia, I've managed to get hold of another transmitter for you. I'm putting you in charge of communications. Relay any information daily, twice if you can. All right, everyone, that's all for now. Let's stay in touch and meet back here in two days."

As Livia and Cosimo hurried back to the apartment, they were horrified to see new Nazi posters had been put up all over the city.

ATTENTION!
FOR THE SAVING OF LIFE, ALL RESIDENTS LIVING WITHIN
THREE HUNDRED METERS OF THE ARNO BRIDGES ARE TO
EVACUATE THEIR HOMES AND APARTMENTS IMMEDIATELY.
BY ORDER OF COLONEL FUCHS, COMMANDING OFFICER,
GERMAN HIGH COMMAND

"They're really going to do it," said Livia as they hurried upstairs to the apartment. "Where are these people supposed to go?" she asked.

At their meeting two days later, they heard from their counterparts on the southern side of the river that the Boboli Gardens had become a temporary refuge.

"There are thousands of families camping there," Adreana said, "sleeping in the open air, cooking on barbecues. Last night, some Nazi snipers were taking potshots at them."

"But that's awful. Is there something we can do to protect them?" asked Livia.

"It's terrible, I know," said Marco. "But we have to stay focused. The attack on the bridges could come anytime. Keep up your patrols and report back."

But days later, the Nazis issued a new order that no one was to leave their home for any reason.

"Even windows and doors are to be kept closed," Livia complained to Cosimo and her father. "They're saying that anyone appearing at a window will be shot. I have no idea how we are going to manage. How can we continue with our patrols? Short of killing every German soldier between here and the bridges, we're effectively trapped."

"Doctors and priests are allowed out," said Cosimo, "my father told me."

"So what are you suggesting?" asked Livia. "That we dress up as doctors and priests?"

"Why not?" replied Cosimo. "I can borrow a doctor's bag from my father. And perhaps we can persuade our friends in the clergy to lend us some cassocks and habits?"

"It's a good idea," agreed Giacomo. "They can't check every priest who goes about his business out there."

"All right," Livia agreed. "Let's do it."

The following day she appeared in the kitchen, dressed as a nun.

"What do you think?" she asked Cosimo, who was eating a thin piece of bread smeared with the remains of Luisa's fig jam.

"It's fantastic!" He cut his bread in half and pushed it toward Livia. "Where did you get it?"

"Marco has a cousin who is a nun. She donated a couple of habits. They were delivered to the roof this morning."

"You look very convincing," said Cosimo. "But it's too dangerous. I should go instead."

"With your leg?" Livia replied. "No, you'll only draw attention to yourself. I can do this, don't worry."

Livia set off toward the river, her hands held piously together, her head modestly bowed, her habit concealing trousers and a pistol. Anyone with a keen eye would have wondered at the number of clergy out and about that afternoon.

She and others from her team carefully noted the placement of wiring, and quantity of dynamite fixed to each of the bridges—there was enough to blow them sky-high. To their relief, the historic Ponte Vecchio appeared to have been excluded, but the buildings at either end were festooned with sticks of dynamite, meaning that even if the bridge survived, access would be impossible.

Soldiers patrolled the area closely, and as she and her colleagues walked along the Arno, eyes reverentially lowered, it became clear that defusing the explosives would be impossible. Livia returned to the apartment and transmitted the depressing information to the Allies. After that, all everyone in Florence could do was wait.

Later that evening, Livia, Cosimo and Giacomo crept up onto the roof terrace. It was a fine warm evening and the night sky was filled with stars. At ten o'clock, the first explosion ricocheted through the city. Livia would describe it later as feeling like "an earthquake." Clouds of dust and smoke filled the air and even up on their roof terrace half a mile away from the explosions, Livia, Cosimo and Giacomo were forced to retreat back down the staircase to the apartment to escape the acrid smoke and fumes.

The explosions went on throughout the night, but at dawn Livia crept back up onto the roof terrace. She looked down and saw the street littered with pieces of stone and mortar from the dynamited bridges.

She went back downstairs to find Cosimo cleaning his pistol at the kitchen table.

"I think we should go out and see what's happened," she said.

"All right, I'll come with you." He slipped his gun into his belt, and pulled on his jacket.

The pair ventured out, picking their way across the rubble-strewn streets. As they approached the Arno, the stench of dynamite and smoke nearly overwhelmed them. Creeping closer, they saw that the Ponte Vecchio had miraculously survived, but all the other bridges to the left and the right had been destroyed. They were just tangled heaps of stone, metal and smoking timber.

Over the next couple of weeks, the Germans continued to hold the citizens of Florence hostage. But in spite of being ordered to remain indoors, people crept out of their houses after dark, searching for food and water for their families.

The partisans meanwhile fought bravely back. Marco made contact with Allied troops on the south side of the Arno, going through a secret corridor that ran above the Ponte Vecchio. He brought back a telephone line laid along the passage. Now, with links to the Allies, and with German troops withdrawing north of the city, the Resistance began to kill off any remaining German soldiers.

Livia, who until then had never killed anyone, hit a sniper stationed on a rooftop. As his lifeless body fell to the street below, she stood over him as he lay crushed on the cobbles. Young, fresh-faced and dark-haired, he could have been her brother, she thought. But he was her enemy, and now he was dead, and she was glad.

Within two weeks, the Allies had built a bridge across the river, and set up their headquarters in the Hotel Excelsior. Meanwhile, the Germans, positioned in the hills behind Florence, began to rain down cannon fire onto the city. Fortunately, there was only minor damage to the city's historic buildings. Within days, any remaining German troops had fled, their hilltop gun emplacements overrun. The Germans had been defeated and the battle for Florence was finally at an end.

In September, came the celebrations. Livia, Cosimo, Elena and all their partisan compatriots lined up in the courtyard of Fortezza da Basso. Sitting to one side, in the audience, were Giacomo and Luisa with other members of the Pd'A council. As General Hume, the Allied Commander, arrived to make the inspection, the American flag was raised beside the Italian Tricolor.

After the ceremony, Giacomo came over and shook Cosimo's hand and hugged his daughter and Elena. "I think a drink is called for," he said. "Where shall we go?"

Cosimo, Livia and Elena looked at one another. "Café Paskowski?" Cosimo suggested.

They chose a table outside on the piazza, and Giacomo ordered sparkling wine. They sat in the evening sunshine and chatted and laughed and shared their memories.

"I have something I would like to say," Giacomo said, standing unsteadily on his feet, and raising his glass to them. "This war has brought out the worst and the best in us all. I cannot be alone in thinking that I am the luckiest of men to have a wife who has stood by me through everything." He raised his glass to Luisa, who blushed.

"To Mamma," Livia called out.

"And," Giacomo went on, "to have a daughter like Livia, who, along with her good friends, Cosimo and Elena, displayed a depth of courage that I would never have thought possible. To Livia, Cosimo and Elena—our brave young people!"

Livia stood up next. As the sun went down over the piazza, she replied to her father. "Papa, I'm sure I speak for us all when I say that we were just following your lead. Your determination to see a fairer world has never wavered, and we salute you!"

Later that evening, the group broke up. Giacomo and Luisa went back to the apartment, leaving Cosimo and Livia to take Elena home. Outside Elena's apartment, Livia hugged her friend.

"Sometimes, I can't believe that we all survived," Elena whispered to Livia.

"Me neither," Livia whispered back. "But we did, and we will go on surviving. I'll see you tomorrow, yes?"

As Cosimo and Livia strolled home in the evening light, they passed through the Piazza del Duomo, and stood quietly admiring the cathedral.

"I never tire of looking at it," Livia said quietly. "I sometimes have to pinch myself that I actually live here."

"I can hardly believe it's still standing," replied Cosimo. "Just a few weeks ago this city was being assaulted by cannon fire. And yet the cathedral is untouched, and more importantly, the spirit of the people is undimmed."

"And what of us?" she asked, as they reached the end of their road. "Will normal life ever live up to what we've gone through?"

"You almost sound as if you're sorry it's over." He kissed the top of her head.

"Not sorry, exactly," she replied, "but I worry that life will never again have the intensity of these last few years."

"Well I, for one, will be glad of that," he said, smiling. "And as long as I have you with me, that will be enough excitement for a lifetime."

And he leaned down, cupped her face in his hands and kissed her.

PART FOUR

THE AFTERMATH

"I like melodrama because it is at the junction
between life and theater."

Luchino Visconti

Chapter Thirty-Seven

Rome
June 1945

Isabella had been invited to lunch at Hotel Flora—no longer headquarters of the German ruling forces, but now back to being a smart hotel for Rome's elite. The lunch had been organized by her friend, Princess Matilda of Savoy, who was keen to introduce Isabella to a young British officer stationed in the capital.

"I'm sure you'll like him," the Princess had insisted. "You've always had an eye for a handsome soldier, and Peter is not just good-looking, he's also the aide-de-camp to General Alexander. He speaks fluent Italian and is utterly charming. Really, he's perfect for you."

In spite of her friend's enthusiasm, Isabella was reluctant. "It's sweet of you to think of me," she said, "but I don't go out much these days."

"I know!" retorted the Princess. "We hardly ever see you, but you can't hide away forever."

Isabella hesitated. The memories of what had happened between her and Vicenzo and Pietro Koch were still raw. As a result, she had lost confidence in herself and her judgment. She had been wrong about so many things, and fearful of making another mistake, she shied away from all social gatherings. But the Princess was insistent.

"All right," Isabella had said finally. "As long as it's just lunch."

"Of course!" said the Princess. "You won't regret it, I promise."

As Isabella entered the hotel, she had a sudden flashback of the last time she had been there. She blushed at the memory of Wolff chasing her down the hotel corridor, as she fled from his bedroom.

The Princess was waiting for her in the lobby. "Isabella, darling," she said, "how lovely you look. The others are already in the dining room."

They walked toward the mirrored doors of the grand banqueting room, but Isabella's eye was drawn to the newspaper stand, and in particular to the headlines.

Fascist Torturer Found Guilty!

"Just a moment," she said to the Princess. She picked up one of the newspapers and scanned the first paragraph of the story. Pietro Koch, it seemed, had been in the High Court in Rome the previous day.

"Isabella!" the Princess called impatiently. "Are you coming?"

"I'm sorry." Isabella looked up at her friend distractedly. "Just a moment." She handed the bellboy a few coins, folded the paper and put it into her handbag.

Isabella was placed next to Peter at lunch. The young officer turned out to be everything the Princess had promised—charming, amusing, kind—and with a good command of Italian.

The lunch, attended by several of the Princess's friends, was a gossipy affair. The guests joked and entertained one another with witty stories, but Isabella could think of little else but Pietro Koch's trial.

"You seem rather lost in thought," Peter said quietly.

"Oh, I'm sorry," she replied, "you must think me very rude. I've just had a bit of a shock. A newspaper story that took me back . . . to the war, you know?"

"The Princess mentioned you'd had a rather difficult time."

"Yes," she replied wearily, "you could say that."

"Do you want to talk about it?" he asked sympathetically.

"I don't think so." She smiled at him bravely. "It's a rather long story."

"I understand—perhaps another time. I gather you're a keen golfer," he said, diplomatically changing the subject.

"Oh, yes, I like the odd round. I'm a member of the Acquasanta. Do you know it?"

"I certainly do! It's considered to be the most beautiful course in Europe. It was laid out by a British groundsman—did you know that?"

"Yes," she said, smiling, "I think I did know that."

"Entire bombing raids were designed around preserving it. 'We can't bomb the Acquasanta,' said the Generals. 'We might want a game after the war.'" He laughed.

"Well I have to confess I didn't quite realize its significance," she replied, "but thank God for the British upper classes' love of golf." She laughed a little herself. It was the first time in months, and it felt good. "You'll be pleased to know," she went on, "that it's just as beautiful today as it was before the war. I'll take you there if you like."

"That's a date," he said, covering her hand with his. His skin felt cool and smooth. His touch was kind and gentle. She looked into his green eyes, admiring his sandy hair, and smiled.

The lunch over, they said a polite goodbye in the lobby.

"May I call you?" he asked.

The Princess, hovering in the background, winked irritatingly at her.

"Yes," she replied. "I'd like that."

But as she hurried home across the park, she forgot the handsome Englishman. Her mind was racing back to the time when she had found herself in an agonizing triangle between Vicenzo and Koch.

Back home, she closeted herself in her bedroom, took out the newspaper, laid it on the bed and began to read:

> *Pietro Koch, the notorious Fascist police chief, was found guilty yesterday of "aiding the enemy during the Nazi occupation of Rome, and the torture and death of Italian patriots."*

Isabella read on, mesmerized, as the details of Koch's crimes were laid bare.

> *Appearing in Rome's High Court, Pietro Koch was found guilty of the beating and torture of hundreds of prisoners, and the illegal invasion of Rome's Vatican City, in order to arrest*

anti-Fascist leaders. He was also accused and found guilty of supplying the Germans with a list of hostages who were later massacred in the Ardeatine Caves.

Throughout his twenty-minute court appearance, the defendant sat bolt upright in the dock, his neck shaved like a German, his eyes bloodshot.

Isabella could picture him—the neat mustache, the pressed blue suit.

As the charges were laid out and the prosecution witnesses detailed his crimes, Koch looked around at the court with a condescending sneer. He appeared fearless and defiant throughout.

Just three witnesses had been called—the two for the prosecution were both ex-police chiefs who gave detailed accounts of his crimes. But it was the name of the defense witness which made Isabella sit up in shock.

Appearing as the only witness for the defense was Count Vicenzo Lucchese, who, in addition to being a well-known film director, was also a leading member of Rome's Resistance movement. Although he was imprisoned by the defendant for many weeks between April and June 1944, Koch's defense hinged on his claim to have secured Count Lucchese's release.

"Koch ordered me to be shot one night," Count Lucchese told the court. "I was kept in 'the hole'—a basement room in Pensione Jaccarino—without food for several days. Finally, they moved me; I understand they needed the space for a couple, a man and a woman, who I later was told were hung up from a hook in the ceiling by their hands. Fortunately for me, I was taken before a judge who declared I was too unfit to be interrogated further."

Reading Vicenzo's testimony, Isabella recalled when Koch had invited her to Pensione Jaccarino "for lunch"—the day she had heard screaming and shouting coming from the basement, which sounded just like a woman and a man being tortured.

She read on, and was horrified to find her own name mentioned at the trial.

> *The prosecution asked the witness if he had ever seen the actress Isabella Bellucci while he was in Pensione Jaccarino. The Count replied that he had not, but that he had later discovered that she had been brought there by Koch, arrested, released and then rearrested.*
>
> *When asked how he had finally been released from Pensione Jaccarino the witness replied that he had first been sent to San Gregorio prison, from where he was finally released by the Americans.*

This final answer was both elusive and hurtful. Vicenzo made no mention of Isabella's involvement in either his removal from the Pensione, or from prison. He made it sound as if the Americans, not her, were entirely responsible for his release.

When Koch finally took the stand, he too was asked if he had known her.

> *"Yes, I knew Isabella Bellucci," said the defendant. "She was arrested and thought to be part of the Resistance, but she was released without charge." When asked by the prosecuting counsel if the actress had ever been his lover, the defendant assured the court that she had not.*

That, at least, Isabella thought, was a relief. But it was disconcerting that she should be mentioned at all. She read on.

> *At the end of the trial, the defendant was asked if he had any further witnesses. "No," he replied.*

Three hours later, the judges delivered their verdict: the prisoner was to be condemned to death.

When asked to make a closing statement, Koch said simply: "It's sad dying at twenty-seven."

Isabella threw the paper down angrily onto the bed. She had hoped the whole episode was behind her, that it was a dark and distant memory. But the thought that here, in open court in Rome, her name was once again being dragged up, as if she had been central to Pietro Koch's regime of terror, was both unfair and alarming.

Peter called her the following morning. "How are you today?"

"Oh..." she began, "not too good."

"Let me take you somewhere lovely for lunch. I think you need a bit of cheering up."

"You're very sweet," she said. "But I'm not sure I'll be very good company."

"Look." His voice was calm and gentle. "I'm all alone in a strange city, and to have you sitting opposite me is all the company I need."

It was such a touching thing to say. "All right," she agreed.

"Meet me at Hotel De Russie? It has the most marvelous garden, do you know it?"

"Yes, I know it," she replied, "it's beautiful there."

Peter had reserved a table in the garden. The sun was shining, the food was delicious, but Isabella was withdrawn.

"I don't like to pry," Peter said eventually. "But you seem very troubled. Is there anything I can do to help?"

She began to weep silently. Peter handed her a handkerchief. "Just cry," he suggested gently, "sometimes it's the best thing to do."

"You're very kind." She wiped her eyes and slowly, falteringly at first, began to tell the story of the last two years. Of falling in love with Vicenzo, of discovering his involvement with the Resistance, of how she had done everything she could to save him, including having to befriend the Fascist Koch, while also keeping him at arm's length.

"I felt trapped in the end," she said, "between the two of them. I was constantly frightened."

Peter reached across the table, and took her hand. "I think you've handled it all brilliantly. I can't imagine having to conceal your true feelings day after day like that."

She blew her nose and wiped her eyes. "When I read the reports yesterday of Koch's trial," she explained, "it brought it all back. After Koch moved away up north, I tried to forget him. And I've not seen Vicenzo since that day of the party—he just appears to have abandoned me. I think what hurt most, reading the reports of the trial, is the way Vicenzo denied my involvement. Every day, for months on end, I put myself in danger for him, but he has never acknowledged it."

"What disgraceful behavior," said Peter. "He put you in an impossible position. He used you mercilessly in my opinion. They both did."

"I just wish I could get some film work again." She smiled bravely at Peter. "That might help to put the whole ghastly thing behind me, but I worry that even my career has been destroyed by it."

"Surely not," Peter said encouragingly.

"You'd be surprised," she went on miserably. "The other day I read the most awful piece about myself in a movie magazine."

"Really? What did it say?"

"I can hardly bring myself to tell you."

"I imagine it's all lies anyway," he said loyally.

"As it happens, I remember it word for word. 'Bellucci,'" she announced theatrically, "'is devoid of any dynamism. She and her fellow actors have become lazy and stylized.'"

"Ouch." Peter grimaced. "That's tough, and I'm certain it's also quite untrue." He smiled.

"I feel as if my whole career has been destroyed."

"You mustn't give up," he encouraged her. "Now the war is over, these things will be forgotten and there will be plenty of work for you. I suppose it's just been so complicated. The involvement of your industry with the regime muddied the waters. But that doesn't mean that you have no talent, quite the reverse I'd have said. And you're certainly beautiful enough to light up the silver screen."

"That's such a sweet thing to say."

"Well it's true; you're the most beautiful girl I've ever seen."

A few days later, Peter rang her to say he had to go away. "I'll be back in a few weeks, but do please take care of yourself."

"I will," she said. "And I have a little good news."

"Go on," he said.

"I had a call the other day from a director who is looking to shoot a film in Sicily. I've decided to do it."

"Well, that's wonderful," he exclaimed. "Will you stay in touch? I'd very much like to see you again."

"Of course," she replied. "Let's meet when we're both back in Rome."

With the prospect of a new job on the horizon and a new man in her life, Isabella began to feel a little more optimistic.

Walking into town one afternoon, intending to visit the hairdresser, she passed a newspaper stand. The headline was unmissable.

Koch Executed.

Her heart racing, she bought the paper, and took it with her to the hairdresser.

A footnote to the story mentioned that Count Vicenzo Lucchese, the famous film-maker, had apparently filmed the execution. Compelled to witness the final chapter in this nightmarish saga, Isabella hurried to the nearest newsreel cinema. Wearing sunglasses for fear of being recognized, she bought her ticket.

Inside the cinema, protected by the darkness, she waited for the newsreel to begin. She wondered about Vicenzo's motivation for filming such a ghoulish event. Had he been driven by a desire to see the job done, to prove to himself that Koch was really dead? Or was it an opportunity to have the last laugh, to be standing behind the camera observing the final disgrace of his enemy?

When the Koch newsreel began, Isabella found herself both mesmerized and horrified in equal measure. The film started with a wide shot of a rough clearing, somewhere in the middle of the countryside. Soldiers stood to one side carrying rifles. A police van was driven into the clearing and Koch was led out of the back doors. He was wearing a smart light-colored suit and white shirt, his hair neatly combed. Apart from the fact that his hands were tied together, he could have been off for a pleasant lunch, Isabella thought. Koch appeared quite calm as he was briefly addressed by a small group of officials. He then calmly walked a few yards to the place of execution, where he knelt before the chaplain. Kissing the crucifix, he made the sign of the cross, before sitting down on a small white chair, facing away from the firing squad. He refused the blindfold. Tied loosely to the chair with a rope, he turned to look directly at his executioners the moment their guns were raised. Defiant to the last, she thought. As he was shot in the head, he fell forward, the blood seeping onto his pure white shirt.

To her surprise, Isabella felt nothing. She sat in the cinema long after everyone else had filed out. Alone in the darkness, she thought about the whole experience. It seemed surreal, almost as if it had never happened. Perhaps now, she thought, it would finally be over and she could begin her life anew.

Her new film, set in Sicily, was hard work; the roads and bridges around Catania had been destroyed during the Allied invasion, and the cast and crew were put up in poor accommodation. But there was a camaraderie on set and Isabella enjoyed it, in spite of everything. It was like an adventure, she wrote later to Peter. She began to feel, at last, her life was returning to something like normality.

Back in Rome, she was woken early one morning by the doorbell. Isabella stumbled sleepily downstairs. A policeman stood on the doorstep.

"You are to come with me," he ordered.

"But why?" she asked.

"You are being arrested."

"Me...what on earth for?" she said, her heart thumping in her chest.

"Isabella Bellucci, I am arresting you on the charge of being a collaborator."

Chapter Thirty-Eight

Milan
April 1946

Livia arrived at the courtroom in Milan, dressed in a new cream linen suit. She wore small tortoiseshell glasses and carried a white stick. "Partially sighted" was how her doctor had described her. She could still read, although her eyes wearied more quickly than she would have liked. Graduating from university the previous year, she had decided to go into journalism, and had recently been appointed as a court reporter for a newspaper in Florence. When the trial of a famous actress had come up, she had begged to be allowed to cover it. After all, this was going to be the trial of the year.

"We had friends in common," she told the editor when making her pitch. "Good sources I can go to for background material—people who were intimately involved. I'll do a good job, I promise."

Impressed by her enthusiasm and her contacts, not least Vicenzo Lucchese, her editor agreed. Livia was thrilled. The opportunity to cover such a famous story was obviously part of its appeal. But Livia had to admit that she was fascinated to see "close up" the woman who had falsely denounced her three years before.

The trial was presaged by lurid headlines in the national newspapers:

Isabella Bellucci Arrested—Accused of Collaboration

Another blared:

Is Italy's Little Sweetheart Innocent or Guilty?

It was a hot day in April when Livia took her place in the press gallery, alongside a cartoonist named Antonio who had been employed to make sketches of the proceedings.

"Antonio," Livia whispered, "you must be my eyes. Tell me exactly what the witnesses look like, describe their expressions for me, all right?"

"Of course," he said.

As the trial began, Isabella was brought into the court-room, accompanied by muttering from the crowd in the observation gallery.

"What does she look like?" Livia asked. "I can see she's wearing a dark suit of some kind; how is it cut?"

"It's very elegant," Antonio said. "She looks beautiful."

"That's no help. Describe the suit. How is her hair done?"

"It's navy blue, very fitted, with a pearl choker. Her hair is brown and nicely done, shoulder-length, you know? For a woman who has been in prison for the last few weeks, she looks like a movie star."

Isabella sat down next to her defense counsel, Arturo Orvieto. He had offered his services when she was first arrested, and in a state of shock and confusion, she had gratefully accepted. She glanced up toward the observation gallery, where Peter sat in his military uniform. He smiled at her and winked, as if to say, "It will be all right."

First to speak was the prosecution counsel, who stood up and began theatrically to address the court.

"The prosecution will show that the accused, Isabella Bellucci, in the years 1943 and 1944, did closely collaborate with the Italian Fascist Party and the occupying German Forces. In particular, she was the intimate of two enemies of the State: General Karl Wolff of the SS and Pietro Koch, the traitor, murderer and torturer who was sentenced to death last year in Rome. We will be producing witnesses of the utmost probity who will testify that she used her relationships with these men for a variety of nefarious purposes.

"I first wish to establish with the court the evidence that Koch and Signorina Bellucci had a close personal relationship. I have here a letter which Koch asked his driver to hand-deliver to her, shortly before he fled from Rome up north. Fortunately the driver disobeyed orders, never delivered the letter and handed it over to the armies of liberation. It consists of nine closely handwritten pages."

Isabella leaned forward anxiously, as the prosecution lawyer dramatically waved the pages at the judges, and continued.

"The letter is replete with passion, esteemed gentlemen. By my count, the words 'I love you' occur not less than six times, and 'I think constantly of you' eight times. But the key passage occurs after Koch refers to a dinner at the well-known society restaurant, Albergo dell'Orso, and I quote: 'I know you said you couldn't come north with me because of your family in Rome, but please reconsider. The house I hope to be moving into is a small palazzo, and would easily accommodate both you and your family. Of course, you and I would have a suite of rooms of our own.' Well, gentlemen, we are men of the world, and I think that last sentence says it all."

Isabella blushed and hung her head. "The man was a fantasist," she sighed to her lawyer. "I would never have gone with him, let alone shared his bed. What I said about my family was just a desperate excuse."

Her lawyer patted her hand, and she glanced up into the visitors' gallery, where Peter was smiling supportively, as if to say, "I know it's not true—and I believe you."

There followed a succession of prosecution witnesses. Hotel staff said they had seen Isabella socializing with high-ranking Nazis, and even knocking on a VIP Nazi's bedroom door. Other witnesses said she had enjoyed Koch's hospitality at Pensione Jaccarino, while at the same time his men were torturing partisans in the basement.

Isabella scrawled a note to her lawyer: *That's a complete lie, I never ate at Jaccarino. I thought I was being taken there to be interrogated.*

Next on the stand was a telephonist who testified that Koch had invented a code name for Isabella—Ambrosia—the word he used to instruct the switchboard to put a call through to her house. Another witness said that Koch had befriended Isabella in order to persuade her to spy on Vicenzo Lucchese and ultimately to trap him.

As the evidence for the prosecution was laid out, Isabella became increasingly distressed, occasionally gasping audibly and muttering "That's just not true!" under her breath.

"She looks genuinely shocked," whispered Antonio, scribbling on his pad. "Incredulous... you know?"

"Do you believe her?" Livia asked. "She's an actress, after all."

"I'm not sure..." he said. "I think I do... she was never known for her guile."

When the court adjourned at midday, Orvieto invited Isabella and Peter to lunch.

"It's all going to be fine," said Peter, trying to encourage Isabella.

"Really?" said Isabella gloomily. "They're twisting everything. Things that I know were completely innocent are being made to sound as if I was the worst and most immoral woman in Rome." She began to cry. "Surely, I must take the stand and defend myself."

"Now, now, my dear." Orvieto's voice was like silk. "You mustn't worry. The prosecution's case is completely circumstantial, and their witnesses are mere minnows. Whereas our witnesses are much bigger fish—in fact very big fish indeed."

Back in court after lunch, Orvieto stood up to his full height and bellowed amid the hubbub. "With the court's permission, I wish to call my first witness," he paused dramatically, "one of the heroes of the Resistance—Signor Salvato Cappelli."

Up strode Salvato into the witness area in front of the judges. He glanced briefly at Isabella, who smiled faintly.

"What's he like?" whispered Livia to Antonio.

"He's about forty-five, dark hair, graying slightly, and dressed in a dark suit."

"I am the editor of a newspaper in Rome," Salvato began confidently. "During the war, I came to know Isabella as a good friend and a loyal supporter of the partisan movement." He went on to describe how he had tried to recruit her as a decoy to effect Koch's murder, but that she had understandably found that morally difficult. He concluded with a strong defense of her. "It was common knowledge among those of us in the Resistance that Signorina Bellucci's relationship with Pietro Koch was an elaborate fabrication on her part, done solely in order to save Count Lucchese from almost certain death. I know for a fact that she detested the man. She took huge risks every day to support the Resistance, including stealing a list of people who Koch intended to arrest, which she brought to me. Those men would be dead now if not for her. This whole trial is a farce."

Isabella mouthed, "Thank you," to Cappelli as he walked off the stand.

The next defense witness caused a murmur in the courtroom. A beautiful woman—tall, with dark hair, dressed immaculately in a black suit, took the stand.

"Signora Luciana Torelli," began the lawyer, "you are the sister of Count Vicenzo Lucchese?"

"I am," said Luciana, looking directly at Arturo.

"You knew Isabella Bellucci during the war?"

"I did," Luciana replied.

"And would it be true to say that Signorina Bellucci helped to secure your brother's release from prison?"

"It would," said Luciana. "Isabella Bellucci performed some very valuable services for my brother, Count Vicenzo Lucchese, during the war. She cared for his home while he was in hiding, she carried messages between my brother and family members. Ultimately, I, and other members of the Lucchese family, will forever be in her debt. I have nothing further to say." With that, Luciana turned on her expensively shod heel, nodded to Isabella, and headed straight toward the exit.

Orvieto seemed taken aback by her swift departure. "I am most grateful to my distinguished witness who has taken time out of her busy life to say those kind words about my client. But moving on..." he cleared his throat. "I now call my final witness, Count Vicenzo Lucchese."

Isabella froze. "You didn't tell me he would be coming," she whispered to her lawyer. "What on earth is he going to say?"

Orvieto took her hand in his. "Don't you worry, my dear."

Vicenzo walked into the court, dressed in his customary black. He looked slender and tanned, like a black panther, Isabella thought. For a moment she felt the familiar longing for him.

He glanced at her and she saw a flicker of a smile playing on his lips and her heart jumped. But after everything they had been through together, she was nervous of what he might say. Could he really be relied on to defend her?

His voice was calm, his delivery almost matter-of-fact. He confirmed others' testimony that Isabella had supported the Resistance in general, and him in particular. "I would like especially to praise her," he paused, momentarily turning to her, "for her extraordinary bravery in retrieving a vital document from my house under the noses of the Fascist Police. In addition, she cared for my house for a period of time, a house filled with weapons for the Resistance, putting herself at considerable personal risk."

Isabella sat transfixed, the familiar welling-up of love returning, almost despite herself. But would he acknowledge her crucial role in saving him from execution? The answer soon came.

"After my transfer to San Gregorio prison, I was able to finally communicate with the outside world. I discovered then how much help had been given to me—by both my sister and Isabella. It soon became clear that, of the two women, I owed most to Isabella."

Isabella felt a huge sense of relief. For the first time in the two long years since his release, Vicenzo was publicly admitting she had helped him. But her feeling of gratitude was short-lived. Why hadn't he clearly said she had saved his life? Why did he mention his sister, who had done nothing for him? Most hurtful of all, why hadn't he publicly thanked her?

As Vicenzo left the witness area, he looked over at Isabella and nodded his head. She smiled back, before glancing up into the gallery. Peter was grinning from ear to ear. Orvieto was once again on his feet.

"That concludes the case for the defense, esteemed gentlemen," he intoned to the judges. "It is abundantly clear from the testimony of my distinguished witnesses that my client is completely innocent of all charges against her. Furthermore, I would argue that her conduct during the war, far from being a criminal matter, actually deserves our praise. The testimony laid before you clearly shows that the very mounting of this trial has been an insult to a remarkable woman, who, at some considerable personal risk, generously used her fame, intelligence and undoubted beauty to ensnare a vicious enemy of the people. In so doing, she succeeded in saving the lives of many partisans, and not least the life of a celebrated man of the Italian cinema."

Orvieto paused, opened his arms wide, and turned theatrically to the courtroom behind him. "For such extraordinary selflessness," he declared, "we in this court, and indeed all Italians throughout our beloved country, owe this very brave patriot our deepest thanks."

The judges' verdict, however, was ambiguous. Isabella was acquitted, but only for "lack of proof of her collaboration." She was devastated. After all she had done for the Resistance, and Vicenzo in particular, it felt like a betrayal.

Outside on the steps of the court, Isabella put on a brave face as she posed for photographs, smiling radiantly to the throng of pressmen. But inside she was filled with a confusing cocktail of emotions.

When the crowds and photographers had finally gone, she shook her lawyer's hand. "Thank you, Arturo. I am so grateful. You must let me know what I owe you," she said.

"It has been an honor, signorina. This war has destroyed too many good people. I was determined you would not be one of them. As for your bill...please don't worry. It has already been paid."

"By whom?" she asked.

"By Count Lucchese," he said, "who else?"

Isabella was stunned. It was the final piece in a complex jigsaw of unrequited love and passion. "Vicenzo paid?" she murmured. "I see—thank you for telling me."

Arturo bowed and walked away down the steps of the courthouse.

Isabella turned and looked up at Peter. "What sort of woman have you got yourself involved with?"

"An impressive one," he said, kissing her. "A woman who is brave, noble and without ego, and who deserved much more from those around her. Let's go. It's time to put this behind you, and get on with your life."

Livia, who had stood aside from the rest of the press pack, watched as the actress put on a show for the photographers. Livia had thought the judgment unfair. It seemed obvious that Isabella was completely innocent. Perhaps she had been naïve, Livia thought. She'd become involved in something larger than herself, had been manipulated from the start by men—Vicenzo, Koch, Wolff. She could imagine the stories the other reporters would submit, and determined that hers would represent the actress as fairly as possible. She bore Isabella no malice for her betrayal. She had long ago forgiven her for that. Now, as she walked away from the court, she felt sad that someone so beautiful and talented should have been so badly treated by the world.

Chapter Thirty-Nine

Giacomo's car wound up the long drive toward the Luccheses' villa. It seemed quite unchanged from its pre-war days. The gardens were as lush as ever, the clay of the tennis court had been freshly raked and glowed red in the sun.

Livia sat in the back seat with Cosimo, delighting in her memories.

"Can you see the court over there? That's where Vicenzo and his brother taught me to play tennis."

"It's quite a place," Cosimo murmured appreciatively.

"The Luccheses are very old family friends," Luisa said from the front. "I had thought at one time that Livia and Vicenzo..." she paused.

"Mamma," said Livia, "don't be ridiculous. He was never going to marry me, he doesn't like women in that way."

Luisa tutted.

"Besides," Livia went on, "I had found my future husband on the first day of university." She gazed up at Cosimo and kissed his cheek.

The car pulled up in front of the pink villa and they all clambered out, stiff from their journey. The front door was opened and two greyhounds ran out of the house, barking. They snaked around the visitors, sniffing hands, and nudging them to stroke their heads.

"Dogs! Come back here!" It was Vicenzo; he was striding toward them, dressed in cream linen trousers and a navy-blue shirt. "Livia!"

he said, hugging her tightly. "How wonderful to see you again—and with your husband too!" He shook Cosimo's hand and led them all into the house.

Over the following week, while Giacomo and Luisa sat in the gardens of the villa, Livia and Cosimo spent most of their time on the beach with Vicenzo and his younger brother, Raffaele. Lying on the sand, they talked of their wartime experiences.

"It seems we have all suffered," said Vicenzo. "I emerged relatively unscathed. Whereas both of you—to lose your sight, Livia, and Cosimo his foot. I am in awe of your bravery."

Cosimo squeezed his wife's hand.

"It's really not that bad," said Livia. "Cosi is used to his injury now, aren't you, caro?"

He nodded. "It's made me reevaluate things—my career for a start. I was originally studying philosophy and art, but during the war I saw so much suffering. Now I'm training to be a doctor. Medicine is something I can be passionate about—and that I can do, even with my disability."

"And although my eyesight is poor," Livia added, "I can still see well enough, as long as I wear my glasses. What's extraordinary is how one's other senses begin to compensate—my hearing, for example, is acute!" She laughed.

"Well, I still think you're remarkable," said Vicenzo.

"And what of your time, Vicenzo?" Livia asked. "I know you were tortured when you were imprisoned—I remember hearing about it during the trial."

"It all seems a lifetime away now, doesn't it?" Vicenzo replied, rolling over onto his side. "As if it happened to someone else, you know? At first, I was locked away in Pensione Jaccarino in Rome. That man Koch was in charge. I think he was cut of the same cloth as your torturer, Carità. These men had the most extraordinary capacity for cruelty. It was a terrible place and I saw some monstrous things—the most awful suffering."

"You were fortunate to get out," Livia said.

"I was." Vicenzo sighed.

"One thing I'd like to ask you, if I may?"

"Of course."

"At the trial of Isabella Bellucci, which I covered as you know, I got the impression that she had played a more significant part in getting you released than you let on. I wondered why you felt unable to publicly thank her for what she did. I thought the judgment was rather unfair, and that she should have been properly vindicated."

"Livia," Cosimo interjected, "I really don't think you should—"

"No," said Vicenzo, sitting up and looking out to sea, shading his eyes. "It's a fair question. And you're right, Livia. Isabella saved my life. "

"So why not make that clear?" asked Livia.

"Her involvement became compromised. She got too close to that monster Koch."

"But she did it for you," Livia persisted. "It was obvious that she was in love with you."

"I know." He looked at her mournfully, wiping a tear from his eye with the back of his hand.

"You did care for her, didn't you?" Livia asked, gently.

"Very much. Although after what she did to you, I struggled to forgive her for a while."

"But I survived," said Livia cheerfully. "She did what she did because she was scared—scared of losing you. Besides, they didn't hurt me, not at that time, anyway. In many ways, I'm grateful to Isabella. Because of her, I became an interpreter and that allowed me to help so many people escape the authorities. Just think how many people might have died without my help."

"What a positive attitude you have to life," said Vicenzo. "You're a lucky man." He patted Cosimo on the back. "She's a remarkable woman, your wife."

"And I think," Livia went on, "that Isabella must have loved you very much to do what she did. To put herself in harm's way every day, to deal with Koch's obsession with her, to risk interrogation and torture—all to protect you, and all because she was hopelessly in love with you. And the tragedy is that she never really stood a chance with you, did she?"

Vicenzo looked deeply into her eyes and blushed slightly. "No, I was never going to be able to offer her the sort of love she wanted. And I'm sad about that. She deserved more. But I did care for her, loved her in my own way—you must believe that."

Epilogue

Livia sat at the same table at Café Paskowski that she always chose. Angelo, the head waiter, had kept it for her, and at ten o'clock she sat down, leaned her white stick against the chair, and ordered her coffee. She unfolded her newspaper and laid it carefully in front of her. Using her silver-handled magnifying glass, she perused the headlines, when she was suddenly interrupted.

"Buongiorno, signora."

She looked up. She could see the outline of a tall man with dark hair. He looked somehow familiar.

"We met yesterday, do you remember?"

She did remember—the young man who had taken her arm and propelled her across the road. Her heart sank. She had thought she had got rid of him. "Oh yes," she replied politely. "I do remember now, how are you?"

"Well, thank you. I wondered, might I sit with you?"

"If you must," she replied. She felt trapped, unable to refuse.

Angelo arrived with her coffee. "Signora, your coffee. Is this gentleman staying?"

"I'm not sure," she frowned.

"Yes, I'll have an espresso please," interjected the young man. "I won't stay long," he assured Livia. "I just wanted to talk to you about someone we have in common."

Livia put down her magnifying glass. "You must forgive me," she said, "if I appear rude. It's just that I am used to my own company and

I rarely see friends or acquaintances. So many of the people I knew are gone now, and I've become irritable. Losing my sight doesn't help."

"It must be difficult." The young man drummed the table with his fingers, as if he was nervous. "Do you have cataracts, if you don't mind me asking?"

"No, if only it was that simple; my sight problems began during the war."

"Oh I see," he replied awkwardly. "In fact, it was the war I wanted to talk to you about."

"The war? But surely you're too young to know anything about it."

"Yes, but my grandmother lived through it and she told me a great deal. It's her that I would like to talk to you about."

Livia thought back to those she had known in the war. To her friend Elena who had only died the previous year after a long and happy life running a vineyard in Puglia. To Sara, who had died just after the war giving birth to her third child. To have survived so much, and then die of something so innocent and life-affirming as having a child had been a real tragedy. Perhaps, she thought, this young man was related to Valentina, who had moved to America soon after the war, and become a politician.

She was intrigued. "Tell me, young man, who was your grandmother?"

"Isabella Bellucci," he replied. "The actress."

Livia paused, her cup held in mid-air. "I see."

"I noticed you were reading her obituary yesterday."

"Yes, although I never actually met her, but our paths…intersected. Our lives became intertwined for a while."

"I know," he said, as the waiter laid his espresso on the table. "She often talked of you, and of the others involved."

"The others?" Livia asked.

"Vicenzo, and Luciana—the whole Lucchese family, and of Koch of course."

"I see," Livia replied. "Well you must forgive me, my memory is hazy. I am a very old lady and I may not be able to supply the information you seek."

"I seek nothing," he said. "I merely come on an errand from my grandmother."

"An errand? But she is dead."

"Yes, but before she died, she made me promise something."

"Go on," Livia said.

"She made me promise that I would come and find you and tell you how very sorry she was that she betrayed you."

"Oh," replied Livia. "I don't consider she betrayed me, exactly."

"She had misunderstood something," he went on. "She was in love, you see—hopelessly in love with a man who couldn't love her back. She was so desperate, she would do anything, anything at all to gain his love."

"It must have been awful," said Livia, "to be so in thrall to someone. I knew a little of her situation—I was a friend of the man she loved, you see. And I felt genuinely sorry for her."

"Did you? I wish she could hear you say that. She lived with this terrible guilt all her life."

"Dear boy," Livia reached across the table, and covered his hand with hers. "That's all forgotten now, surely. It was all such a long time ago. And she suffered enough, I think, don't you? The terrible lies that were told about her in the press. I covered her trial, you know, I worked as a journalist," she said, by way of explanation.

He nodded. "She read your stories and often spoke of you, of how fair you were. You were the only journalist to cover her trial in a dispassionate way."

"I'm glad she thought so. I thought much of the coverage was disgraceful, sensationalist. I know she was hounded for years. And then she seemed to just disappear."

"She struggled to get work after the war. The new wave of Italian cinema rejected her. Fortunately, by then she'd married my grandfather, Peter. He was an English officer who had been stationed here. I don't know exactly how they met, but he was a blessing for her—a kind man, who accepted her complicated past. Their only child, my father, was very unwell as a boy. He had a heart defect, and I think it took all her courage and strength to bring him up. But he improved gradually, and eventually grew up, and married, and I was born."

"Was Isabella happy, at the end?" Livia asked.

"Happy enough. But it still hurt, I think, that people in the film industry believed such terrible things of her. She spoke at a film festival a few years ago in Bologna, but even then, the coverage was complicated and unfair. That slur, that she had collaborated, never left her. What really hurt was that Vicenzo Lucchese would never publicly acknowledge what she had done for him. She rationalized it later that a man like Vicenzo—noble, aristocratic and proud—was incapable of acknowledging the part that a mere woman, and an evil fascist like Pietro Koch, could have played in his release. But even though she could rationalize it, I don't think she ever really got over it. To her it was the ultimate betrayal."

"I'm so sorry. I think Isabella was right about Vicenzo. I challenged him about it afterward. He did care for your grandmother, but his pride got in the way. Still, to live a life full of such pain and regret, as Isabella did, must be terrible."

"But your life has not been so straightforward, has it, signora?" he asked. "I read an article about you once, of the extraordinary things you did in the war."

"I wasn't extraordinary. We all did remarkable things back then. Every day was frightening and beautiful at the same time. I think adrenaline got us all through. We had no time for reflection, only action. It was life afterward that could be hard to bear—the normality of it could be claustrophobic. That's why I became a reporter—it gave me some excitement." She smiled.

"And did you marry?"

"Oh yes. I married a wonderful man I met during the war. We used to come to this café when we were students; he introduced me to it, actually."

"Is that why you come here every day?"

"I suppose so," she replied. "He died a few years ago now, but I feel close to him when I'm here. And it brings back memories—some good, some bad. My friend Elena was arrested here—she attempted to blow up Mario Carità, the Fascist policeman, the man who tortured me, as it happens."

"She tried to blow him up here...in this café?"

"Yes—she and my future husband, Cosimo. It was a mad plan, but brave." She smiled.

"I presume he was about the same age as me when he did these things. I wonder... how do you live a normal life after an experience like that?"

"It's difficult. Nothing else can ever have the same intensity. But Cosimo became a doctor," Livia said, "so his life had meaning. And we had four marvelous children—a couple of them are grandparents themselves now."

"And you still live here, in Florence?"

"Yes, in the same apartment I spent the war in. When my husband was alive, we brought our children up in the family villa in the country. But it needed a lot of upkeep and I decided to move back here after he'd died. My son lives in the villa now with his family, but I am content in this city, with my memories." She paused and looked around her.

"I wonder if I might take your photograph?" the young man asked.

"My photograph? Why would you want that?"

"To show my children, if I ever have any. My generation owe you so much."

She covered his hand with her own. "If it would make you happy then of course," she said.

He stood up and took his phone out of his pocket. He backed away across the piazza, anxious to get a picture of her sitting in front of the now famous café. She looked so small and frail, he thought, as he clicked the shutter. He zoomed in, and took a second photograph. Her face, though lined, was beautiful and strong. Her white hair pinned elegantly on top of her head. For a second he saw a glimmer of the young woman she had been, fighting fiercely for what she believed in.

The piazza was buzzing with life. Market stalls around the edges were thronged with people. The café itself, always popular, was busy serving coffee. Lunch guests would be arriving soon. In the distance he heard the bells of the Duomo chiming twelve o'clock. He thought of all the people like her, some who survived, many who didn't, and the enormous sacrifices they had made.

Returning to the table, the young man took her small hand in his and kissed it. "I'm so glad to have met you," he said. "I just wish my grandmother could have had the chance to talk to you before she died. She would have been so happy to know that your life was not ruined by her betrayal."

"My dear boy," said Livia, smiling up at him, "I had a wonderful life—it wasn't ruined at all."

ACKNOWLEDGMENTS

I am grateful to the following people for their support:

My editor, Cara Chimirri, and the whole team at Bookouture, who have provided unwavering support and enthusiasm for this project.

My family, who put up with my locking myself away for months on end to research and write; my husband, Tony Edwards, who translated Maria Denis's book, *Il Gioco della Verità,* into English and assisted with the historical research; and my daughter, Charlotte Edwards, who has used her skills as a photographer and social media expert to help with publicity.

Finally, my sincere thanks to Vanessa Nicolson for her generous introduction to her remarkable mother, Luisa Vertova, who had been a young partisan in Florence during the Second World War and who partly inspired this book. The book is dedicated to her.

I am grateful too for the fascinating insights I received during my various research trips to:

The Museo Storico della Liberazione, in Rome: This building in Via Tasso was one of the two Fascist torture centers in Rome. It chronicles the history of the period and the terrible sufferings of the brave men and women who attempted to defy Fascism in the country's capital city.

Ardeatine Caves: This site just outside of Rome witnessed one of the worst atrocities committed by the Germans in Italy—the murder of 335 Italian men, in retribution for the death of 33 German soldiers in a bomb attack by Roman partisans in March of 1944.

Cinecittà: This famous Roman film studio was founded by Mussolini, and some of its original 1930s buildings still survive. Tourists can enjoy guided tours of its permanent modern sets.

Acquasanta Golf Club: This golf club on the outskirts of Rome is as beautiful today as it was back in the 1940s.

The very fine cities of Rome and Florence!

READING GROUP GUIDE

Discussion Questions

1. Of the two central characters, Isabella and Livia, which one did you sympathize with the most?

2. The Fascist government in Italy was on the same side as Hitler during World War II, but many of the people of Italy despised Fascism and fought against it. How much did you know before reading the book about the complexities of the political situation in wartime Italy?

3. If you were trapped in a war-torn country, would you risk your life by joining the Resistance, as Livia did?

4. This novel is a blend of fact and fiction, with many historical people making appearances as characters. Livia is the amalgam of several actual women who fought for the Resistance in Florence. Is historical fiction a justifiable method of presenting history?

5. The Fascist movement had total control of the media and the film industry in Italy. Do you see any parallels in today's world?

6. The character of Isabella was based very closely on the actress Maria Denis. By befriending the chief of the Fascist police, she ultimately saved the life of film director Luchino Visconti. After

the war, Maria was shunned, whereas Visconti went on to have a hugely successful career. Why do you think they received such different treatment?

7. Isabella took enormous risks with her own safety. Do you think Isabella was brave or foolish?

8. If the novel became a film, who would you like to see playing the two central roles of Isabella and Livia?

The Story Behind the Book

All of my books to date have involved some element of truth—a person or events that have inspired me to tell their story—but this novel is the most closely aligned to real events and personalities.

The character of Isabella Bellucci is based in very large part on the Italian actress Maria Denis. Working for Cinecittà before the war, "Italy's little sweetheart" starred in many "white telephone" films, Italian movies modeled on American comedies of the time. After a successful career making five or six films each year, Maria fell hopelessly in love with the highly intellectual and artistically gifted director Luchino Visconti.

Many actresses had fallen in love with Luchino—such were his legendary good looks and captivating personality. But his relationship with Maria was unique. She, above all others, was so devoted to him that when he was arrested for being part of the Resistance in Rome, she was prepared to risk her life to save him. For this devotion, she was never truly appreciated. Instead, she was hounded by the Italian press and accused of being a collaborator and traitor, accusations from which she never truly recovered. She can be accused of many things—naïveté, certainly, and an almost childlike optimism—but I believe she was no traitor.

Many of the events in this novel were taken from her memoir, *Il Gioco della Verità*. Published in 1995, this was Maria's attempt to set the record straight about her desire to save the life of her friend Luchino Visconti through a "relationship" with Koch, the Fascist police chief.

There is one important part of Isabella's story that is *not* true and not based on the life of the "real" Maria in any way: Isabella's betrayal of Livia. This was, however, based on another true story—something that happened to a young woman in Florence, whom I had the pleasure of meeting in 2019. At the age of ninety-nine, she could still recall her wartime experiences. Falsely accused of being in the Resistance by the jealous mistress of an aristocratic acquaintance, she was denounced to the Fascist police. As a result, she had to report to Villa Triste each day and work for them as an interpreter. This struck me as such an extraordinary experience, and I was keen to reflect it in my novel.

Livia's storyline was also inspired by a remarkable Resistance *staffetta* named Gilda, who helped to run Radio Cora. Gilda was nearly blinded during an interrogation by Mario Carità in Florence and subsequently imprisoned in a camp in northern Italy, and this novel re-creates details of her escape and subsequent adventures.

As a novelist, it is my job to "imagine" the feelings and conversations of my characters. In this novel, many of the episodes that triggered those feelings are true. I am indebted to the women of Italy who fought Fascism during the Second World War with such bravery and selflessness and who coped daily with the confusion of living in a country at war with both itself and its oppressors. May we never forget them.

Suggestions for Further Reading

The Other Italy: The Italian Resistance in World War II, by Maria de Blasio Wilhelm (W. W. Norton & Co., 1988)

Mussolini's Enemies: The Italian Anti-Fascist Resistance, by Charles F. Delzell (Princeton University Press, 1961)

Il Gioco della Verità, by Maria Denis (Baldini & Castoldi, 1997)

The Battle for Rome, September 1943–June 1944, by Robert Katz (Simon & Schuster, 2003)

Partisan Diary: A Woman's Life in the Italian Resistance, by Ada Gobetti, translated and edited by Jomarie Alano (Oxford University Press, 2014)

Mussolini's Dream Factory: Film Stardom in Fascist Italy, by Stephen Gundle (Berghahn Books, 2013)

The War Diaries of Count Galeazzo Ciano, 1939–1943, by Galeazzo Ciano (Fonhill, 2015)

Forgotten Blitzes, by Claudia Baldoli and Andrew Knapp (Continuum, 2012)

ABOUT THE AUTHOR

Debbie Rix tells the stories of real women whom history has overlooked. As an ex-journalist, she believes historical accuracy is key and she strives to weave her stories around real-life events. Her novels have been published in several languages, including Italian, Czech, and Russian.

Debbie spends a lot of time in Italy, but when not traveling, she lives in the Kent countryside with her journalist husband, children, chickens, and four cats.

You can learn more at:
DebbieRix.com
Twitter @DebbieRix
Facebook.com/DebbieRixAuthor
Instagram @DebbieRix